PRAISE FOR
DONALD E. WESTLAKE AND
SMOKE

◆

"Explaining what happens in a Donald Westlake novel is like reading a recipe for meringue instead of eating the results. . . . I strongly suggest you buy a copy now and squirrel it away for emergency use the next time you find yourself stuck in an airport lounge with a departure time of maybe. The bartender may resent the fact that you're too busy laughing to order another drink, but you'll definitely feel better in the morning."

—*New York Times Book Review*

◆

"Westlake is a consummate pro. . . . SMOKE is one of his best books in years."

—*Washington Post Book World*

◆

"This is one of the funniest books I've read in a long time. The dialogue is outrageous, the situations implausible, the humor nonstop. Freddie is the most likable fictional scamp you're likely to ever encounter."

—*San Francisco Examiner*

◆

"More effective than a nicotine patch, and much funnier."
—*San Jose Mercury News*

◆

"Glorious Westlake comedy. . . . Full of hilarious characters, crackpot conversations and narrative sleight of hand."
—*Publishers Weekly*

◆

more . . .

By Donald E. Westlake

NOVELS
Humans • Sacred Monster • A Likely Story
Kahawa • Brothers Keepers • I Gave at the Office
Adios, Scheherazade • Up Your Banners

COMIC CRIME NOVELS
Trust Me on This • High Adventure
Castle in the Air • Enough • Dancing Aztecs
Two Much • *Help* I Am Being Held Prisoner
Cops and Robbers • Somebody Owes Me Money
Who Stole Sassi Manoon? • God Save the Mark
The Spy in the Ointment • The Busy Body
The Fugitive Pigeon • Smoke

THE DORTMUNDER SERIES
Don't Ask • Drowned Hopes • Good Behavior
Why Me • Nobody's Perfect
Jimmy the Kid • Bank Shot • The Hot Rock

CRIME NOVELS
Pity Him Afterwards • Killy • 361
Killing Time • The Mercenaries

JUVENILE
Philip

WESTERN
Gangway (with Brian Garfield)

REPORTAGE
Under an English Heaven

SHORT STORIES
Tomorrow's Crimes • Levine
The Curious Facts Preceding My Execution and Other Fictions

ANTHOLOGY
Once Against the Law (coedited by William Tenn)

DONALD E. WESTLAKE

SMOKE

THE MYSTERIOUS PRESS

Published by Warner Books

A Time Warner Company

MYSTERIOUS PRESS EDITION

Cover design by Jackie Merri Meyer
Cover illustration by Jeff Fitz Maurice

The Mysterious Press name and logo are registered trademarks
of Warner Books, Inc.

 Mysterious Press Books are published by
Warner Books, Inc.
1271 Avenue of the Americas
New York, NY 10020

Visit our web site at
http://pathfinder.com/twep

A Time Warner Company

Printed in the United States of America

Originally published in hardcover by The Mysterious Press.
First Printed in Paperback: October, 1996
10 9 8 7 6 5 4 3 2 1

This is for Knox Burger and Kitty Sprague, with
affection, admiration, and gratitude

1

Freddie was a liar. Freddie was a thief.

Freddie Noon his name was, the fourth child of nine in a small tract house in Ozone Park. That's in Queens in New York City, next door to John F. Kennedy International Airport, directly beneath the approach path of every big plane coming in from Europe, except when the wind is from the southeast, which it very rarely is. Throughout his childhood, the loud gray shadows of the wide-body jets swept across and across and across Freddie Noon and his brothers and his sisters and his house as though to wipe them clear of the table of life; but every shadow passed and they were still there.

Freddie's father worked, and still does, for the New York City Department of Sanitation, hanging off the back of a garbage truck. He's in a good union, and gets a decent salary and benefits, but not quite enough for a family with nine kids. And that may be why, at the age of seven, in the local five-and-dime's toy department, Freddie Noon became a thief.

His becoming a thief is why he became a liar. The two go hand in hand.

Freddie's junior high school was the big rock-candy mountain. In no time at all, Freddie became enthralled by, and in thrall to, any number of products that could set him up to soar *above* the flight paths of the inbound jets. The trouble was, the more potent the product and the higher it let him soar, the more it cost. By the age of fourteen, Freddie's reason for being a thief had changed; he did it now, as they say in the solemn magazine articles, to support his habit. His other habit, really, since his original long-term habit was already set: to be a thief. Habit number one supported habit number two.

Freddie took his first fall at sixteen, when he set off a silent alarm in an empty house he was burglarizing out in Massapequa Park on Long Island—they hadn't stopped their *Newsday* delivery when they went on vacation—an error he didn't know he'd committed until all those police cars showed up outside. He was sent to a juvenile detention center upstate, where he met youths his own age who were *much* worse than he was. A survivalist, Freddie quickly caught up. Fortunately, the joint was as awash in drugs as any high school, so the time passed more quickly than it otherwise might.

That was the end of Freddie's formal schooling, though not the end of his incarceration. He did one more term as a juvenile, then two clicks as an adult, before he found himself in a drug-free cell block, a situation that almost seemed against nature. What had happened, the white inmates who'd been born again as Christian fundamentalists and the black inmates who'd converted to Islam joined *together* for once, and policed that prison like a vacuum cleaner. They were more efficient, and they were a lot more mean, than the regular authorities, and they kept that building of that joint *clean*. You're found with so much as a Tylenol on you, you'd better have a damn good explanation.

Freddie was twenty-five when he went in for that stretch. He'd been flying above the flight paths for eleven years. The landing he made inside that clean house was a bumpy one, but he did walk away from it, and as the pilots say, any landing you walk away from is a good landing.

And here Freddie met a new self. He hadn't made his own

acquaintance since he was fourteen years old, and he was surprised to find he liked the guy he'd become. He was quick-witted, once he had his wits about him. He was short and skinny, but also wiry and strong. He looked pretty good, in a feral-foxy sort of way. He liked what he saw himself doing, liked what he heard himself thinking, liked how he handled himself in the ebb and flow of life.

He never reformed, exactly, never became born again or changed his name to Freddie X, but once he was clear of drugs he saw no reason to go back. It would be like infecting yourself with the flu all over again; back to the stuffy nose, the dull headache, the dulled thought processes, the dry and itchy skin. Who needed it?

So that was why, when Freddie Noon hit the street once more, two years later, at twenty-seven years of age, he did not go back on drugs. He stayed clean, alert, quick-witted, wiry, good-looking in a feral-foxy way. He met a girl named Peg Briscoe, who worked sporadically as a dental technician, quitting every time she decided she couldn't stand to look into one more dirty mouth, and she also liked this new Freddie Noon, and so they set up housekeeping together. And Freddie went back to being a thief. Only now, he did it for a different reason, a third reason. Now he was a thief because he liked it.

And then one night—just last June, this was—when he was twenty-nine and had been two years out of prison, Freddie broke into a townhouse on East Forty-ninth Street, in Manhattan, way east over near the UN Building. He chose this particular townhouse because the front entry looked like a piece of cake, and because the bottom three floors of the four-story building were dark, and because a little brass plaque beside the main entrance read

LOOMIS-HEIMHOCKER
RESEARCH FACILITY

A research facility, in Freddie's extensive experience, was a place with many small valuable portable salable machines: word processors, faxes, microscopes, telephone switchboards, darkroom equipment; oh, all sorts of stuff. It made this particular townhouse seem a worthwhile place to visit.

So Freddie found a legal parking space for his van only a few doors away from the target, which was already a good omen, to find a parking place at all in Manhattan, and he sat there in the dark, eleven o'clock at night, and he watched the research facility across the street, and he bided his time. Faint candlelight flickered behind the top-floor windows, but that was okay. Whoever lived up there wouldn't get in Freddie's way. He'd be quick and quiet, and he wouldn't go above the second floor.

No cars coming. No pedestrians on the sidewalks. Freddie stepped out of the van, whose interior light he had long since removed, and stepped briskly across the street. He hardly paused at the front door for his busy fingers to do their stuff, and then he was in.

2

"Uh-oh," said David.

Peter peered across the candle flame, then turned his head to follow the trajectory of David's eyes. In the dimness beyond the kitchen alcove, in the hall, on the elaborate alarm panel mounted on the wall beside the maroon elevator door, a dull red light burned. "Ah-huh," Peter said.

"Do you suppose it's a malfunction?" David asked. It was clear he hoped it was.

But a sudden idea had come into Peter's mind, connected with what they'd just been discussing. "Someone has broken in," he said, sure of it and glad of it, and got to his feet, dropping his napkin beside his plate.

Dr. David Loomis and Dr. Peter Heimhocker were lovers. They were also medical researchers, both forty-three years of age, currently funded by the American Tobacco Research Institute to do blue-sky cancer research. Their work, reports of which looked good in tobacco-company annual reports, and references to which invariably formed a part of tobacco-industry spokespeople's testimony before congressional committees, was sincere, intelligent, and well funded. (Even the alarm system had been paid for with tobacco money.) David and Peter were encouraged by their funders to come up with anything and everything that might help in the human race's battle against the scourge of cancer, except, of course, further evidence that might recommend the giving up of the smoking of cigarettes.

David and Peter had met twenty years earlier, in medical school, and had soon realized how much they had in common, including a love of non-result-oriented research and an infinite capacity for guile and subterfuge in the suspicious sight of the outside world. Their coming together strengthened both. They'd been inseparable ever since.

The tobacco-money project was now in its fourth year. Early on, David and Peter had decided to focus their efforts in the direction of melanoma, the fatal form of skin cancer, for the avoidance of which one was advised to keep away from the sun, not cigarettes. It seemed both a safe and a worthwhile area of study, but it had also proved, so far, quite frustrating.

It seemed to David and Peter that the key lay in the pigment. Pigmentation is what gives our skin and hair and blood and eyes and all of us their color. David and Peter did not think pigment was the culprit, they thought it was the carrier. They thought that certain cancers could be reduced or even reversed if particular pigments could be temporarily eliminated. They had been working on various formulas for some time, and felt they were near a breakthrough, but they were stymied by an inability to perform a real-world practical test.

They had two formulas at this time, both more or less ready to go, neither of which seemed *quite* to do the job, though there was no way at this stage to be sure. One of these formulas was in the shape of a serum, to be injected into the buttock. The other was a kind of small black cake or cookie, looking much like an after-dinner mint, which was meant to be eaten. The serum was called LHRX1, and the mint was called LHRX2.

Both formulas had been tested on animals, as a result of which two translucent cats now roamed the townhouse on East Forty-ninth Street. Buffy had been given LHRX1 and Muffy LHRX2. These cats were quite startling, at first, for David and

Peter's friends from the worlds of ballet, fashion, art, academe, and retail, when they would come over to the townhouse for parties. "No one *else* has cats you can *see through!*" everybody cried, giving in to both admiration and envy, watching these gray ghosts amble around, silent as the fog.

But what was needed, and what David and Peter had been discussing over late dinner when the alarm's red light went on, was human volunteers. The research had gone as far as it could without real test data, which meant actual human beings. Translucent cats can only tell so much. To finish refining the formulas, to be certain which of the two was the likelier candidate for further study, to achieve the breakthrough they could sense was out there, just beyond their grasp, they needed to try the stuff on people.

It was true, of course, that there were two formulas and two researchers, being David and Peter, so that in theory they could experiment on themselves, as so many heroic nineteenth-century medical discoverers were alleged to have done, but David and Peter were not *mad* scientists. Who knew what side effects there might be, what long-term consequences? Who would be around to record the data if something were to go wrong? And how could a translucent scientist hope to be taken seriously in the medical journals?

No, the volunteers must come from elsewhere, from outside David and Peter and their immediate circle. They had been discussing this problem over dinner. Could the governor of New York be approached, to offer inmates from the state prisons as guinea pigs? Would a tobacco company be prepared to open a clinic somewhere in the Third World? Could they advertise on the back page of the *Village Voice*?

Then that red light bounced on, and a sudden idea clicked on, a much brighter light, in Peter's mind. He stood, and dropped his napkin beside his plate. "Our problems may be solved," he said. "Just wait while I get my gun."

3

Freddie put a fax machine on top of a printer and carried both out to the van, juggling them there with one hand and one knee while unlocking the van's side cargo door. It was a pain having to unlock and relock the van every trip, but anybody who leaves a vehicle alone and unsealed for even a second in Manhattan is looking for trouble, and will soon be looking for a new radio.

It may be that the pervasive air of theft and chicanery forever floating like an aggressive cloud bank over New York City had played some part in Freddie's original decision to become a thief. In a different part of the world, where both property and human feelings are respected—oh, someplace like Ashland, Oregon, say—even the scurviest villain will have the occasional bout of conscience, but in New York's take-or-be-taken atmosphere moral suasion goes for naught.

Not that most New Yorkers are thieves. It is merely that most New Yorkers expect to be robbed, all the time, everywhere, in all circumstances, and in every way imaginable. The actual thieves in the city are statistically few, but very busy, and they set the tone. Therefore, whenever a New Yorker *is* robbed, there's no thought in anyone's mind, including the victim's, of a community outraged or a moral ethos damaged. There's nothing to be done about it, really, but shrug one's shoulders, buy better locks for next time, and rip off the insurance company.

Having relocked the van, Freddie went back to the neatly appointed front office on the first floor of the townhouse, and by the light of his muted pen-flash stacked a keyboard on a VDT, picked them up with both hands from underneath—van keys hooked in fingers of right hand—turned toward the front door, and a bright light hit him smack in the face.

Oh, shit. Freddie immediately slapped his eyelids shut; he knew that much. Don't lose your night vision. Eyes closed, he started to turn back to the desk to put down the VDT and keyboard, but a voice from the darkness said, "Don't move," so he stopped moving.

A second voice from the darkness said, "I think you're supposed to say 'freeze.'"

"It means the same thing," said the first voice, sounding a little testy.

The second voice said, "Maybe not to *them*."

"Them," Freddie knew, was him. And "him," at this moment in the history of the world, was a guy in trouble. Third conviction as an adult. Good-bye Peg Briscoe, good-bye nice little apartment in Bay Ridge, good-bye best years of his life.

It was very depressing.

Well, let's get on with it, then. His eyes still squeezed shut, Freddie said, "I'll just put this stuff down here."

"No, no," said the first voice. "I like you with your hands occupied. Search him, David."

"I don't have any weapons, if that's what you mean," Freddie said. At least they wouldn't be getting him for armed robbery, which might count for something twenty-five or thirty years from now, when he first came up for parole. Jesus Christ.

A lot more light suddenly flooded onto his eyelids; they'd switched on the room fluorescents. Still, he kept his eyes closed, jealously guarding that old night vision, the one asset he still had that might prove useful, God knew how.

"Of course you have weapons," said the second voice, David, approaching. "You're a hardened criminal, aren't you?"

"I'm kind of semisoft," Freddie said, quoting a remark Peg had made one night, comparing him to some crime show they were then watching on television (hoping for a little human contact there, but not expecting much).

And not getting much. If the two voices found the remark as amusing in this context as Freddie had in the context of being in bed with Peg watching television while stroking her near thigh, they kept it to themselves. There was ongoing silence while hands patted him all over, and then David, now directly behind Freddie, said, "He's clean."

Everybody watches television. "Told you so," said Freddie.

"What a trusting person you must be," said voice number one.

David, who had now moved around to Freddie's front, said, "His eyes are closed, Peter, do you see that?"

"Maybe he's afraid of us," Peter said.

"Maybe it's deniability," said David, his voice receding toward Peter. "You know, so he'd be able to swear in court he couldn't identify us."

Sounding flabbergasted, Peter said, "For Christ's sake, David, *him* not identify *us*? Good God, *why*?"

"*I* don't know," David said. "I'm no lawyer."

I'd like to see these idiots, just once, Freddie admitted to himself, but he still thought there might be some value in retaining whatever night vision he might still have with all this fluorescent glare greenish-red on his eyelids, so he kept his eyes squeezed shut and his hands cupping the VDT—which was beginning to get heavy—and waited for whatever would follow from here.

Which was Peter saying, "David, where did we put those handcuffs?"

Freddie couldn't help it; his eyes popped open, night vision be damned. Scrunching up his cheeks against the sudden on-slaught of fluorescents, he said, "Handcuffs! What do you people want with handcuffs?"

Meanwhile, David was saying, "*What* handcuffs? We don't have any handcuffs."

Peter, the tall skinny one with fuzzy black hair, answered Freddie first. "I want them for you, of course. You can't stand there holding our office equipment all night." Then, to David, he said, "From that Halloween thing. *You* remember."

David, the blond one with the baby fat, said, "Do we still have those?"

"Of course. You never throw anything away."

"You don't need handcuffs," Freddie said.

Peter said, "David, look in the storage closet with all the costumes, all right?"

"I'll look." David glanced at Freddie again, and back at Peter. "Will you be all right?"

"Of course. *I* have a gun."

"You don't need handcuffs," Freddie said.

"Be right back," David said, and left.

"You don't need handcuffs," Freddie said.

"Hush," Peter told him. "Turn to face that desk there, will you?"

So Freddie made a quarter turn, to face what was probably by day a receptionist's desk, and Peter sat at the desk, put the pistol down on top of it, and searched the drawers for forms. Freddie looked at Peter and the gun on the desk. He thought about throwing the VDT and the keyboard at Peter, or at the gun, and running for the front door. He thought Peter seemed pretty self-confident. He decided to wait and see what would happen next.

Which was, surprisingly enough, that Peter took his medical history. "Now," he said, having found the form he wanted and a pen to go with it, "I'll need your date of birth."

"Why?"

Peter looked at him. He sighed. He put down the pen and picked up the pistol and aimed it at Freddie's forehead. "Would you rather I knew your date of death?" he asked.

So Freddie told Peter his date of birth, and his record of childhood diseases, and about his parents' chronic illnesses, and what his grandparents had died of. And no, he was not allergic to penicillin or any other medicine that he knew of. He'd had no major operations.

"Drug history?" Peter asked.

Freddie clamped his mouth shut. Peter looked at him. He waited. Freddie said, "Reach for that gun all you want."

"I don't actually need to know your entire drug history," Peter acknowledged, as a clicking of handcuffs announced the return of David. "I just need to know your current status in re drugs."

"They were," David said, "in *your* underwear drawer."

"I've been clean over two years," Freddie said.

"Absolutely clean?"

"That's what I said, isn't it? What's going on here, anyway?"

David, jangling the handcuffs, said, "Put those things down and put your hands behind your back."

"I don't think so," Freddie said. He held tight to the VDT, ready to throw it in whatever direction seemed best. "Why don't you guys," he said, "just call the cops and quit all this fooling around?"

"There's a possibility," Peter said, seated over there at the desk, "that we won't have to call the cops at all."

Freddie squinted at him. He understood that these guys were the kind who in prison were known as faggots but who out here in the allegedly normal world preferred to be called gay, even though very few such people were even moderately cheerful. He didn't know what they wanted with him, but if it turned out that he did have some sort of honor on which they had nefarious designs, he was prepared to defend that honor with everything he had, which at the moment was a VDT and a keyboard.

David, apparently reading in Freddie's face something of his thoughts and his fears, abruptly said, with a kind of impatient sympathy, "Oh, for heaven's sake, there's nothing to worry about."

Freddie looked at him sidelong. "No?"

"No. We're not going to deflower you or anything."

Freddie wasn't sure what that word meant. "No?"

"Of course not," David said. "We're just going to experiment on you."

Freddie reared back. He very nearly tossed the VDT. "Like hell!" he said.

Rising from the desk, holding the pistol pointed alternately at David and Freddie, Peter said, "That's enough. David, you have the bedside manner of Jack the Ripper. Look, you— What's your name?"

"Freddie," Freddie said. He could give them that much.

"Freddie," agreed Peter. "Freddie," he said, "we are medical practitioners, David and me. Doctors. We are doing very valuable cancer research."

"Good."

"We are at a crossroads in our research," Peter went on, "and just this evening at dinner—"

"A dinner," David interpolated, giving Freddie a reproachful look, "which *I* prepared, which *you* interrupted, and which is now stone cold upstairs."

"Sorry about that," Freddie said.

"And not entirely relevant," Peter said, pointing the gun at David again.

"Point it at *him!*"

"Stop interrupting, all right, David?"

"Just point it at him."

"I'm trying to explain the situation to our friend here."

"Fine. Point the gun at him."

Peter pointed the gun at Freddie. He said, "Just this evening at dinner, we were discussing the next step in our research program, which is to test our formulae on human volunteers."

"Not me," Freddie said.

"We weren't thinking of you in particular," Peter told him, "because we didn't know you yet. We were thinking of calling our friend, the governor of the state of New York, and asking him for some prison volunteers. You know how that sort of thing works, don't you?"

As a matter of fact, Freddie did. Every once in a great while, in the pen, not often, the word would come around that some pharmacy company or the army or somebody wanted to test some shit on some people, and who would like to volunteer to drink the liquid or take the shot, in return for extra privileges or money or sometimes even early parole. There was always the guarantee that the shit was safe, but if the shit was safe why didn't they try it on people outside these prison walls?

Also, those times, they also always guaranteed they had this antidote available if anybody turned out to be allergic or something, but if they couldn't know for sure the shit itself would work how come they were always so positive the antidote would work? Anyway, Freddie had never volunteered for any of that stuff, but he knew people who had, usually long-termers, and there was always something weird happened. They gained a lot of weight, or their pee turned blue, or their hair fell out. One guy came back to the block talking Japanese, and nobody could figure out how they'd worked *that* on him. Sounded like Japanese, anyway.

Peter was still talking while Freddie'd been skipping down memory lane. When Freddie next tuned in, Peter was saying, "—takes so long. We'll get our volunteers, we'll run our experiments, everything will be fine, but it's just going to add six months of unnecessary delay to get the paperwork filed and the state legislature to approve and all that."

"The thing is," David said, sounding more eager than his partner, jingling the handcuffs as he talked, "the thing is, we've gone through all this bureaucratic red tape before and it's *so* costly in terms of time lost, and when we're talking cancer research, time lost is lives lost. You can see that, can't you?"

"Sure," said Freddie.

"Which is where you come in," Peter said.

"No," Freddie said.

"Listen to the proposition first," Peter advised him.

Freddie shrugged, which reminded him this VDT was getting *heavy*. "Can I put this down?" he asked.

"Not yet," Peter said. "Here's the proposition. If you agree, you'll sign a release here, and we'll give you the medicine, and you'll stay in this house for twenty-four hours. We'll have to lock you up, of course, but we'll feed you and give you a decent place to sleep."

"The rose room," David said to Peter.

"Exactly," Peter agreed. To Freddie he said. "The point is, we'll need to observe you, for reactions to the medicine. After the twenty-four hours, you'll be free to go. Without our equipment, of course."

"Heh-heh," Freddie said, acknowledging the joke.

"If you decide, on the other hand, not to cooperate—"

"You'll call the cops."

"I knew you were quick," Peter said.

Freddie considered. These guys were legitimate doctors, okay, and this thing was even called a research facility, the very phrase that had brought him in here. And it's on the East Side of Manhattan, so it's all gotta be on the up and up, right?

And what's the alternative? Good-bye to all that, that's the alternative. Police, prison, guards, fellow cons. That's the alternative.

So, if worse comes to worst, Peg can learn Japanese, that's all.

Freddie said, "And if something goes wrong, you got the antidote, right?"

"Nothing will go wrong," Peter said.

"Not a chance," David assured him.

"But you do got the antidote, right?"

The two doctors exchanged a glance. "If necessary," David said, jingling the handcuffs, "and it won't be necessary at *all*, but just in case it should be necessary, we would have an antidote, yes."

"And I get to put this thing down," Freddie said, meaning the VDT.

"Of course," David said.

Freddie looked from one to the other. "One thing," he said, "and one thing only. You don't need the handcuffs."

4

Both Peter and David would have felt more comfortable with the burglar in handcuffs, but that had turned out to be actually a sort of deal-breaker, so finally they'd agreed, and that meant the only restraint they had on this fellow Freddie was Peter's pistol. Fortunately, it was clear that Freddie believed Peter might be capable of using the pistol, a belief neither Peter nor David shared, but a belief they were willing to encourage.

Freddie having signed the release form with an unrecognizable scrawl, they moved him at last up one flight from reception to the rear lab room, where they seated him in a metal chair and did a cursory examination to be sure he was as physically fit as he claimed, and he was. There was no evidence of alcohol or drugs, no irregular heartbeat, no troublesome sounds in his lungs, and a perfectly average blood pressure. So that left nothing to do but give him the formula and see what happened.

No, actually there was still one thing more to be done. Before the experiment could get under way, they first had to decide which formula to try on him, since they could only hope to test one of the two formulas per experimental subject. LHRX1 and LHRX2 were both put out on the chrome table, side by side, the syringe and the after-dinner mint, and there they waited while David and Peter discreetly argued over which one was the likelier to succeed, therefore which one should be tried in this first human experiment. They argued for several minutes, at an impasse, and then the subject said, "I get it. That's always the way."

They turned to study him. Peter said, "What is?"

The subject pointed. "The shot is the stuff I got to take, and the cookie's the antidote, that I probably won't even need."

They looked at him. They looked at one another. Peter, who'd been arguing for LHRX1, the serum in the syringe, smiled and said, "An omen, clearly. David, we'd best do what it says."

"Oh, very well," said David, who hadn't really expected to win the argument anyway.

Peter smiled again as he crossed to pick up the syringe. Holding it point upward beside his shoulder, he turned to the subject. "In the buttock, I'm afraid," he said.

"And I saw that one comin', too," the subject said. But he made no trouble about it, merely stood and dropped his trousers and bent over the lab table and jumped a foot when Peter swabbed the spot with the cotton wad dipped in alcohol. "Jesus!" the subject cried. "That hurt!"

"I didn't do it yet," Peter told him, and did it, and the subject didn't move at all, because he was too confused. "There you are," Peter said, stepping back a pace. "You may adjust your clothing."

The subject did.

"You may sit down again," Peter said.

"Not yet," the subject said. "My ass cheek is real sore."

It was not, and Peter knew it, but he also knew how childish patients are, so he merely said, "Stand, then, if you like."

The subject stood. He said, "What happens next?"

"Nothing, not at first," Peter told him. "We all stand around here like idiots—"

"While our dinner dies upstairs," David said.

Peter turned to him. "We'll microwave it, David, it will be good as new."

"Hardly."

Peter turned back to the subject. "We'll stand here bickering about nothing at all," he explained, "for fifteen minutes, and then we'll take your pulse and look in your eyes and do a few more things like that, and then we'll close you away in the guest room upstairs—"

"It has its own john," David assured him.

"—and then," Peter said, "we'll examine you again at . . ." He consulted his watch. "It's nearly midnight now. Every two hours. We'll disturb your beauty sleep, I'm afraid, at two, and four, and six, and so on."

"Disturbing our own, as well," David added, as though the subject cared.

"During the day tomorrow," Peter went on, "the staff will be down here, in the research area, but only David and I ever go up to the living quarters, so no one else needs to know you're here. We'll feed you at appropriate times, and go on observing you at two-hour intervals, and at midnight tomorrow we will be happy to let you go."

"Me, too," said the subject. "Can I call my girl?"

"Sorry," said Peter.

"She'll worry," said the subject.

"I imagine she's used to that," Peter said, "given you for a boyfriend."

So that was the end of that. Conversation grew more desultory, time crept by, and at last the fifteen minutes were up. David and Peter gave the subject his first postserum examination, found no abnormalities, and wrote everything down on a long yellow legal pad. "Fine," Peter said. "Now we go upstairs. The elevator's too small for three, I'm afraid."

As they were leaving the lab, the subject pointed back to LHRX2, saying, "What about the antidote? Doesn't that come along with us?"

"Don't worry," Peter said. "You won't need it."

"Besides," David said, "that isn't—" But then he broke off, at a warning glare and headshake from Peter, behind the subject's back. Oh, of course. The point was to keep the subject soothed, not permit him to get more than necessarily tense. "We know where it is," David said, "if we need it. Which we won't."

"Okay."

With no more complaint, the subject went on ahead of them up the stairs two flights and then past their cold dinners and down the hall and into the rose room. "See you at two," Peter said, and locked the door, and he and David went back to their main living quarters, where David mourned their dinner a while before nuking it in the microwave, and Peter said, "We can't take turns, of course. This is still a criminal here, we'll both have to wake up every two hours."

"Assuming we sleep at all," David said. "Oh, Peter! Wouldn't it be wonderful if it works?"

"Not wonderful, exactly," Peter said. "We did struggle very hard on this, David, you and I, after all."

"You know what I mean, though."

Peter unbent. He smiled at his partner. "I do know what you mean. And you're right, wonderful *is* the word."

It was not, however, the word for their dinner, when at last they got back to it. They finished it just the same, their attention elsewhere, on the guest in the rose room and the serum even now coursing through his veins. Affecting his pigment? They discussed what they would do if the experiment proved a success. If the subject, Freddie, became even a little translucent, they would photograph him from every angle, they would document the fact as much as possible, they would even bring in one or two trusted staff members during the day tomorrow to see the subject for themselves. Then, armed with that documentation—but not with Freddie; they'd keep their side of the bargain and release him—they could go to the governor of New York or the president of a tobacco company or almost anybody and get permission and funding for much broader experimentation, with volunteers who could be thoroughly documented and checked and observed by all the impartial medical men you want. No problem.

This prospect keyed them up so much they didn't go to bed at all between midnight and 2 A.M., when it was time for the first check on the subject. They unlocked his door to find him in bed sound asleep, but he quickly and amiably awoke, yawning. How could he be so calm under such circumstances?

David and Peter examined him once more, found no changes at all, locked him in the room again, and this time went to bed, setting the radio alarm for 3:50. It went off at that awful hour, with the kind of ungodly modern music the classical stations like to put on when no one's listening, and they got up, brushed their teeth, dressed hurriedly, and went down the hall to find the door of the rose room gone.

Well, no, not gone. It was leaning against the wall inside the room. The subject had removed the pins from the hinges, moved the door, and left. "Oh, Christ!" said Peter.

But that wasn't the worst. The alarm system had been dismantled, not carefully: wires dangled from the box next to the elevator door. "Hell and damn," said Peter.

They went down to the first floor, where they found that Freddie NoName had taken all the rest of their office equipment with him on his way out. "Bastard," said Peter.

Then they went back up one flight and looked around the lab, and it was David who noticed that the LHRX2 was gone. "Oh, Peter, my God," he said, pointing at the empty space where that black after-dinner mint had lately stood.

Peter looked. "Oh, no," he said.

Half-whispering, David said, "He thinks it's the antidote."

"Oh, wow," Peter said.

5

Peg Briscoe dreamed of open mouths, huge open mouths with great red sluglike tongues and teeth that were huge and filthy and alive, writhing like Medusa's snakes. And she was being drawn into them, drawn into the horrible foul-smelling mouths.

This is very scary, she thought, in the dream. This is really very scary. I better quit working for Dr. Lopakne.

The mouths were getting closer, the writhing tongues reaching for her, the snakey teeth glaring at her with their shiny chrome-filling eyes. This is truly scary, Peg told herself in the dream. I think I better wake up now.

So she did, to find a hand on her breast. She opened her eyes in the blackness of the bedroom and whispered, "Freddie?"

"Who else?" Freddie whispered, his breath warm on her ear, his hand roaming over her body.

"You're late," she whispered.

"I had a hell of a thing happen," he whispered, moving her legs apart. "I'll tell you all about it."

"I had such an awful dream," she whispered, as he moved around under the covers, getting closer to her. "I'm going to have to quit at the dentist."

"That's okay," he said. He was on top of her now, supporting weight on his elbows. "I got a bunch of stuff in the van."

"Mmm, nice," she whispered, feeling that gentle pressure, feeling him find his way home. Her left hand reached out in the darkness, toward the bedside table. "Oh, let me see you," she whispered, and her fingers found the pull chain. She pulled, and the light came on, and she SCREAMED.

"Wha?"

Her eyes snapped shut. She thought, Take me back to the dream! Back into the mouths, anywhere, anywhere but here!

Thrashing on top of her. "Whasa matter?"

She opened her eyes, wide, and stared at the ceiling. "There's nobody here!" she screamed, "Oh, my God, I'm going crazy!"

"What? Whadayou—Holy *shit*!"

The thrashing redoubled. A weight lifted from her, and the covers flung themselves back from her body, down to a heap on her ankles. In the light of the bedside lamp, she stared down at her own naked body, the white sheet all around, the sudden indentation in the sheet beside her and then that indentation just as suddenly gone.

She was alone in the room. Alone! Is this a dream? she asked herself.

Drugs! All at once, she was sure of it. Years ago, she'd experimented, the way everybody experimented, she'd tried some pretty wild chemicals that nobody knew what the side effects were, or how long they could hang around inside the body. Was this a—was this a bad trip, five years late?

Over to the right was the dresser, with the mirror above it. From over there came the voice that sounded so much like Freddie's: "Holy Jesus!"

Peg whimpered; she couldn't help it. She wanted to reach down to the flung covers and pull them up over herself, but she was afraid to move. She whimpered again and said, in a new tiny voice, "Freddie?"

"What the *fuck* has happened?"

"Freddie, where are you?"

"I'm right *here,* for Christ's sake!"

"Freddie, what are you doing?"

"I'm looking at myself," said the voice, from over by the dresser and the mirror. "I'm looking *for* myself."

"Freddie, don't do this!"

"It's those goddamn doctors! That goddamn stuff they shot me with!"

"What? Freddie?"

"The fucking antidote didn't work!"

"Freddie?"

A big indentation came into the sheet beside her, as though someone had sat down on the other side of the bed. She screamed, but not as loudly as before. She kept staring at that indentation.

"Listen, Peg," said a voice from somewhere above the indentation. "What happened to me was—hey!" the voice suddenly interrupted itself, as though surprised and pleased by something.

Fearful, trembling all over, Peg said, "Hey? Hey what?"

"When I close my eyes," said Freddie's voice, "I can still see!"

"Oh, Freddie, I'm gonna have a heart attack, I'm gonna have an accident right here in the bed, Freddie, don't *do* this, whatever you're doing, don't do it!"

"Listen, Peg, listen," Freddie's voice said, and something horrible touched her arm.

This time she SHRIEKED—she let out a good one—and recoiled half off the bed.

"Jeeziz, Peg! The neighbors are gonna call the cops!"

"What was that? What was it? Something touched me!"

"*I* touched you, Peg."

"You? Who *are* you?"

"I'm Freddie, for Christ's sake."

"*Where* are you?"

"I'm right here, I—listen, let me explain."

"I can't *stand* this!"

"Peg," the voice said, "Peg, turn off the light."

"What? Are you crazy?"

"Believe me, Peg, it'll be better. Turn off the light."

Afraid to disobey—what if something horrible touched her again?—she reached out and pulled the chain and turned off the light, and in the blessed shield of darkness she sat up, reached forward, grabbed the covers, and pulled them up over herself as she lay back down. All the way over herself, head and everything.

"Peg?"

"Wha?"

She could feel him shifting around, changing position on the bed, sitting there beside her. "You feel a little better, Peg?"

She did. It was stupid, but she did. Just not seeing him—well, she wouldn't be able to see him anyway, but in the darkness there was no way to *know* you couldn't see him. "A little," she admitted, but kept the covers over her head just the same.

"Peg," said Freddie's voice in the darkness, outside the covers, "let me tell you what happened. I went to a place to get some stuff tonight, and these two doctors grabbed me and held a gun on me."

"Doctors?"

"Some kinda doctors. It was a lab kinda place, with equipment I could turn over pretty easy, so I went in, and they got me, and they made me this deal."

"Freddie, that *is* you there, isn't it?"

"*Sure* it's me, Peg," Freddie said, and patted her through the covers, and the funny thing was, the pat was comforting. As long as she couldn't see that she couldn't see him, things were okay. Almost normal.

She sighed. She relaxed one tiny notch. She said, "Okay, Freddie. What happened?"

"They made me this deal," Freddie said. "I'd help them with this experiment, or they'd call the cops. I mean, one option was, they *don't* call the cops. They were doing cancer research and they had this medicine and they needed to test it on a person. And there was this other stuff that was the antidote, in case something went wrong. So I went along with them—"

"Sure."

"—and as soon as I could I got out of there and took the stuff I came for and took the antidote and come right home. And you know I don't like to turn the light on when you're asleep . . ."

"I know."

"So that's what it is," Freddie said, and sighed.

Peg tentatively moved her head out from under the covers, like a turtle. She looked in the blackness toward the sound of his voice, pretending she'd be able to see him if the light was on. "*What's* what it is, Freddie?" she asked.

"The antidote didn't work," Freddie said. "I don't know what the hell all this has to do with cancer research, but I see what they did to me. Peg?"

"Yes, Freddie?"

"I'm invisible, Peg," Freddie said. "Isn't that a bitch?"

He sounded so forlorn, so lost, that she couldn't help it, her heart went out to him. "Oh, come here, Freddie," she said, reaching out, finding his arm, pulling him close.

"I'm sorry, Peg," Freddie said, sliding in under the covers.

"It's not your fault," she said, arms around him, caressing him.

"Aw, thanks, Peg," Freddie said, and kissed her, and pretty soon they were heading back toward where they'd been going in the first place.

"One thing," Peg said, as Freddie's comforting weight settled upon her.

"What's that, Peg?"

"Don't turn on the light."

"Don't worry," Freddie said.

6

It's hard to service a body you can't see. Freddie's bathroom experiences in the morning were more complex than usual. Shaving turned out to be the easiest part of it—if maybe the least necessary, all things considered—since he was used to shaving in the shower, where he couldn't look at his face anyway. The worst, particularly in the shower, was that he could see through his eyelids. Now, when a person closes his eyes it's because he wants them *closed*. He doesn't want to see water spraying straight down from the shower fixture onto his eyeballs, and he certainly doesn't want to watch the soapy outline of knuckles, in extreme close-up, squidging deep into his eyes.

Still, he eventually finished, his towel swooping and swirling in what seemed to be an empty room, and came out to dress—shoes and socks and pants okay, but the polo shirt had these round openings for arms and neck, and nothing there—and by that time Peg was back. She'd taken one look at him this morning—or, rather, she'd taken one look at where she'd thought he might be, judging by the sounds he was making—and she'd said, "I don't need this, Freddie. I'll be right back." And off she'd gone.

And now she was back, in the kitchen, and when Freddie walked in she stood up from her breakfast of dry toast and black coffee, looked at the round openings in the polo shirt, and said, "I thought it was gonna be like that. I can't do anything about the hands, but there's your head." And she gestured at the butcher-block counter between the sink and the refrigerator.

Freddie went over to look. Peg had gone to one of those party-supply places, or tourist-junk places—whatever. And here on the butcher block were four full-head latex masks: Dick Tracy, Bart Simpson, Frankenstein's monster, and the Ayatollah Khomeini. Freddie said, "Khomeini?"

"It was marked down. The way I look at it," Peg said, "you've got kind of a mood thing there. You go through the day, you can decide who you feel like."

"If I ever feel like Frankenstein," Freddie said, "you better worry."

"I figure you'll mostly be Bart Simpson," Peg told him.

"Have a cow," Freddie agreed morosely, beginning to feel sorry for himself. He sighed, and said, "Peg, how do I eat through one of those?"

"I don't wanna know about it." Picking up her toast and coffee, she said, "I think we don't eat together anymore. I'll be in the living room. When you come in, be one of those fellas, okay?"

"Okay, Peg." Freddie sighed again. "Being an invisible guy," he said, "is kind of a lonely job, isn't it?"

Taking pity on him, Peg said, "Maybe it'll go away pretty soon."

"Maybe."

"Or we'll adapt, we'll get used to it."

"You think so?"

"Eat your breakfast, if you can find your mouth," Peg told him. "Then come in and we'll talk."

She left the kitchen, and Freddie poured orange juice and coffee, then popped a couple fake waffles into the toaster. Sitting alone at the small kitchen table, feeling more and more sorry for himself, he ate his breakfast, lifted his shirt to find out if he could still see the food he'd just eaten, and looked in at a bowl of succotash and soy sauce, without the bowl. Lowering the shirt and averting his gaze, he decided he wouldn't mention this part of the experience to Peg. Nor let her discover it for herself, if at all possible.

The visual replay of breakfast so discouraged him he almost went into the living room without his new head. In the doorway, in the nick of time, he remembered, and made a U- turn.

His choosing of Dick Tracy was a kind of self-therapy, an attempt to lighten his mood through the therapeutic use of comedy. He was a crook, see, and Dick Tracy was a cop. Get it? Well, it was a try.

Peg didn't help much. Looking up from *Newsday*, "Ah, the Dick head," she said.

"Thanks, Peg."

"That isn't what I meant. Sit down, Freddie, let's talk."

"It's hot inside here," Freddie complained, sitting in his favorite chair, across from the TV.

"If you want to talk to me," Peg told him, "you'll keep it on."

"I'm just saying." Whenever Freddie sighed, inside the latex mask, it ballooned slightly, as though Dick Tracy had recurring mumps.

Peg frowned at him, discontented. After a minute, she said, "Freddie, could you possibly put on a long-sleeve shirt?"

"This is becoming a pain," Freddie announced, but he obediently got up and went into the bedroom, coming back two minutes later in a long-sleeved blue work shirt with the cuffs turned back just once and the bottom of the Dick Tracy head tucked into the collar. "Okay?"

"Fine," Peg said. "I'm sorry to be a pest, Freddie, but I'm just not used to it yet. I'll *get* used to it, I really will, but it's gonna take time."

"Maybe we won't need a whole buncha time," Freddie suggested, sitting again in his favorite chair, constantly aware of the nothing just beyond his turned-back shirt cuffs. "Maybe it'll go away soon."

"Maybe."

"The sooner the better," Freddie said. "I wonder if I oughta go back to those doctors, make up some kinda deal, see have they got an antidote that works."

"That could be trouble, Freddie," Peg said. "If they had you arrested or something."

"Still. To get my, you know, my *self* back."

"Well, I've been thinking about that," Peg said, "and maybe this thing isn't such a tragedy after all."

"It's not a *tragedy*," Freddie agreed. "It's just a pain in the ass."

"Or maybe," Peg suggested, "an opportunity."

The Dick Tracy face gave her a skeptical look. "What kinda opportunity?"

"Well, what is it you do for a living?"

"Steal things."

"And if nobody can see you?"

Freddie thought about that. He rested Dick Tracy's chin on the heel of his invisible right hand, which looked worse than he knew, and he said, "Hmmmmm."

"You see what I mean," Peg said.

Freddie shifted position, nodded Dick Tracy's head, and said, "You mean, get naked and sneak into places."

"Yeah, that's right, you'd have to be naked, wouldn't you?"

"Warm places," Freddie decided. "Sneak into warm places. But then what?"

"Steal," Peg said.

"Steal what? I grab a handful of cash, I head for the door, people see this wad of cash floating through the air, they make a jump for it, what they grab is *me*."

"Too bad you don't have a, like a bag that's invisible, too."

"I got trouble enough with just me invisible."

"Well, it won't be all trouble, Freddie, will it?"

He sighed; Dick Tracy's mumps recurred. "What else is it, Peg? Look how I am."

"Well, I can't look how you are, can I?"

"That's part of the problem right there. And I have to sit around with my head inside this microwave oven here—"

"We'll punch airholes around the top."

"After I take it off."

"Okay," she said. "But, you know, Freddie, maybe we don't have to be so completely negative about this situation."

"Oh, no?" He waved his round empty sleeves at her. "You call this positive?"

"Possibly," she said, musing, thinking. "Possibly it's positive."

Freddie loved it when Peg thought. In the first place, she was so good at it, and in the second place, she looked so lovable while doing it. So he didn't interrupt, merely sat there, invisible inside his clothes and Dick Tracy head, and watched her think, and after a while he saw the slow smile of success spread across her face. "Yeah?" he said.

"Yeah," she said.

"Now it's all hunky-dory?"

"Not exactly," she said. "It's true there's still stuff we're gonna have to adapt to here, we both know that—"

"Like don't make love with the lights on."

"Don't remind me. But that isn't all there is to what's happened here, just problems and adaptations."

"No?"

"Freddie," she said, with a broad smile at Dick Tracy's latex-chiseled features, "it just might be, when we get used to it, invisibility, just maybe, it could be fun."

7

To be a tobacco-company lawyer is to know something of the
darkness of the human heart. Little surprised Mordon Leethe,
nothing shocked him, not much interested him, and there was
nothing in life he loved, including himself.

A stocky heavy-shouldered man of fifty-six, Mordon
Leethe had been a skinny six foot two when he'd played bas-
ketball all those years ago at Uxtover Prep, but caution and
skepticism had worked on him like a heavy planet's gravity,
compressing him to his current five foot ten, none of it muscle but all of it hard anyway, with tension and rage and dis-
dain.

Mordon was going over the latest PAC regulations regard-
ing corporate donations to political campaigns—he loved
Congress; hookers defining how they'll agree to be fucked—
when the phone rang. He picked it up, made a low sound like
a warthog, and the voice of his secretary, Helen, a nice ma-
ternal woman lost in these offices, said in his ear, "Dr. Amory
on two. R&D."

Helen was a good secretary. She knew her boss could not
possibly keep in his mind the name and title of every person
listed in his Rolodex, so whenever someone he wasn't used to
was on the line, Helen would identify the caller when an-
nouncing the call. By just now saying, "R&D," she'd jogged

Mordon Leethe's memory, reminding him that Dr. Archer Amory was head of NAABOR's research and development program, a three-pronged project that attempted to (1) prove that all proof concerning the health dangers of cigarette consumption is unproved; (2) find some other use for tobacco—insulation? optical fibers?—should worse come to worst; and (3) prepare for a potential retooling to marijuana, should that market ever open up.

Which of these R&D tines had led Dr. Archer to call an attorney? All Mordon Leethe knew was the equation: Doctor = bad news. Shrinking, condensing yet another tiny millimeter, he punched "2" without acknowledging Helen's words, and said, "'Morning, Doctor. How are things in the lab?"

"Well, the mice are still dying," said a hearty brandy-and-golf voice.

"I know that joke," Mordon said sourly. "The elephants are still alive, but they're coughing like hell."

"Really? That's a new one. Very funny."

It was really a very old one. Mordon said, "What is it today, Doctor?"

"You're going to be getting a visit from two of our independent-contractor researchers."

"Am I."

"Their names are—"

"Wait."

Mordon drew toward himself today's yellow pad, flipped to a new page, picked up his Mont Blanc Agatha Christie pen with the ruby-eyed snake on its clip, and said, "Now."

"Their names are Dr. David Loomis and Dr. Peter Heimhocker, and they—"

"Spell."

Amory spelled, then said, "I want to emphasize, these two

are not employees of my division, nor in fact employees of NAABOR at all. They're independent contractors."

This is something very bad, Mordon thought. He said, "And what's their problem?"

"I'd rather they told you that themselves. When today would be a good time to see them?"

Very *very* bad. Mordon looked at his calendar. "Three o'clock," he said.

"Do keep me informed," Archer Amory said.

Fat chance. "Of course," Mordon said, and dropped the phone like a dead rat into its cradle.

Since it was dangerous for Mordon to drink at lunch—his real self kept trying to come out—he refrained, taking only Pellegrino water, which meant his mood in the afternoons was *much* worse than his mood in the mornings. Into this foul presence came the two doctors, at five minutes before the hour of three, tension in their every aspect. Mordon remarked their sexual proclivity without regard; he didn't dislike any human being more than any other human being. "*Doctor* Amory," he said, with slight savage emphasis on the title, "tells me you two have some sort of problem."

"We think we do," said Dr. Peter Heimhocker. This was the one Mordon had the most trouble looking at. White men in Afros are hard enough for normal people to take; for Mordon, after lunch, that fuzzy halo of black hair above that skinny pale face was practically incitement to amputation. Of the head.

The other one, Dr. David Loomis, looked at his partner with frightened outrage. "You *think* we do! *Pee*-ter!" He was the somewhat heavier one, a soft-bodied, earnestly petulant man with thinning hair on top, unnaturally blond.

Meanwhile, Heimhocker was saying, "David, do you mind?"

It was going to be necessary to look at Heimhocker. Looking at him, Mordon said, "Why not tell me what happened?"

While Heimhocker opened his skinny mouth and took a long deep breath, visibly gathering his thoughts, Loomis, in a sudden spasm of words, cried out, "We kidnapped a man and gave him an experimental formula and he got away!"

Mordon moved backward in his chair. "Did you say 'kidnapped'?"

Heimhocker said, "David, let me. David, *please*." Then he turned to Mordon, saying, "I don't know how much Archer told you—"

"Pretend Dr. Amory told me nothing."

"All right. David and I run a small research facility here in New York. Last night, a burglar broke in, and we captured him. We're just at a point here—well—you don't want to know about our research."

Mordon drew a noose on the yellow pad.

Heimhocker at last went on. "Suffice it to say, we're just at the stage in our work where we need practical field results."

"Guinea pigs," Mordon translated, being well familiar with the creation of smoke-screen phrases.

"Well, yes," Heimhocker said, and coughed delicately. "Human guinea pigs, in point of fact."

"Volunteers," the fidgety Loomis volunteered. "Or prisoners in a state penitentiary. Also volunteers, of course."

Mordon drew fuzzy hair above the noose. "What is the subject of this research?"

"Melanoma."

Mordon stared. "What the fuck has *that* got to do with cigarettes?"

"Nothing!" cried Loomis, appalled, waving his hands in front of his face like a man afraid of bats.

Simultaneously, Heimhocker practically leaped to his feet

as he shouted, "There has never been the *slightest* link! Never!"

Then Mordon understood, and came close to smiling, but refrained. "I see," he said, and did see. "So you tried your whatsit on this burglar, but he then escaped, and you want to know what your legal exposure might be."

"Well," Heimhocker said, "us, of course, but also the American Tobacco Research Institute."

Now Mordon did smile, not pleasantly. "Is that what NAABOR calls itself with you two? Dr. Amory assures me they've already cut you loose."

"What?"

Mordon said, "Let me explain the situation. If your problem turns out to be a simple matter, I will handle it for you, and charge my normal corporate client, NAABOR. But if it turns out to be a police matter, a matter of felonies, I will direct you to a colleague of mine who handles criminal cases, and you'll work out your arrangements directly with him."

Loomis breathed the words, "Criminal case?"

"The first question, I suppose," Mordon said, writing the number *1* on his pad and circling it, "is, What is the likelihood your stuff killed the fellow?"

"Killed him!" They stared at one another, and then Heimhocker said, "No, there should be nothing. I mean, nothing *lethal.*"

"In one," Loomis said, "or the other, Peter. The combination, how do we know *what* that cocktail could do?"

"Not kill anybody," Heimhocker insisted, irritably. "We've been over this and over this, David."

Mordon said, "Cocktail? Would you explain?"

"The fact is," Heimhocker said, "we have two formulae. We gave the burglar one, but he got the idea—"

"We *gave* him the idea, Peter."

"All right, David, we gave him the idea." To Mordon he explained, a bit shamefacedly, "He thought the other one was some sort of antidote."

"And took it, is that what you're saying, on the way out?"

"Yes."

"And now he's somewhere in the world," Mordon summed up, "a felon, a burglar, not likely to consult a doctor or an emergency room, with two experimental medicines floating around inside him that you aren't absolutely totally sure what either of them would do, much less both."

"Not precisely, no," Heimhocker agreed, sounding defensive, "not before *much* more testing and—"

"Yes, yes, I'm not impugning your methodology," Mordon assured him. "At least, not before last night. What were these products of yours *supposed* to do?"

"Affect the pigment of the skin," Loomis said, eagerly, pinching his own pink forearm to demonstrate the concept *skin*.

"You mean it could give him a bad burn, something like that?"

"Oh, no, not at all," Loomis said, briskly shaking his head, and Heimhocker said, "Quite the reverse. The object is the elimination or alteration of pigment."

Mordon waited, but nothing more was forthcoming. At last he said, "Meaning?"

"Well, we've discussed this, David and I," Heimhocker said, "ever since it happened—"

"We had *no* sleep."

"No. And we talked it over and we think it's possible," Heimhocker went on, and cleared his throat, and said, "that the fellow is, at this point he might very well be, uh, well . . . invisible."

Mordon looked at them, at their serious frightened faces. He did not write anything on his pad. In fact, he put down the pen. "Tell me," he said, "more."

8

There are vans with many large windows all the way around, so the kids can look out on their way to Little League. And there are vans with a minimum of windows—windshield, and rectangles to both sides of the front seat—so the cops can't look in on its way to or from the felony. Freddie's van was of the latter type, with two seats in front, a floor gearshift between them, and a dark cavernous emptiness in back where an electrician would mount shelves but which Freddie kept bare because he was never exactly sure what size object he might want to put back there. The van had two rear doors (window-less) that opened outward like the library doors in a serious play, plus a wide sliding door on the right side in case he ever desired to steal a stove. The floor in back was carpeted with stubbly gray AstroTurf, and the bulb was gone from the interior light.

Bay Ridge is one of the more crime-free neighborhoods of Brooklyn, mostly because it is populated by so many hot-headed ethnics who take crime personally and who in any case like to beat up on people. Therefore, most residents leave their vehicles parked at the curb, no problem. But Freddie felt about his van much the way he felt about Peg, and he wouldn't leave *Peg* at the curb, so he'd worked out an inexpensive rental arrangement for space in the parking lot next to the neighborhood firehouse, where the firepersons kept their own private vehicles and where *nobody* messed around.

This morning, after their separate breakfasts, Peg took the keys and walked the two blocks to this firehouse, waved to a couple of the persons sitting around on folding chairs out front enjoying the spring sunshine and the spring clothing on the persons passing by—they waved back, knowing Peg and Freddie and the van all went together as a package—then got the van and drove it back to their apartment building. Usually Freddie did the driving, but Peg had taken a shot at the wheel several times before this, and was used to the stick shift on the floor.

What she wasn't used to was Freddie, not like this. She pulled up in front of the building, and out came a tall Bart Simpson, in normal shirt and pants and shoes, but with weird peach-colored hands that were actually Playtex kitchen gloves. Not being a kitchen sort of person, and so not used to Playtex kitchen gloves, Freddie had a little trouble at first opening the passenger door of the van, but then he got it, and got in, and said, "Peg, these gloves are hotter than the mask."

"Keep them on," Peg advised, and drove away before anybody in the neighborhood could get a good look at her traveling companion.

"We'll go to Manhattan," Freddie said. "Nobody looks weird there because everybody looks weird there."

"Well, you're sure gonna test that theory," Peg said. "You know, Freddie, I didn't notice it in the apartment, but in this little space here, when you talk, you sound kind of muffled."

"Well, no wonder," Freddie said. "I'm inside this condom here."

"Poor Freddie," Peg said, and concentrated on her driving.

There were some looks from surprised other drivers while they were stopped at red lights along the way, but not enough to be real trouble. Freddie sat well back in the passenger seat, usually with his face turned toward Peg—or Bart's face, actually—and anyway it was pretty dim inside the van, so probably the worst the nosy parkers in the other cars could say, to themselves or their fellow travelers, was, "That's a weird-looking guy," or, "That weird-looking guy looks familiar," or, "Doesn't that weird-looking guy look like Bart Simpson?" And even if somebody said, aloud, in the privacy of his or her own vehicle, "There's a guy in that car in a Bart Simpson mask," so what? They sell them, don't they? For people to wear, don't they? So what's the problem?

They took the Brooklyn-Battery Tunnel—well, what else would you do?—and once they were in the tunnel Freddie said, "Time for me to get ready." He clambered through the space between the seats, into the empty rear of the van, sat down on the floor back there, and began to unwrap himself.

Since the van was without back windows, it had only exterior rearview mirrors, for which Peg was now grateful. It meant she couldn't see her guy gradually disappear. Nevertheless, it was startling, just before they left the tunnel at the Manhattan end, when what was clearly a forearm rested on the back of the driver's seat and Freddie's voice just behind her right ear said, "All set," but when she turned her head for a quick look, there was nobody in the van except her, and nothing back there but a crumpled pile of clothes on the floor.

The sudden adrenaline rush made her veer too close to the cab on her left, which yawped in angry response. Pulling back into her own lane, emerging from the tunnel into sunlight—even Manhattan gets sunlight, some days—Peg said, "Neaten up those clothes, Freddie, you're gonna have to put that stuff back on."

"You're right," said the voice, and the forearm left her seatback, and she heard but did not turn around to watch Freddie's clothing arrange itself more neatly in a rear corner.

"Where do I go from here?" Peg asked, since big green

signs dead ahead were giving her a number of choices, and not much time to make one.

"West Side," Freddie's voice said. From the sound of it, he was now leaning on the back of the passenger seat, and when Peg glanced over there, yes, that was the indentation of his arm. This, she thought, not for the first time, is going to take some getting used to.

Peg took the West Side Highway, Freddie's disembodied voice telling her to bear to the right at Twenty-third Street and then make the right turn onto Forty-second Street, which she did, only then saying, "Where we going, Freddie?"

"West Forty-seventh. The diamond district."

"Oh, yeah?" Peg was pleased. "I've never been there."

"Neither have I," Freddie said. "At least, not in the day-time."

9

There are a couple of centers of the wholesale diamond trade in New York City, one down by the Manhattan Bridge and the other on West Forty-seventh Street between Fifth and Sixth Avenues. Diamonds are the principal business of this block, but they also deal in other precious stones, and gold and silver, and platinum, and whatever else is small and shiny and very very valuable. Here entire buildings are given over to the buyers and sellers of costly stone and metal, all seated at the small wood-and-glass tables under the extremely bright lights, protected by layer after layer of security, negotiating in Yiddish or Dutch or Japanese or Boer or Portuguese or Bantu or even, if all else fails, English. Millions of dollars in value change hands on this block, not every month, not every day, but every minute, most of the transactions handled by somewhat shabby-looking people who seem to take no pleasure from riches or even the idea of riches but only from the process itself. They don't live to make money, they live to make deals, and they've gotten pretty good at it.

When Peg made the turn from Seventh Avenue, Freddie could sense it already, the buzz and stir of furious life all up and down the block. There's something here for me, Freddie thought, as he often did, adrenaline surging, and as usual it was a happy thought. "Park anywhere, Peg," he said.

Peg gave the air around him a caustic look, then turned her attention back to the street, lined solidly on both sides with parked trucks, vans, station wagons, and sedans armed with company names on their doors. (A civilian vehicle would be eaten alive on this block.) "Oh, sure," she said. "How about on top of that cable-company van?"

"Whatever works for you, Peg," Freddie said. He was too excited by the street to worry about details. The bowl of succotash and soy sauce (without the bowl) was gone now, happily digested, and he was ready to roll.

Midway down the block, on the right, stood a fire hydrant. A roofing company truck was parked next to it, of course, but whatever had recently blocked the rest of the legal clearance must have just this minute left, so Peg slid in there, backed and filled into the tiny space, and at last said, "There."

"Leave the motor on and switch on the blinker lights," Freddie advised. "That way you're not parked, you're stopped. And I tell you what, Peg. After a few minutes, move over to the passenger seat here. When I knock on the window, you open it, okay?"

"How will I know it's you?"

"Because you won't see me, Peg," Freddie said. "If you *see* somebody, don't open it. If you don't see somebody, it's me."

"Of course," Peg said. "I'm sorry, Freddie, the traffic got me rattled."

"S'okay. Close the door after me, okay?"

The side door of the van opened on the curb side. Freddie slid it slowly back, sorry for once there wasn't a window in it so he could see exactly what was just outside there, and when it was ajar barely enough he wriggled through and stood silent a moment, back against the van, checking it all out, while Peg reached over to slide the door shut.

The first thing Freddie didn't like was the sidewalk. It wasn't what you would call clean. It was also crowded with people, rushing, scurrying, sidestepping, side-slipping people. Tall skinny black messengers with many-shaped packages strapped to their backs; black-coated and black-hatted Hasidim, some pushing wheeled black valises; short round Puerto Rican file clerks in Day-Glo clothing; tourists from Germany and Japan, gawping at what might have been theirs; MBAs in their last suit, looking for work; lawyers and process servers and bill collectors, sniffing the air as they prowled; white-collar workers taking fifteen minutes to do an hour of errands; Central American delivery boys with white aprons, bearing cardboard trays of paper cups; cops and rental cops and undercover cops, all eyeing one another with deep suspicion; mail-persons and United Parcel persons and FedEx persons hurrying past one another, pretending the other persons didn't exist; druggies visiting Terra in search of supplies; and the homeless with their empty cups, trying against all the odds to get at least a little attention, if not sympathy, from this heedless throng.

All those bodies in motion formed a constantly changing woven fabric, a six-foot-high blanket of rolling humanity, and it was now Freddie's job to weave himself horizontally through this fabric, slipping through the weft and warp without any of the textile becoming aware of his existence; to be, in short, the ultimate flea. To do all of that, and to do it successfully, would require every bit of his concentration, leaving nothing for the careful self-protective study of this dubious sidewalk that the surface really deserved. Freddie knew his bare feet were just going to have to get along as best they could.

Freddie took one tentative step away from the van, and here came hurtling two hooky-playing kids in big sneakers, waving cigarettes and laughing at each other's dumb jokes. Freddie dodged them, but then almost ran into a guy carrying a roll of tarpaper on his shoulder, coming out of the roofing-company truck. A rollout in the other direction put Freddie in the path of three middle-aged Japanese women, marching arm in arm, cameras dangling down their fronts, forming a phalanx as impenetrable as the Miami Dolphins' defensive line.

Freddie recoiled, back against the cool side of the van, heart beating, doubt rising to the surface of his brain. This mob was *dangerous*. It was true they rarely crashed violently into one another, hardly did anything worse than the occasional shoulder bump, but that was because they could see one another and take whatever minimal evasive action might be necessary to avoid a head-on collision. But they couldn't see Freddie, and would have no notion of getting out of his way or even accounting for his presence on the sidewalk. They would tromp his toes, knee him in the groin, elbow him in the breadbasket, and pound their foreheads into his nose, all without ever having the slightest clue that his toes, groin, breadbasket, or nose were anywhere in the vicinity.

Maybe this wasn't such a good idea after all. Maybe what he needed was someplace quiet, uncrowded. But then, when he tried to move the loot, he *would* be noticeable. Still, the question was, how to deal with this never-ending crowd?

As Freddie stood there, pressed against the side of the van, staring at the surge of people and trying to figure out his next move, if any, a United Parcel guy bumped into him on his way past and kept going without even a backward glance to see what he'd hit. Coming the other way, a pale overweight tourist skipped out of the United Parcel guy's path and would have run head-on into Freddie if Freddie hadn't automatically fended him off with an elbow. The tourist threw some words in some language over his shoulder, perhaps an apology, and kept going.

Wait a minute. It was true the people couldn't see Freddie,

but in fact they weren't really *seeing* anybody, except as necessary to avoid full-scale collisions. If Freddie were to bob and weave just enough to keep the jostling to a minimum, no one would even notice there was an invisible man in their midst.

Well, it was a theory worth testing. Freddie's goal was a narrow building, six stories high, just a few doors back up the block, with the words DIAMOND EXCHANGE among other words in gold on its bullet-proof glass display window. A truly homicidal-looking black security guard in a brown uniform sat on a stool behind the showcases in this window, looking out at the world like a fish-store cat, daring anybody to try to come in and take any of these goodies away. Beside this window, a locked black iron gate led to a small square vestibule and a solid door, and then who knew?

From time to time a person would approach this building, pause at the gate, and ring the bell beside it. He would then speak into the microphone grill set between gate and window. The security man in the window would engage him in suspicious conversation, would eye him with carnivorous hostility, and at last grudgingly the new arrival would be admitted. Sometimes two people showed up together, and while Freddie watched there was even a trio allowed in all at once, which meant there was certainly going to be room in that vestibule and those doorways for one entrant accompanied all unknowing by an unseen stranger.

The unseen stranger, at last emboldened to make his move, waited till he saw a black-coated, black-hatted, black-bearded, spit-curled skinny fellow who looked to be about seventeen approach DIAMOND EXCHANGE and ring the bell; then he pushed away confidently from the van, tiptoed rapidly across the iffy sidewalk, caromed off two or three pedestrians who merely kept on truckin', and reached the iron gate just as the nasty little buzzer began to sound. The skinny fellow in black

pulled at the gate, it opened, he stepped through and the unseen stranger zipped through behind him, close enough to
smell the combination of Palmolive soap and old wool coat
that was his new associate's personal scent.

The iron gate very nearly nipped Freddie's heels and right
elbow, but he scrinched himself just in time. The gate snicked.
The inner door buzzed. Freddie and his dancing partner did it
again.

He was inside. Here, Freddie and his new friend parted
company, the skinny fellow in black moving purposefully
across the floor toward a narrow door to what appeared to be
a very narrow elevator, where he pushed another button, and
waited, while Freddie didn't move forward at all, but pressed
his naked back against the cool side wall, and took a moment
to case the joint.

He was in a long narrow room, about twenty-five feet wide
by sixty feet long, illuminated by a ceiling composed almost
entirely of fluorescent tubes. Down both sides and down the
middle of this space were three long rows of booths, waist-
high cubicles separating each dealer and his desk and safe and
display case from the dealers on either side. Armless wooden
chairs for the customers stood outside each cubicle, facing in.
Customers and security people moved up and down the two
aisles, everybody constantly looking at everything. In their
compartments, the dealers haggled, or read in little books, or
talked on their telephones, or added up strings of numbers, or
looked at tiny stones through their loupes.

Across the way, the elevator arrived, and was very small indeed. In that elevator, two was a crowd. A crowd of two
emerged from it, shrugging their shoulders and adjusting their
clothing after the unwelcome proximity of the ride, and Freddie's former friend boarded in lonely splendor to ride up—or
possibly down—to some other selling floor.

There was a kind of loose unofficial flow to the movement

in the long room; it mostly went counterclockwise, from the door here at the front right, then on back to the rear, then across to the left aisle, and thus back to the front again. Occasional customers swam briefly upstream, moving from one dealer to the next, but most of the traffic was one-way.

Fine by Freddie. He joined the throng, moving along at the general pace, tucking in close to one person or another, so as not to be bumped into from behind. And as he walked, he looked.

Jewels. Blue sapphires, green emeralds, red rubies. Blue turquoise, green jade, red garnet. Purple amethyst, black onyx, violet alexandrite. Opalescent girasol, creamy chalcedony, pearls of a thousand shades of white.

But what Freddie cared about, and only what he cared about, were the diamonds. Winking and blinking under the glass counters, nestling in clusters or in solitary grandeur on trays of felt, tumbled like sprays of magic moondust from palm to palm; little hard concentrations of light, colorless yet filled with color, prismatic, faceted, tiny, fabulous.

Freddie made one circuit of the place, getting used to it, getting used to himself in this new format, and by the time he got back to the front he was so comfortable, so at ease, so sure of himself, that he even tapped the homicidal sentry on the arm on the way by. The guard's head swung around, he looked, saw no one, and brushed away the nonexistent fly.

Freddie had his target picked out. On the left side, near the front, two dealers were dealing with one another as well as with a customer seated in front of one of them. The dealers would stand to speak across the cubicle wall at one another, then sit, then stand to hand across a tray of stones or take them back. The customer looked, discussed, moved back and forth between the two dealers. It had been going on for some time, it looked as though a lot of money was going to be involved once the deal was finally set, and the three thus engaged in the transaction were deeply engrossed in what they were doing.

Also, there were these factors: The site was not far from the front door. It was on the left side, where the movement of the customers was toward the front. And near the right elbow of the dealer nearest the front were several trays of small exquisite diamonds.

Freddie made a second circuit, partly to go with the flow and partly to keep an eye open for other opportunities, either to be accepted now or at some later time. But nothing better attracted his eye, not for this excursion, so when he came around to those two dealers once more, he tucked in next to the empty chair in front of the dealer on the right, leaned against the front of the cubicle, listened to the foreign languages going off all around him like popcorn, and waited for just the right customer to come along. He'd already spotted her, and now merely had to wait.

Most of the people in this room, but not all, were men, from sallow sharp-nosed teenagers to wrinkled heavy-jowled ancients. Most, but not all, were professionals, the customers as much as the dealers, the customers being also dealers in their own right, with shops or private clients. The few civilians in here were rich people being courted by a particular jeweler, who had emphasized their special status by bringing them here to this wholesale trading floor. The civilians could be told at once from the dealers: they were eager, their attention was not sharply focused, and they were well dressed. (The few female dealers tended to scowl a lot, and to wear very expensive tasteful jewelry with brown or black silk dresses.)

There was one civilian Freddie had particularly in mind to help him make his move out of this place, and here she comes now. Accompanied by a tall suave pale man in black whose languages seemed to include Dutch, Yiddish, German, French, and a heavily Dutch-accented English, she was a compact woman in her fifties, as round and solid as a beer keg, with madly curled hair the color of Pepto-Bismol and clothing so bright and sparkly you could read by her. This woman had either at one time been the toast of Broadway or with the help of a therapist had raised a submerged false memory of having been the toast of Broadway. Her whiskey voice was large, the gestures of her jeweled hands larger, her enthusiasms strong enough to knock over a horse. As she made the circuit of the sales floor, she would point, cry out, bend to study, rear back to gain perspective, and all the while her companion would speak to the dealers in his languages, consult briefly with the woman in his broken-spring English, and make notes in a small pad, sometimes handing a memo to a dealer on the way by.

Here was Freddie's escort. Of course, if this woman and her companion decided to take the elevator to some other floor, it could make an awkward moment for Freddie, but sometimes you just have to take a chance, and this was one of those times. (It seemed to Freddie, in any case, that for the Toast of Broadway, after this appearance, the only possible exit was grandly out the front door to the public street, not meekly into a tiny elevator box.)

Here she was, with her tall man. Nothing at the counters of Freddie's two dealers interested her. She barely slowed, turned her cotton-candy head to look at the dealer on the other side of the aisle, and kept going. Freddie watched her feet. If she'll take the elevator, that foot will angle to the right . . . *now*.

It didn't. Relieved and excited, with the woman past him, about four feet away toward the front door, Freddie reached with both hands to the trays of diamonds, made a double dip, and scampered. The dealer who'd just been robbed, deep though he was in tense negotiation, nevertheless caught movement from the corner of his eye, looked quickly around,

frowned, stared this way and that, then had his attention
snagged by something the other dealer said, and turned back.

Freddie meanwhile had tucked in close behind the Toast of
Broadway, holding his double-fist of diamonds close to the
back of her glittery sparkly dress. Gazing at these rocks from
above, and up close, Freddie could clearly see that he'd done
well. He smiled as he looked down at the diamonds floating
there, inside his invisible hands. For anybody else in the
room, involved as they all were in their own concerns, the diamonds would be barely visible, if at all, against the shiny
statement of that dress. So long as they kept moving . . .

The woman halted, barely ten feet from the door. Freddie
damn near ran right into her, but stopped himself just in time,
teetering off balance. "That aquamarine," the woman said,
with the plaintive loudness of someone bemoaning the loss of
a loved one.

The tall pale man bent over her. "No, no, Marlene," he said,
soothingly, "I don't tink so. Dot flaw—"

"Couldn't it be set so we could hide . . ."

This was going to go on. Now that the woman was not
moving, and with that security guard so damn close, these diamonds would soon become noticeable. Freddie looked all
around, becoming desperate, and near the front door he spied
a fairly large trash can with an open top and black plastic
liner. It was just a few feet away. Freddie *leaped* over there,
stuck his hands down in among all the papers and plastic
cups, and waited while the woman and her guide continued
to discuss whether or not the flawed aquamarine was worth a
return visit.

This was a bad situation. Of course, Freddie could merely
open his hands and permit the diamonds to fall away into the
trash, then saunter off unseen to try again, but he was so
close. If only this woman would *forget* the aquamarine, just
forget it.

In the meantime, people were coming in and going out, many of them brushing very close to Freddie. He didn't dare tuck in behind any of those exiting black coats, not with these handfuls of electric light, to stand out against the black like moons in the night sky.

At last, the tall pale man's views prevailed. He and the gaudy woman moved forward, and as they passed Freddie he yanked his hands out of the trash, causing a minor volcano in there, and put them back close to the woman's dress, where they belonged. (The security guard glared briefly at the trash can, knowing something had happened but not sure what.)

But now there was a *real* problem. Three in the vestibule was a rather tight squeeze, and the security arrangements here included that the street-side gate, which opened outward, would not work until the inner door, which opened inward, was closed. Also, the tall pale man, being a gentleman, held the inner door open for the lady, then followed her through the doorway, much too close for Freddie to sandwich in between. Freddie had to duck under the gentleman's door-holding arm, scoot through the narrow space between the gentleman's left leg and the closing door, hold the glittery little sausages of diamond right down at floor level, and remain hunkered in the same position in the corner until the door closed and the gate opened.

The woman had some sort of problem getting through the gate. She stuttered and skipped, the tall pale man backed up, Freddie bounced off him, and the man turned to frown directly into Freddie's face from one foot away. Then the woman called something and the man turned back, expression bewildered and dissatisfied as he moved forward through the gate to the sidewalk, where he promptly and firmly slammed the gate shut before Freddie could get through.

Well, *shit.* That was vindictive. Freddie stood there, looking out at the sidewalk, but there was nothing to be done, no

way to get out there until someone else came along, to persuade the guard to hit that button. In the meantime, waiting,
Freddie stood with his hands in the corner next to the hinged
side of the gate, hiding the diamonds from passersby, while
nothing at all happened for minute after minute.

Come on, will ya? Somebody's got to pass through here, in
or out, either way. In the meantime, since this was merely an
iron-barred gate that the breeze (if not Freddie) could go
through, he was beginning to get a little chilly (June is June,
but naked is naked), while the bottoms of his feet were chafed
and sore (who *knew* what they might have picked up?) and his
hands were tired of making fists. Looking catty-corner through
the gate, he could see the van down there, just beyond the fire
hydrant and the roofing-company truck, and from time to time
he could even see Peg move her head inside there, looking
back, wondering how he was doing, looking for him even
though she knew she wouldn't be able to see him.

A customer. An Arab, in a white head towel and a long
gleaming gray robe. He had appeared just outside the gate and
stopped to press the button there.

Freddie looked at him, and his heart sank. This was a *large*
Arab, a hugely fat man who, in the pearly gray robe, looked
mostly like a diving bell. He would fill this damn vestibule all
by himself. How was Freddie to get by him and *out* of here?

The hell with it, that was how. The nasty buzzer sounded, but
before the Arab could pull on the gate Freddie pushed against
it, shoving it out forcefully, holding it wide open as he sidled
through between the iron bars and the very large customer.

Who looked at the door in surprise, and then in pleasure.
An innovation, since last he was here! A self-opening door, as
in the supermarket! Very good!

Smiling, the Arab entered the vestibule, as Freddie released
the door and ran for the van, juking and jinking through the broken field of pedestrians, his hands with their packs of diamonds

held down at his sides at thigh level, where people were not likely to be looking when he went by. And when that Arab left DIAMOND EXCHANGE, he'd probably whomp his big belly a good one against that gate when it didn't open, wouldn't he? Ah, well.

Freddie reached the van. He bunked the window with his elbow bone, not wanting to raise a visible cluster of diamonds to window height, and inside he saw Peg leap, startled, then stare at him—through him, around him—and push the button to lower the window.

Freddie turned to the van and raised his hands. He knew there was no point in shielding the movement with his body, it was just habit; nevertheless, he shielded the movement with his invisible body as he lifted both hands, stuck them through the open window, and dropped a lot of diamonds onto Peg's lap. "Yike!" Peg said.

Passersby would have seen, if anything, a flash, come and gone. "Hide them," Freddie advised.

Peg brushed at her lap with both hands, while saying, "Should I open the side door?"

"Not yet." She couldn't see him grin, but he grinned anyway. Maybe she'd be able to hear the grin in his voice. "I'm not done," he said.

She stared toward his voice, which meant that actually she looked at his mouth. "Freddie? Why not?"

Now that all the disasters had been avoided, now that he'd been freed from the vestibule, now that no one had seen the floating diamonds and grabbed him by the wrist, Freddie was feeling a sudden elation. The nervousness was gone, the apprehension was gone, the—whatchacallit—*stage fright* was gone. Now that he'd done it, Freddie was really ready to do it. This was a long block, a street full of trade, a street full of commerce. A street full of diamonds.

"I'm gonna do it again, Peg," Freddie said. You *could* hear the grin in his voice. "This is fun!"

10

It was five days after his meeting with the two burglar-doping researchers—and a further confirming meeting here in the office later that day with their astonishingly translucent cats—that Mordon Leethe got to meet at last with his ultimate authority, the CEO of NAABOR, his lord and master. It had been clear to him from the outset—as clear as those cats—that this situation could not be resolved or made use of at any lower level.

The initial problem was, the situation could also not be *described* at any lower level—this was not news that Mordon wanted publicly aired. But unless he could explain to an entire ladder of underlings just why he wanted a private meeting with Jack Fullerton the Fourth, the boss of all bosses, they wouldn't approve it. Sarcasm, anger, cold aloofness, and vague threat were the tools Mordon had used in lieu of candor—the last arrow in his quiver anyway, under any circumstances—and at last, on Friday afternoon, a reluctant PPS (personal private secretary) had informed Mordon that Mr. Fullerton would see him for thirty minutes on Monday morning, promptly at eleven.

CEOs understand the word *promptly* differently from thee and me. Mordon arrived at five before the hour, and was ushered into Jack the Fourth's football-field office in the World

Trade Center at ten past the hour, to find its owner not yet
there. Mordon refused an underling's offers of coffee, tea,
seltzer, or diet soft drink, and contented himself (if that's the
right word) with standing near the windows, gazing out at the
broken playground of New Jersey across the broad sweep of
heaving gunk of New York Harbor until twenty past, when the
click of a door opening far behind him caused him to turn
about, an obsequious oil automatically filming his face.

Mordon watched as Jack Fullerton the Fourth wheezed
himself into a room, carrying his oxygen machine in a Pebble
Beach tote bag at his side, the slender plastic tube snaking up
out of the bag and up along his back and over his shoulder, to
cross his face just above the lip, extending a pair of tendrils
into Jack the Fourth's nostrils on the way by to provide him
the extra oxygen he now required, then back over his other
shoulder and thus downward once more into the machine in
the tote bag. Some users wear that tube as though it's a great
unfair weight, pressing them down, down into the cold earth,
long before their time; on others it becomes a ludicrous mustache, imitation Hitler, forcing the victim to poke fun at himself in addition to being sick as a dog; but on Jack the Fourth,
with his heavy shoulders and glowering eyes and broad forehead and dissatisfied thick mouth and pugnacious stance, the
translucent line of plastic bringing oxygen to his emphysema-
clenched lungs was borne like a military decoration, perhaps
awarded by the French: *Prix de Nez*, First Class.

Jack Fullerton the Fourth had been chief executive officer
of NAABOR the last seven years, having assumed the title
after the cardiac-disease death of his uncle, Jim Fullerton the
Third, who had himself taken over the helm nineteen years
earlier, upon the lung-cancer demise of his cousin Tom Fullerton, Jr. All in all, the Fullerton family had for almost the entire length of the twentieth century controlled what had
originally been National Tobacco, then (after the merger with

American Leaf) N&A Tobacco, then (after the absorption of the Canadian firm Allied Paper Products) N.A.A. Corporation, then (after the horizontal expansions of the fifties and sixties) N.A.A. Brands of Raleigh, then (after a Madison Avenue face-lift) NAABOR.

Jack the Fourth was accompanied everywhere these days by two "assistants." These assistants knew nothing about corporate work, but were well skilled both as nurses and as bodyguards. The dark suits and conservative neckties they wore did not disguise their true callings, but did at least serve to soften their professional silence and alertness, and distract from their bulging muscles and bulging coats.

This trio made its laborious way across the lush expanse of Virgin Mary–blue carpet toward the broad clean desk at the far end, Jack the Fourth not yet attempting to speak but contenting himself along the way with a nod and a small two-finger salute in Mordon's direction, to which Mordon responded by nodding his head, smiling his mouth, and wagging his tail.

At last seated at his desk, tote bag on the floor at his side, assistants in armchairs behind him and to his right, Jack the Fourth wheezed three or four times, then nodded at Mordon once more and gestured at the comfortable chair just across the desk. "Thank you, Jack," said Mordon, coming over to settle himself into the chair (Jack liked imitation informality). "You're looking well," he lied.

"Had a good enough night," Jack the Fourth wheezed. "Had a good enough shit this morning." His voice was like the wind in the upper reaches of a deconsecrated cathedral, possibly one where the nuns had all been raped and murdered and raped.

"That's good," Mordon said, expressing interest.

Jack the Fourth brooded at Mordon. "Haven't seen you since the victory party," he wheezed, "when we whupped the widows and orphans."

"Grand days," Mordon agreed.

Jack the Fourth's interest in small talk had never been very strong. "Cartwright tells me," he wheezed, "you want to talk about something, but you won't tell him what it is."

"Jack," Mordon said, with a significant look at the assistants, "I won't tell anybody on this earth but *you* what it is."

Jack the Fourth fixed Mordon with a watery but cold eye. "You aren't about to suggest," he wheezed, "that my assistants leave us alone in here."

Mordon at once shifted ground. "Not at all, Jack," he said. He had no idea if Jack the Fourth felt he might need his assistants to protect him from murderous attack from Mordon Leethe, or if he simply had in mind their nursing skills: CPR, all that. In any event, Mordon smoothly said, "I just wanted you to hear it *first*. After that, of course I'll be guided by your decision."

"Fire away," Jack the Fourth wheezed, opening a desk drawer and removing a fresh pack of cigarettes.

While his CEO's shaky fingers worked on opening the package, Mordon said, "We fund, under our American Tobacco Research Institute arm, two blue-sky medical researchers named Loomis and Heimhocker."

"Do we." Jack the Fourth's clean nails scrabbled at the cigarette pack, finally breaking through.

"They've been studying melanoma."

Jack the Fourth tapped a cigarette loose, while that word circled down into his brain, searching for a definition with which to mate. Got it; Jack the Fourth frowned massively at Mordon. "Melanoma! What the fuck for?"

"Research."

Jack the Fourth held up the cigarette for Mordon to see. "Let them make *these* fuckers less lethal," he advised. "Melanoma! Who gives a fuck about melanoma?"

"I think," Mordon said carefully, not knowing how much

Jack the Fourth wanted to know about his own business, "I think it's mostly window dressing."

Again, Jack the Fourth thought that over, while one of his assistants took his cigarette, lit it for him, and gave it back. Taking a drag, coughing his guts out, heaving in the chair, tapping ash that didn't yet exist into the hubcap-size clean ashtray on his desk, at last he wheezed, in utter disgust, "Public relations," much as another man might have said, "There's vomit on this seat."

"Yes, Jack," Mordon said. "A smoke screen, you might say."

"That's not bad." Jack wheezed a chuckle.

"But the point is, they've been working on two formulas to reduce skin pigmentation—it doesn't matter, it's just something to do with their research—and they both work pretty well, to the extent that they turn you translucent."

"Trans"— hack hack hack herack *hok hok hok* HOK HOK *hack* hack hack hack—"lucent? What do you mean?"

"Well, these researchers gave the formulas to their cats, one each, and now you can see through the cats."

Jack the Fourth waved smoke away from his face with his free hand. "You mean they're invisible?"

"No, you can see them, the shapes of them, sort of grayish, but you can see *through* them. They're like"—Mordon pointed at the air between himself and his master—"they're like smoke."

Jack the Fourth shook his big head. "I'm not following this. They want to make cigarettes out of *cats?*"

"No, no, I—"

"Not that I'd be against it," Jack wheezed, "if they were lower in tar and nicotine. But you've got to factor in those damn animal-rights people, you know, they're *much* nastier than the human-rights people, human beings mean nothing to them."

"The cats," Mordon said firmly, "were merely an early part of the experiment."

Jack the Fourth considered that. "Do cats get skin cancer?"

"Not as far as I know. Jack, could I just tell you about this?"

"I think you'd better."

"They have these two formulas," Mordon said, and held his hands up as though they gripped test tubes. "They have to experiment with them," and he poured the test tube contents onto the carpet. "They experimented on their cats," and he spread his hands, palms up, forgiving the researchers on behalf of animal-rights activists everywhere. "But now," and he brought his hands together as though hiding a baseball greased with illegal spit, "they need to experiment on human beings."

"I won't be a part of that," Jack the Fourth wheezed. "They'll have to go offshore for that. Set them up a dummy corporation."

"Well, they already did it," Mordon said, dropping his hands into his lap, and jutting his jaw forward like Il Duce. "They caught a burglar, tested one of the formulas on him, locked him up—very ineptly, I might say—and the burglar took the other formula, thinking it was the antidote, and escaped."

"Probably dead in a ditch somewhere," Jack the Fourth commented, and paused to cough before adding, "No legal problem I can see. Not for us."

"No, Jack," Mordon said, and his hands reappeared, to conduct the slow movement of a sextet. "The researchers say it's almost impossible the burglar's dead. I wouldn't come here, Jack, to talk to you about a dead burglar."

"I would hope not." Jack the Fourth took a puff, strangled, retched, coughed his guts out, lost his oxygen tube out of his nose, replaced it with the help of both calm assistants, blew his nose on a Kleenex out of a desk drawer, wiped his eyes on another Kleenex, gasped and panted a while, clutched the arms of his chair as though it were mounted on the rear of a sports-fishing boat in a heavy sea, and at last wheezed, "Well, Mordon, if they don't think this burglar's dead, what *do* they think he is?"

"Invisible."

For a long moment, there was silence in the room. Jack the Fourth didn't wheeze. The assistants even looked at one another, briefly. Then, with a long shuddering inhalation, very like a death rattle, Jack the Fourth wheezed, "Invisible?"

"They can't be sure, of course, but it seems very likely."

"Invisible. Not smoke, not . . . ghostly. Somebody you can't see at *all*."

"Yes."

"Hmmm," wheezed Jack the Fourth.

Briskly, Mordon said, "We're pretty sure he left fingerprints at the researchers' place. He's a burglar, he'll have a record. We don't want to make an official complaint in this case, Jack, but surely we know someone somewhere in law enforcement—"

"We know half the fucking Senate," Jack the Fourth wheezed.

"Half the Senate, Jack," Mordon said, "is on the wrong side of the law. We need a lawman, someone with access to the FBI's fingerprint files—"

"You want this invisible man."

"*You* want him, Jack," Mordon said. "He'll work for us, if we give him the right inducement. The fly on the wall, Jack. In jury deliberations, in advertising-campaign strategy sessions, in closed congressional hearings, in private *pricing* discussions . . ."

"Jesus Christ on a plate," Jack the Fourth wheezed, and almost sat up straight. Reaching for his phone, stubbing out his cigarette in the big ashtray—almost out; it smoldered, reeking like an old city dump—Jack the Fourth even rose briefly above his wheeze. "Don't you move, Mordon," he stated. "We're about to *get* this boy."

11

As fences go, Jersey Josh Kuskiosko was no more scuzzy than the average. As *human beings* go, of course, Jersey Josh was just about at the bottom of the barrel, down there in the muck and the filth and the fetid stink where thoughts just naturally arise of retroactive abortion. But as far as fences are concerned, he wasn't bad.

Still, it wasn't often that Jersey Josh's phone rang, so when it did on that Monday evening a little after six, while he was watching several children being burned alive in their tenement apartment on the local news (their mother had only left the place for a *minute,* to get milk, Cheerios, and crack), Josh turned a very suspicious head to glower at the telephone, daring it to repeat that noise.

It did; damn. Hadn't been a glitch in the wires after all. It could still be a wrong number, though, or bad news. Aiming the remote at the TV to hit "mute"—now he could watch the children burn without listening to the newscaster's play-by-play—he mistrustfully picked up the phone, an old black rotary-dial model some scumbag had sold him long long ago, and warily said into it, "R?"

"Josh?"

"S?"

"This is Freddie Noon, Josh."

"O."

"You gonna be around?"

Where else would he be, but around? Nevertheless, this answer was going to require more of the alphabet. Hunching over the phone, as though he didn't want the burning children to watch, he said, "Maybe."

"I got some stuff to show you," Freddie Noon said.

Meaning, of course, stuff to *sell* him. So why didn't he just come over and announce himself around midnight, like a normal person? "S?"

"I'll send Peg. She's my friend."

"Y not U?"

"I'm kind of laid up," Freddie said.

"U sound OK."

"It's my leg."

"O."

"When should she come over?"

Shower. Shave. Change underwear. "8."

"Okay. Her name's Peg."

"S."

Jersey Josh Kuskiosko lived over a onetime truck-repair place near the Lincoln Tunnel. The building was squat and brick, with a tall ground floor and a normal-size second floor, its grubby windows overlooking a tunnel approach; open one of those windows, you're dead in ten minutes. Nobody had ever opened them.

In the old days, the upstairs had been used only for storage of parts and files, since the downstairs had at that time been full of the noise and stench of big trucks, many of them not stolen, undergoing repair. But some years ago the owners of the business moved to the other end of the tunnel, over in Jersey, where the rents are lower and law enforcement even more slack. This left the owners of the structure, the British royal family, with yet another lemon on their hands. Fortunately, the British royal family is used to thinking in the long term, so they simply held on to the parcel, as they've continued to hold on to so many Manhattan parcels, waiting for the idea of gentrification of the world's most important city to come around and be popular again.

These days, the downstairs was rented as storage space by a restaurant-supply company, so on that thick oily concrete floor down there stood big restaurant stoves, walk-in freezers, industrial dishwashers, wooden boxes full of dishes and cutlery, all kinds of stuff, much of it not stolen, and all of it protected by locks, bolts, chains, alarms, razor wire, and two Doberman pinschers who were never fed quite enough.

Upstairs—you got up there through a door at the right front of the building, next to the two big wide green accordion-metal overhead garage doors—were Jersey Josh's apartment, office, and storage area. Some of the restaurant-supply company's security measures also protected his space, but in addition to that he had his own double layer of doors at the foot of the stairs, both metal, both wired for a variety of things, including a disagreeable but probably not fatal electric shock should you insert anything at all into any of those inviting-looking keyholes.

The stairs themselves were steep and narrow, so that only one person could ascend at a time. The door at the head of the stairs was also metal, and contained a peephole for looking through, a slit for shooting through, and a small hinged openable panel for accepting pizzas through.

Behind this door was a large living room with two natural brick walls and two plaster walls painted a kind of dirty white. These weren't dirty walls, these were walls painted a specific white only found in New York City, variously known as landlord white or cockroach white; it goes on gray and drab, and therefore will always look the way it does the first day it's spread, and so it doesn't have to be repainted as often as walls painted more esthetically pleasing colors.

The furnishings here are, you might say, eclectic, since everything was bought from thieves, including the saggy green sofa, all the lamps (he paid a premium, three dollars, for the table lamp that represents a Moor in a turban and scimitar and wide lavender pants), and the rug on the floor, on which can clearly be seen the traffic patterns of its previous owners.

Almost no one penetrates deeper into Jersey Josh's domain than the living room, but then, almost no one except police with warrants would want to. His bathroom is large and contains a big old clawfoot tub (stolen), but is otherwise unspeakable, as is his kitchen. His bedroom is as large as his living room, and furnished out of the same back doors. The floor-length mirror on its farthest wall is actually a door, leading to Jersey Josh's business space: a room with a desk and two safes, plus several rooms of watches, fur coats, TV sets, and SaladShooters. At the farthest end is the wall-less ancient elevator for which only he has the key, used to bring larger goods up or send shipments down for resale to dealers from Pennsylvania and Maine.

When Jersey Josh uses this elevator, it descends into a cage on the first floor, which separates his realm from the territory of the restaurant-supply company; always, when he and the elevator lower into that cage, the Doberman pinschers are there, slavering, in such a frenzy to tear his flesh they bite the bars of the cage. Good-humoredly, Jersey Josh spits at them and makes obscene gestures in their direction, before turning to open the overhead garage door which only he can operate without electrocution, and which leads to a side alley, where the customers await, with their trucks.

Usually, Jersey Josh was content in this comfy little nest he'd carved for himself from the cold heart of the city, but tonight he was to have a lady visitor, and tonight he wasn't sure the place was absolutely up to snuff. He fussed around, dusting the Moor, running water in the bathtub to redistribute the grease in there, spraying the rooms with an aerosol product that was supposed to make them smell like a mountain glade but which in fact gave them an odor strongly reminiscent of an Eastern European chemical plant. But it was the best he could do.

Also, there was his personal self. Short, heavyset, out of condition, with long lank gray hair and a deeply lined face the exact color of Egyptian mummies, Jersey Josh was not at the best of times easy to look at, and his best of times had been some decades ago. Nevertheless, when he was ready—seven-thirty, half an hour early, agog with anticipation—and looked at himself in his mirror/secret door, he saw an image that did not displease him totally. Wasn't there something of Henry Kissinger in his stance, a soupçon of Ari Onassis in the debonair tilt of his brow? If he were a little taller, couldn't he give Tip O'Neill a run for the money? Wasn't there more than a trace of Ed Meese in his whole self-confident air?

7:32. Jersey Josh put Blue Nun on ice, *Centerspread Girls* in the VCR ready to roll, and sat down to wait.

8:04. Doorbell. Josh jolted awake from a warm dream. Doorbell. The lady. Right.

He struggled out of the saggy sofa, wiping drool from his chin, and lumbered across the room to push the intercom button: "R?"

"It's Peg, uh . . . Peg."

Female. Young. Nervous. Check, check, and check. "S," Josh said, and pushed admittance button number one. Then he peered through the peephole in the upstairs door, and didn't push button number two until he heard her thud into the interior door down there, expecting it to open. Push. Open.

In she came, holding the door open a long time down there, as though thinking she might turn around and go back after all. She even muttered to herself, showing more of the nervousness he liked, then looked up toward his door, and at last released the door down there and started up the stairs.

Nice. Good-looking, but not a real beauty, not enough to scare a person. Good strong legs, coming up those steep stairs. Good long fingers holding the rail. Nice round head, slowly rising toward him.

He didn't make her ring the bell at the top, the way he did with most people, including the pizza kid. Instead, just as she reached the last step he opened his final door, smiled at her in a way he hoped wouldn't show his teeth too much, and said, "I."

"Hello," she said, blinking at him, taken aback. She almost seemed to lose her balance for a second in the doorway, maybe from the long climb, causing her to lean against the door, opening it more widely than normal, while Josh automatically resisted, gripping the knob. Then she got her footing again and smiled a little shakily and went past him into the living room.

Josh closed the door, metal door chacking into metal frame with a satisfying finality. He turned to see his guest surveying his room, so he took the opportunity to survey her, the black shoes, black slacks, black spring coat, the blond hair, the little winks of gold at her earlobes. "S'just my place," he said, shrugging, sorry to hear himself apologize for it.

She turned and smiled at him; nice teeth, better than his. "It's very individual," she said. Inside the black coat was a bit of white blouse, moving with her breath.

"S." He smiled back, forgetting about his teeth till he saw her look at them, then quickly stopped smiling, but was still pleased, no longer unhappy about his living room. "Take your coat," he said. She frowned at that, and he hurriedly added, "No, no, I'll give it back!"

That made her smile again. "I know you would," she said. "But I'm a little . . . chilly, I guess. I'll keep it on."

Disappointed, he said, "OK," then gestured at the sofa: "Siddown?"

"I'll sit here," she said, and took the wooden chair off to the side, on which somebody long ago had painted, pretty poorly, some Amish hex signs.

"But," Josh said, as she sat on the hex signs, "you can't see the TV!"

She looked at him. "So what?"

"Well." His imaginings scrambled in his brain. He motioned at the VCR atop the TV. "You could watch a movie."

"No, I'll just sell you these things," she said, taking a white tube sock from her coat pocket. The sock was clean, and had red bands around the top. Softening the rejection, she said, "Freddie's waiting for me at home. He's pretty sick, you know."

"He said leg."

"That's *right,* it went to his leg! He told you that, did he? I guess you and Freddie are pretty good friends."

"Pretty good," Josh agreed. How could he ask this woman to go to bed with him? What were the exact words, to go from here to there? Did he have anything he could put in a drink, knockout drops? Maybe roach poison, he had plenty of that around here. Or maybe he could just hit her on the head when her back was turned, do what he wanted, and then when she woke up he'd say she tripped or something, knocked herself out, and she'd never know anything at all had happened.

Meanwhile, she was holding the damn tube sock, saying, "Where should I put all this?"

"What's in?" he asked her, reluctant to engage in the wrong conversation.

"Diamonds. Some other jewels, too, but mostly diamonds. All unset."

"Sit there," he said, pointing again to the sofa. Then he pointed to the coffee table—kidney-shape avocado-colored Formica—and said, "Put 'em there. I'll get wine."

"I don't need any wine," the damn woman said, and extended the sock toward him, dangling it in the air like some damn scrotum, as though to make fun of him, smiling at him but not getting to her feet, not coming forward, not letting him get his hands on her at all. "Here, you do it," she said.

Grumpy, stymied, Josh snatched the sock from her hand, sat himself down on the sofa, and emptied the sock onto the coffee table.

Well, well. Unquenchable lust for the moment forgotten, Josh stared at the little mountain of diamonds, like the world's richest pile of cocaine, with here and there a dozen other kinds of gems visible on its slopes. Small stones, mostly, but choice.

Jersey Josh knew his business, you could say that much for him. He would check and double-check, but he already knew what he was looking at here. Somewhat over a hundred thousand dollars in gems, unset, untraceable. Probably not so much as a hundred and a half, but certainly more than a hundred.

Since Jersey Josh and Freddie Noon had done business together for quite a while, Freddie normally would get the favored rate, which was ten cents on the dollar, which would be ten thousand in cash for this pile of crystallized carbon here. But that wasn't Freddie Noon over there, was it? That was a lady Jersey Josh didn't know, who wouldn't sit with him on the sofa, who wouldn't look at a movie with him, who wouldn't drink any of his Blue Nun, who almost certainly would not have sex with him without a struggle, and bad feeling from everybody afterward. Ten thousand dollars would this lady not get.

"Minute," Josh said, palmed a couple diamonds, and got to

his feet to go into the bedroom and get his jeweler's loupe, pausing to drop the diamonds into a dresser drawer and to pat his hair a couple times in front of the mirror.

A sound like a giggle came from the other room; was she loosening up, this woman? Josh lumbered back to the living room, and she was seated as before, knees together, arms folded, with her head bent forward now and shaking back and forth as she muttered something or other, then stopped when she saw he'd returned.

Woman talks to herself. Prays? Giggles. Maybe Josh'd be better off, have nothing to do with this woman, could be crazy. Nothing worse than a crazy woman. So *loud*.

Sitting up straighter, hands now in her lap, the woman said, "Did you bring those diamonds back?"

He stared at her. She could not have seen him palm them, could *not*. "What diamonds?" he asked.

"The ones you carried into the other room," she said, cool, calm, and collected.

He was rattled, but he shook his head anyway, and clamped his jaws tight shut.

She smiled easily at him, and as though to give him an out, she said, "I figured, maybe you wanted to weigh them or something."

"Did not," Josh said.

She considered him, then looked around, and pointed at the phone. "Should I call Freddie?"

A confrontation with Freddie Noon? Bad idea. Josh snapped his fingers, as though suddenly realizing what she was talking about; it wasn't much of a snap. "Weigh them," he agreed.

"I thought so," she said.

Feeling put-upon, Josh sat on the sofa again, in front of the little stack of diamonds. He screwed the loupe into his right eye, put a few of the stones in his right palm, studied them one by one.

Nice, very nice. Good quality. Excellent resale value. "Not so good," he said.

"Oh, sure they're good," the woman said, unruffled.

She was very annoying. Josh dropped the diamonds back onto the table, lifted his eyebrow to drop the loupe into his now-empty palm, and looked at her. "I know diamonds," he said.

"So does Freddie."

Hmm, yes. Whatever he gave this woman, she would take back to her friend Freddie, whose leg illness, whatever it might be, wouldn't last forever. Freddie Noon had for some time been a good source for Josh, and from the look of these diamonds Freddie was just now hitting his stride as a source.

Then there was the woman herself, named Peg; why make her angry or irritable? If she goes to bed with cheap burglars, why wouldn't she go to bed with Jersey Josh Kuskiosko?

All right. Time to lighten up. Taking a deep breath, Josh aimed an utterly false smile at . . . Peg . . . and said, "Peg."

She looked perky and alert. "Yes?"

"Wait," he announced, and heaved himself to his feet. At her look of surprise, he patted the air as though in reassurance, repeated, "Wait," and waddled off to his unspeakable kitchen, where he not only took the Blue Nun out of the refrigerator, but also the cheese spread he'd put in there last Christmas after nobody showed up. He gave it the sniff test— still fine. Crackers, crackers, crackers, here they are.

Speaking of crackers, the woman was muttering to herself in the other room again. Josh could hear her. That's okay, that's okay. Maybe crazy women aren't so bad, maybe they're better in bed, more . . . uninhibited. Josh tried to imagine what an uninhibited woman in his bed would be like, and had to lean briefly against the drainboard until the image faded. Then he opened the Blue Nun—the *tock* of the cork coming out silenced the muttering in the other room—chose his two least unspeakable glasses, put everything on an unspeakable tray, and carried it all to the living room, where he smiled at . . . Peg . . . as she looked at him in some surprise, gazing in particular at the wine bottle as he bore the tray across the room and put it down on the coffee table next to the little alp of diamonds.

"Oh, you shouldn't," Peg said.

"Peg," Josh repeated. His instinct told him, if you say her name, she'll think you care about her. About *her.*

She shook a finger at him, with a smile to show she was only teasing. "If you think," she said, "you can get me drunk so I'll take less money, you're wrong."

Well, that was one reason, of course. Josh smirked as he poured into the two glasses, and extended the cleaner one toward her. "Both drunk," he said.

"Well, that's fair," she admitted, and took the glass, and even held it up while he clinked his against it.

He drank down half a glass of the cold stuff, while she held the glass to her lips. Then he put down the wine and gestured at the cheese and crackers. "Eat," he suggested.

"Oh, I'm on a diet," she told him, putting her glass on the floor beside the Amish chair. "I have to watch my figure, you know."

There was some sort of clever response to that, he knew there was, having to do with *him* watching her figure, something like that, but his mind tripped over the phraseology, and the moment was lost. "OK," he said, and put down his own glass on the coffee table with a little thunk that made tiny avalanches on the diamond slopes. Then he lumbered across the room to kiss her on the point of the chin, painful for his teeth.

He hadn't been aiming for the point of her chin, of course, he'd been aiming for her mouth, but she'd moved, the damn woman, she'd thrown off his aim. She was still moving, as he pressed forward, fumbling at her, holding her in the chair.

"I DON'T THINK SO!" she yelled, very loudly, unnecessarily loudly.

He'd known she'd be loud, dammit. "Coats," he muttered, pawing at her, meaning he had other coats in the back he'd give her after he'd finished ripping this one to shreds to get it off her.

"DAMMIT, FREDDIE!"

"Not here," he panted, shoving coat out of the way, blouse out of the way, one knee now in her lap, holding her down. Faintly he registered the squeak of the hinge of his mirror/door, far away, but his own loud breathing and his own tense concentration kept him from heeding that impossibility, or remembering it later. His hand found a breast, an actual real-life throbbing warm human breast! This so electrified him that he froze, glary-eyed, not even breathing, and was like that when he felt the sharp hard pain at the back of his head, and darkness fell, like a tree.

So did Josh.

"Are you all right?"

Josh swam into painful consciousness. There was a sticky smell in the air, a pain in his head, a nasty wetness around his collar and the back of his shirt. He groaned, and moved, and found he was stretched out on his back on the very thin carpet on his living room floor. The woman . . . Peg . . . leaned over him, expression concerned. "Mr. Kuskiosko? Jersey Josh? Speak to me!"

". . . Wha . . ."

"I'm sorry I had to do that."

". . . Wha . . ."

"You understand, if I'd had to go home and tell Freddie you

misbehaved, he'd come here and do something *terrible,* and I wouldn't want *that.*"

Josh raised a shaky hand and touched the wetness at the back of his head, then looked at the fingers and it wasn't red. Shouldn't his blood be red, like anybody else's? He sniffed his fingers, and it was wine. Blue Nun. Looking past his fingers at Peg, finding it hard to focus, he said, "Wha . . ."

"We can be friends, Mr. Kuskiosko, but not if you're going to be silly. Are you all right now? Can you sit up?"

"Wha . . ."

"Here you go. Try to sit up."

She didn't touch him, but she did make a lot of hand movements to encourage him, and, following them, leaning into them, he did manage to sit up. He looked around. Pieces of broken wine bottle littered the wet carpet. The Amish chair was overturned. But the mountain of diamonds still sat on the coffee table, the tube sock still lay on the sofa. "Wha . . ."

"Mr. Kuskiosko," she said, "I think we should just conclude our business and I'll go on my way, and neither of us will ever mention this misunderstanding again, and from now on we can get along with one another and be friends. Okay?"

She extended her slim long-fingered hand toward him, her nasty schoolteacher smile fixed on her nasty pretty face. Josh looked at that hand, those long fingers, and he knew in his heart they would never be used in any of the ways he had imagined them being used. Hating everything about this situation, but seeing nothing else to be done, he took that nasty hand and shook it briefly, feeling the delicate bones in there, quickly letting go.

She had been kneeling beside him, her coat again fastened, looking none the worse for wear, dammit. Now she got to her feet, brushed off her knees, and briskly but smilingly said, "There. We're friends now."

"S," he muttered.

"Can you get up?"

"S."

He could, and he did, and stood tottering there, while she nodded at him in satisfaction and said, "You're fine now, I know you are."

"S."

"So shall we talk about the diamonds?"

"S."

"How much are you going to give me for them, Mr. Kuskiosko?"

He beetled his brows, and glowered at her. "2."

She pretended she didn't understand. "Two? Two what?"

"K."

"Two thousand dollars?" She laughed, as though perfectly naturally, and said, "I didn't know you told jokes, Mr. Kuskiosko, Freddie never told me that. But he *did* tell me I shouldn't take less than ten, so unless that *was* a joke I guess I'd better take all this back to Freddie." And she crossed the room to pick up the sock from the sofa.

Damn woman. "Wait."

She turned, sock in hand, one eyebrow lifted, and waited.

Now she does what I tell her to do. Josh brooded. Dicker? Haggle? Negotiate? Or just get the damn woman out of here, so he could remove his wine-soaked clothes and take aspirin and watch *Centerspread Girls* all by himself? "OK," he said.

"Oh, thank you, Mr. Kuskiosko," she said, as sunny as a field of daisies. "Freddie will be *so* pleased."

"Wait," he commanded again. Then, not looking directly at the woman, he lurched away, holding the bruise on the back of his head, moving through the bedroom and past the mirror/door and on into his office, where many items were just subtly disarranged, which he was too distressed to notice.

In the office, he opened one of the safes, removed from it two white envelopes that each contained five thousand dollars in wrinkled bills, shut the safe, and staggered back to the living room, which was empty.

Oh, God, what now? Josh stared around, his headache redoubling, and in she came from the kitchen, smiling, saying, "I put the cheese and crackers away. It was the least I could do, Mr. Kuskiosko."

It damn well was. "Here," he said, and thrust the envelopes at her.

"I *know* I don't have to count these," she said, chirpy chirpy *chirpy,* as she put the envelopes in her coat pockets. "Besides, we both know Freddie *will* count them. Well, bye-bye."

Josh stood there, in his violated living room, while she crossed to the door, opened it, and then held it open an unnecessarily long time while she turned back and waved at him like Audrey Hepburn or somebody, and then at last she left. Chack of metal door sardonically into metal frame.

Josh sank onto the sofa, drained and miserable. He gazed at his new diamonds without joy. Hit him on the head, she did, just because he wanted to be friendly.

How in *hell* did she do that? Get the wine bottle from all the way over here and hit him with it all the way over there, while he was holding her down in the chair?

It just goes to prove it yet again, Jersey Josh thought. You simply can't trust women.

12

Getting chilly. Freddie jogged in place to keep warm, watching out for the sudden appearance of employees around the hall's far turn. One skinny black kid who kept zipping into sight behind a wheeled garment rack full of fur was the worst menace, having actually knocked Freddie over during one of his abrupt flybys. Fortunately, Freddie had managed to roll out of the way before those flashing feet stumbled over him, so the kid remained unaware—as did everybody else in this building—that Affiliated Fur Storage contained at the moment an extremely unauthorized visitor.

Eight days, and no change. Not a hint of Freddie had come back into view, not a shadow, not the faintest smudge of smoke. He was as invisible as on the night those mad doctors had done their experiment on him. Was this condition going to be permanent?

Freddie was torn on the subject. On the one side, invisibility was certainly a decided asset in his occupation. On the other side, there was Peg.

Peg was being very good and supportive about this situation, mostly, and was a great help on the professional side, driving the car and dealing with Jersey Josh Kuskiosko and all of that, but on the *personal* side, there was a definite sense of strain here, which was not getting better. You could even say it was getting worse. Freddie had noticed a new pattern in Peg the last few days, a habit she had developed of facing half away from wherever she thought he was, as though she had to pretend to herself that he wasn't really invisible, it was just that she didn't happen to be looking in his specific direction at this specific moment.

Denial, in other words. Not being able to see Freddie was a problem for Peg that she had clearly not figured out how to deal with, and it seemed to him that one result was a growing distance between them, a certain coolness, that worried him a lot.

All right. The thing to do, he'd decided, was pile up a lot of scores very quick, accumulate a lot of money, and then make contact with those crazed doctors, open negotiations, and work out some way to get his hands on an actual working antidote without getting himself arrested the second somebody could see his wrists to put the cuffs on.

But money first, the scores first, and that was why Freddie, naked as an empty water glass, was bouncing around in this hall here in Affiliated Fur Storage, with clerical offices on one side and chilled rooms full of fur coats on the other, trying not to get killed by a supersonic black kid with huge sneakers and an evident fantasy in which he won the Indianapolis 500 driving a wheeled garment rack.

It isn't true that all small business has been driven out of New York City by high rents and high taxes and high crime and a workforce whose only skill is pilferage. All small business has been driven out of *Manhattan* by the above, but many thousands of these little companies still exist in Queens and Brooklyn, where they can draw from the labor pool on Long Island, people at the competency level of the smiling Burger King kid who gets your order right the second time.

Among these surviving small companies is Affiliated Fur Storage—and who knows how many failed furriers are entombed in that cemetery of a word, *Affiliated?*—here in Asto-

ria, Queens, in a long low cinder-block building flanked by a
seltzer bottler and a uniform laundry. Behind it, facing the
next street, is a smaller similar structure housing a manufac-
turer of bowling pins. The fur storage building sits inside an
eight-foot chain-link fence topped by razor wire, with two
gates, both at the front, both hedged from street to building
past the weedy dirt moat by more tall chain-link fence. The
narrow gate at the right is for pedestrians, the wider gate at the
left for delivery trucks.

The interior of this building, except for the administrative
offices, is a maze of windowless rooms, air-conditioned to a
fur-loving forty degrees. Here is where many of the more for-
tunate women of New York store their minks in summer, to
protect them from deadly heat and humidity. Here, if you've
a mind to steal fur coats, is the place to go.

And here is where Freddie came, this afternoon at four-
thirty, slipping in with a delivery truck, filled with another
load of arriving mink. Once inside, he'd tucked out of the
way, taking it easy, expecting the place to close at five. But it
did not.

Problem. By June, the fur coat owners really should already have called Affiliated to make their arrangements for
the pickup of their coats, but you know how people procrasti-
nate, how they forget to do something unless it's staring them
right in the face, how they don't even *think* about the fur coat
until one day they open that closet looking for something else
entirely—sunglasses in a coat pocket, usually—and there it
is! And *then* they make that call, and that's why June is the
busiest month of the year at Affiliated, and that was why, at
ten past six on Wednesday, June 14, this year, Peg was still in
the van parked up in the next block, waiting for the signal—
something waving by itself in the air, in front of the just-
opened delivery gate—while Freddie, inside, still bobbed and
weaved around that damn kid.

He'd come in here in the first place figuring half an hour was all he'd need to watch the security systems, see how they were armed and how they could be disarmed, and he'd been right; once everybody finally did get the hell out of here, he'd open the building like a banana, no sweat. But when would they call it a day, goddam it, and go *home*?

And now it was six-twenty, and a person came around the corner of the hall. Not the speed demon, this was a middle-aged woman shrugging into a light cloth spring coat. Freddie pressed himself against the wall as she went by, and here came three more, chatting together, taking up the entire width of the hall. And more behind them.

Whoops. Freddie fled in front of the staff, and found that the receptionist had been among the first to leave, which meant her desk was empty, which meant Freddie could skip around behind it, and even sit in the receptionist's chair, still warm from her bottom, and from that vantage point watch everybody leave.

This place had rent-a-cops, three of them in brown uniforms and shoulder patches, with holsters containing walkie-talkies, and the seriously humorless faces of drunks who aren't drinking yet today. These were the last to leave, having checked every room to be sure there were no stragglers, having set every alarm, and having called their security office from the receptionist's desk—Freddie leaped nimbly out of *that* guy's way—to report all secure and solid and shut down. Then they left, arming the final alarm system behind them. Freddie stood by the windowed front door—shatterproof window with what looked like chicken wire in it—and watched the security guys close and alarm the outer gate, then get into their little white security car with all the words and numbers on it, and putt-putt away.

Ain't no security against the invisible man; no, *sir*.

The first thing Freddie did, when he knew he was alone in

the building, was skip down the hall, waving his invisible arms and kicking his invisible feet, knowing *nobody* would be coming around that corner to knock him down, not even his old friend Superfly. And the second thing he did was go into the nearest storage room and find a fur coat that fit and put it on.

June, shmoon; Freddie was *cold*.

13

By five-thirty, Peg had to go to the bathroom *bad*. Freddie should have signaled to her by now, but he hadn't, because of course the employees should have left by now, and they hadn't, which meant she couldn't avail herself of the fur-storage building's ladies' room.

Before they'd come out here, she'd talked this situation over with Freddie, or at least with the volume of air she'd assumed contained Freddie, and she'd asked him how come they had to deal with Jersey Josh Kuskiosko all the time? Aside from Jersey Josh's personality, which was the pits, why not just steal cash, and cut out the middleman? Take 100 percent instead of 10 percent? And Freddie had said, "What cash? There aren't any big piles of cash around. Payrolls are by check. Big stores take credit cards."

"Banks have cash," she'd pointed out. "You could sneak in, wait till they close—"

"Bank security is not simple, Peg," the air had told her. "Bankers are serious about money, that's one thing I'm sure of. You never know what you're gonna find in a bank. Heat sensors, motion sensors; they don't have to *see* me to know I'm there. The real money is locked away so no one naked guy without tools is ever gonna get at it. I know Jersey Josh is kind of an irritation—"

"I can put up with him, if I have to," Peg had said, being brave. "As long as you're there with me."

"I'm sorry, Peg, but that's just the way it is. All I can take is merchandise, and convert it to cash. I could start, maybe, a new relationship with a new fence . . ."

"Would he be any better?"

"Probably worse. You know, guys who go into that business, being a fence, they're not your Albert Schweitzer mostly."

So here they were, in pursuit of more merchandise. Over there, *more* delivery trucks backed in to the loading zone, maneuvering backward up a driveway so hemmed in by tall chain-link fence that most drivers didn't even try to get out of their vehicle. Peg watched them, and thought about the diner she and Freddie had passed on Astoria Avenue on their way over here, and thought about Freddie finally coming out of that building to make the signal and nobody around to receive the signal, and at last she decided enough was enough. Bladder-wise, enough was too much.

Leaving the area, Peg drove past the fur building and noticed that across the street from it was a parking lot with a sign that read AFFILIATED FUR STORAGE PARKING ONLY. The lot was better than half full. Employee cars, they must be. If they're gone when I get back, Peg told herself, then Freddie will be ready for me. So there is a signal after all, whether I'm here or not.

At the diner, Peg relieved herself and ordered a coffee and a doughnut to go, because she didn't feel right about just using the ladies' and then walking out. When she drove back to take up her vigil, the cars were all still in that lot, so nothing had changed. Peg settled down again, a bit more comfortably, to wait.

An *hour* went by. The second hour since Freddie'd left the van. An hour in which Peg drank the coffee but didn't eat the doughnut. An hour that gave her a lot of time for thought, for private rumination. And the longer she had to think, and the more she pondered this situation in which she found herself, the gloomier she became. Gloomier, and then gloomier.

What it came down to was, an invisible boyfriend was no fun. You just didn't get used to being around such a person, having their voice suddenly come at you from over *there* when you thought they were over *here,* having the TV channel-changer float in the air while Freddie was surfing for something to watch, seeing those sudden indentations and abrupt puffings-up, and other signs of Freddie's movements, his presences and absences.

What made it even worse, you could never be sure when *he* was looking at *you.* We all like privacy sometimes, to be alone with our thoughts, or our bodies, but these two hours in the van were the longest stretch Peg had had to herself—to *be* herself—in the last eight days. There was *no* privacy when you lived with an invisible man. *He* got all the privacy, and you got *none.* Never knowing when you're under observation, whether he's behind you or in front of you, never knowing how *you* look. At this particular moment, do you look sexy and pretty and thin, or do you look foolish or ugly or stupid? Or just merely cranky, probably, most of the time.

And of course Freddie, being a man, hadn't the slightest idea anything was wrong. He just went blithely on, being invisible, half the time in the apartment forgetting his Bart Simpson head, *never* wearing the gloves, never giving a second thought to the effect he was having on the person with whom he shared the apartment.

Which might be unfair, actually, though Peg wasn't in much of a mood to give Freddie the benefit of the doubt. But the other problem with living with an invisible man was the fact you can't *see* him. It wasn't merely that you can't see him, you can't *see* him. You can't see the expression on his face, can't tell if he's pleased or miserable, can't tell if he's bored or excited, can't tell what's going *on*. We all of us to some extent chart our voyages through life based on the weather occurring in our loved ones, but with an invisible man you can never tell what the weather is. The voice gives some clues, the words give some clues, but where are the facial expressions? Where's the body language? Where's the goddamn *body*?

I don't know how much more of this I can put up with, Peg thought. There, the thought was out.

So were the people. All at once, people were coming out of the fur-storage building a block and a half away, streaming across the street to the parking lot, calling out words to one another, waving, getting into their cars. A little pocket rush-hour now took place on the street in front of Affiliated Fur Storage, and then they were all dispersed, leaving only a little white security-company car parked at the gate. Five minutes later, as Peg watched, no longer impatient, no longer bored, happy and interested now that something was *happening*, three bulky men in brown uniforms came out of the building, paused to lock the front gate, then clambered into the little car and drove away.

Peg didn't wait for a signal from Freddie. She knew that place down there was empty, she knew he was in there dismantling the alarm system, she knew it would be only a very few minutes before he came out with a white towel or a roll of fax paper or something to wave at her, so she started the van and eased it slowly forward, through and beyond the intervening intersection.

The seltzer bottler and the uniform laundry, not being seasonal businesses with a high-volume June, had both shut for the day more than an hour ago. This was strictly a commercial area around here, with no pedestrians ever and no traffic after business hours. Peg had the world to herself as she drove on down the street, and was pulling up in front of the loading entrance to Affiliated when the garage door back in there lifted and out walked a fur coat, holding a white plastic in-tray in its nonexistent hand. "Oh, Freddie," Peg muttered, and just for a moment closed her eyes.

The fur coat, seeing she was already there, retired into the building to put down the in-tray, then came out again and un-locked the gate, while Peg backed and filled, getting the van into position. The fur coat opened wide both sides of the gate, then waved an arm at Peg, and she backed into the driveway, looking left and right, this mirror, that mirror, not quite scrap-ing the sides of the van, moving slowly as the fur coat re-treated, and finally kabunking against the black rubber edge of the loading dock. She switched off the engine as the van's rear doors opened and the fur coat said, "Peg, I thought they'd never go home."

"Freddie," Peg said, trying to sound calm and dispassion-ate, "why are you wearing that *coat*?"

"I'm cold, Peg. Believe me, it gets cold in there. I need my shoes and socks."

The van jounced as the fur coat clambered in, then sat on the floor. Socks moved through the air. Peg said, "You're going to get dressed, aren't you? I mean, regular dressed, your own stuff."

"Let's do the job first," he said. "Here, put my things on the seat, okay?" Freddie's clothing floated toward her, as he said, "I'll put the rest on when I'm done loading up the van."

Peg took the mound of clothing, mostly to stop it from floating like that. "You want help?"

"No, you stay with the van, in case there's some kind of trouble. If you gotta take off, I'll make my way home later."

"Take off?" Peg looked out at the street. Police patrols, that was what Freddie was thinking of. But if the police came along, and if they didn't like the look of the situation here, all they'd have to do was park across the front of this driveway, blocking her in.

Get arrested? Do eight years of prison laundry upstate? This, Peg thought, is not what I signed on for.

She might have said something, she wasn't sure what, but the fur coat, now sporting loafers and white socks, was skidding back out of the van. She watched him go, and there was just something so stupidly comical about a shin-length mink coat wearing white socks and brown shoes and no head that she forgot the awful possibility of getting Jean Harris's old room, and simply watched as the mink coat made a dozen trips in and out of the building, bringing great armloads of fur, dumping them into the back of the van, shoving them in, pushing them in, piling them in, until the leading edge of the pile, like a furry iceberg spreading, began to intrude into the driver compartment. "Enough, Freddie!" Peg yelled through the muffling mountain of mink, not sure he'd even be able to hear her back there.

But he did. "Right!" his voice shouted, dulled but intelligible. Thunk thunk, the rear doors closed. "Drive it out!"

She did. Stopping in the street, looking in the right-hand outside mirror, she watched the mink coat with the white socks and brown shoes, and what a busy mink coat it was! First it ran inside the building one last time, then ran back out as the garage door lowered, then came forward to close and lock the gates, with itself on the outside. Finally, it came up to the van and opened the passenger door. As Peg watched through the open door, the mink coat paused, then suddenly went mad and then limp, as Freddie took it off. The coat then appeared to stuff itself in among the other coats crowding the back of the passenger seat, and Peg looked away, watching the street for police patrols, until Freddie said, "Okay, Peg, you can look now."

He was back, or Bart Simpson was back, standing out there

beside the van. She smiled, relieved, actually liking Freddie when all was said and done. Putting the van in gear, she said, "Now what?"

"On to Jersey Josh," Bart said, sounding like a cartoon character with a head cold, and climbed into the van.

14

"9," Jersey Josh repeated, with more emphasis.

"The thing is, Josh," Freddie Noon's voice said in his ear from this old telephone, "I'm making these deliveries, see, I mean I'm already loaded up here."

Obviously, as Josh well knew, there was only so much one could say under such circumstances, because who knows how many telephones are tapped? All of them, probably; after all, this is the information age. But what Josh understood, from what little Freddie could say, and from the traffic noises in the background, was that Freddie was calling from a pay phone somewhere out on some street, and that his van was already loaded up with whatever it was he wanted to sell Josh, and he didn't like the idea of driving around the city for hours with his van full of felony convictions.

However, that was Freddie's problem, and had nothing to do with Josh. Josh's problem was, he would not, repeat not, repeat never, never ever lower the elevator and open the delivery entrance at the side of the building in daylight. Period. June is the worst of months for a fellow like Josh, with daylight practically all around the clock, which meant he was not going to *think* about opening that door down there until 9 P.M. Two A.M. would be better, but 9 P.M. he could live with.

But not a second earlier. "9," he said, for the third time.

Freddie sighed. "Okay, Josh, I understand. I just don't like Peg out by herself at night, that's all."

The woman again? Josh flinched, his head suddenly aching at the memory, as he said, "Not U?"

"Naw, you know, I pushed myself, I shouldn't have got out of bed so soon, I just can't make it. You know Peg now, so that's okay."

"S." He knew Peg, all right.

"So she'll be there at nine o'clock."

And this time, Josh thought, she doesn't get off so easy. This time, no more Mr. Nice Guy. This time, no subtlety, no wine and cheese, no *Centerspread Girls*. This time, direct action. Hit her on the head, start from there. "9," Josh said, and hung up, and went to look for something heavy.

Nine. Josh stepped onto the thick wooden-plank floor of the freight elevator, turned the key in the lock, and the oil-smeared motor in its housing up on the roof growled into action, sounding like an old lion with emphysema. Slowly the open-sided platform lowered, shaking under its cables, and as Josh descended, the growl of the motor became blended with the snarls and threats and bitings of the Dobermans, flinging themselves at the heavy metal cage. Josh amused himself with the dogs in his usual fashion as the platform settled down into its lower position, then turned his back on them, ostentatiously farted, and used his key to open the ground-level garage door.

The van was there. In the darkness, Josh couldn't see exactly who was at the wheel, but assumed it was the woman. "N!" he cried, and waved for the driver to back the van in onto the elevator platform.

The van's windows had been shut. Now the driver's window slid down and the woman's head appeared, looking back at him. "Just unload it," she called.

Oh, no, not that easy. "Up," Josh insisted, pointing toward his lair upstairs.

As usual, the woman was nothing but trouble. "Why not unload it right here?" she asked.

"2 much work," he said, which happened to be true, though not the reason. Jabbing his thumb skyward, he repeated, "N. Up."

"Oh, all right."

She closed her window before backing the van into the elevator. Did she think she was going to *stay* in there? No way.

With the van inside, Josh used his keys to close the door and raise the elevator, leaving the key in the elevator lock for later. He opened the rear doors of the van, and looked in at enough fur to clothe an entire Norse horde. "M," he said, his word of satisfaction, rarely heard. Going around to the driver's window, he looked in through the glass at the woman and said, "Help."

She lowered her window less than an inch. "What?"

"Help."

"You mean, unload?" She shook her head as he was nodding his. "I don't do heavy lifting," she said, and closed the window.

Heavy lifting. *All* women can lift fur coats, they've got special muscles for the job. Grousing, muttering letters of the alphabet to himself, Josh sloped on back to the rear of the van and started pulling out furs, hanging them on garment racks he kept around for just this purpose, every coat still equipped with the hanger it had worn at the fur-storage place.

A lot of furs. Good furs, too, Freddie always had a good eye. Four garment racks crammed with minks in shades of brown and black, giving off that cold warmth peculiar to natural fur.

Valuable. More than the diamonds, last time. There had to be two hundred thousand dollars' worth of fur bending the metal bars of these garment racks. In the normal course of business with Freddie Noon, that would be a twenty-G payment, and of course Freddie would know it, so his woman would know it, so there was no point arguing, was there? No.

Josh went around to the driver's window, rapped on it, and the damn woman lowered it that same inch. "Twenty," he said.

She smiled at him, sweetly, the lying little bitch. Her *smile* lied. "Freddie said," she said, also sweetly, "twenty-five."

Josh frowned. Had he estimated wrong? Or had Freddie? "Wait," he decided, and went back to look at the furs again, paying more attention to labels this time, and lengths, and finally deciding he'd been right the first time around.

But then he decided it didn't matter. He'd give her the twenty-five, and a little later he'd take it away from her again, and let her explain herself at home. He'd tell Freddie she'd left with the money, that's all, and Freddie would have to know what a sneaking liar this woman was, so he'd have to believe his old friend Josh, wouldn't he? And if he didn't, if he took the damn woman's part against his old friend, well, fine. If Josh never saw Freddie Noon again, that would be okay, too.

So he went back to the driver's window, and of course it was shut. He rapped more sharply on the glass this time, and when she opened it the usual inch he said, "S."

"Oh, good. Freddie will be very happy. This'll make him get healthy even faster."

"Out," Josh suggested, and turned the door handle, and it was locked. *Damn* woman!

"I don't need to get out," she told him. "You can just give me the money right here, and I'll be on my way. I don't like to leave Freddie alone when he isn't feeling well."

Stupid woman. The van's *back* doors were open; he could just crawl in that way and get his hands on her. So he turned away from her nasty smiling face and walked toward the rear of the van, and she started the engine. He looked back, betrayed, and she'd lowered the window more now and was looking back at him. "Don't go right behind there," she advised. "It might back up and hurt you."

He stood glowering, unable to think of a single thing to say. She waited, smiling, then said, "Just get the money, all right, Josh? And I'll be off. I don't want to smell up your place with the exhaust."

Money. All right, get her the money. We'll get her the money. And more. We'll see who's so smart around here.

Josh went through his storage rooms to his office, opened a safe, and took out five of the five-thousand-dollar envelopes. This time, he'd make her count the money, so she'd be looking away when . . .

Here was the rack of auto keys, the master keys for every kind of car, for this kind of car, that kind of car, and . . . Freddie Noon's van. Josh slipped the key off its hook on the rack.

This evening, a part of Josh's fashion statement was grimy shirttails hanging out. He pulled up the tail on the right side so he could put the key in the pocket of his baggy rotten trousers, then wiped his sweaty hands on the shirttail, picked up the five envelopes, and plodded back to the van.

It still sat there with its engine running, but the rear doors were now shut. The exhaust smell *was* getting pretty strong. Don't want her to knock me out again, Josh thought, and grinned to himself, because this time he'd be the one doing the knocking out.

Window open one damn inch. Giving her the envelopes one at a time was like mailing letters. "Count," Josh ordered.

"Oh, that's okay, I'll just—"

"Count!"

"Okay, okay, I'll count," she said, shrugging, and as she looked down at the envelopes in her lap, reaching for one, he reached for the key in his trouser pocket and found his shirt-tail on fire.

Ipe! Josh jumped around like a Watusi, whacking at his right hip like a move in a Bob Fosse dance, while the damn woman in the van looked at him with the first honest smile he'd ever seen her wear.

How could he catch fire? Holy Batman, his whole shirt was on fire! What had he touched, what had he brushed against, how—

Yanking the shirt off to reveal the tattered and filthy sleeveless undershirt beneath, staring around in wild surmise, Josh saw, against the far wall, forty million dollars in counterfeit twenties in brown paper bags burning like a Magritte tuba.

Fire! Disaster! Shrieking, leaving the shirt to burn itself out on the elevator floor, Josh scampered to the bags of money, grabbing fur coats along the way, throwing the coats onto the flames, throwing himself on top of the coats, smothering the fire.

Creak/groan/creak/groan. Supine atop the smoldering minks, Josh looked up to see the van descending out of sight. Somehow, the damn woman had gotten *out* of the van and started the elevator. Josh couldn't run after her, not with everything on fire here. He slapped at flames, rolled around on flames, scrambled to his feet, threw more coats on the smoking mess, jumped up and down on it all, and at last felt it was safe to turn his attention to the elevator.

It was already at the bottom, down in the darkness there. The woman had the garage door open and was driving out. Josh stood panting at the lip of the big square opening, his nose full of burning fur and car exhaust and his own self, and her vicious voice came up to him from the blackness below. "I'll send the elevator back up."

Huh.

"And I'll send along a little something to remember me by."

What did she mean by *that?*

"And next time, Josh, *you be nice.*"

Grungle-grungle, the delivery door closed down there. Kerough-kerough, the elevator started up. Snarl snarl . . . Josh peered, trying to see the rising wooden platform. Something was on it, moving . . . the Dobermans!

Josh ran for his life.

After eighteen rings, Josh finally gave up and answered the telephone: "Y."

"Peg tells me she had to set the dogs on you," Freddie Noon's voice said.

Four in the morning, and the Dobermans were still snarling and biting and hurling themselves at the other side of his secret mirrored door. God *knows* what they'd destroyed back there in the storage area. Tomorrow, the downstairs people would figure out how to get those murderous beasts back where they belonged, but for now, Josh's private space was ass-deep in Doberman pinschers. "Y," he repeated.

"Peg knew what you had in mind," Freddie said, infuriatingly calm. "She saw you get that key, she knew you were gonna try to attack her again."

Saw him get the key? Impossible, she was two rooms away in the van. Did she follow him? Was that possible? But how did that fire start? Did *she* start it? Did he brush by it without seeing it, and that's how it got his shirt? It *couldn't* have happened that way. "No," Josh said, meaning no to just about everything in the world.

Freddie said, "Josh, you and me, we've always had a good professional business relationship."

"S."

"And I want us to go on having that good professional business relationship, Josh."

"S."

"But, you know, I figure I'm gonna be laid up a while longer, so it's Peg you're gonna be dealing with, and she and me, we don't want her to have any more trouble with you."

She's having trouble with *me*? Josh gritted his teeth, but kept silent.

"Josh? You hear me?"

"S."

"When Peg comes over there, she's gonna have the same good professional business relationship with you that I do. Right? Right, Josh?"

Josh's fantasies lay in crumbled ruins around his feet. Nearby, a Doberman flung himself yet again at the secret door. "S," Josh said, and hung up.

15

So this is what tobacco money buys when it's blowing the stink off, Mordon Leethe thought, as he got out of the taxi at the Loomis-Heimhocker Research Facility on East Forty-ninth Street. The taxi, driven by a recent immigrant from Alpha Centauri, zipped away, rattling, and Mordon climbed the slate steps in late-morning sunshine toward the well-polished old wood front door with beveled lights, his hand stroking the smooth thick paint on the rail. Thursday, the fifteenth of June, beautiful weather, three days since Mordon's meeting with Jack Fullerton the Fourth, and at last it looked as though some progress was about to be made. But first, ID.

Mordon reached the landing at the front door, saw the bell button beside the door, saw the small sign above it—PLEASE RING BELL—and rang it.

In the oriel to his right, a young black woman sat typing on a very new word processor atop a very old mahogany desk. When Mordon pressed the bell button, she paused in her typing, turned her head just enough to give him a look as flat and impersonal as the gaze of a parakeet, and then, having apparently decided he looked like the sort of person who was permitted onto these premises, she reached under her desk. A faint buzzing sound came from the direction of the door; Mordon pushed on it, the door swung open, and he entered.

The immediate interior impression was of the entry to an Edith Wharton novel. Emotionally constipated people should now come down those carpeted stairs into this flocked-wallpaper entryway, not telling one another the important things. Instead, the slender black girl, having risen from her desk, appeared in the doorway to the right, hands clasped at her waist as she said, "Yes?"

"I'm Mr. Leethe, I phoned earlier."

"Oh, yes, the doctors are expecting you. I'll tell them you're here."

She receded back into her room, and he followed into the doorway, where he gazed around at the neatly efficient office while she murmured briefly into the phone. When she hung up, he said, "You had a robbery."

"Yes, we did," she agreed, with a wry little smile; someone she would not have approved of had gained entry.

"All the equipment is new," he explained, displaying his powers of observation,.

"I'm still not used to it all yet." Her fleeting smile came and went. "I thought technological obsolescence was fast. Robbery's faster."

"I suppose it is."

"The doctors are one flight up. You'll see them, just at the top of the stairs."

"Thank you."

Mordon climbed the stairs, thinking that in fact he would not be revealing any emotional privacies in this coming meeting, nor could he expect—or want—any from the doctors Loomis and Heimhocker, so the Wharton setting would be honored, after all.

Dr. David Loomis, the blond one with the baby fat, stood at the head of the stairs, smiling nervously and offering a hand, which trembled when Mordon shook it. "It's good to see you, Mr. Leethe."

"And you," Mordon lied.

Loomis gestured with his spastic hand. "We can talk in the conference room."

"Of course."

Loomis led him down the hall, and the conference room turned out to be Edith Wharton's parlor, without the ferns and plant stands. Two red Victorian sofas set at a welcoming angle flanked the fireplace with its polished brass andirons and tools. Tall windows overlooking Forty-ninth Street were discreetly curtained. Garden prints hung on the dark-papered walls.

Dr. Heimhocker, the skinny one with the Afro, rose from one of the sofas as Loomis and Mordon entered. "You have news, I guess," he suggested, coming forward to offer a firmer handshake.

"Possibly," Mordon said. "A start, anyway, or we think so."

"Tea?" asked the skittish Loomis. "Perrier?"

"No, thank you." Mordon had no desire to elongate this meeting into a social call, Edith Wharton be damned.

Heimhocker, who seemed to have better antennae than his partner, said, "Sit down, Mr. Leethe. What kind of start?"

Mordon took the sofa on the right. Heimhocker (relaxed) and Loomis (tense) sat across from him. An elaborate low Oriental table with inlaid teak filled much of the space between the sofas. Taking a small manila envelope from his inner jacket pocket, Mordon said, "We think we've identified your burglar." He shook out the mug shots onto the Oriental table, slid them across to the others. "He told you his name was Freddie, and that much was true."

There were two sets of the mug shots, front and side views, about five years old, courtesy of the Kings County (Brooklyn) District Attorney's office. Each doctor picked up a set. Loomis gasped, "That's him! Peter, that's him!"

" 'Fredric Urban Noon,' " read Heimhocker, and raised an eyebrow at Mordon. "Urban?"

"I believe that was a pope. Perhaps more than one."

"That explains it," Heimhocker agreed, and looked at the pictures some more. "He wasn't happy when these were taken, was he?"

"He was going to jail."

"Of course." Heimhocker placed the mug shots before him on the table. "When do we go talk to Mr. Noon?"

Mordon looked blank. "We?"

"David and I are his doctors," Heimhocker said.

"Oh, come now."

"We gave him the injection, that makes—"

"One moment, Doctor," Mordon said. Reaching across the table, he picked up the one set of mug shots from its surface and plucked the other from Loomis's trembling hand. "You met this fellow once," he pointed out, "as he was robbing your offices. You gave him one injection, one unethical and probably illegal injection. You can't—"

"The patient left our care without our approval," Heimhocker interrupted. It seemed he could be as steely cold as Mordon himself. Mordon waited, alert, and Heimhocker went on, "It was never our intention to leave him without proper medical care, without thorough medical observation. We brought the problem of his disappearance to *you*, which makes you our agent in this matter. You now say—"

"Hardly, Doctor, hardly your agent. I'm employed by—"

"You were talking, a minute ago, about ethics?"

A slippery slope here. Mordon asked himself, Do I want to make enemies of these people? What's the profit in it? On the other hand, what do they want? He said, "Dr. Heimhocker, I don't believe we have a disparity of interest here. You want to see the result of your experiment, naturally, and NAABOR wants to see if the result of your experiment is useful in any other way."

Heimhocker's reaction was to display even greater hostility and suspicion. "*What* other way?"

Mordon's irritation broke the surface of his professional calm. "Nothing to do with you," he snapped. "We're not talking vivisection here, for God's sake."

"What *are* you talking?"

"I don't see in what way that matters to you. The fellow's a *thief,* he robbed you, he stole all your office equipment, what are you trying to *protect* him for?"

"All we're trying to protect," Heimhocker said, while beside him Loomis's head bobbed in frantic agreement, "is the integrity of our experiment. What we are thinking about, quite frankly, Mr. Leethe, David and I, what we are thinking about is the judgment of our peers, *our* peers, when we publish. We made a mistake, I grant you that, but the mistake wasn't using whatsisname, Fredric Noon, Fredric *Urban* Noon, using him for our experimental subject. The mistake was in letting him get away. You say you know where he is, and *we* say, we're not going to let—"

"No, I didn't say that."

"—him get away again. What do you mean? Of course that's what you said."

"I did not."

"We heard you," Loomis chimed in. "We both heard you."

"What I said," Mordon carefully explained, "was that we know who he is. He left fingerprints in your guest room, our expert lifted them—"

"*And* left a mess behind."

"Irrelevant, David."

"Still."

Mordon said, "May I go on?"

"*I'm* sorry," Loomis said. "Yes, please do. You know *who* he is, but you don't know *where* he is? That's silly."

"Is it? The man is not on parole, not wanted for any crime—"

"Except the burglary here," Heimhocker interrupted.

"Well, no," Mordon said. "In the first place, it was a robbery, not a burglary, and in—"

Loomis said, "What's the difference? It's the same thing."

"A burglary is a theft in unoccupied premises," Mordon explained. "If the premises are occupied, it's robbery, a more serious crime. Whether or not the occupants and the criminal interact."

"Then he's wanted for robbery," Heimhocker said.

"The robbery was reported, by you," Mordon told him, "but there's been no official report linking Fredric Noon to the crime."

"For God's sake, why not?"

"Well, just from your point of view," Mordon said, "how much do you want Fredric Noon in jail from now on, for the rest of his life, absolutely unavailable to you for observation and experimentation?"

"We've *done* the experiment."

"And the observation?"

Loomis said, "Peter, he's right." Turning to Mordon, he said, "But the fingerprint man was from the police."

"Moonlighting," Mordon explained. "A few members of the New York Police Department are unofficially helping NAABOR in this matter. I'm going to see one of them next, on the question of how we make contact with Mr. Noon." Tucking the mug shots away again in their envelope, and returning the envelope to his jacket pocket, he said, "Before seeing him, I needed a positive identification that we were on the track of the right man." Rising, he said, "Now I know we are, I can proceed."

The two doctors got to their feet, Heimhocker fixing Mordon with a stern eye as he said, "You'll keep us informed of progress, of course."

"Of course," Mordon said, and thought, I'm lying. He knows I'm lying. I know he knows I'm lying. But does he know I know he knows I'm lying? And does it make any difference? Well, time would tell. "I can find my own way out, thank you," he said, and departed.

16

A restaurant can be a very satisfying business. Barney Beuler found that so, certainly. It had so many advantages. For instance, it always gave you a place to go if you wanted a meal, but *you* it didn't cost an arm and a leg. It gave you, as well, a loyal—or at least fearful—kitchen staff of illegals, always available for some extra little chore like repainting the apartment or standing on line at the Motor Vehicle or breaking some fucking wisenheimer's leg. It also made a nice supplement to your NYPD sergeant's salary (acting lieutenant, Organized Crime Detail) in your piece of the legit profit, of course, but more importantly in the skim. And it helped to make your personal and financial affairs so complex and fuzzy that the shooflys could never quite get enough of a handle on you to drag you before the corruption board.

The downside was that, in the six years Barney Beuler had been a minor partner—one of five—in Comaldo Ristorante on West Fifty-sixth Street, he'd gained eighty-five pounds, all of it cholesterol. It was true he'd die happy; it was also true it would be soon.

Another advantage of Barney's relationship with Comaldo was that it made a perfect place to meet someone like the attorney Mordon Leethe. The NYPD frowned on its cops using department time and department equipment and department clout on nondepartment matters, but what did Barney Beuler have to sell to a big multinational corporation like NAABOR except his NYPD access? I mean, get real. A man with three ex-wives, a current wife, a current girlfriend, a very small drug habit (strictly *strictly* recreational), two bloodsuckers he's paying off to keep their mouths shut and himself out of jail, a condo on Saint Thomas, a house and a boat on the north shore of Long Island, and a six-room apartment on Riverside Drive overlooking the Hudson from eleven stories up needs these little extra sources of income to make ends meet, as any sensible person realizes.

Barney was having lunch at "his" table near the front (it was his and the rest of the partners' table every midday till 12:45, when, if none of them had showed up, it would be given away as needed, Comaldo always doing a brisk lunchtime trade) when he saw Mordon Leethe come in with a tall skinny young guy who looked like Ichabod Crane. Ich would be one of the recent law school graduate employees of Leethe's firm and would not know he was the beard in this meeting between Leethe and Barney; the sap would think he was being earmarked for the big time. Well, maybe he was; stranger things have happened. Every day.

Barney, who was lunching with one copartner and two Long Island boating friends, gave Leethe the smiling nod of a restaurateur spying a good customer, and Leethe responded with the dignified nod of that good customer. He and Ich were shown to a table near the rear, one selected earlier by Barney because the acoustics at that back-corner location were particularly good if you didn't want your conversation overheard.

Barney kept his attention on his own table and food and companions, but nevertheless was also aware when Leethe and Ich ordered their lunches, and when they were given their bread, their water, and their olive oil. Only then, "Be right back," Barney told his pals, filled his mouth with gnocchi, and got to his feet.

Every year, it seemed, it was a little harder to squeeze between the tables. Seemed like the customers sat with their
chairs farther back than they used to. Maybe *everybody* was
getting fat.

Still, Barney eventually forced his way through the clien-
tele to that rear table, where he did his complete boniface
number, smiling broadly, extending his hand out across the
table, bowing from the general vicinity of his waist as he said,
"How are ya, Mr. Leethe? Been a while."

"I've missed the place, Barney," Leethe said, showing one
of his own false smiles as he laid a dead bird into Barney's
hand.

Barney shook the dead bird, returned it, and said, "How
you been keepin, Mr. Leethe?"

"Just fine, Barney. That tip you gave me on the brandy was
perfect, thank you for it."

The "brandy," of course, was the minor punk and thief called
Fredric Urban Noon, who had turned out to be the perp Leethe
was looking for. Barney grinned and said, "My pleasure, Mr.
Leethe, I'm glad it worked out. Speaking of brandy and suchlike,
you and your companion having some wine this lunchtime?"

"No, Barney, not today, we've got a lot of work ahead of us
back at the shop." The false smile took in Ich Crane: "Right,
Jeff?"

"Right," Ich said, and sat at attention. He was mostly
Adam's apple, over a yellow tie. Who'd told him yellow ties
were still in?

"Nevertheless, Mr. Leethe," Barney said, "I'd like you to
just cast an eye over our new wine list. I'm not trying to tempt
you—"

"You couldn't, Barney," Leethe said, chuckling at his underling, who chuckled back.

"I'm sure I couldn't. But for your future reference, I'd just
like you to see some of the Italians we got in. Okay?"

"Be happy to look at it, Barney," Leethe agreed.

"Be right back."

Barney went into the kitchen, took the sheet of paper he'd earlier worked up on the restaurant's computer—the same computer that did the menus, the billing, and the inventory—slipped it into the middle of one of the restaurant's large wine books, and went back to Leethe's table, where he presented the book with a flourish and said, "Just take a look at that."

Leethe found the insert right away, of course, and Barney watched him study it with just as much pleasure as if it had actually been a list of fine Italian wines. What the insert was, though, was a letter. Printed in three colors and four different typefaces, it looked like an expensive print job, and what it said was:

NEW YORK STATE GAMING AUTHORITY
WORLD TRADE CENTER TOWER #2
NEW YORK, NY 10001
212-555-1995

June 16, 1995

Mr. Fredric U. Noon
124-87 130th Crescent
Ozone Park, NY 11333

Dear Mr. Noon:

CONGRATULATIONS!

As you may know, the New York State Gaming Authority, in response to a consent order from the New York State Supreme Court, dated September 25, 1989, has been required to make a reimbursement of a certain percentage of the "tote" in the various gaming operations under the Authority's control, due to a computer malfunction between February 9, 1982, and October 1, 1986. The class-action suit brought against the Gaming Authority was completely satisfied by that court action.

It was directed by the Court, and agreed to by the Authority, that all citizens of the state of New York who, according to the records of the Authority, engaged in gaming activities under the control of the Authority between the dates of February 9, 1982, and October 1, 1986, shall be given equal standing in a lottery drawing to be held on the fourth of July, 1994, and the fifteen hundred (1,500) citizens whose names would be drawn would share equally in the court-directed judgment against the Authority of three million, one hundred seventy-six thousand, seven hundred dollars ($3,176,700.).

It is my happy duty, Mr. Noon, to inform you that yours was one of the names thus drawn by television star Ray Jones on July fourth of last year. Your share of the judgment comes to two hundred eleven thousand, seven hundred eighty dollars ($211,780.).

CONGRATULATIONS, Mr. Noon! If you will call me at 555-1995 before the fourth of July of this year, I will be happy to give you further details in re this judgment. It will be necessary, of course, for you to provide identification, and the judgment is fully taxable, but otherwise, the money is yours.

Unfortunately, Mr. Noon, if I do not hear from you before July fourth, I will have to assume that you have passed away or are not the correct Fredric U. Noon, and your two hundred eleven thousand, seven hundred eighty dollars ($211,780.) will be shared on a pro rata basis with the remaining lottery winners.

Congratulations again, Mr. Noon. I hope to hear from you
soon.

> With all best wishes,
>
> *B.L. Wickos*
>
> Banford L. Wickes
> Deputy Controller
> New York State Gaming Authority
> BLW:dw

This letter, with several variants, had been used sparingly
but effectively over the last decades by a number of different
law enforcement agencies, including the NYPD, to find and
apprehend criminals who had dropped out of sight. The letter
was sent to the criminal's last known address, in hopes it
would be forwarded, or sent to some close relative.

In this case, the only address for Fredric Noon that Barney'd been able to find in police records, since he was neither
in jail nor on parole at the moment, was the perp's parents'
home in Ozone Park. The phone number had been provided
by Leethe, who would have somebody of his own answer that
dedicated line the one and only time it would ring. From there
on, it was Leethe's task to reel the sucker in; Barney suspected
he was up to it.

"Very nice," Leethe said at last. Closing the wine book, he
returned it to Barney and said, "I'm looking forward to tast-
ing some of those."

"I'm sure it won't be long, Mr. Leethe," Barney said, and
carried the wine book back to the kitchen, where he removed
the letter, folded it twice, put it in the official-looking envelope he'd had the guy at the copy place around the corner
knock together, and tossed the envelope into the basket with

the outgoing paid bills. Then he went back to his chums and his gnocchi.

Leethe hadn't told him what all this was about, of course, and Barney was too cool to show the slightest curiosity, nor was he so incautious as to stick his nose in anywhere until he found out what the story was. But a story was here, all right, he could tell that much. Profit in it for Barney Beuler? Hard to say.

Fredric Urban Noon was a nobody, a penny-ante sticky-finger from Queens, not connected to anything except other people's goods. Why would a major corporation like NAABOR want him? What had he been doing in a cancer research place? Did he steal a cancer cure? Barney ran that scenario in his mind, but it just wouldn't play.

So was it maybe something in the other direction? Did the little gonif make off with some proof of something bad about the tobacco company that they didn't want known? Was he shaking them down right this minute? Did he need a partner?

The only problem with that second scenario was, with everything that was already known about the tobacco companies that didn't bother them, or bother their customers, or their stockholders, or the feds, what could they possibly have left to hide?

It was seeming to Barney that he too might like one little word with this Fredric Urban Noon.

17

Freddie never got over how weird it felt to walk around naked in the public streets in the middle of the day, particularly in your own neighborhood, passing people you'd seen on these blocks for years. Not people you actually know, just people you recognized, but still.

For instance, that fat young mother coming out of the supermarket pushing the stroller full of fat baby and Cheez Doodles and Dr Pepper. She seemed to be staring right at him, but of course she wasn't, though still it seemed that way. On the other hand, he'd been seeing her around for a couple of years, but now for the first time he could pause and study her and marvel at how fat she'd managed to get herself while still in her twenties.

But that wasn't all. He could also look at the good-looking women, so far as this neighborhood had any, and he could watch the old guys in front of the social club and how they talked with their hands and their chins, and he could watch the different ways people wait for a bus, and he could thumb his nose at the patrol car when it drove slowly by, the cops inside there telling each other war-hero lies and laughing in their own private party; you could rob the Cheez Doodles right out of that fat kid's stroller, those cops would never even notice.

He could, in other words, do a thousand different things to

help fight off boredom, without ever actually fighting off boredom.

What he was doing out here, just before lunch on a warm sunny Saturday in June, was making Peg happy. Trying to make Peg happy, anyway. He and she had a long talk in the van the other night, Thursday night, after they left Jersey Josh Kuskiosko. It was somehow easier lately for Peg to talk to Freddie after dark, so while she drove and he wore his Bart Simpson head she explained how she felt about things, and how she didn't want to break up with him or anything like that, but not being able to see him while he was all the time able to see her was really getting her down.

He made very sympathetic noises while she explained all this, and said he understood, and in fact he did understand, at least partially. Since she couldn't be with him completely while he was invisible like this, she had to have some time when she could be completely by herself. Of course, when you said it like *that* it didn't make any sense, but Peg had ways of saying it where it did make sense, or anyway it was important to her, so finally in the van Freddie suggested something that might help, and Peg agreed to it at once.

The idea was, since they weren't eating their meals together anymore—Peg still didn't know that food took a couple of hours to fully join his invisible body, and with luck she never would know—Freddie would leave the apartment at lunchtime any day it wasn't raining, go for a walk or take in a matinee movie (he wouldn't have to pay, after all) or whatever he wanted, while Peg ate her lunch and did whatever she had a mind to do in her own home without any thought that Freddie might be lurking somewhere, watching. (That was Peg's word, *lurking*, which Freddie himself wouldn't have used, but which he'd made no beef about, merely nodding his agreement, which of course she couldn't see.) Then, after an hour or so, Freddie would come home and have his own lunch, which Peg would have left on the kitchen table. It wasn't a *solution* to the problem, but it ought to at least help.

There was only one movie house in the neighborhood, and it showed a matinee only on Thursday, Friday, Saturday, and Sunday, but all four days of one week the same movie. So Freddie yesterday went in and watched an action movie where guys get blown up and you see them arc through the air like off a trampoline and afterward their *machine guns* still work, never mind the guys.

This is not a movie you can see two days in a row. One day in a row is a lot. Also, it turned out the matinee was senior discount time, and seniors in a movie theater in the middle of the day act *exactly* they way they did when they were eight years old in the same circumstances, talking and yelling at each other, changing their seats, eating stuff and throwing the wrappers on the floor, asking each other what just happened up on the screen. The only difference is, they totter up the aisle instead of running, and it's the toilet they're headed for, not the candy counter.

So Freddie wasn't looking forward to a repetition of that experience anytime soon, except maybe to go in with an Angel of Death kite and swoop it around over their heads until the theater emptied.

Anyway, today he was viewing the rich panorama of street life while time crawled by, and also incidentally looking for a telephone. Peg had suggested he phone her every day when he was ready to come home, and although she said it was because she wanted to be sure she got his lunch on the table at the right time, he knew it was because in her innermost heart she didn't entirely trust him, and wanted him to prove he was actually out of the apartment by phoning her from someplace else.

So yesterday he'd snuck into the manager's office in the movie theater, while the manager was out separating two codgers who were beating on each other with canes in the process of their discussion of whether or not Walter O'Malley was totally culpable in the felonious robbery of the Dodgers from Brooklyn. He'd made his call, assured Peg he was enjoying the movie——*Holy Shit III*, or whatever it was called—then got out of the way as the manager returned to his office to tend to his nosebleed.

Today, though, was a little different. He was *not* going back into the Megablok Star, no matter what, not even just to use the phone in the manager's office. He couldn't use a pay phone because he didn't have a quarter on him; in fact, he didn't have anything on him. And pay phones were the only kind of phones to be found out here on the street. But to go inside, into the storefront dentist, or the deli, or the copy shop, or the dry cleaner's, would mean somehow using a telephone right under the eyes—and ears, let's not forget ears—of employees, customers, dentists.

Still, to go home without having made a call would leave Peg convinced he'd never gone out in the first place, which would be *not* good. The last thing Freddie wanted to do was feed her doubt and paranoia. He was, after all, well known to be a liar and a thief insofar as other people were concerned, so if Peg gave way to occasional suspicion or skepticism she couldn't really be blamed.

And here came a guy talking on the phone. A guy in a tan suit and pale green shirt and dark green tie and brown shoes. A guy in his thirties, with a narrow sandy mustache and sandy hair cropped close all around so his big ears stuck out. One big ear, anyway; the other one would probably stick out, too, but at the moment the cellular phone was pressed against it as the guy walked along, swinging a briefcase in his other hand, chatting away.

It was only envy at first that made Freddie lope along beside this guy, ducking around oncoming pedestrians as he lis-

tened to the guy's half of the conversation, learning that he
was an insurance salesman calling his office, reporting on his
appointments so far today, wondering if there'd been any
messages. It should have been a short call, since there weren't
any messages for this guy, and not a lot had happened in his
appointments till now, but he dragged it out, prolonging it, obviously getting a kick out of walking there on a semicrowded
shopping street in Brooklyn in the sunshine talking on his
brand-new toy.

Still, the conversation eventually had to wind down, because the secretary or whoever it was at the other end of the
call had work to do, couldn't just sit there and play games all
day. But the so-longs also stretched out, and then Freddie saw
the stocky older woman coming slowly the other way, fresh
from the supermarket, weighed down by full plastic bags
dragging at each downward arm, slogging ahead flat-footed,
oblivious to the world and even to the sight of a tall insurance
man in a tan suit talking on the telephone as he walked along
the sidewalk.

Good-bye good-bye good-bye. Timing is everything. The
woman approached, the guy said yet another good-bye, then
thought of one more irrelevant question to ask, started to ask
it. The woman passed, headed the opposite way. Freddie
plucked the phone out of the guy's hand and dropped it into
the woman's right-side shopping bag.

The guy talked another two syllables before he realized the
phone wasn't there anymore. Then he stopped dead, said,
"Wha?" and moved his now-empty hand, still cupped for the
phone, around in front of his eyes, where he could stare at it.

Meanwhile, Freddie backed away out of the flow of foot
traffic, stood with his back against the cool glass of the nearest storefront window—ladies' garments, latest styles, large
sizes a specialty—and watched to see what would happen
next, which was that the woman kept trudging homeward with

her groceries, unaware of anything at all occurring anywhere in the world, while the guy in the tan suit started spinning in circles, looking down, out, up, around, everywhere. A couple of little kids, bopping along, deep in their own conversation, stopped to look at this weird grown-up, and the grown-up stopped his whirling to glare at *them* and shout, "Where is it?"

"Where's what?" one of the kids asked, while the other kid, wiser in the ways of adults, said, "We don't have it."

"I want my phone!"

"There's a phone on the corner," the wiser kid suggested, pointing.

"I want *my* phone!"

An older guy with half a dozen magazines under his arm stopped to say, "What's the problem?"

"My phone, I—" The guy would have torn his hair if it weren't too short to get hold of. "I was talking on it, and it disappeared!"

"Your telephone disappeared?"

"Yes!"

"Right out of your hand?"

"Yes!"

"That's like the missing Ambroses," the older guy said.

Freddie and both kids now gave this new arrival a lot closer attention, realizing he was going to be more interesting than they'd thought. The insurance man, glaring pop-eyed, cried, "Ambroses? Ambroses?"

"Sure," the other guy said. "Somebody was collecting Ambroses, Charles Fort wrote about it."

The insurance man had expected skepticism, scorn, disbelief; he hadn't expected Ambroses. "What the hell has that got to do," he cried passionately, "with my *phone*?"

The other guy took his magazines out from under his arm and started to leaf through them, as though one might contain an article explaining where the insurance man's telephone had gone. "Then there's Judge Crater," he said. "Now, in parapsychology—"

"I don't want any of your *crap!*" the insurance man screamed, waving his arms around. "I want my phone!"

It seemed to Freddie the insurance man was doing a very nice job of drawing attention to himself and away from anything else that might happen on this block, so, while all eyes turned toward this unexpected entertainment on the sidewalk, Freddie skipped through the gathering throng and went off in pursuit of the woman with the shopping bags. She was still plodding forward, step after step, doggedly homeward bound.

Unfortunately, just as Freddie arrived, the woman stopped. She frowned. She gazed down at the shopping bag into which Freddie had dropped the phone. Her eyes widened. "Hello?" she said.

Now what? Freddie had just caught up, and had been about to reach into that bag to retrieve the phone, but he couldn't very well do that with the woman staring at the bag that way.

Then things got worse. One-armed, the woman raised that plastic bag toward her head, a listening expression on her face. And then Freddie could hear it, too. In a tiny tinny voice, the plastic bag was saying, "Hello? Hello?"

The woman screamed, sensibly enough. Then she dropped the plastic bag onto the sidewalk—something glass broke in there, Freddie heard it—and legged it down the street at a milk-horse trot, listing to the side where she still toted groceries, but making good headway nonetheless.

So now while most of the people on the street were watching the insurance man do his mad lost-telephone dance, the rest of the people on the street turned to watch the fershlugginer woman with the one plastic bag, trotting and shrieking. A great moment for Freddie to retrieve the phone, which he did, and scoot with it into the tapered recess of the storefront dentist's entryway. Hunkering down there, so he could keep the phone below the level of the storefront window—he didn't want the receptionist in there to have to wonder why a cellular phone was flying solo in her doorway—he raised it and heard the thing still going, "Hello? Hello?"

What persistence. "Sorry, wrong number," Freddie told it, and closed the two halves of the phone together, which made it hang up. He waited a couple seconds, then opened it again, put it to his ear, and the plaintive hellos were gone at last, replaced by the welcome dial tone. Quickly he punched out his own number, and Peg answered on the second ring: "Hello?"

"It's me, Peg, I'm gonna come home now."

"Okay. Your brother Jimmy called."

"Oh, yeah?"

"He said don't call him back, he'll ring again later."

"What's it about?"

"He didn't say."

Freddie looked up, and there was a kid of maybe eight years of age standing in the doorway, looking with deep interest at the floating cellular phone, which was just now saying, "I'll make you a turkey sandwich, okay?"

"Ssshhhhh," Freddie said.

The kid said, "I didn't say anything."

Peg said, "Freddie? Something wrong?"

"I got to hang up now," Freddie said, and folded the phone on itself.

The kid gazed, neither frightened nor excited, just intensely interested. He said, "Are you a magic phone?"

"Yes," Freddie said.

"Do you belong to that man back there?"

"I didn't like him anymore," Freddie said, "so I went away from him."

"He's really mad."

"That's it," Freddie told the kid. "He's just got too excitable a personality, I get yelled into all the time, that's why I left."

"What are you going to do now?" the kid asked.

"I'm going to fly away," Freddie said. Standing up, he held the phone in both hands, then opened and closed it, opened and closed it, which made it look like something with wings.

Freddie left the dentist's doorway and headed toward home, holding the phone in front of him at about wrist level, opening and closing, opening and closing; every time he looked back, the kid was still there, watching.

Other people were watching, too, their attention caught by the vision of something weird flying by. Nobody tried to grab the phone, though, and Freddie made sure to steer himself so he never got too close to anybody.

Moving like that, he made it to the corner, and turned away from the shopping street onto a residential side street, where maybe he could get a little peace and quiet. His idea was, he'd stash the phone under a bush or a rock or something, so he could come back and use it every day at lunchtime and solve his telephone problem for good and all.

But when he looked back, an army of the curious was coming around the corner behind him, led by that damn kid, who was loudly explaining to anybody who'd listen that that was a magic flying telephone up ahead there, and that it didn't want to be yelled into anymore.

Freddie sped up, waggling the phone wings like mad. Behind him, the crowd also sped up, and some of them were considerably speedier than Freddie, mostly because they were wearing shoes and he was not.

Too damn many people, that was the problem. You can distract a thousand of them, there's still another hundred to give chase. The downside of city life.

Freddie could see his plan was not going to work. If he didn't abandon this telephone, before the end of this block somebody would catch up, reach for it, touch him, yell like mad, touch him some more, and then grab. And then a lot of people would grab.

Come to think of it, since they wouldn't be able to see him, they wouldn't know *what* they were grabbing, or *where* they were grabbing it. They could knock him down onto the sidewalk and trample him and never even know it.

Would they be able to see his blood, once it was outside him, all over the sidewalk?

These were not comforting thoughts. At the moment, Freddie was running past narrow yellow-brick two-story houses, all alike, two feet apart from one another, built up a tiny slope and back from the sidewalk, with gray-brick steps and walks, and scrubby little plantings in front of their enclosed porches. As he ran on by them, the shouts behind him closer and closer, and as he came to understand at last how the fox feels when all those loudmouth hounds are in his near background, Freddie finally tossed the telephone up and away, toward the shrubbery in front of house number 261-23.

Good-bye, telephone. Tomorrow we'll work out something else.

Freddie kept running, but the shouts behind him receded, and when he at last dared to look back the crowd had all run up the steps to 261-23 and were diving into the bushes there. More and more of them came, ripping greenery out by the roots in their frenzied search for the magic flying telephone.

Freddie was winded. He stood where he was, panting, holding his side where the pain was, and watched people toss the phone into the air and leap to catch it and fight over it and toss it some more, trying to make it fly. A throng of people had gathered in front of 261-23 now, ballooning out onto the sidewalk and even to the street, and nobody even paid any attention when the lady of the house, outraged at this attack on her brushwork, came roaring out of her enclosed porch to stand on her top step with an Uzi in her hands, at port arms. She yelled a lot, but everybody else was also yelling, so what else was new?

Would she shoot the damn gun? She looked mad enough. Meanwhile, the insurance salesman in his now-rumpled tan suit was way out at the periphery of the mob, jumping up and down and screaming that he wanted his phone back. And above it all, the sound of approaching police sirens.

Enough. Figure out telephones some other time. Turning his back on the follies of the human race, Freddie trudged on home.

"I'm home!"

"Did you go to the movies?"

Peg wouldn't come out of the bedroom, as Freddie well knew, but would shout to him from in there until he'd lunched and dressed.

"No, I saw it yesterday," he called back, and made his way toward the kitchen

"What'd you do?" she shouted.

"Went for a run," he shouted, and entered the kitchen.

His sandwich and coffee were on the table there. On one of the two chairs lay his clothing and all four masks, so he could make his own choice. He sat on the other chair, ate, considered his recent experiences in the outside world, and at the end of the sandwich he had no difficulty at all selecting the mask to put on.

It was Frankenstein's monster in a long-sleeved shirt and pink rubber gloves who at length sloped on into the living room, where Peg sat reading a paperback novel about a rich beautiful woman who owned her own successful perfume business but had trouble keeping a guy. She looked up from the deck of a yacht in the Med, anchored off Cannes at film festival time, to say, "Frankenstein? You haven't wanted to be *him* before."

"Frankenstein's *monster*," Freddie corrected. "Frankenstein was the doctor. I don't think the monster ever had a name."

Peg marked her place in the book with a twenty-dollar bill. "What's the matter, Freddie? You seem depressed. Or is it just the head?"

"No, I don't think so," he said. "I think I'm probably kind of depressed all over. I was just chased by a mob. A Brooklyn mob. It made me kind of identify with this guy," he explained, pointing at his head.

"Chased by a mob? How could they even *see* you?"

He began to relate his adventures, assuring her he didn't blame *her* for his complex need to find a telephone (while making it clear in the subtext that he did blame her, for not trusting him to really leave the apartment), and he'd just reached the dentist's doorway when the phone beside Peg rang. "If it's the insurance guy," Freddie said, "tell him I don't need any."

"Oh, yes, you do," she said, but picked up the phone and spoke and then said, "Yeah, he's here now, hold on." She extended the phone toward Frankenstein, or his monster. "It's your brother."

"Oh, yeah."

Freddie crossed to take the phone, which felt strange with the rubber gloves on. Holding the phone to the side of the mask, he said, "Hey, Jimmy, what's happening?"

"Where are you, man, in a tunnel?"

Jimmy was one of Freddie's younger siblings, so Freddie didn't have to take any shit. "No, I'm not in a tunnel," he said. "Is that why you called?"

"You sound like you're on one of those speakerphones or something."

"Well, I'm not. This is how I sound these days, is all." Through the eyeholes, he could see Peg wincing in sympathy, which made him feel a little better. He said, "I'll tell you all about it sometime, Jimmy. What's going on?"

"Well, I'm calling from a pay phone," Jimmy said.

Ah-hah. The message in that was that Jimmy wanted to tell him something that the law might want to know about, and Jimmy's own phone might be tapped, since Jimmy had also in the course of his life at times drawn himself to their attention. But, since Freddie's phone likewise might have additional listeners, Jimmy's comment was also a warning: Be careful what we both say here.

"Okay," Freddie said. "How's the weather out there, by your pay phone?"

"Not bad. You got one of those sting letters, sent to the folks' place."

Whoops. Again Freddie knew exactly what his brother was talking about. Whenever the cops wanted to round up a whole bunch of really stupid people who had warrants outstanding, they'd send out these letters, which had come to be known on the street as the Superbowl letters, because usually they told the recipient he'd won tickets to the Superbowl and all he had to do was come to such-and-such an address and pick them up. Instead of which, *he* was what would be picked up, by a lot of unfriendly cops. This was a real cull, sweeping the streets of the most boneheaded of the crooks, leaving a clearer field to everybody else.

On the other hand, it was kind of an insult to be sent one of those letters. Voice dripping scorn, hoping his phone *was* tapped, Freddie said, "I *got* tickets to the Superbowl."

"It wasn't exactly that," his brother said, "but you got the idea. I don't know what you been up to recently—"

"Nothing! There's no sheet out on me at all!"

But even while he was saying that, and just for that moment believing it, Freddie was also thinking, Those damn *doctors*! Frankenstein and Frankenstein. They must have turned him in, and he must not have cleared away every last fingerprint from all the places he'd been in their damn house.

Meantime, Jimmy was saying, "Well, the folks got the letter, and it gave them a start, you know what I mean?"

"Tell them everything's fine, Jimmy, okay?"

"But is it? I mean, really? You know, just a yes or a no."

"Yes, Jimmy," Freddie said, and hung up, and said to Peg, "Let's get outta town for the summer."

18

At the end of 1993, Congress passed an obscure amendment to the tax law declaring that employer-provided free parking garage space worth more than $155 a month was to be treated as taxable income. The purpose of this obscure amendment was to skim just a little more off a few rich businessmen in New York and Los Angeles and Chicago, it never occurring to the good burghers of Congress that *they* receive from their employer—us—free parking garage space worth considerably more than $155 a month; have you ever tried to park near the Capitol? This fact, however, did not escape the notice of the IRS, no respecter of persons, so we can assume it's an amendment that won't be on the books for long.

In the meantime, however, the partners of Mordon Leethe's law firm were faced with an agonizing choice. Either pay the tax on their convenient parking spaces in the basement of their office building, or remove the glass from the barred high windows of the basement garage area, thus making the parking area one "exposed to the elements," thus presumably outdoors, thus worth less than $155 a month; whew, close one.

In June, the breeze wafting through the basement garage where Mordon parked his Mercedes was sweet and soft, redolent of the islands, or at least of the Cajun restaurant half a block away. Mordon locked his car—he also locked it inside

his own garage, attached to his own house, in Oyster Bay—
and as he turned toward the elevator a nearby car door
slammed and there was Barney Beuler, the corrupt cop, strid-
ing fatly toward him, smiling that smug smile of his. (The
man, did he but know it, was far more credible as a maître d'
than a police officer.) "Good morning, Mr. Leethe," Barney
crowed, pleased with himself. "Long time no see."

This was why Mordon locked his car. "How did you get in
here?" he snapped.

Some men might have been insulted by such a greeting, but
not Barney. "Are you kidding?" he said, and beamed more
and more broadly in self-satisfaction. "I can get in anywhere
I want."

"I thought you liked to be careful where you went," Mordon said, sour because he hadn't been looking forward to an
encounter like this at the very beginning of the business day.
"I thought you were worried about surveillance from— What
do you call them? The police that police the police."

"Shooflys," Barney said, and grinned again, and pointed a
thumb upward. "At this very moment," he said, "I am at my
dentist's, in this building."

"When did he become your dentist?"

"Very recently."

The difference between Barney and me, Mordon told himself, and the reason I am automatically repelled by the man, is
that when we meet, I am doing my job, but he is betraying his
job. It makes all the difference. "What's this about, Barney?"
he asked, and made a point of looking at his watch. "If you
have news about that fellow Noon, why not get to me the normal way?"

"Because it isn't normal news," Barney said. Gesturing at
Mordon's Rolex, he said, "You got nothing that won't keep.
Come on and siddown a minute, lemme tell you a story."

Reluctant, but curious despite himself, Mordon followed

Barney to a long black Lincoln, where Barney opened a rear door and gestured for Mordon to enter.

Mordon reared back to study the car. Connecticut plates. Chauffeur's cap on front passenger seat, on top of today's *New York Post*. Extraspacious rear seat, with TV. "This isn't your car."

"I never said it was. Get in, will ya?"

Mordon couldn't believe it. "It was unlocked?"

"Not when I got here. Come on, we don't wanna stand out here in the wind. You people oughta glass in those windows or something."

Mordon was *not* going to get into a discussion of tax law with Barney Beuler. Instead, he bowed forward and climbed into the Lincoln, sliding over on the black leather to make room. Barney settled in next to him, pulled the door shut, and leaned back with a sigh and a smile. "Not bad."

"Are you here to sell me this car?"

"That's one of the things I like about you, Mr. Leethe," Barney told him. "You're always a pistol, you never let up."

Mordon closed his mouth, observed Barney from a great distance, and waited.

Barney got it; he was always quick. "Right," he said, and looked out at the parking garage, then back to Mordon. "This fella Noon," he said. "He's an interesting guy."

"Just a little crook, you told me the other day."

"That's his record," Barney agreed. "Not even a blip on the old crime meter. But here you are taking an interest in him."

"My client is taking an interest in him."

"Even better. So this fella Noon, there's more to him than meets the eye."

Mordon permitted himself a wintry smile. "That's truer than you know."

"There's been no answer to our letter," Barney said.

"Surely he's gotten it by now." Today was Tuesday, and the letter had been sent last Thursday.

"Either he's not gonna get it," Barney said, "because his people don't know where he is, or he's too smart to fall for the stunt."

"This isn't what you're here to tell me."

"Last Wednesday," Barney said, "there was a break-in at a fur storage place out in Astoria. Looks like an inside job, nothing busted to get in, alarms switched off, a bunch of valuable mink coats just up and walk off the property. But the Burglary Squad takes prints, just to see if there's any strangers that the inside man let in, and there's our friend Fredric Urban Noon."

"He stole the coats?"

"You can't prove it, not in a court of law," Barney said. "Fingerprints will tell you *where* a guy was, but they can't tell you when he was there. Anyway, the week before that, either Wednesday or Thursday, they can't be sure, a bunch of diamonds went missing on West Forty-seventh Street. Again, looks like an inside job, no alarms touched, nobody suspicious around, just the diamonds are gone."

"And they found Noon's fingerprints," Mordon finished.

Barney grinned at him. "You know they did."

"Of course," Mordon said, realizing. "He can't wear gloves."

Barney raised an eyebrow. "What's that supposed to mean?"

"Nothing. Go on."

Barney thought about that, then shrugged and decided to let it go, to get back to his own flow of events. His smile when he looked at Mordon now was proprietary, the way he might smile at his restaurant. "Fredric Noon's an interesting guy, isn't he?"

"You said that before."

"I'm saying it again. He's an interesting guy. And you're gonna tell me why."

"I don't think so," Mordon said, "but I'll be happy to tell my client what you just said." And he reached for the door handle.

"Don't be stupid, Mr. Leethe," Barney said.

Mordon looked at him in surprise, and Barney wasn't smiling anymore. "Am I being stupid?"

"Not yet. It's true some of the shooflys would like to nail my nuts to a courthouse bench, but I also got friends here and there in the department, what with one thing and another."

"I'm sure you do."

"Now, if I was to go to those friends," Barney said, "and tell them you tried to suborn me and bribe me to pass along classified NYPD information—"

"They'd laugh at you," Mordon said. "*I'd* laugh at you."

"You think so?" Barney's eyes were now cold as ice. "You think I haven't been wired with you, Mr. Leethe? You think *I'm* so stupid I don't have selected tapes from our conversations that make *you* the heavy and *me* the virgin? Do *you* have tapes, Mr. Leethe?"

It had never occurred to Mordon that he might need such items. He stared at Barney, unable to think of a thing to say.

Barney could think of what to say. Patting Mordon's knee, the gesture sympathetic, he said, "You got a partner now, Mr. Leethe. So tell me the story."

Mordon told him the story.

19

"The house is haunted, you know," Mrs. Krutchfield said.

The young woman signing the register looked less than overwhelmed. "Oh, yeah?"

"Many of our guests have seen . . . strange things."

"I do too sometimes," the young woman said, and extended her credit card.

Dealing with the card, looking at the information the young woman had written on the register—Peg Briscoe, and an address in Brooklyn and the license number of that van outside—Mrs. Krutchfield was not at all surprised that this guest was a New Yorker.

City people, they think they know it all. Mrs. Krutchfield, a buxom motherly woman rather beyond a certain age, was sorry, but she just couldn't help it, New Yorkers rubbed her the wrong way, they always had. They were never *impressed* by anything. You can take your tourist families from faraway places like Osaka, Japan, and Ionia, Iowa, and Urbino, Italy, and Uyuni, Bolivia—and Mrs. Krutchfield could show you all of them in her visitors' book with their very *excellent* comments—and you could show them your wonders of the Hudson River valley, and you could just happen to mention that this lovely old pre-Revolution farmhouse, now The Sewing Kit bed-and-breakfast outside Rhinebeck, was known to be haunted by a British cavalry officer slain under this very roof in 1778, and those people are, in two words, im pressed.

But not New Yorkers. It was such a pity, then, since The Sewing Kit was a mere 100 miles straight north of Manhattan, into the *most* scenic countryside, that New Yorkers were so much more important to her operation than all the Osakians and Ionians and Urbinos and Uyunis put together. Mrs. Krutchfield just bit her lip and kept her own counsel and tried not to look at the "wives'" ring fingers, and did her level best to treat the New Yorkers just like everybody else.

Including this Briscoe snip. Handing over the large iron key dangling from an even larger wooden representation of the sort of drum that goes with a fife, Mrs. Krutchfield smiled maternally and said, "You'll be in General Burgoyne."

The snip frowned, hefting the heavy key and drum. "Is that usual?"

That was the other thing about New Yorkers: they kept saying things that made no sense. Ignoring that remark, Mrs. Krutchfield said, "We've named all our rooms after Revolutionary War figures, so much nicer than numbers, I think. General Burgoyne, and Betsy Ross, and Thomas Jefferson—"

"The usual suspects."

Mrs. Krutchfield got that one. "Yes," she said, miffed. But she couldn't help going on with her patter. "All except the colonel, of course, we wouldn't name a room after *him*."

So it *is* possible to attract the attention of a New York snip. The girl said, "The colonel?"

"Colonel Hesketh Pardigrass," Mrs. Krutchfield explained, and looked over her shoulder before lowering her voice to add, "the one who was slain in this very house in 1778. It was because of a *woman*. He's the ghost."

"Ah," the young woman said. "Haunted house equals ghost equals your colonel."

"Well, yes." It was so *hard* to be civil to New Yorkers, but

Mrs. Krutchfield would not give up. "You can read all about him in your room," she confided. "I wrote up his history and made copies, so there's one in every room. You're welcome to take it with you if you like." She didn't add, but might have, most of the decent people do. Particularly the Japanese.

"Thank you," the girl said, noncommittal; *she* wouldn't take the colonel's history with her, you could tell. And now she hefted the drum-and-key once more, and said, "Are they alphabetical?"

Mrs. Krutchfield went blank. "Are *what* alphabetical?"

"The rooms. I was wondering how to find General Burgoyne."

"Oh, well, I'll give you directions," Mrs. Krutchfield offered. Alphabetical? she wondered. What did the girl *mean*, alphabetical? "You just drive your vehicle around to the back," she said, "and park anywhere. You'll see the outside staircase, just go up and in the door there, and it's the first door on the right. You'll have lovely views of the Catskills."

"Oh, good."

"And you'll be staying just the one night?" This customer was a bit unusual, at that; a lone young woman on a Wednesday in June, arriving at almost six in the evening, for one night only.

Which the girl confirmed. "Yes. We're up looking for a house to rent for the summer, but we didn't find anything today."

Mrs. Krutchfield frowned past the girl toward her van parked on the circular drive. "We? I thought you were alone."

"Oh, I am. My, uh, my friends had to drive back to the city tonight, because of their cats."

Oh, yes, New Yorkers also have cats. Some had even been known to ask if they could keep their smelly cats in the actual rooms at The Sewing Kit, to which the invariable response was a gentle but firm no.

The girl said, "You wouldn't know any houses for rent, would you?"

"I'm afraid not, no."

"Well, we'll look some more tomorrow. Thank you."

Mrs. Krutchfield was at heart a good woman, which is why she said, "There's a television set in the parlor, some guests like to watch in the evening," even though New Yorkers never want to watch the same programs as everybody else.

"Thanks." The girl turned away, paused, seemed to think about something, and turned back with her brow all furrowed. "Your ghost," she said. "You say there's a write-up about him in the room?"

"Yes, every room. You're welcome to take it with you, if you like."

"Yes, you said that." The girl seemed obscurely troubled, and even sighed a little. "Well, we can only hope for the best," she commented, as though to herself, and left Mrs. Krutchfield steaming in a stew of irritation and bewilderment.

New Yorkers!

There was only one empty room at The Sewing Kit tonight, Nathan Hale, the one Mrs. Krutchfield always rented last because it was downstairs in back, too near the kitchen and the TV, and with no view at all to speak of, unless you like extreme close-ups of pine trees. But it was a nice group tonight, a nice mix, with some Germans in Betsy Ross, making marks on maps, and a family of Canadians in Ben Franklin washing their clothing in the sink—they'd particularly asked for a room with a sink, since The Sewing Kit did not offer private baths, but only communal bathrooms shared by two or three guest rooms—and in other rooms were several groups of mid-westerners, whom Mrs. Krutchfield had always found to be the very *nicest* of Americans, if somehow not all that stimulating. And of course the retired couple from Detroit—"Motor

City!" they kept calling it, with the exclamation point solidly present in a silvery saliva spray—were still here, and still had *more* of their postcard collection from all over the "Lower Forty-eight"—as they called America—to show to their innkeeper or the other guests or anyone else who didn't move fast enough.

And of course there was the New Yorker in General Burgoyne.

Somehow, not entirely sure why, Mrs. Krutchfield found herself hoping the Motor City! couple and the girl from Brooklyn never crossed paths.

The Sewing Kit did not serve lunch or dinner, offering instead a typed-up list of suggestions of fine restaurant experiences to be had in the general Rhinebeck–Red Hook area. Mrs. Krutchfield did serve a breakfast of which she was proud, enough baked and fried food to pin any traveler to the seat of his or her car for *hours* after departure from The Sewing Kit, but the other meals she prepared only for herself, in her private quarters off in the left front wing of the sprawling structure, from which she could watch the main entrance and the circular drive for late arrivals or unexpected departures.

Usually, after dinner, Mrs. Krutchfield would join in the side parlor any of her guests who might like to watch TV. She herself was always in bed by ten, but she didn't mind if the guests continued to enjoy television by themselves, so long as they kept the volume down and turned the box off no later than the end of Jay Leno at 12:30. (New Yorkers always wanted to watch David Letterman.)

This evening the parlor was comfortably full, mostly with midwesterners, plus the Canadians (who smelled of Ivory Liquid), all spread out on both sofas, the three padded armchairs, and even the two wooden chairs. The girl from Brooklyn came in a little later than everyone else, looked around, smiled, said, "That's okay," waved the midwestern gentlemen back into their seats, and settled cross-legged on the floor in front of the sofas more gracefully and athletically than a city girl should be able to do.

Mrs. Krutchfield was justifiably proud of the big black gridwork dish out behind The Sewing Kit, bringing in television signals from all over outer space, but the truth was, she didn't make much use of its potential, limiting herself almost exclusively to the three networks, except when it so happened that one of the guests knew of a particular old movie afloat on some obscure brooklet crossing the heavens, and asked if they might tune in: a Martin and Lewis comedy, perhaps, or *Johnny Belinda*, or *Fail-Safe*.

There was nobody like that tonight, though, so they contented themselves with sitcoms. Mrs. Krutchfield sat in her usual place, the comfortable armchair directly opposite the TV. On the maple end table beside her lay the remote control, atop the satellite weekly listings open to tonight's schedule. (It was better not to let any of the male guests near the remote control.) And so another evening began at The Sewing Kit.

At first, everything was normal and serene. Then, at just about four minutes past nine, as everybody was contentedly settling in to watch a program broadcast from some parallel universe in which, apparently, there was a small town where the mayor and the fire chief and the high school football coach spent *all* their time joshing with one another at a diner run by a woman suffering from, judging by her voice, throat cancer, *all at once* the TV set sucked that picture into itself, went click, and spread across itself an image of three people moving on a bed, with no covers on. With no *clothing* on! Good gracious, what are those people *doing?*

Some horrible corner of the satellite village, some *swamp* beside the information highway, had suddenly thrust itself— oh, what an awful choice of words!—onto their TV screen.

Gasping and shaking and little cries of horror ran through the room as Mrs. Krutchfield grabbed frantically for the remote control, only to find it had somehow fallen to the floor under her chair.

The people on-screen were also gasping and shaking and emitting little cries, though not of horror. "Mrs. Krutchfield!" cried a midwesterner, a stout lady from Loose Falls, whose chubby hands were now a bas relief on the front of her face. "Mrs. Krutchfield, *help!*"

"I'm, I'm—"

Scrabble, scramble—there! A different channel. On this channel, in a bare room, garishly lit, several men in ski masks and gray robes waved machine guns over their heads and yelled at the camera in some foreign tongue, urging who knew what depredations to be directed against the decent people of the planet, but at least they were *clothed,* and none of them were *women,* so they afforded Mrs. Krutchfield that calm moment of leisure she needed to figure out how to get back to Kitty's Diner, where the coach was saying: "—and that's when you throw the long bomb."

The sound track laughed, God knows why, and most of the people in the parlor dutifully laughed along with it, and life got back to normal.

For eight minutes. *Im*-plode, click, and now it was two people on what looked like a hockey rink in a large empty arena. These two weren't entirely naked, since they were both wearing ice skates, but what they were doing together was certainly *not* an Olympic routine.

Cries and shrieks from the sofas. Great wafts of Ivory Liquid essence from the Canadians. Mrs. Krutchfield *lunged* for the remote, and it was *gone again!*

Under her chair again—how could she keep knocking the blame thing off the end table like that, without noticing?—but this time she was more sure-fingered in fighting her way back to Kitty's Diner, where Kitty was rasping: "—and that's why you can't get today's special today."

The sound track laughed, the people in Mrs. Krutchfield's parlor laughed, and the world returned to its accustomed orbit.

For four minutes this time, before the implode*click*picture, during which half the guests either squeezed their eyes shut or protectively slapped their palms to their faces. But this time it was something entirely different. The picture on the screen was in black-and-white, to begin with, instead of those all-too-real flesh tones. Also, the woman walking along the cliff-edge above the stormy sea was fully clothed. Not only that, she was . . .

"Gene Tierney!" cried a midwestern gentleman who had not shut his eyes.

"*She* wouldn't do things like that!" cried a midwestern lady, whose eyes were still firmly sealed.

"It's a movie!" cried another midwestern gentleman.

Eyes opened. On-screen, the action had moved indoors, into an extremely cute cottage not unlike The Sewing Kit itself, though perhaps a bit more cramped. In this setting, a recognizable Rex Harrison marched and harrumphed, dressed like a pirate captain or something, and behaving in a rough-and-ready way that didn't at all suit him. Also, you could see through him, which was odd.

A midwestern gentleman said, "It's *The Ghost and Mrs. Muir.*"

A midwestern lady said, "I remember that series. But it wasn't Rex Harrison."

"No, no, no," said the gentleman. "This is the original movie."

"There was a movie?"

A Canadian, somewhat younger, said, "There was a television series?"

A midwestern lady gave out a sudden shriek. "It's the ghost!" she cried.

"And Mrs. Muir," said her companion on the sofa.

"No! The *ghost*! Colonel Pardigrass!"

That shut them up. For a minute or two everyone in the room just sat and gazed at Rex Harrison and Gene Tierney, finding love—or something—across the centuries. So much pleasanter to contemplate than those *other* people.

Timidly, a midwestern lady said, "Mrs. Krutchfield, does this happen often?"

"My goodness, no," Mrs. Krutchfield said. "I couldn't bear it."

"What does the ghost usually do?" asked a gentleman.

"Well, uh," Mrs. Krutchfield stammered, all undone by events. "Just, oh, rapping and, and creaking, and that sort of thing. The *usual* sort of thing."

"This is a completely different manifestation from anything that ever happened before?"

"Lord, yes!"

The snip from Brooklyn, seated on the floor in their midst, turned toward them an excessively innocent face as she said, "Looks like, after all these years, the colonel's getting a little randy."

"The ghost wasn't like that with Mrs. Muir," a lady objected.

"Frankly," a gentleman said, "I don't see how it's possible to suffer the pangs of the flesh if you don't *have* any flesh."

"It doesn't bear thinking about," a lady announced, in an effort to forestall speculation.

Another lady said, "Mrs. Krutchfield, what should we *do*?"

Mrs. Krutchfield had been pondering this problem herself. The ghost of Colonel Hesketh Pardigrass had never been any trouble before, had been, in fact, merely another charming part of the decor, like the Laura Ashley curtains and the Shaker reproduction furniture and the print in the entranceway of George Washington crossing the Delaware. An insubstantial insubstantiality, in other words, which was exactly the way Mrs. Krutchfield preferred it.

It wasn't that Mrs. Krutchfield had *made up* the ghost, or not exactly. The real estate agent, years ago when she'd bought this wreck of a place to fix up for its present use, had told her about the old tales of ghostly goings-on here, though without any specific history or even anecdotes attached. (Privately, Mrs. Krutchfield had always believed that much of what the real estate agent had told her was malarkey, meant to intrigue her, but that was all right. She'd been spending her school-administration retirement funds plus her dead husband's insurance money, and had been in a mood for a bit of malarkey, anyway.)

Then, shortly after buying the place, when Mrs. Krutchfield had been ripping out some horrible old linoleum in the kitchen, with newspapers lining the floor beneath, one ancient newspaper had contained a feature story about ghosts in the Hudson River valley, in which Mrs. Krutchfield had read about this Colonel Hesketh Pardigrass, who had been having some sort of liaison with the wife of a farmer in the area and had been murdered in the farmhouse, presumably by the farmer, though possibly by the wife. In any event, it had been claimed for a while that Colonel Pardigrass roamed the site of his demise on windy nights, still vainly trying to get back to his old regiment, though no one, even at the time this old newspaper had been printed, claimed to have had personal experience of the wayward colonel. As to the farmhouse, the description of the place and its whereabouts had been vague, but this house here could just as well have been the one where it all happened, so why not say so? What was the harm?

And how much cosier for a nice B-and-B like Mrs. Krutchfield's to come equipped with a ghost. A nice gentlemanly ghost, like Rex Harrison over there, though less intrusive. And that was how it had been.

Until tonight, that is.

After a few minutes of *The Ghost and Mrs. Muir,* when nothing further of an untoward nature happened—and now, more than ever before, Mrs. Krutchfield understood the concept of happenings of an untoward nature—one of the Canadians timidly asked if it might be possible to return to Kitty's Diner, but one of the midwestern gentlemen said, "Seems to me, *this* is what the colonel wants to watch. I don't know that we oughta cross him."

Which ended that discussion, and everybody settled down to make some sense out of *The Ghost and Mrs. Muir,* if possible. However, without color to soothe their eyes and a laugh track to let them know when things were supposed to be funny, they soon became restless and uneasy. There were murmurings among the guests, who were clearly suggesting to one another it was time to give up television for this evening and go to sleep instead—what else was there?—until Mrs. Krutchfield, who was not a timid woman, suddenly said, "Well, I'm sorry, but I'm just not in the mood for this particular movie this evening. *I* want to go back to Kitty's Diner."

"So do I," said several other people.

"Good," Mrs. Krutchfield said, and reached to the end table, and found nothing. She looked—the remote wasn't there. On the floor again? Grunting, she leaned forward to look under her chair, and it wasn't there either. "*Now* where's that remote doodad?" she asked, and implode*click*picture it was those people on the bed again!

Indefatigable, inexhaustible, and now there were four of them! A second naked woman had joined the other depraved souls, and this one had something strapped around her midsection. What *is* that?

"Aaaaa!" said many people in the room.

A mad scramble took place to find the remote, while on-screen the four naked people displayed various mathematical formulae. Two into one *does* go, as it turns out.

The remote was in a midwestern lady's purse, which caused her to turn as red as Rudolph the Reindeer's nose. "I'm sure I—I'm sure I—I'm sure I—" was all she could manage to say.

"No one blames you, Edith," her husband assured her, patting her arm.

Mrs. Krutchfield had, the instant the remote was in her hands, used it to off the TV, with extreme prejudice. "I think," she said, "that's enough television for this evening."

No one disagreed. One of the ladies, on quitting the parlor, said rather waspishly in Mrs. Krutchfield's ear, "I don't think much of that colonel of yours."

"I don't know *what* to think of him," Mrs. Krutchfield replied, which was only the truth. A dubious character from two dubious sources, dubiously yoked together into one fanciful whole, and now was it to come to life? Would Mrs. Krutchfield never be able to watch television peaceably in her own parlor ever again? Would she have to remove those handsome write-ups about the colonel from her guest rooms, the ones the guests were free to take along with them on departure, if they so chose? (No one from this group would so choose, you could be sure of that.)

How did one find an exorcist? Were they in the Yellow Pages?

Mrs. Krutchfield went to bed with a severe headache, and tossed and turned all night; alone, at least, thank heaven.

Most people, including the grinning snip from Brooklyn, left the parlor when Mrs. Krutchfield did, but a few of the midwestern gentlemen stayed behind to try to find those naked people on the bed in the airwaves just one more time. They never did succeed.

20

"That wasn't very nice."

"Then how come you're still laughing?" came the unrepentant voice from the rear of the van.

"I didn't say it wasn't *funny,*" Peg pointed out, "I said it wasn't *nice.*"

In both exterior mirrors, The Sewing Kit and its collar of pine trees receded in bright morning sunlight, appearing to shiver slightly, as though not yet over last night's trauma. Everyone had seemed subdued at breakfast this morning in the overly cutesy sunroom, and Mrs. Krutchfield most subdued of all. As she brought out platter after platter of scrambled eggs and sausage and English muffins and fried potatoes and heavily buttered toast, her professional smile had been less than perfect and her doting attention to her guests hampered by an unremitting distraction. Jugs of orange juice and coffee and milk sloshed as she brought them from the kitchen, and she constantly darted glances over her shoulder. From time to time, she trembled all over, like a hard-ridden horse.

Peg had offered to sneak some food back for Freddie, but he'd said that was okay, he could wait until they left and get something at a deli somewhere, so Peg ate by herself while Freddie packed, and now they were on their way north in their continuing search for a nice place to spend the summer.

The problem was, most nice places were already gone. To be looking for a summer rental in the mountains north of New York City in the last week in June was an exercise in frustration. Most real estate agents had nothing left to show, and those few rentals that *were* still on the market were there for a very good reason: nobody could possibly want them.

Still, they were here, so, once they'd gotten Freddie a sandwich and a Coke to eat in the back of the van, on they went in their quest.

Most of the real estate agents Peg talked to wanted to use their own cars, naturally, to show this potential client around, but she always refused, saying she just wasn't comfortable as an automobile passenger anymore, not since that horrible accident that had led to so much reconstructive surgery; you can't see the scars, can you? Tell the truth, now.

So the real estate agents invariably agreed to travel with Peg in the van, unaware of the naked Freddie, lolling in the back. And wherever they went to look at a house, Peg would always leave her van door open. That way, Freddie could look the places over, too, and once Peg had returned the agent to his or her office, they could discuss what they'd seen.

Not that there was much to discuss. Kennels and chicken coops, chicken coops and kennels, and that was how the morning sailed by. For lunch, they picnicked on opposite sides of the van in a field full of flowers, with cows on the other side of a barbed-wire fence, and in calling back and forth to one another, their mouths full of take-out sandwiches, they admitted a certain discouragement. And not just with the house-hunt, either.

"I'll tell you the truth, Freddie," Peg called from her side of the van, waggling a pickle for emphasis, "this eating business is getting to be a drag."

"For me, too, Peg," Freddie's voice came back, floating around the van. "I'd like to go to a restaurant again, the two of us. I'd like to eat with you even at *home* sometimes, order out Chinese like we used to."

"That's the way I feel, too, Freddie."

Freddie could be heard chewing thoughtfully for a while, and then he said, "Peg, the fact is, there's a lot of advantages to this invisibility thing, I don't deny it, but there's a whole bunch of disadvantages, too."

"*That's* the truth."

"If I could turn it on or off, you know, whenever I wanted, it would be a different thing."

"Exactly."

"On the other hand, Peg," Freddie said, "I think maybe all these doghouses we've been looking at the last couple days have depressed us."

"Even more, you mean."

"Yeah. Even more. Maybe we should pack it in. Quit now, and go back to the city."

"We've only got one more guy on the list around here," Peg said. "Let's go see him, take a look at what he's got, and then we'll give it up, we'll go home and forget it."

"We can take a plane somewhere," Freddie said. "First Class is never full, we'll take one First Class seat, and I'll sit beside you."

"And spook the pilots, just for fun?"

"Did you like that? The ghost and Mrs. Muir?"

Peg laughed, and then Freddie laughed, and things were all right again for a while.

"I have something you're going to love," said Call Me Tom. He was a hefty amiable guy in a small office in what had once been a gasoline station back before OPEC, and he'd jotted down Peg's particulars on a form, asked her about price range, and then he'd smiled and said he had something she was going to love.

Fine. On the other hand, every other real estate agent had also had something to show Peg that she was going to love, and every one of them had been wrong. So Peg was restrained in her joy. "I'll look at it," she allowed.

"It just came on the market," Call Me Tom explained, "or it would have been snapped up already. The owners didn't leave till Tuesday, we needed the cleaning lady to go through, so it's only today I can start to show it."

Peg said, "How come the owners left in such a hurry?" Because if it didn't mean the owner was on the run from the Mob so the house was likely to get itself firebombed, it must mean the house was full of asbestos that the owner just found out about.

But Call Me Tom said, "He's a scientist with a big pharmaceutical company, they had some kind of problem in their plant out on the West Coast, all of a sudden he had to transfer out there for the next four months. He doesn't like to leave the place empty, so that's why it's for rent. Fully furnished. Within your price range."

"Let's take a look," Peg said.

Okay. Here's the house: It's a small old farmhouse, built in the early nineteenth century, a center-hall Colonial with entrance and second-floor staircase in the middle. Downstairs is a big living room, medium-size dining room, small kitchen, and tiny bath. Upstairs, two bedrooms and two more baths.

Modern windows and screens and central air. A wooden deck behind the house. The swimming pool, small but very nice, was in a wooden-fenced enclosure just beyond the patio. The circular asphalt drive in from the secondary country road included a spur to a two-car garage, built to match the style of the house; it contained a 1979 white Cadillac convertible up on blocks and space for another vehicle, such as Freddie's van. The house, tastefully furnished with American antiques and every known modern appliance, came with a cleaning woman and a guy to mow the lawn and take care of the pool, each showing up once a week.

All the way through the place, while Call Me Tom was pointing out features and Peg was trying to see and listen and comprehend, she kept getting insistent little jabs in the side and taps on the elbow from her invisible playmate. In the master bathroom, just as Call Me Tom was leaving and Peg was about to leave, steam appeared on the medicine cabinet mirror, which would be Freddie's breath, and a moving but not observable finger wrote TAKE IT.

Peg, who already knew that, rolled her eyes and would have left the room, but Call Me Tom had turned back to remark on something or other, and when Peg looked at him he was frowning past her toward that mirror.

Immediately, she turned back. Keeping her own head visible in the mirror, blocking Call Me Tom's view of the message, she stepped forward, saying, "I forgot to look in the medicine cabinet."

"*That's* funny," Call Me Tom said, musing, following her.

As Peg neared the medicine cabinet, an invisible palm swiped over the steam, removing it. Peg opened the door fast, hoping to whack her playful companion a painful one, but missed. The interior of the cabinet was empty. All the personal goods the owner had not taken with him had been stored away in the attic.

"Very nice," Peg said, and shut the cabinet door, to see in its mirror Call Me Tom's face looming over her right shoulder, frowning deeply at his own reflection. She lifted an eyebrow.

"I could have sworn," he said.

She lifted both eyebrows. "What?"

"Oh, nothing."

The tour continued, and so did the jabs and jostles, until finally, back downstairs in the kitchen, while Call Me Tom was pointing out the food disposal in the sink, Peg yanked away from one poke too many, and cried out, in exasperation, "I know! I know!"

Call Me Tom gazed at her, hurt. "You don't have one of these in New York," he said, justifying himself. "They're not legal in the city."

"I'm sorry," Peg told him, "I just, uh, I didn't mean that, I was thinking about something else. Anyway, we'll take it."

"Good," Call Me Tom said, well pleased, but then looked confused. "We?"

"My boyfriend," Peg explained. "He couldn't come up today, he's working, but he'll visit me on weekends. We'll share the cost."

"Are you sure he won't want to see it first, before you take it?"

"Oh, no. I know Freddie's taste," Peg assured the agent. "I'm as positive of how he'll feel about this place as if he were standing right here next to me."

"That's beautiful," Call Me Tom said. "When a couple have that much understanding of one another and confidence in one another."

"We understand each other pretty good," Peg said, and on the way out she did at last manage, with a sudden unexpected shove of the front door, to give Mr. Smartaleck a satisfying whump. She distinctly felt and heard it hit, and definitely heard that sharp intake of breath.

Peg smiled, all the way back to the van.

21

At just about the same moment that Peg was looking into the empty medicine cabinet up north in Columbia County, "A very frustrating guy, your Freddie Noon," Barney Beuler was telling Mordon Leethe in the backseat of a maroon Jaguar sedan in the underground garage where they'd met before. Barney liked this way of meeting, except for the dental bills; he really did have to keep those appointments. On the other hand, his teeth had needed work for some time, as both his wife and his lady friend had more than once pointed out. And the main point was, he liked the idea of these secret meetings in the underground garage here, these shadowy figures together. Like he was Deep Throat, in the backseat of this car here. The other Deep Throat.

Anyway, "A very frustrating guy," he repeated, and settled more comfortably into the luxurious cordovan-tone leather of the Jaguar upholstery.

"Is that right," said Leethe. Sour as ever, which was *his* problem, wasn't it?

The other nice thing about meeting here instead of at the restaurant was, down here Barney didn't have to do his restaurant grovel with this asshole. They could meet as . . . what? Partners.

"Lemme tell you about Freddie Noon," Barney told his

partner. "He's got no phone listed in his name, he isn't registered to vote—"

"That's a surprise," Leethe said, with deep sarcasm.

"No, there's a lotta guys registered you wouldn't think so," Barney told him. "Your serial killers, for instance, they tend to be very scrupulous voters. I dunno, maybe it's a way to meet people."

"You were talking about Fredric Noon."

"His pals call him Freddie," Barney said. "And he's got a true scoundrel's take on life. No vehicle registered in his name, no account with Con Edison, no way to get a handle on him. A guy that's ready to cut and run at any second."

"Are you saying it's impossible to find this fellow?"

"Well, we know he's in town," Barney said, "with those fingerprints of his showing up in all the wrong places. Pretty good, huh? The invisible burglar." Barney'd been getting a kick out of that idea ever since he'd browbeaten Leethe into telling him the secret.

"We would prefer him," Leethe said, "to be an invisible burglar for *us*."

"Well, naturally. Okay, the other thing is, besides he's in town, we can figure he's got himself a lady friend. *Somebody's* got to get those electric bills, put their name on the apartment lease. The question is, how do you find the lady friend?"

"I take it," Leethe said, "you wanted to speak to me because you've succeeded."

"Wait for it," Barney told his partner. He refused to let Leethe's sourness spoil the occasion. "It happens," he said, "I have a friend in the department has a friend in probation has a client that's an old pal of Freddie Noon. So my friend asks his friend to ask Freddie's friend how Freddie's doing these days, and Freddie's friend says he thinks Freddie went straight—"

"Hah."

"Well, yeah, but what would you expect the guy to say? Except, he says he thinks Freddie went straight when he took up with a dental technician named Peg."

"There must be a lot of such people," Leethe said.

"Yeah, but they're all licensed," Barney said. "Dental technicians are licensed. So we're talking about somebody that lives in New York, that's named Peg, that's on the list of licensed dental technicians, that's the right age and race and sex and marital status."

"She could be black," objected Leethe. "Or Asian. Or married. Or the wrong age group."

"You go with the probabilities," Barney said. "And when you go with the probabilities, you find she's a single white broad in her twenties named Peg Briscoe and she lives in Bay Ridge."

"Very good," Leethe allowed, which was about on a par with a normal person having an orgasm.

"On the basis," Barney said, "of those fingerprints found at the furrier and the diamond center, and on the basis of Peg Briscoe being a known associate of Fredric Urban Noon, and on the basis of I'm the one that found the connection, I got an okay to go question Peg Briscoe on her knowledge of the whereabouts of one F. U. Noon."

"F.U.?"

"Think of him as F.U.N."

"Slightly better," Leethe acknowledged. "But why go through all that hugger-mugger?"

Barney pointed at the top of his head. "See this scalp? There's shooflys want to wear this on their belt. Everything I do, every goddam thing, I gotta take it for granted they're watching me. So I *always* cover my ass."

"If only my corporate clients," Leethe said, "could absorb that concept into their thinking."

"Civilians think like civilians," Barney said, and shrugged. "There's no point trying to change them."

"You're probably right. What happens now?"

"When I'm done at the dentist," Barney said, "I'll go see this Peg Briscoe. You wanna come along?"

"What about those shooflys of yours?"

"I've already signed out that I'm going to interview Peg Briscoe. That's where I'll go, and when they see that's where I'm going they'll forget me for today. They don't have the manpower to watch every red-flag cop twenty-four hours a day."

"I should think not."

"So you'll go there, too, you'll drive, and you'll park near the place—"

"Where is it?"

"Bay Ridge, I'll give you the address. When I get there, I'll go around the block a couple times, make sure I'm alone. Then I'll park and go in, and when you see me go in *you* go in. Then we go talk to Briscoe together. And with any luck our pal Freddie."

"This is very good news," Leethe said. He damn near smiled, the bastard.

22

Driving south toward New York City on the Taconic Parkway, the keys to their new summer house in her pocket, Peg said, "I thought he looked a little funny when I gave him cash."

Beside her, Freddie was being Dick Tracy again, always a sign he was in a cheerful mood, sometimes a sign he was in *too* cheerful a mood, might decide to get playful or something. But at the moment he was just sitting there, being a good boy, wearing his head and his pink Playtex gloves. Using a gloved finger to scratch Dick's nose, he said, "Whaddaya mean, money? Why wouldn't he want money? You're telling me they still use wampum up here?"

"Checks," Peg said. Having lived a more or less normal life until she'd met Freddie, it was frequently her job to explain the straight world to him. "Nobody uses cash anymore," she explained.

"Whadda they use?"

"When you go the supermarket, you use your credit card."

"Don't have one."

"I know. When you rent a house, you pay by check."

"Don't have a checking account."

"I know. Freddie, we might have to get us one."

Freddie really and truly didn't get it. "Why? Peg, cash is money. You know? The green stuff, that's the actual money."

"But nobody uses it."

"Big companies don't use it."

"*Nobody* uses it," Peg insisted. "So when you use it, you stand out, people look at you."

"They don't look at *me*, Peg."

"You know what I mean, Freddie, don't be a smartaleck. You know, I used to have a checking account."

"What, and you miss it?"

"The problem is," Peg said, "when you move a lot of money around in a bank, they have to report it to the feds. I forget, it's either five or ten thousand. You move more than that, whichever it is, the bank tells the IRS, and they look at you to see what's what."

Dick Tracy's mask managed to look astonished, even skeptical. He said, "Regular citizens they do this to?"

"Anybody. Sure."

"And the citizens put up with it?"

"Well, yeah."

The Dick Tracy head shook, in mournful wonder. "Peg," Freddie said, from down inside there, "that's a world I never wanna be a part of."

"I don't think you'll be asked," Peg told him. "But what I think I'll do, I'll reactivate my old checking account, or start a new one, and put three or four grand a week in it, so we can pay our bills like regular people."

"Peg, I don't know about this," Freddie said.

"And I'll get a credit card," Peg said. "Dr. Lopakne'll give me a reference, if I ask." Dr. Lopakne was the dentist she'd most recently worked for.

"Peg!" Freddie cried. He sounded really alarmed now. "I don't like this, Peg. In our life, we don't need all this stuff."

"I tell you what I'll do," Peg said. "I'll use the address in the country. That way, when we move back to town, I can just cancel everything."

"Okay," he said, but he still sounded dubious.

"We don't want people wondering about us, Freddie," Peg said.

"Yeah, you're right, I know you're right," Freddie said. "It's just such a weird way to live, though. Afraid of the feds. Don't believe in cash money. Putting stuff down on paper all the time. How do the squares stand it?"

"They get used to it," Peg said.

The deal was, they were taking the house for four months, July through October, two thousand a month, and the owners were throwing in the last week in June, but they wanted a one-month deposit, so, four thousand in front. It was when Peg had opened her shoulder bag and taken out the envelope with five grand in it and counted it out on the desk until she got to four thousand, and then put the rest away again, that Call Me Tom began to look a little glassy.

Peg had seen that reaction, and understood it, and explained that her boyfriend was avoiding checks and normal paper trails at the moment because he was in a legal battle with his ex-wife, which was why Peg was signing the lease by herself and her boyfriend had given her cash to seal the bargain. Call Me Tom understood, of course, about legal battles with ex-wives, so that was okay, but still, at the end, after the signature and the handshake, as he escorted Peg out of his office, and over to her van, parked where the gas pumps used to be, he said, "I hope your friend's legal problems get worked out."

"Me, too," Peg said, and smiled, but she knew what he meant. Normal people really and truly don't trust cash.

The place was theirs right now, to move in whenever they wanted. Driving back, they discussed their plans. It would be nice to make the move, do it and be done with it, but on the other hand did they want to drive *another* hundred and some miles today? Probably not. So they go home to Bay Ridge, pack, make grocery lists and stuff, sleep in the apartment, and tomorrow morning head north.

It might have worked out that way, too, if they hadn't been interrupted. Freddie was in the bedroom, his two beat-up suitcases on the bed, drawers open as he transferred stuff, and Peg was in the kitchen, deciding what to take from the refrigerator and the shelves and what to toss out, when a banging sounded at the front door. Freddie and Peg both moved, meeting in the living room, giving each other wary looks. Peg called at the door, "Who is it?"

"Police!"

Already Freddie's head was coming off, as he dashed back into the bedroom. Peg called, "Just a second till I get dressed!" Then she returned to the kitchen, closed the cabinet doors, and ran some water from the sink over her head, dabbing it quickly with a dish towel.

Meanwhile, the pounding started up again at the front door. Crossing the living room, Peg called, "Here I come! Here I come!" Opening the door, she said, "I just got out of the shower."

It was plainclothes cops, which was worse than usual cops, because that meant already they were taking it seriously, whatever it was. One of them was your typical beefy cop, tough guy, looking for a chance to throw his weight around. He came in first, flashing his shield in its leather case, saying, "We're looking for Freddie Noon."

"Not here," Peg said. "You came to the wrong place."

"No, we didn't, girlie," the tough cop said. He put away his shield, then pulled out a folded document on thick paper. "This is the warrant," he said, waving it around like an incense holder, sanctifying the apartment for his search. "It says we can go through this place, look for your boyfriend."

"He isn't my boyfriend."

"Oh, yeah?" The cop opened his warrant and studied it, as though for the first time. "Are you," he said, frowning over the document, "Margaret Elizabeth Briscoe?"

Hard to believe; oh, well. "Sure," Peg said.

"Then we're in the right place," the cop said, and some ghostly stew came floating across the room; it looked something like chicken à la king.

Uck—she hadn't known about *that.* "Let me see that paper," she demanded, to distract both the cops and herself.

The cop held it up, so she could see but not touch, then frowned and said, "What are you standin there with the door open?"

"This all of you?" Peg made a production out of leaning out to look up and down the hall. A voice whispered in her ear, "*Train, tomorrow, Rhinebeck.*" Ghostly lips touched her cheek. She grinned at the air, winked, and turned back, saying, "The way you came in, I thought you had like an army with you."

The tough cop ignored all that. "Where is he?"

"I don't know. I haven't seen him in weeks," Peg said, which was, of course, the literal truth. "I threw him out, I didn't like the way he carried on."

The tough cop said to his partner, "Keep an eye on her, I'll toss the place."

"Right," said the other one.

The tough cop left, to thud through the other rooms of the apartment, and Peg now took a closer look at his partner, and was surprised by what she saw. An older guy, sour-looking, deeply lined face, sloping shoulders. Not in good physical shape at all, but not in bad shape in that beer-and-weightlifting way that cops get. There's something weird about this guy, Peg thought. She said, "What did Freddie do this time?"

The guy shook his head. He seemed faintly embarrassed. "We don't have to have a conversation," he said.

What? Cops *always* want to have a conversation, particularly when they've got the upper hand. Now Peg was *really* leery of these guys. "I want to see that warrant," she said.

"Oh, it's real," the guy told her.

Meaning you're not, Peg thought, and the tough cop came back into the living room. "The bedroom's full of some guy's stuff," he said. "Freddie Noon's stuff, right?"

Peg said, "Don't you see the suitcases on the bed? I'm packing that crap up, taking it to the Good Will."

"He left without his things?"

"I threw him out, I told you. Let me see that warrant."

The tough cop laughed, fished it out, handed it to her. "Always happy to help a citizen," he said. "Especially if the citizen's gonna help us."

Peg looked at the warrant. It seemed real, but what did she know? "I think," she said, looking at the tough cop, "I think this is legitimate, and I think you're a cop, but who's this other guy?"

"Detective Leethe," said the tough cop.

The other one, "Detective Leethe" bullshit, said, "Let me handle this, Barney."

So this is the power, he's letting the cop march around and be tough out in front. Peg said to him, "You're no cop."

"I want to talk to Freddie Noon," the guy said, and took a little leather case from his inner pocket. From it, he withdrew a business card, extended it toward her. "I mean him no harm. It's to his advantage to talk to me."

Peg took the card. Leethe, that part was right. Mordon Leethe. The guy was a *lawyer!* Wishing she had a crucifix to hold up, Peg said, "You still came to the wrong place." She held the card out, wanting him to take it back. "You'll have to get the message to him some other way."

The tough cop wasn't finished. "Don't waste our time with all this shit, okay, Peg?" he said.

The lawyer wouldn't take his card back. Still holding it, Peg said to the cop, "I won't be seeing Freddie, all right? I guarantee it."

The lawyer said, "Is that some sort of joke, Miss Briscoe?"

Peg was so startled that she let him see she was startled, which was of course stupid. He knows! she thought, as she saw the look of satisfaction touch his sour face. Trying to save the situation, even though they both knew it was too late, she said, "Whaddaya mean, a joke? Freddie *Noon's* the joke, that's why I threw him out."

"If you have the opportunity to speak with him," the lawyer said, "would you tell him I represent the doctors?"

Peg shut down. This lawyer already knew too much. "I'm not going to see him," she said.

The lawyer offered a wrinkled kind of little smile, as though he didn't use those muscles often. He nodded at Peg, nodded at the card she still held, then looked at the cop. "Come on, Barney," he said. Once more, he nodded at Peg. "Sorry to disturb you," he said.

After they left, Peg went back to the kitchen to try to concentrate on what she'd been doing before those two had come crashing in here. But it was hard not to be distracted. And she couldn't bring herself to throw away the lawyer's card.

23

"Frankly," the attorney said, "I believe you've been avoiding me."

Well, of course Mordon had been avoiding the fellow. It was sufficient reason merely that this attorney, one Bradley Cummingford, had left a series of messages over the past week describing himself as representing the doctors Loomis and Heimhocker, and leaving a number at Sachs, Fried, one of the most prestigious old-time law firms in New York. However, had Mordon known that Cummingford was also someone who said "frankly," he would have gone on avoiding him forever.

Anyway, so far as Mordon was concerned, Loomis and Heimhocker were cut out of this matter, no longer involved. Besides which *he* was their attorney, through the beneficent goodwill of NAABOR; the idea that the doctors might feel the need for outside counsel—independent counsel, if you will—was aggravating, but no more.

At least, not until today's phone memo, which had been waiting on Mordon's desk when he'd arrived this morning. He hadn't returned to the office after yesterday's unsettling session with Miss Peg Briscoe, a self-possessed tart with rather a quicker brain than Mordon had expected. After they'd left Miss Briscoe's residence yesterday afternoon, with a pretty good idea that Fredric Noon had been somewhere in the vicinity, but was no more, Barney had said, "Leave it to me from here," and Mordon had been happy to agree. He knew his own uses for an invisible Fredric Noon were essentially benign—NAABOR would pay the fellow well, for what amounted to no more than industrial espionage—and he suspected that Barney's ideas were cruder and probably more dangerous and less legal, but they could work out their differences later, once they actually had their hands on the man.

In the meantime, Loomis and Heimhocker were no more than irrelevancies, if irritating ones. But now, this morning, the latest message from their "attorney," Bradley Cummingford, was: *The doctors intend to go public.*

Go public? With what? To whom? How? Nevertheless the threat was enough to force Mordon at last to return Cummingford's call, only to hear him say "frankly."

Twice. "Frankly," Bradley Cummingford said, "I had expected more courtesy from a firm of your standing."

Had you. "What surprises *me*," Mordon said, "is that you represent yourself as attorney for my clients."

"I believe," Cummingford said, "your client is NAABOR."

"I represent Drs. Loomis and Heimhocker," Mordon said, "in matters concerning their employment by the American Tobacco Research Institute. Any invention, discovery, product, commodity, or theorem they produce as employees of the institute naturally belongs to the institute. It is my job to protect the interests of both the institute and the doctors in any matter concerning or relating to that employment."

"And if the interests conflict?"

"How can they?"

"Frankly," Cummingford said, doing it again, "I was thinking of the invisible man."

Mordon blinked rapidly, several times. "I'm not sure I—"

"Frankly, Mr. Leethe, my clients are afraid you have it in mind to make off with their invisible man."

"*Their* invisi—"

"Leaving them to fret over questions of medical ethics, not to mention laws that might be, perhaps have already been, broken. My clients have no intention of being made the goats in this matter, which is why, against my advice, they have expressed the desire to go public with the facts of the case."

Against Cummingford's judgment; well, at least there was that. "What do they hope to gain by going public, as you put it?"

"Frankly, they hope to distance themselves from any legal fallout that might ensue."

"Have you told them, Mr. Cummingford, that they'll simply make fools of themselves? That either they won't be believed, which will ruin them as researchers forever, like those cold-fusion idiots from Utah, or they *will* be believed, in which case they are already at legal risk?"

"Frankly," the damn fellow said, over and over again, "my clients have, I would say, minds of their own. Which is why, Mr. Leethe, I strongly suggest a meeting among the four of us, before my clients do anything irrevocable."

No way out of it, Mordon saw. But Cummingford, apart from his infernal "frankly"s, seemed rational enough. "Where?" Mordon demanded. "When?"

"The sooner the better. Four this afternoon?"

"Fine. Where?"

"The conference room here is very—"

"Bugged."

A tiny silence, and then a laugh. "Well, yours over there will be, too, won't it?"

Mordon didn't dignify that with a response.

Cummingford said, "How about the doctors' facility? You've been there before, I understand."

Facility—oh, yes, that place. "The townhouse, you mean."
"At four?"

Damn you all. Is Barney Beuler accomplishing something
or not? Is there any point in delay? Or is there too much dan-
ger? "At four," Mordon agreed.

24

Rhinebeck. What was the damn woman doing in Rhinebeck? Meeting three trains so far, and so what?

Yesterday, after tossing Peg Briscoe's apartment and reassuring himself that Freddie Noon actually did live there, Barney had sent lawyer Leethe on his way and had then driven slowly and purposefully around the neighborhood. He had earlier collected, from Motor Vehicle, the make, model, color, and tag number of a van registered to Margaret Briscoe at that Bay Ridge address, so all he had to do now was find it.

But that took a lot longer than he'd expected. It was over an hour before he saw the damn thing, so smug and demure and unnoticeable and safe, tucked away in the parking lot next to the local firehouse. "Goddam, Freddie," Barney said out loud, driving by, grinning at that van behind the chain-link fence. "You're a pretty clever fella, Freddie. But so am I."

Barney parked half a block away, and from the glove box he took the tailing transmitter he'd lifted years ago from Stores at Organized Crime Detail, for just such a situation as this. The tailing transmitter came in two parts, one being a tiny dome-shaped black bug with one sticky side when you peeled off the tape, and the other being a small flat metal box, about the size and shape of a TV remote control, but with a round compass dial where the remote would have had all its buttons. Leaving the compass in the glove box, Barney pocketed the bug and took a walk.

At the firehouse, Barney ID'd himself as a member of a collateral uniformed force. He explained that a blue Toyota had been involved earlier today in a fender-bender with a car driven by a well-known mafioso, and that the Organized Crime Squad was trying to find that Toyota to tell its driver he might be facing more retribution than he expected. No, Barney didn't have the Toyota's tag number, but there was a blue Toyota of the right model parked next to that van in that parking lot there that matched the description. Okay if he looked it over?

The owner of the Toyota, a young red-haired Irish fireman with last night's hangover lying on him like the results of a poison gas attack, assured Barney his vehicle had been in no fender-benders at all, but go ahead and look. So Barney went ahead and looked, studying the Toyota's exterior from every angle, and along the way sticking the transmitter bug onto the frame of Peg Briscoe's van. Then he thanked the fire guys for their help, and left the firehouse.

All afternoon and evening, Barney sat in his car, parked where he could see Peg Briscoe's building, and all afternoon and evening nothing happened. Which gave him time to think, and what he thought was that he was involved in something a little different here. If you're on the lookout for an invisible man, it isn't business as usual. For instance, forget descriptions. Forget tailing the guy through the streets. All you can hope to do is find out for sure where he is, close down that spot, and when you know you've got him inside a perimeter he can't get out of, you make your proposition.

Barney knew exactly what his proposition would be when the time came, and he thought he knew how to make Noon go along with it. His proposition was a straightforward one: assassination. Forget industrial espionage, tiptoeing around cigarette-company meetings, all this penny-ante stuff. There were those two guys, for instance, that he was endlessly paying off to keep their evidence about Barney to themselves. They were still alive only because Barney Beuler would be the prime suspect if either of them went down. The prosecutors were right now trying to get something on those guys, to force them to give up Barney, and he knew it. Take them out, and nobody would ever be able to put together an indictment against Barney Beuler; nobody, ever.

But how to do it? How to terminate those dear old friends? Barney had brooded on this problem for months. He couldn't do it personally; they'd have him in a second. And who could he hire that wouldn't turn on him, set him up, sell him for their *own* rotten reasons?

But if you had yourself an invisible man, and if that invisible man had a big family he liked, and a girlfriend he wanted to protect, you could be in *Europe* if you wanted, safe and clean and absolutely untouchable, while those two dangerous guys went down. And then after that, Noon could still be useful. Through his job, naturally, Barney knew a few guys in the world of organized crime, and those people were *always* looking for the clean hit. Farm Freddie Noon out. Why not? Retire on the little son of a bitch.

The only snag that Barney could see, other than finding Noon in the first place, was that violence had never been part of the guy's MO. But that was okay; everybody's *capable* of violence. Noon had just never been motivated before, that's all.

In the meantime, there was still the first step to accomplish. Find Noon, box him in. So Barney sat in his car as the long June twilight descended on Bay Ridge, and he watched Peg Briscoe's apartment, and nothing at all happened. It would be nice, wouldn't it, if she came out? It would be even nicer if the

the door opened and *nobody* came out. Barney was looking forward to that one, hope against hope.

But no, it didn't happen. Around eight, he drove away to find a fast-food joint, then swung around the firehouse on the way back and the van was still there, so he took up his position again, parked where he could see Peg Briscoe's front door.

A little after nine, he called home, told his wife he was on stakeout and she could call him on the car phone if she needed anything. Around ten, he called his girlfriend on West Seventy-fourth Street in Manhattan and told her he'd probably come over around midnight, why not have a nice little supper ready? And at eleven-thirty, he quit for the night.

One of the things Barney had that he hoped nobody knew about was a second car. He kept it in an apartment building's garage on the block behind his girlfriend's place, and he had bribed the supers involved so he now had the keys he needed to take the elevator from his girlfriend's place down to the basement, go through several locked doors and one narrow open areaway, and eventually wind up in the garage. If the shooflys *were* watching his girlfriend's place they'd just have to assume he was spending entire *days* in the sack, while they were sitting in cars surrounded by empty cardboard cups. Good, ya fucks.

Barney and his second car, a nondescript older Chevy Impala, reached Bay Ridge a little before eight-thirty in the morning, and the van was still there. He drove over to park near Briscoe's building, and was barely in position when out she came, by herself—well, maybe by herself—and walked away toward the firehouse.

At last. Barney placed the transmitter compass on the dashboard and waited; the thing would make a low buzzing sound once the van was in motion, and he'd be able to follow it without ever having to be within sight of it.

It's funny, he thought, waiting for the buzz, how quickly you get used to an impossibility. A week ago, he would have said there was no such thing as an invisible man, that was old movie shit. But all he had to hear was that some serious people said there *was* an invisible man, and that they were willing to spend serious bread to find him, and doubt vanished like . . . well, like an invisible man. What it comes down to is, you don't question the real world, right? Because if you do, they put you away where the walls are soft, right? Right.

Buzz. Barney started his engine. But then, instead of the buzz getting fainter, as it would if the van moved away from him, it got louder, so Barney switched off his engine, and here came the van, Briscoe at the wheel. She stopped in front of her building, opened the van's side door, and then proceeded to go between van and building several times, lugging heavy suitcases and liquor-store cartons.

O-kay! Pay dirt! Barney sat and watched, grinning from ear to ear, and pretty soon Briscoe slid the side door shut, got behind the wheel, and took off. Barney waited till she was out of sight, then followed.

And now Rhinebeck, ninety miles north of the city beside the Hudson River, long ago a port town, when river traffic meant something. Peg Briscoe had driven straight here, like a homing pigeon, north out of the city, up the Taconic Parkway, then west to the river. The whole way, Barney hung back out of sight, listening to the transmitter buzz and watching the compass, and it wasn't until they were in Rhinebeck itself that he saw the van again, five vehicles ahead at the town's only traffic light. He considered dawdling here to get himself caught by the next red, but the hell with it. In town there was enough traffic to hide among, even if she was looking for a tail, and it was clear she wasn't.

They went on through Rhinebeck to its even smaller suburb, a steep village called Rhinecliff, where the Amtrak trains from New York, on their way to Albany and Buffalo and Montreal, pulled in a dozen times a day. The station building was midway down a steep slope, with a small full parking area above and a downhill entrance drive clogged with parked cars. The van drove down in there, found itself a niche in among the others, and Barney parked at the curb up top, where he could look down through the parked cars and just barely see the van.

Nothing happened for about twenty minutes, and then a train must have come in, because people suddenly began emerging from the station building down there, maybe a couple dozen, lugging their luggage. Barney watched Briscoe get out of her van and open its side door and lean against the front passenger door like she was waiting for a Little League team. This was interesting; what was the woman up to?

The last of the passengers came out of the station, to be greeted by friends or to climb into their cars or to take off in the two taxis that had showed up at the last minute. Briscoe waited a little longer, then shut the van's sliding door, got behind the wheel, and drove off, back the way she'd come. Barney waited till she was out of sight, then U-turned and followed, to see where she was going.

To have lunch. There was a cafeteria on the main street in Rhinebeck, and that was where she went, in no hurry at all, worried about nothing. Damn.

Barney couldn't find another lunch place nearby, and since she knew his face he couldn't go in where she was, so he stopped at the local supermarket to get himself a sandwich and coffee from their deli department, which he ate in the car. Do something, Peg, he thought. Do something.

She did something. After lunch, she got in the van and drove back to the damn railroad station. This time, the wait was half an hour, then what looked like the same couple dozen ex-passengers appeared, did the same things as before, and left. And again Briscoe opened the van's side door and waited. And again, once all the passengers were gone, she shut that door and got back into the van.

But this time she didn't drive away. Instead, she backed into a parking space that had just been vacated, and when Barney got out of the Impala to walk back to where he could see her, she was in there behind the wheel reading a magazine. Waiting for the next train, right? Had to be.

There was another side street that went downhill behind the station, and when Barney walked down that way, out of sight of the parking area where Briscoe sat, he found, as he'd hoped, another entrance to the station. Going in there, he got a copy of the schedule and carried it back to the Impala, to study it and figure out what was going on.

Okay. Judging from the times on this schedule, the first two trains she'd met had been northbound out of New York. And then Barney got it, all of it. The son of a bitch had *been* there yesterday! When he and Leethe had showed up. Noon had skipped out, invisible, and arranged with Briscoe to meet him here today. The Amtrak out of New York City was carrying an invisible man. Freeloading.

I hope somebody sits on the son of a bitch.

All right. All Barney had to do now was wait until Briscoe left here, and he'd *know* she had Freddie Noon inside that van. Then he'd follow, out of sight, to wherever they were hiding out, up here in the north country. *High Sierra* time, right? Too bad there wasn't snow on the ground. *That'd* slow down your goddam invisible man.

Barney looked at the schedule, and the next train out of New York wasn't for another two hours and a half. Hell.

Okay, he'd been on long stakeouts before. If Briscoe could do it, Barney could do it.

But he didn't have to stay here the whole damn time, did he? No, he didn't. So he U-turned again, and went back to Rhinebeck, and had a second lunch there, at the place where Briscoe had eaten, and then used the pay phone and a charge card the shooflys didn't know about to make some calls, square himself in his world. He called the Organized Crime Detail and said he was in Brooklyn following up some possibilities about the Paviola family. He called his wife and said he was calling from the office but was about to go on stakeout again, this time in a department car, so no phone, and he'd get in touch with her when he got in touch with her. He also made a couple more calls, concerning other matters he had cooking, and heard nothing too troublesome. Then he walked down to the drugstore on the corner, where he bought four magazines and two newspapers and two maps of the general area.

Back at the railroad station, having double-checked that Briscoe and the van were still there, he U-turned and parked up the block, out of her sight, and spread out the maps on the steering wheel to see where he was and where they might all be headed.

And the first thing he saw was a big bridge just a couple miles north, and no passenger service on the other side of the river. So Briscoe could be planning to cart Noon somewhere over there. But not too far, or this wouldn't be the right train stop.

Finished with the maps, he went through the two newspapers, and was about to turn to *Playboy* for the haberdashery tips when a disgorgement of cars up from the railroad station told him the next New York train had arrived. Dropping the magazine, he waited and watched, but after the last of the cars and taxis had come up and run off, the van had still not appeared.

Barney got out of the Impala and walked back to where he could see down the driveway, and there it was, still there, Briscoe still at the wheel. Shit. He went back to the car to look at the schedule, and it would be *another* three hours before the next train. Dammit, the local people ought to complain, they really ought to, get themselves better service.

Barney almost missed it. He was just picking up *Playboy* when a tiny movement in his rearview mirror caught his eye, and when he looked there was Briscoe, walking up out of the driveway, stopping at the top to look left and right, then turning right to walk along past the upper-level parking area.

Now what? Barney watched in the mirror, and Briscoe took the same route he'd taken earlier, down to the next cross street, then right toward the rear entrance to the station.

He had to know what was happening, but he also had to be very damn careful. Getting out of the Impala, he walked back toward the station, following her. He could see the top of her head far away on the cross street, past the cars parked in the upper area. He hung back until she'd disappeared past the corner of the building, then followed, and when he got to the corner she was well down the street, still going straight. Past the railroad station the street became some kind of overpass, leading to a low wall and a sharp left turn angling down. More cars were parked along there, on the right side; Briscoe walked down the middle of the street to the end, then made the left.

Barney trotted forward once she was out of sight. He saw that this overpass went above the railroad tracks, and that the left turn carried the roadway, now a kind of bridge or ramp, down a long slope to a launching site at the river. A few vans and pickups were parked down there, with empty boat trailers hitched at their backs, and Briscoe was walking straight down to join them.

Had Barney been wrong? Was she waiting for Noon to arrive by boat? Or, worse thought, *had* he arrived, and they were *leaving* by boat? That would be a true pain in the ass.

But, no. After a minute, Barney saw what was happening. Briscoe was just killing time, that's all, sightseeing while she waited for the next train. Barney couldn't blame her.

Just in case, though, he kept watching. Briscoe walked on down to the launching area, strolled around there a few minutes, looked out at the river and the green cliffs and white mansions over there on the other side, and Barney leaned against the wall at the top of the overpass, feeling warm in the sunshine in his dark jacket, watching her.

She hung around down there maybe five minutes, and then turned and started the long trudge back up the slope, and Barney retreated all the way to the far corner, past the parking area, waiting there until she made the turn, then moving back again, holding at the head of the station driveway until her head would appear again, over there beyond the parked cars, and it didn't.

He waited. He frowned. He looked down into the blacktop area in front of the station, where the van was parked, and here she came, out of the building. She just hadn't known ahead of time about that back entrance, that's all.

Okay. Time out for everybody. Barney walked back to his car, got behind the wheel, reached for *Playboy,* and the van drove by.

What? The damn buzzer wasn't working! What a hell of a time to break down! Knowing he'd have to do a visual tail, hating the idea of it, Barney quickly started the engine, shifted into drive, and the car went *klomp* forward *klomp* forward *klomp* forward. A mile an hour. Less. And shaking all over the place.

Barney hit the brakes. The *bastards*. He already knew, but he got out of the Impala anyway, as the van disappeared around a curve far ahead.

All four tires. Flat. Slashed. And a little later, when he lifted his maps and newspapers and magazines from the front seat, there under them lay the bug, almost as good as new.

25

"I don't like that guy on our necks like that," Freddie said.

He was still dressing in the back of the van, so Peg kept her eyes firmly on Rhinebeck's only traffic light, now red, two cars in front of her.

She said, "He isn't on our necks anymore, Freddie. You took care of that."

"Damn good thing those guys told you about him."

"Yes, it was."

Those guys were the guys in the firehouse, who had told her, when she went to pick up the van this morning, about the cop who'd come in with a cockamamie story that nobody believed for a second, so everybody watched the cop when he was supposedly looking over a blue Toyota, and he was obviously taking too much of an interest in Freddie and Peg's van, and maybe she ought to know about it. The guy, from their description, was the tough cop who'd come to the place yesterday with the lawyer, Leethe.

Because the fire guys had given her that warning, she'd been extremely alert, looking in every direction at once on her way back to the apartment to pick up the stuff they were taking upstate, so that was why she spotted him, lurking in that big old Chevy, a faded green like an old shower curtain or something, parked half a block from her place. I'll have to lose him somehow, she thought, and went on to load up the van.

But then she didn't see him again. Had he been that easy to lose? She drove all the way upstate on the Taconic, and over the local road to Rhinebeck, and never saw him at all. Until all at once, as she was stopped at this very light, there he was, just a few cars behind her.

That was when she realized what he must have done at the firehouse yesterday: put some kind of bug on this car. Every new piece of police technology is immediately described to the citizenry via cop shows on TV, so Peg knew all about long-distance tailing of other cars with these radio bugs. What she didn't know, now that she found the cop in his washed-out green Chevy behind her, was what to do about it. I'll let Freddie decide, she decided, and ignored the cop and his car from that point on.

It was a long wait, all in all—three trains—before at last she heard that whisper in her ear: "Hi, Peg." Then the van sagged beside her, so he was aboard.

Relieved, glad to be reunited, grinning like an idiot, Peg shut the van door, got around to the other side, slid in behind the wheel, got serious, and said, "Freddie, he followed me, he put something on the van."

"The cops from yesterday?"

"Just one of them's a cop. He's up there in an old Chevy the color of a lima bean."

"And he put a bug on the car?"

"He must've."

"Go take a walk somewhere for maybe five minutes," the voice behind her said. "Get him to follow you. I'll take care of it."

So she did, and the cop followed her, and Freddie took care of it, and now, as she waited for the Rhinebeck traffic light to turn green, Bart Simpson came up and sat next to her, saying, "Only one of them was a cop?"

The light changed; traffic moved. As she drove on through town and out to the countryside, Peg told him her story, and then said, "How've things been with you, since yesterday?"

"Weird," he said. "I took the subway to Manhattan—it's really dirty down there, Peg, after a while you could see my feet, I think a couple little kids *did* see my feet—"

"That must have been kinda scary."

"Good thing it wasn't rush hour. I got off at Times Square and went to a movie and washed my feet in the men's room—"

Slyly, she said, "Not the ladies' room?"

"I don't know why I didn't thinka that," he said. The Bart Simpson face was deadpan. "Anyway, then I sat there and watched a Disney movie five times. You can't believe, Peg, you just can't believe, how not funny after a while it is to see a wet Labrador retriever in a station wagon with six little kids and an actress on coke. And every time you see a can of housepaint you say, 'Oh, boy, here comes *that* one again.'"

"Sounds like no fun."

"They oughta change the rating system," Bart said. "They oughta have a 2D rating, for movies that are Too Dumb to put up with."

"It might bring more people in," Peg suggested. "Especially out-of-towners."

"Good for them," Freddie said. "Finally, after the fifth time, the movie stopped and everybody went home, and I got a good night's sleep."

"On a movie chair?"

"No no, the manager had a nice sofa in his office. Smelled like Dr Pepper, that's all. They have these dust cloths they put over the popcorn stand at night, so I used a couple of them for sheets and blankets, and it was pretty good."

"Be glad nobody walked in."

"The first movie's at noon," he said. "I was up long before then, had breakfast at the food stand, and took off when they unlocked the doors, before Disney could get at me again."

"And went to the railroad station?"

"I was on my way," he assured her, "but those city streets are *crowded,* you know, and this time of year most of them seem like they're Europeans, talking all these other languages, and they got no radar at *all,* they bang into each other all the time and they can *see* one another. So I had like fifteen blocks to go to get to Penn Station, and I just wasn't gonna make it, so I ducked into Macy's and went up to furniture and fell asleep again on a sofa in there and woke up when a fat lady sat on me."

"No!"

"Yes. She let out a holler and so did I, but with her holler nobody heard mine, so I got outta there, and she was saying that was the *lumpiest* sofa she ever felt in her life."

"I bet. *Then* what'd you do?"

"I made it over to Penn Station—*another* dirty place, believe me—and saw when the next train was, which was like over an hour—"

"They don't go very often," Peg agreed. "I think we'll travel mostly by car."

"Me especially," Freddie said. "Anyway, I tried to keep out of the way, but what you got in railroad stations is people *running,* and wherever I went that's where somebody wanted to run, so finally I hid behind a homeless guy against a side wall, and when he accidentally leaned back and found me there I told him just to mind his own business."

"You *talked* to him?"

"I was tired of gettin out of people's way, Peg. So I said, 'You just do what you're doin, don't mind me back here, I'm not gonna bother you, just do what you're doin,' which was nothin much except to hold up a message on a piece of cardboard and stick out a used plastic coffee cup for people to put quarters in, which mostly they don't."

"But what did he *do?*" Peg wanted to know. "When you talked to him, and he couldn't see you?"

"Well, first he jumped—"

"Naturally."

"But then he just got sad and shook his head and said, 'It's my old trouble comin back. And I was doin so good. And now it's my old trouble comin back.' "

"Oh," Peg said, brought down. "I feel sorry for the guy."

"Me, too," Freddie said. "So I told him, 'You shoulda took your medicine, like they told you.' And he said, 'Oh, I know, I know.' And it was gonna be my train then, so I said, 'Take your medicine and I'll never bother you again. Is it a deal?' And he said, 'Oh, I will, I will.' And I gave him a little pat on the back, and his eyes got all wide, and when I went away he was thinking it over, and I think maybe I did some good there today, Peg."

"That's nice," Peg said. "That was good of you, Freddie."

"So then I got on the train," Freddie said, "and it was only like half full, so I had no trouble about a seat by myself, and here I am, except I'm hungry. All I had was breakfast at the movie."

"Which brings up an issue," Peg said. "You didn't tell me food doesn't disappear right away."

"Uh-oh. Yesterday, huh?"

"Yes."

"I thought maybe you wouldn't want to know."

"You were right. But now I do. How long does it take, anyway, to uh, you know, disappear?"

"Couple hours," Bart said, looking hangdog. "I'll make sure, Peg, I don't remind you again. You know, if those cops hadn't showed up—"

"I know, Freddie," she told him. "You're doing your best, I know you are."

"Thanks, Peg."

"And we'll be home pretty soon." They were driving through bright green June scenery, rounded hills, tiny white villages, red barns, wildflowers on the roadsides, horses in fields, cows in fields, even sheep in one field, afternoon sun smiling down on the countryside, corn and tomatoes growing in tight rows, the gray van with Peg Briscoe and Bart Simpson running deeper and deeper into the landscape. "From here on," Peg said, "we've got it made."

26

Peter and David *dressed* for the meeting. Fumbling with his necktie, getting it wrong *again,* David said, "I don't know what's wrong with this tie."

"You're nervous, David," Peter explained. His tie was perfect, he was even now shrugging into his blazer, shooting his cuffs. "Calm down, why don't you?"

"Of *course* I'm nervous. Peter, for God's sake, you're nervous, too, you're just covering it, keeping it inside, you *know* that's—"

"Tie your tie, David," Peter said, not unkindly. "We'll be all right."

That trace of sympathy in Peter's voice was enough; David calmed down at least enough to tie his tie so the end neither dangled at his crotch nor covered a mere two buttons of his shirt. Slipping into his rough jacket with the brown suede elbow patches—his defensive garb was professorial, while Peter's was aristocratic—David said, "All right. I'm ready. For whatever comes."

What came first, by prearrangement, was Bradley Cummingford, a large sandy-haired man with a big round open face and eyebrows of such a pale pinky-orange as to almost disappear. He wore a blue pinstripe suit, white shirt, muted blue tie, and black tassel loafers, and he carried an attaché case of extremely expensive leather, and he greeted them with a firm handshake and a clear eye and no nonsense. This was a Bradley Cummingford seen in a whole new light. Prior to this, they had only known Bradley in playful mode, when he was a very different person, in a very different place.

Many of David and Peter's friends summered up in the central Hudson Valley, around the river town of Hudson and eastward from there toward—but not into—New England. This influx into the rural dairy world of upstate by all these sophisticated New Yorkers of a certain type had done wonders for the region, particularly in culinary ways: an unusual range of restaurants; arugula and goat cheese in the supermarkets, for God's sake; excellent variety in the local wine shops. David and Peter, wedded to their research and happy as Darby and Joan—Darby and Darby, anyway—in their city townhouse, had never bought or rented a summer place in the country, but they'd frequently accepted weekend invitations to this or that hideaway in the woods, where the goings-on tended to be . . . unbuttoned.

Until now, that was the only way they'd ever known Bradley Cummingford, merely as a fellow guest at summer outings, but they'd always been aware that he somehow or other had a serious side as well, in which he wore grown-up male clothing and was treated with respect by lawyers and judges and businessmen. When they found themselves at the mercy—to put too strong a word on it—of the tobacco lawyer, Mordon Leethe, and when it became evident there was no one around who was both knowledgeable in the arcane and frightening world of the law *and* reliably on their side, one of them—it doesn't matter which one, it really doesn't—remembered Bradley, and they made the phone call, and met with him in his offices in a downtown skyscraper—high floor, tall windows, lovely view of La Liberty lifting her skirts above that awful sludge in the harbor—and once they got him to believe that *yes,* they had strong reason to believe they had created an invisible man, on whom a large tobacco company had some sort of nefarious designs, he looked somber, almost severe, and said, "Well, you two *have* been silly, haven't you?"

Peter, not used to this more responsible Bradley, said. "Is that a legal term, Bradley?"

"You don't want to know the legal term, Peter," Bradley said, and gazed levelly at him until Peter coughed and looked away and muttered, "I'm sorry. I'll be good."

"Better late than never," Bradley said. "Now tell me the rest."

So they told him everything, and he made many tiny notes on a long yellow legal pad, and said he'd see what he could do. Then, for a week, he couldn't do a thing; every time they called, Bradley had the same news: "He's ducking me. But he can't do it forever." Until, late yesterday, when they called him—*he* never called *them,* you notice—he said, "Tomorrow morning, you will threaten to go public."

"Oh, *please,*" they cried. (They were on the speakerphone in their office at the time.) "Bradley, are you out of your *mind?* A premature disclosure of this experiment would make us *laughingstocks,* Bradley, it would *ruin* us in the field forever, we'd be lucky to get published in *Omni!*"

"I didn't say you were going public," he corrected them, infuriatingly calm.

"Well, it certainly *sounded* like it."

"I said you will, tomorrow morning, *threaten* to go public, to protect yourselves from unknown consequences of Mr. Leethe and his friends' activities. You will make this threat against my counsel and advice, I might add."

In their office, Peter and David smiled in relief at one another. They hadn't been wrong about Bradley, after all. Peter said, "Bradley, you are a slyboots."

"Well, we'll see," Bradley said, and now they had seen, and Bradley *was* a slyboots. Mordon Leethe had been flushed from his lair, was on his way *here*, would meet with them *and with Bradley*.

But first Bradley by himself. In he came with his expensive attaché case, briskly shook hands, and surveyed their parlor with a critical eye. "Haven't you anything less comfortable?"

David stared. *"Less* comfortable?"

Peter said, "This is where we talked with him last time."

"It's obviously too small for four," Bradley said, gazing around a room that could have—and often had—accommodated eight with no problem. "What else do you have?"

"Well," David said, dubiously, "there's the conference room downstairs."

"Oh? What's that like?"

"Very plain," David told him. "Comfortable chairs but, you know, officelike. TV and VCR and all that at one end, a long rectangular table."

"Fluorescents in the ceiling," Peter added. "Nothing on the walls. When we eventually *do* make a public announcement about our work here, that's where we'll hold the press conference."

"Sounds ideal," Bradley said. "Lead me to it."

So, having brought him upstairs, they now brought him downstairs again, where Shanana the receptionist read her correspondence-school lessons and watched the street outside and answered the occasional phone call. Peter said to her, "Shanana, when Mr. Leethe gets here, show him to the conference room, will you?"

She looked at him, alert and willing but uncertain. "The conference room? Where's that?"

"The coffee room," he explained, because the coffeemaker was kept in there.

"Oh." She looked just as alert and just as willing, but even more uncertain. "You're going to be in *there?*"

"Yes," he said firmly, and went after David and Bradley, who'd already gone on into the . . . conference . . . coffee . . . press-announcement room.

In there, Bradley was looking about in happy satisfaction. "This is perfect," he said, and plopped his attaché case onto the table down at the far end, opposite the entrance, with the TV and VCR and the pull-down slide-show screen all behind him. "You two both sit on my right here," he directed, "along this side. When Leethe arrives, he'll sit down there, with his back to the door. People always feel slightly uneasy with their backs to the door in an unknown room. Whether they're aware of the feeling or not, the unease is there."

"Bradley," David said, sitting nearest him, "you're brilliant."

It was clear that Bradley agreed with this assessment, but, "We'll see," he said, and opened his attaché case and brought out both his yellow legal pad and a manila folder. "Sit down, Peter," he said, since Peter was still standing, then Bradley sat down himself and said, "Before Leethe gets here, let's define exactly what it is you two want."

"We want our invisible man back," Peter said.

"Unharmed," David added.

"*Without* publicity," Peter said.

"You also, I take it," Bradley said, twiddling his Mont Blanc pen, "want to retain your relationship with NAABOR."

"I never thought we *had* a relationship with NAABOR," David said.

Peter said, "We're funded by the American Tobacco Research Institute."

"A golem belonging to NAABOR," Bradley pointed out, "as their own annual stockholder statements are proud to claim."

"We're not stockholders," David said.

"You aren't totally unworldly either," Bradley told him. "You know who's financing you, and why. And the point is, you don't want to put that relationship at risk by whatever happens in connection with this current matter."

"God, no," David said. "We don't want to lose our *funding*."

"What we want, in fact," Peter said, "is everything. We want our invisible man, and we want our funding, and we want our privacy maintained until *we* are ready to go public."

"The question is," Bradley said, "what in all that is negotiable, and to what extent—"

"None," Peter said, and Shanana entered, saying, "Mr. Leethe is here."

Bradley offered her a big moonlike smile, and probably raised those invisible eyebrows of his. Getting to his feet, motioning for Peter and David to rise as well, he said, "Thank you, dear. Show him in, please."

She stepped back, and Leethe entered, carrying his own more battered but equally expensive attaché case. Peter and David stood where they were, like minor servers at some arcane Mass, while Bradley strode around the table, hand out, high-wattage smile agleam as he said, "Ah, Mr. Leethe, at last we meet. Bradley Cummingford."

Leethe took Bradley's hand as though it were part of the membership ritual for a club he wasn't sure he wanted to join. Then he lifted an eyebrow at the room, gazed at David and Peter, and said, "Farewell to elegance, I see."

"This seems more businesslike," Peter said.

"It certainly does."

Bradley gestured at the chair he wanted Leethe in. "Do sit down, Mr. Leethe," he said.

"Thank you."

As Bradley returned to his own place at the head of the table, Leethe followed him partway and took a chair midway along the side, facing David and Peter, with the allegedly uneasy-making door down to his left. David and Peter both looked at Bradley, to see how he'd take this development, but Bradley didn't appear to have noticed it at all. Sitting down, picking up his pen, smiling again at Leethe, he said, "It does seem to me we do have some goals in common here."

"That's because we have the same clients," Leethe said.

"Ah, if only that were so," Bradley told him. "In fact, our firm *has* done some work for NAABOR over the years, but on this matter, I'm sorry to say, we have not been retained."

Gesturing at David and Peter, Leethe said, "I meant the doctors here."

"Oh, Mr. Leethe," Bradley said. "We aren't going over that stale ground, are we?"

"I suppose not," Leethe agreed, and shrugged. "I want my position clear, that's all." Raising that eyebrow at David and Peter, lifting his hands from the table to gesture with upheld palms, like a slow-motion demonstration of pizza-tossing, he said, "You want something. Something you couldn't discuss with me without the presence of your friend here."

"We want our invisible man," Peter said.

Leethe's smile could give you frostbite. "We all want the invisible man," he said.

"You're looking for him," Peter pointed out. "You have . . . people, looking for him."

"Granted."

"We want to be a part of it, when he's found."

Bradley said, "Well, no, Peter, that isn't exactly what you want."

Peter looked at him in surprise. "It isn't?"

"May I?"

"Go ahead."

To Leethe, Bradley said, "David and Peter here created that invisible man while employees of your client. To the extent that a human being may be property, therefore, he is the property of your client, or the discoveries and techniques he embodies are your client's property. However, legal practice, medical practice, scientific practice, all agree that while your client holds ultimate ownership, or whatever rights would take the place of ownership in this instance, David and Peter are the ultimate authorities as to when their creation is in a fit and proper condition to be *turned over* to your client. As of this point, since the experiment was altered by the experimental subject away from the original intentions of Peter and David, and since they have not as yet had the opportunity to examine the subject to see what other unforeseen effects may have been caused by this flawed experiment, they wish me to put NAABOR and the American Tobacco Research Institute on notice, through you, their agent, that the experiment must be considered at this point in time tentative and inconclusive and incomplete, and that David and Peter are thoroughly averse to turning over to your clients any experimental data, including but not limited to the invisible man himself, until they are satisfied with the results of their researches. It is only a *completed* discovery or invention they are required to deliver to your client and toward which your client would enjoy a proprietary relationship." Opening the manila folder, he said, "I have a number of citations of court cases tending toward—"

"That's all right," Leethe said, patting his right hand toward Bradley's manila folder, as though to tell a dog he didn't feel like playing fetch. "We can citation one another for a month, if we wish," he said, "but I don't think we need waste the time, do you?"

"Fine," Bradley said. But he left the folder open, and lifted from it a packet of white paper. "I have prepared," he said, "a statement outlining the position I've just described, that David and Peter acknowledge that at the end of the day all research results adhere to the American Tobacco Research Institute, and the institute acknowledges David and Peter's right to withhold material they consider flawed or incomplete. They will sign copies today, and we'd like a qualified officer of the institute to sign it as well. Here you are," he said, and handed copies of the two-page statement to each of the other three.

It was what Bradley'd said. David and Peter read their copies, and read their own names under signature lines midway down the second page, and both noticed that the subject of the discussion remained determinedly vague. Invisible men were never directly mentioned, which was a pity; what a thing it would be, to have on a legal document.

Leethe took a lot longer to read it, then removed his own Mont Blanc pen from his inner pocket and said, "I think we need to add here, 'Not to be frivolously withheld.' "

"Where's that?" Bradley asked. Leethe pointed to the spot, and Bradley considered it, then shrugged. "Of course. If you feel you need it."

"I would be happier."

"Then by all means. Peter, David, would you write that in on your copies?"

He showed them where and what to write, and they did, and then he had them sign their copies and initial the addition, then exchange the copies and sign and initial, then take Bradley's and Leethe's copies and sign and initial *them,* and it was all very like buying a house.

Bradley kept one signed copy, and gave the rest to Leethe, who put them away in his attaché case and said, "As a matter of fact, I also have something here for signature."

Bradley waited politely, and Leethe took out his own little stack of papers and put them on the table, saying, "The first point is, the American Tobacco Research Institute never approved experimentation on human beings."

"Oh, *now!*" Peter cried. "It was accepted from the very beginning that at some stage field trials would have to be done, and that means human volunteers, everybody knows that."

"I have searched the relevant files," Leethe assured him, while his fingers demonstrated by running up a slope in midair. The hands then swept to the sides, palms down, clearing snow. "I found nothing." The hands met in prayer. "If it isn't on paper," Leethe said, "it doesn't exist."

Before either Peter or David could reply, Bradley interjected, "Granted."

Peter stared at him, betrayed. "Granted?"

"It would have been better," Bradley gently suggested, "if you'd gotten that understanding in writing at the outset, but we're not going to worry about it now." While Peter continued to look shocked, and almost mutinous, Bradley turned to Leethe and said, "We accept the point. We also accept the fact that the particular experimental subject under discussion was *not* a volunteer."

"Which the institute," Leethe added, the first finger of his right hand playing metronome, "would *never* have approved."

"Agreed."

"At this point," Leethe went on, "the institute, not acknowledging any onus of responsibility in this matter, but certainly aware of an accrual of goodwill that has grown between the doctors and the institute over the last years, is prepared to assist the doctors in finding the missing experimental subject—"

"You're already looking for him!" Peter cried.

Leethe ignored the interruption. "—for the purpose of assuring themselves the subject will come to no harm as a result of their actions. In return, the institute requires the doctors, in writing, to hold the institute harmless in all matters both prior to and proceeding from this date, in connection with this flawed experiment."

"You want carte blanche," Bradley said.

"The institute does not intend to carry the can," Leethe said, and carried a pretty bad bag of garbage out.

"David and Peter could only sign such an agreement," Bradley said, "if the institute places *them* in charge of the search for the experimental subject—"

"Oh, come, now."

"—and places them in charge of the subject himself, once he has been located."

"I'm not sure the institute could—"

"The alternative is that Peter and David will go to the state medical association."

Leethe blinked. He gazed at David and Peter, who did their best to maintain poker faces. "Would you, indeed," he said.

"We need protection from *somewhere*," Peter said.

Leethe pondered, then shrugged and said, "We'll find common ground."

Bradley nodded. "I have no doubt."

Leethe dealt out his documents, saying, "Look these over, and tell me what you feel should be altered."

They all took copies—it was another two-pager—but Bradley said, "Before we do that, Mr. Leethe, I'd appreciate it if you'd bring us up to date on the search for . . ." He turned to David and Peter. "What *is* his name?"

"We're not sure," David said. "We think he lied on his medical form."

"Fredric Noon," Leethe said.

Bradley nodded at him. "Thank you. How goes the search for Fredric Noon?"

"It goes well, I think," Leethe said. His hands gathered a light blanket to his chest. "We have hired a New York City policeman, to conduct the—"

"Police?" David cried.

"Not officially," Leethe assured him, as his left hand, two

fingers up, waved back and forth in benediction. "The gentleman is moonlighting for us."

"Moonlighting," Bradley echoed, and smiled. "What a lovely image."

"Oddly inapt, with this fellow, I think," Leethe said, as his hands lifted, tossing a little stardust into the air. "In any event," while both hands became play guns and shot David and Peter in their stomachs, "he's found Noon's girlfriend, the one he's been living with recently." While his left hand rested, palm down, on the table, his right, finger upraised, pointed out various constellations. "I hope to hear good news very shortly."

"When you find him," Peter said, "we want to be there."

"That's what we're here to iron out," Leethe told him, smoothing a bedspread. "When we do get our hands on friend Noon at last, I assure you, we'll be delighted to have you assist."

David and Peter might have nodded agreement with that, but Bradley said, "What you mean, I think, is that when you find Noon, you'll be delighted to have assisted David and Peter, and you'll want to go on assisting them."

"Semantics," Leethe said, and shrugged.

"Is my business," Bradley said, and picked up Leethe's document. "Shall we see what we have here?"

27

The thing about anger is, it tends to overcome one's sense of self-preservation, even if that one is such a one as Barney Beuler, whose sense of self-preservation had been honed for years on the whetstone of the New York Police Department. Coming off the Amtrak train from Rhinecliff into Penn Station at eight that night—after *dark!*—Barney was so enraged by life in general, Amtrak in particular, and Fredric Urban Goddam Noon in *special* particular, that he couldn't have cared less if shooflys had wired his wristwatch.

Fortunately for him, they hadn't. In fact, fortunately for Barney, all of his many enemies over there on the side of truth, justice, and the American way were otherwise engaged when he stomped up the filthy steps of Penn Station from the filthy platform, bulldozed his way through the filthy homeless living their half-speed half-lives in the terminal, found an exposed pay phone on a stick—not even an enclosed phone booth, for a modicum of privacy—and dialed Mordon Leethe at *home*. At this point, he didn't give much of a shit what happened, so long as revenge was a part of it.

"Hello?"

"Barney."

A second or two of baffled silence, and then, "Barney? Barney who?"

"Oh, fuck you, Leethe!"

"Oh, Barney! I'm sorry, I didn't recognize your voice, you sounded different."

Barney hardly recognized himself; fury had annealed him. "We have to meet," he snarled, while wide-eyed families from Iowa clutched one another close and moved in little clumps farther away across the terminal. "Now," Barney added, and his teeth clacked together.

"I'm engaged this evening."

"With *me*."

Leethe sighed, a dry and rasping sound. Barney almost expected dead leaves to drift out of the telephone. "I could see you at eleven," Leethe agreed at last, reluctance dragging out the words. "There's a bar near me."

Leethe lived, as Barney had made it his business to know, on the Upper East Side, Park Avenue in the nineties. It wasn't a neighborhood he thought of as being rich in bars. "Oh, yeah?"

"It's called Cheval. It's a bit of a bistro, really."

Sure it is, Barney thought. "I'll see you there at eleven," he snarled. "You and the rest of the Foreign Legion."

Derrière du Cheval, if you asked Barney. As with most small side-street Manhattan restaurants, this one was built into the ground floor of a former private dwelling, which meant it was long and narrow, with a not very high ceiling. This particular example of the type was warmed with creamy paint and goldish fixtures and woodlike dark trim. The bar was a C-clamp near the front, against the right wall; beyond it, one would go to the dining area with its snowy tablecloths, most of them not in use at this hour.

In fact, aside from the Israeli owners and Hispanic employees, most of the people still here at 11 P.M. on a Friday night were the adulterers at the bar, hunched in murmuring

guilty pairs on the padded high square stools with the low up-
holstered backs. Among these semilost souls, Mordon Leethe
looked like Cotton Mather in a bad mood, nursing a Perrier
and brooding at his own reflection in the gold-dappled mirror
above the back bar, as though hoping to find somewhere on
the map of his own glowering face the path that would lead
him out of all this.

But no, not tonight. Sliding onto the stool to Leethe's right,
Barney bobbed two fingers at the Perrier and said, "Letting it
all hang out, eh, Counselor?"

Leethe glowered at Barney's reflection in the mirror, then
turned his head just enough to give him the full treatment
from those bleak eyes. "You wouldn't want me to let it all
hang out, Barney," he said.

By God, and that was true, wasn't it? "Keep it buttoned,
then," Barney advised, and turned his attention to the fourteen-
year-old barman with the black pencil mustache. "Beer," he
said.

"Yes, sir?"

"Imported. In a bottle."

"Any particular brand, sir?"

"What've you got that's from the farthest away?"

The barman had to think about that. He wrinkled his mustache briefly, then said, "That would be the one from China."

"Mainland China? Where they have the slave labor?"

"Yes, sir."

"I'll have that," Barney decided, and as the barman turned
away he gave Leethe his own bleak look and explained, "I like
the idea that a lot of people worked long and hard, just for me.
Fifteen thousand miles to give me a beer."

"This isn't why you phoned me," Leethe said. "At home."

"No, it isn't." Barney looked at the hunched backs all
around them. "Isn't this kind of public?"

"These people," Leethe said, "don't care about our problems. I take it something went wrong when you tried to follow the Briscoe woman."

"Oh, everything went ducky," Barney said. He'd had three hours to cool down from his rage, and it was true his rage had cooled, in the sense that it had hardened, but it hadn't abated one dyne, and would not abate until honor—or something—was satisfied. "Just ducky," Barney repeated, and showed his teeth. At moments such as this, he didn't actually look like a fat man at all.

The barman brought the Chinese beer the last few feet of its journey, poured some from the bottle into a glass, and went off to provide more Kleenex for the hefty blond woman at the end of the bar. Barney drank, nodded, put the glass down, and said, "That invisible son of a bitch is pretty cute, I'll give him that. When I do get my hands on him, I just may strangle him to death."

"He wouldn't be much use to us then."

"Almost to death."

"What did Mr. Urban Noon do to you, Barney?"

One thing Barney had learned in his years with the NYPD; how to give a succinct report. Succinctly, he described his day, finishing with the dead Impala sprawled on its broken ankles in Rhinecliff and he himself coming back to the city alone, by train.

At the finish, there was a little silence. In it, Barney sipped more Chinese beer and Leethe sipped more French water—Barney's liquid might have traveled farther, but Leethe's had arguably made a sillier trip—and then Leethe said, "It may be we've been misjudging Mr. Noon."

Barney looked at the grim profile, studying itself again in the mirror. "How do you figure?" he asked. "I've been judging him to be a cheap crook, and he's a cheap crook."

"We've been judging him," Leethe said, "to be stupid because he's small-time. But he didn't bite on that excellent letter of yours, and he understood how you were managing to follow his friend Briscoe, and he threw you off his trail with, you must admit, dismaying ease."

"I'm not *off his trail*," Barney snapped. "I'm on that son of a bitch's trail, don't you worry."

"All I'm suggesting is, we shouldn't underestimate the man."

"Fine." Barney shrugged, making his jacket jump. "I'll brush up my Shakespeare for when we meet," he said, and made a small sword-type gesture. "Have at you, Fauntleroy!"

Leethe gave him a skeptical, even disgusted, look. "And where is that," he asked, "in Shakespeare?"

"How the fuck do I know? The question is," Barney said, lowering his voice as he became aware of the adulterous herd around him disturbed at their grazing, "where is Noon in New York State? I had my maps on the train—"

"Why?" Leethe asked, surprised. "You were on a train."

Barney lowered an eyebrow. "I may practice my strangling on you," he said.

"Never mind," Leethe said, unintimidated. "I understand what you meant. You've determined the area Noon must be in."

"On the basis of the railroad station he picked," Barney said, "I worked out an area where he's got to be. No," he corrected himself, "I'm forgetting, he's a genius. So maybe he took the train north to Rhinebeck because he's *actually* staying on the Jersey shore."

"I don't think so," Leethe said.

"I don't think so, either," Barney admitted. "I think I'll go with the probabilities here, and the probabilities here are limited to four rural counties in New York state plus maybe a little bit of Connecticut."

What might have been a smile ruffled Leethe's features. "So Mr. Urban has gone rural."

"Yeah, and we'll find Mr. Noon at midnight. What are you drinking there? What'd they put in that stuff?"

"Barney," Leethe said, sounding impatient all at once. "Why are you telling me all this? Why are we in *this* place? If your target area is four counties in New York State and a little piece of Connecticut, why aren't you *there*, nose to the ground, tirelessly searching?"

"Because I figure we want to find Freddie Noon within this lifetime," Barney told him. "It's all little villages up there, dairy farms, shit like that, spread out. A lot of people rent summer places up there, a lot of New Yorkers have weekend places there. It's not the kind of territory I know, and it's not a place where I got any clout, and it's not a job for one guy anyway, no matter."

Leethe considered this as he turned the little Perrier bottle around and around on its circle of water on the bar. "You're saying," he decided at last, "that you want to hire somebody, or some several somebodies, to canvass the area, and you couldn't wait till tomorrow to talk to me because I have to approve the expense."

"You got it in one."

"I hired you," Leethe pointed out, "and all at once you're my partner. Now you're suggesting we should hire somebody else."

"I see your problem," Barney agreed, "but let me reassure you."

"I find it very unlikely, Barney," Leethe said, "that you could ever reassure me, on any subject, at any time."

"Let me try, anyway. There's a bunch of private detective agencies—"

"My God. You're going to bring in Mike Hammer?"

"Not like in the movies," Barney told him. Now *he* was getting impatient. "In real life," he explained, "licensed private detectives do guard duty at small museums or private estates, they do industrial espionage to find out who's stealing the lawn mowers or the secrets or whatever, they repossess cars and boats and stuff that people don't make their payments on, but what they *mostly* do is find deadbeats. Skip-tracing is their real art, and they do it all on the phone, and they never ask *why* the customer wants to find so-and-so, they just do it. Mostly, they're little shops with three or four or five people, and that many phones, and the boss has the license, and he's a retired cop. They're all over the country, and they all have WATS lines so they don't care if they have to call Alaska or Florida or whatever, and in a situation like this I wouldn't even use a New York outfit. New York City, I mean. I'd use one from Boston, or maybe Albany or Syracuse, and all they know is they're looking for Margaret Briscoe, formerly of Bay Ridge, Brooklyn, and we believe for the summer she's somewhere in this area. So they'll charge me for the time—overcharge me, that's how they are—and a bonus when they find her, and in the meantime we sit back and wait."

"How long?"

"Maybe a week, maybe less, maybe more."

"Precision," Leethe said, with another brief faux smile. "How much will all this cost?"

"Under a grand."

Leethe considered. He finished his Perrier. He said, "And how much of that will be paid by my partner?"

Barney stared at him. He couldn't believe this guy. "Are you feelin all right?" he demanded. "Maybe it's past your bedtime. Lemme make it easy on you. Just nod your head if I got the okay to spend the grand."

28

Sunday evening, they had a fire. They didn't *need* a fire, the Sunday of the last week in June, but if you're going to rent a house in the country, and if that house has a fireplace, and if it has a stack of firewood outside under a black plastic sheet against the back wall, it doesn't much matter if it's August, you've got to have a fire.

Also, as Freddie pointed out, "You need more warmth in a room when you're naked."

"You could put some clothes on, Freddie."

"If I put on a shirt and pants," he answered, accurately, "you'll get upset unless I put on one of the heads and a pair of rubber gloves and then some socks and shoes and—"

"Okay, okay. We'll have a fire. Let *me* do it!" she cried, as a log started to fly all by itself across the room toward the fireplace.

This was long enough after dinner for Freddie to be completely invisible again, and there was still bluish-pink light to be seen through the windows in the sky outside, above the black soft masses of the trees. In the country, their patterns were changing, they were going to sleep earlier, waking up earlier, living an entirely different life. Call Me Tom had given them a list of nearby—if fifteen miles could be considered nearby—shops and stores, and they'd done their exploring, taking life easy, Freddie not even shoplifting, though in these country shops you hardly had to be invisible to walk out with half their stock. There were places in the little towns to rent videotapes, and the house had a big television set and a working VCR—even the clock in it worked, to show the advantage of renting from a scientist—so in the evenings they could watch movies, except tonight they were having a fire.

A nice one, too, if Peg did say so herself, having done the whole thing and then come back across the room to admire her handiwork. Sitting there on the deep sofa, lights out, rich sky colors in black-framed rectangles at the windows, snuggled against Freddie (it was okay if she didn't look), she gazed into the twisting flames and said, "Freddie, this is pretty okay."

"I kind of like it," Freddie agreed.

"The only question—"

"I know."

"What do you—"

"The cop."

"That's it."

"Here's the way I see it," Freddie told her, adjusting his arm more comfortably around her (she didn't look). "This cop, that you say his name is Barney something—"

"That's what the lawyer called him."

"It could still be true, though. Okay, Barney's a real cop, with all that power, and that was probably a real warrant he showed you, but what I think is, I think he isn't working *as* a cop. I think he's rented himself out to that lawyer—"

"The lawyer was the guy in charge," Peg agreed, "when they were at our place."

"Right. And the lawyer's working for the doctors."

"Do doctors have that kind of clout?" Peg asked. "That they can get a lawyer that bosses cops around?"

"These aren't regular doctors," Freddie pointed out. "These

are research doctors. Who knows who they got behind them? The CIA, maybe, or the Republican National Committee, or some oil sheik."

"Scary people."

"Which is why we want to stay away from them. Keep out of their sight."

"Easy for *you* to say."

"The question is," Freddie said, ignoring that, "what's gonna happen next with this cop and this lawyer?"

"They know we're up here someplace," Peg reminded him. "Someplace around the Rhinebeck railroad station."

"Which I'm not worried about," Freddie said, "if the cop's working on his own. If he can send out a flyer on us, that's different. Then we might actually have to leave here."

"Oh, Freddie! Don't even say it!"

"We still have to think it, Peg. We don't wanna be sitting here like this, cozy and romantic in front of the fire, and outside a SWAT team's surrounding the house."

Peg stared at the darkening shapes of the windows, her eyes wide in the firelight. "Oh, my God, Freddie, do you think it's possible?"

"Not this quick. Maybe not at all."

"But—what are we gonna do?"

"I tell you what," Freddie said. "Tomorrow's Monday. If this Barney the cop is on official business, if he's after me because there's a warrant out on me or something, those doctors swore out something against me, though I doubt it, but if that's the case—"

"Yes? Yes?"

"By tomorrow," Freddie said, "they'll have the bulletin with my name on it at all the police stations around here, and the state trooper barracks, and all the rest of it. So I'll go to one of those places and have a look."

"Freddie!" Peg said, and forgot, and looked at him—at the

sofa, that is—then quickly looked at the fire again. "Could you do that?"

"Peg, I can do anything. That's the upside of this business. I know there's problems and all that with this invisibility thing, but Peg, you know, when it comes right down to it, I can do anything I want."

"I guess that's true."

"So if my name isn't there, on the be-on-the-lookout-for list, then everything's fine. Barney'll never find us here on his own."

"So we're safe."

"Yes." Freddie squeezed her more tightly. "Peg," he said.

"Yes?"

"Close your eyes now, Peg."

"What? Oh, sure."

29

When folks around Dudley said that Geoff Wheedabyx wore a whole lot of different hats, they meant it literally. Geoff lived in the old Wheedabyx place that had been built by his great-great-grandfather along the Albany–Boston road back in the 1850s, when there was still iron under this land (great-great-grandpa was the mine owner) and when all this countryside around here was farms and woods. Some members of the Wheedabyx clan—particularly the ones who had moved away to California—were still sore that the town that had grown up around great-great-grandpa's place was called Dudley and not Wheedabyx, but the fact was the Dudley farm had comprised over seven hundred acres, while Great-great-grandpa never had more than eleven acres around his house, a parcel which in any case he'd bought from the Dudleys.

The Albany–Boston road was now Market Street, the only east–west thoroughfare in the village of Dudley. The iron under the ground was long gone, turned into hard round balls and fired southward in the 1860s, and the farms were recently gone, turned into suburban developments and weekend homes and back into woods, but the Dudley descendants were still here, in and around their namesake town, and the Wheedabyx descendants were represented mainly these days by Geoff, who wore all those hats.

They were hung usually on pegs in his office, that being the big room at the left when you came in the front door. Originally that room had been the best parlor, unused except for holidays and family reunions and visits from the pastor, and at later times it had been a sickroom, whenever there was a Wheedabyx in residence too far gone to make it up the stairs, or sometimes a formal dining room, though too far from the kitchen, but now it was Geoff's office, where, on pegs high on the side wall opposite the entrance doorway, hung his many hats.

Here are the hats, from the left: volunteer fireman's helmet, with CHIEF emblazoned on the front, and goggles and mask and straps dangling from it; yellow construction hard hat, with WHEEDABYX BUILDERS in blue letters on the right side, being the small construction company Geoff ran and spent most of his time at, hammer in hand; white helmet with built-in walkie-talkie and AMBULANCE in red letters across the front, which he wore when driving for the Roe-Jan Volunteer Ambulance Service; dark blue graduation-type cap with tassel, worn when singing with the Unitarian choir (he wasn't a Unitarian, but it was a good place to meet girls); serious black fedora for use at weddings and funerals and outdoor speech-making (by others); and dark blue military officer–style police chief's hat, with silver badge and black hard brim, which is why we're here.

Monday morning, June 26 of this year, Geoff Wheedabyx awoke alone and happy, leaped out of bed, and went off to shower. He didn't always awake alone, but he didn't mind it. At forty-seven, he'd been married twice and divorced twice and, while still friends with both ex-wives, he saw no reason to marry a third time. He essentially agreed with the philosophy of W. C. Fields, who once said, "Women to me are like elephants. I like to look at them, but I wouldn't want to own one."

Geoff liked to look at women, and more, hence the choir-singing cap and the black fedora, but to an even greater extent he liked to go on being an overgrown boy, hence the fireman hat and the policeman hat and the hard-hat hat. For a cheerful grown-up boy, who can actually legitimately wear all those hats, life is a pretty sweet proposition, all in all.

Geoff had a bachelor's kitchen skills: he threw food at the stove, then ate it, then cleaned up. By 7:40 A.M., he was done with all that, and carrying his second cup of coffee into the office, ready to go to work.

Geoff's office, a large room, was nevertheless crowded. His police-department file cabinet stood next to his fire-department file cabinet stood next to his construction-company file cabinet. His firematic books and police manuals and building codes bulletins and lumber brochures were all tumbled together into rough bookcases he'd made himself, evenings. On the walls, wherever there was space among the calendars, safety posters, work schedules, and area maps, Geoff had pinned up FBI wanted posters, not because he ever expected to see any of those hard-looking fellows here in Dudley, but because their pitiless faces helped to remind him that, small as all his operations might be, he was still engaged in serious business here.

As a police department, his operation was about as small as you could get: himself and two part-timers, who were mostly employed for traffic control when things like the circus or the horse show or the bluegrass festival were in the neighborhood. The rest of the time, the Dudley, New York, police department was just him, as backup to the state police, who handled all the real criminal work: burglary, DWI, possession of a controlled substance. (Once, there'd been a small Ziploc bag of some sort of white powdery controlled substance actually here in this office, locked in the bottom drawer of his grandfather's old oak desk over there between the two front

windows, locked in there for two days, waiting for State CID
up in Albany to send somebody down and pick it up. Oh, *how*
Geoff had wanted to open that bag, just take a sniff, maybe a
tiny taste; but he'd been good, and left that evidence alone,
and regretted it ever since.)

This morning, as usual, he phoned the state-police barracks
down toward Pawling to find out if anything he should know
about had happened during the night—like more escapees
from the boys' reformatory over by the Connecticut state
line—but this morning, happily, there was nothing. Next he
called the firehouse out at Futterman—Dudley was just
backup to their fire department—and they'd also had a quiet
night. So then he made some lumberyard and hardware-store
calls, put on his hard hat, and went out, locking both the office door and the front door behind him, because there were
just too many things in the office, like guns and flares and radios, that kids might take too intense an interest in, and he
didn't want to be responsible for some dumb kid blowing his
fingers off or something.

The Dudley PD owned a fine black-and-gray police car,
two years old, equipped with stuff you wouldn't believe possible, but Geoff rarely used it. In fact, he mostly kept it parked
just this side of the town-limit sign at the west end of Market
Street, to remind eastbound drivers they weren't on the
Taconic Parkway anymore and should slow the hell down.
What Geoff drove instead was his 4 x 4 pickup equipped with
flashing red light, police radio, CB radio, walkie-talkie, handgun mounted under the dash, fire extinguisher, and, oh, Lord,
just tons of stuff. Including at the moment, three sheets of C-
D exterior plywood and some boxes of nails and a can of joint
compound and some other construction-company stuff in the
back.

The pickup was parked in the drive outside to the left. Geoff
boarded it and took it the two blocks to the house where he was

enclosing the back porch downstairs and creating a new screened porch on the second floor above it. He arrived at three minutes to eight, to find two of his three construction-company employees already there, yawning and scratching and drinking diner coffee out of plastic cups. The third guy pulled in about ten seconds later, and then they went to work.

The deal is, as everybody knows, construction crews cannot work, can simply not work, unless country-and-western music is playing on a crappy little portable radio under everybody's feet. On the other hand, Geoff had to be aware of his radios in the pickup, just in case there was a fire or an ambulance emergency or some call for the police department, so an electrician friend—who should have been here this week, by the way, but of course he wasn't—had rigged a white light on the pickup's dashboard that would flash through the windshield if anybody tried to call. And Geoff always left one transmitter on in the office, that could be received by the police radio in the pickup, if anybody tried to make contact with him back there. A voice, a phone ringing, anything like that in the offices would transmit to the pickup and switch on that white light.

It came on this morning a little after ten. It would come on like that once or twice a week, and was never any big deal. Today, one of the guys on the crew noticed it first, and said, "Your light's on, Geoff," and Geoff put down his hammer and left the porch and went around to get behind the wheel of the pickup.

He listened. No voice, no telephone, no walkie-talkie. Nothing. So why would the light go on? Did somebody just ring once, at the office, and then hang up? Geoff was about to switch off the light and go back to work when his police-department radio began to make scratching sounds.

Well, hell, so that's what it was. When he'd put in this system, the electrician—where the hell *was* he, by the way?—

had said it was so sensitive it could pick up a mouse eating an apple in the office, which was okay with Geoff since he had no varmints in his house at all. Except maybe now he did. Listen to that scratching—sounded like the damn thing was eating a baseball bat.

The door opened.

What? Geoff leaned closer to the radio. Had he heard what he'd thought he'd heard?

The door closed. Footsteps. A file drawer opened.

"Well, hell," Geoff said, and reached for the handgun under the dash. Tucking it into his jeans, removing his nail apron, flipping the tail of his T-shirt over the gun butt, he got out of the pickup, called to his guys, "I'll be right back," and walked the two blocks back to his house, passing along the way a gray minivan with city plates and a strange woman at the wheel, who didn't look at him as he went by. Something to do with it, whatever it was.

Already he knew this wasn't kids. It was a burglar, picking locks, deliberately breaking into that specific room in that specific house and going right away to the filing cabinets.

Half a block this side of his house, Geoff turned off and walked down a driveway, then across some backyards. He'd grown up in this town, and until the age of thirteen the backyards and fields and lower tree branches and barn interiors had been his primary routes, leaving the ordinary streets and roads for the use of unimaginative grown-ups. You didn't forget those childhood patterns: Geoff could now come at his house from eleven different unexpected directions.

Letting himself quietly into the house through the back door, he paused to remove his work boots, then in his tube socks eased through the house to the closed office door. Leaning close to it, holding his breath, he listened at first to silence, and then to a squeak—his office chair, the son of a gun was sitting in his office chair—and then the undeniable scrape of his bottom drawer opening, the one that was always kept locked, but which this alien burglar son of a gun had picked or pried open. God*dam* it!

Geoff took a deep breath, held the handgun in his left hand—a Smith & Wesson Police Positive .32 revolver, tested semiannually on the firing range but never fired otherwise, up till now—squeezed the doorknob with his right hand, stopped to be sure he was calm enough for all this, then turned the knob, shoved the door open, stepped in, pointed the revolver toward the desk, and cried, "Hold it right—"

There was nobody in the room. Geoff stared around, this way and that, and there was nobody in the room, the place was as empty as when he'd gone out.

There'd been no scratch marks or damage on the door, either, come to think of it. Was he crazy? Was it a mouse after all?

The bottom desk drawer over there was open. From this angle, he could just barely see it. And his office chair was tilted backward at an unusual angle. Geoff squinted, pointing the handgun at that chair. He waited.

The chair squeaked. A tiny, reluctant, embarrassed squeak, but a definite squeak.

"Okay," Geoff said. Now he was sure of himself. Back to the doorway, handgun pointed firmly at the seat back, he said, "I don't know how you're doing that, mirrors or whatever it might be you've got there, some kind of city trick *I've* never heard of, but that's okay. I don't have to see you to know you're there. And I don't have to see you to shoot you, either, so you'd best be very careful."

The chair squeaked again, even more reluctantly than before, this time sullenly, mulishly as well.

"I said be careful," Geoff told it. One small part of him was amazed to listen how he was talking so calmly and self-assuredly in an empty room, but the rest of him was just doing his job. All of his jobs, all the jobs he'd been trained for, taking state-police classes and fire-department classes and CPR training and ambulance-rescue instruction and all the rest of it. Emergencies were what he *did*. If the emergency is you talk out loud in an empty room and point your handgun at a perpetrator you can't see, that's okay. You cope.

Geoff said, "That chair's giving you away, you know. I'll know if you try to stand up out of it, so you shouldn't try that, because then I will have to shoot you, because otherwise I might not know where you are. So just stay in the chair."

Nothing. Silence.

"You're not fooling me, you know," Geoff said.

Nothing. Silence.

"Well, this is just silly," Geoff said. "All I have to do is call a couple of friends of mine, and they'll come here and throw ropes around you *and* the chair while I hold this gun on you, and then we'll turn you over to the state police and let them send you back to the city or whatever they want to do with you. Is that woman in the van with you?"

A sigh sounded, floating in the air.

Geoff nodded. "Yeah, I thought she was."

The chair squeaked again, this time loudly and unashamedly. Papers on the desk ruffled and crumpled. It was Geoff's guess that the perp had put his elbows on the table and his head in his hands. He almost felt sorry for the fellow, and might have, if the fellow weren't in the process of burglarizing Geoff's own house, own office, and own desk. Sympathy in his voice, he said, "You want to tell me about it?"

"Out of all the police departments in all the small towns in all the world," said a faint forlorn voice from the general direction of the desk, "why did I have to pick this one?"

"Maybe you underestimated us hicks," Geoff suggested.

"Oh, don't do that city-country shit on me," the nothing in

the chair said, sounding aggrieved. "We're all just people, goddam it."

"Well, that's true," Geoff said, feeling suddenly abashed. He tried to be a decent person, and didn't like all at once to find evidences of prejudice in himself. "I apologize if I was being anti-city," he said, "but you have to admit, what you're doing there, whatever it is you're doing, it isn't something anybody around Dudley could do."

"That's right. So nobody's gonna believe you," the whatsit in the chair said hopefully, "so you'd just make trouble for yourself, so probably the best thing would be, you just let me go."

"They don't have to believe me," Geoff told him. "They can believe *you*."

The next sigh from the chair was counterpointed by a sudden loud knocking at the front door. An instant later, a woman's voice out there called, "Hello? Anybody home?"

"There's your friend," Geoff said.

"Never saw her before in my life."

"You're not seeing her now."

"If I could see her, I've never seen her before."

Knock knock. "Hello? Hello?"

Geoff said, "Is my front door locked or unlocked?"

"Unlocked."

"Why don't you call her in, then?"

"It's your house."

"You unlocked the door."

Knock knock. "Hello? Anybody? *Freddie*?"

Sigh from the chair, long and heartfelt. "Come on in," the burglar called.

"Freddie?"

"It's unlocked!"

"You be good now, Freddie," Geoff warned, and stepped

back into the doorway, so he could look simultaneously at his office chair and the front door, which opened.

The woman from the van, now that he got a better look at her in his open front doorway, was an attractive girl, like one of those movie actresses that play girls from Brooklyn but aren't really. Except this one probably was. She stared at Geoff, much more astonished and frightened by his appearance than he had been by her boyfriend's nonappearance. "Who—who are you?"

"Well, the householder," Geoff said. "Also the chief of police. Come on in. Might as well close the door behind you."

"No, I, I was just, he's not here, sorry, I was just, uh, looking for my friend."

"Freddie. Come on in," Geoff invited again, being very calm and easygoing, trying not to spook this girl more than she was already spooked. "Freddie's sitting at my desk," he said.

She came in, she shut the door, and she looked at Geoff with deep mistrust. "I don't know what you mean," she said.

Now that she was inside, Geoff let her see the gun. Gesturing with it, he said, "I'd like you to come into the office, please," and he put more of his official tone into his voice.

She stared at the gun. "That's a gun!"

"Yes, ma'am. Which I don't intend to use unless you try to run away or Freddie makes an unauthorized move out of that chair." Looking toward the chair in question, Geoff said, "Freddie, would you ask your friend to come on in?"

Sounding resigned, Freddie's voice said, "Come on in, Peg."

"Freddie?" Clearly, she couldn't believe any of this. "What's happening?"

"Well, I'm caught, Peg. That's the hell of it."

Geoff stepped back from the doorway into the office, and

Peg came forward. Entering the office, she looked around and made one last hopeless try. "I don't see anybody."

"Forget it, Peg," Freddie said. "He's got me pinned in this chair here." And he made the chair squeak, just to prove it. Then, sounding aggrieved again, he said, "You're such a goddam handyman, I can see it all over you, how come you don't oil this chair?"

"Never got around to it. Peg, maybe you could stand beside the desk over there, while Freddie tells me what's going on."

As she moved over, they both started talking at once, then both stopped, then Peg said, "Freddie, let me tell him."

"Okay. You're better at it, I guess."

"That's right." Peg turned to Geoff, her expression as open and honest and clean as the day outside those windows. "Besides," she explained, "you can *see* me, you can see my face and know I'm telling the truth."

"Sure," Geoff said, and looked at that dewy face, and thought, Now *here* we have a first-class grade-A liar. "Go ahead," he said.

"Freddie's a scientist."

Well, that's good, Geoff thought. Start with a whopper. "Uh-huh," he said.

"He's working on a cure for cancer."

"Uh-huh."

"Skin cancer," Freddie added.

"Uh-huh."

Peg said, "He's got this special medicine that takes the color out of your skin and your whole body, and that's why you can't see him."

"That would explain it," Geoff agreed.

Peg now looked more sincere than ever. "But," she said, "there are some very bad guys trying to steal the formula."

"Uh-huh."

Simultaneously, Freddie said, "A chemical company," and Peg said, "Foreign agents."

"Uh-huh," Geoff said.

"A foreign chemical company," Freddie explained.

"Their agents," Peg footnoted. "They're Swiss, I think." Turning desperately to the chair behind the desk, she said, "Is that right, Freddie?"

"Yeah, I think so. Swiss, I think."

"So Freddie had to get away and hide," Peg explained, turning back to Geoff.

"Should be easy for him to do, considering," Geoff agreed.

Sounding bitter, Peg said, "You'd think so."

"I experimented on myself," Freddie said. "To test my formula, because I didn't want to put anybody else at risk."

"I've seen that in the movies," Geoff said.

"Sure. Happens all the time. But now I got to hide out until my experiment's done, and these guys are after me. They're very powerful guys, with these like tentacles into the very highest level of government, and all that stuff."

Peg explained, "It's like a Robert Ludlum novel."

"I was going to suggest that myself," Geoff told her.

"So we ran away," Peg went on, "but Freddie wanted to know if maybe they had some of their powerful friends get the police to look for us—"

"Corrupt city police," Freddie said, in a blatant appeal to Geoff's prejudices—dang!

"So we stopped here," Peg said.

"Of all places," Freddie said.

"And Freddie came in here to see if his name was on any wanted lists."

Geoff lifted an interested eyebrow toward the chair. "Was it?"

"I don't know yet. I mean, not so far."

Geoff pointed the gun at the clipboard on the right side of the desk. "Did you look on that clipboard?"

"No. What's that?"

"If they *were* looking for you, how long would it be?"

"Just a few days."

"Then it'll be on that clipboard," Geoff told him. "Any wanted flyers they fax me, I put them on that clipboard. Anything in the last two, three weeks'll be there."

"Okay if I look?"

Geoff couldn't help a sardonic chuckle. "You break-and-enter my house, and then ask my permission to look at that clipboard?"

"I apologize for breaking and entering."

"Go ahead and look," Geoff said.

That was a strange moment, when the clipboard lifted up into the air all by itself, and then started riffling its own pages. While the clipboard animated itself like that, Geoff took time to consider the baloney sandwich they'd just fed him. He suspected that, here and there in the mix, like flecks of gold in a sandy streambed, there were particles of truth stirred into the baloney. Not a lot of particles, but some.

A sigh of relief from the desk. Peg turned, hopeful, ready to be happy. "Is it okay?"

"We're not there!" Freddie sounded relieved, elated, even astonished. "Peg, by golly, I'm not a wanted man!"

"Well, that isn't exactly true," Geoff said. "Here in Dudley you're wanted, in fact you're being arrested, for breaking and entering."

"Aw, come on, Chief," Freddie said. "I didn't take anything, I wasn't *gonna* take anything, you know that's true. And I didn't hurt any of your locks or anything else, no damage at all. I'll even oil this damn chair before I go, if you want."

"Go? You aren't going anywhere."

"Chief?" Freddie asked. "Won't you give us a break?"

"No."

"Peg?"

All at once, Peg was slinking seductively toward him, smiling, blocking his view of the desk, saying, "Chief? Am I arrested, too? *I* didn't break into anywhere."

"Move over!" Geoff cried, but it was too late. *Squeak!* When Geoff jumped to his right, to see his chair, it was turning in a lazy circle, bobbing slightly, definitely empty.

"Damn it!" Geoff yelled, and pointed the gun at Peg. "Don't you move!"

"I just don't believe you'll shoot me," Peg said, and backed toward the open doorway.

"I'll shoot your leg!"

"*This* leg?" She leered at him. "Chief, what kind of man are you?"

"Now, *stop*! Right there!" Geoff shouted, and his fire-chief helmet came flying out of the air and bounced off his wrist, so that he almost dropped the gun, but held on to it. Peg was now through the doorway, fleet of foot, and before he could get to the hall the front door slammed shut. Geoff spun around, trying to fill the doorway, to at least keep Freddie bottled up in here, and his police-chief hat took him square on the nose.

The son of a gun was throwing his hats at him! Geoff dodged his fedora, waving the useless gun this way and that, and here came his choir-singing cap, tassel streaming out behind it like a kite's tail. Geoff was actually ducking away from that cap when he realized it was moving in too straight a line, and not turning; it wasn't being thrown, it was being carried!

But the trick had worked, doggone it, that cap had made him duck out of the doorway just at the wrong second. Geoff flailed with his free hand, and found a wrist, and clenched on tight to that invisible wrist until he felt invisible teeth crunch *hard* onto his fingers. "Yow!" he cried, and let go, and so did the teeth, and a few seconds later slam went the front door again.

By the time Geoff got out to the porch, the van was picking up speed westward down Market Street; not a chance in the world he could get to either his pickup, two blocks to the left, or his police car, two blocks to the right, before those people were long gone.

Geoff hurried back into his office, sat down at his communications center, and was on the very brink of calling the state police when his second thoughts caught up with him. Report this? Report what? No evidence of a burglary, nothing taken. *He* knew Freddie was invisible, because he'd spent time in this room talking to the guy, but what would the fellas at the state-police barracks think if he called and asked them to pick up an invisible man in a gray minivan?

He had no idea who those two people really were, except not scientists. He had no idea where they were headed or what their true story was or why Freddie had thought he might be on some wanted list. All he knew for sure about Freddie, in fact, was that he was *not* on any wanted list, which seemed improper, somehow.

Well, he did know a couple things more about those two, when he thought it over. He knew Freddie had enough burglar skills to be a first-rate burglar, so probably was. He knew their first names, Freddie and Peg. And he knew their minivan's license number.

It took about two minutes to radio in and get the registration information, and learn that the owner of the van was one Margaret Briscoe—Peg, check—with an address in Bay Ridge, Brooklyn, New York.

So he'd been right about one thing today, anyway.

30

"That was too close a call," Freddie said. He was staying in the back of the van, clothes off, just in case they got stopped by some law sicced on them by the chief. It hadn't happened so far, which meant it was increasingly unlikely to happen, but nevertheless. Freddie's wrist still burned where the chief had grabbed it, and his mouth still remembered the bad taste of the chief's work-roughened fingers.

Up front, Peg concentrated on her driving. "What got me about that guy," she said, "was how easy he took it. Like he talked to invisible people all the time."

"I don't like a cop that doesn't get rattled," Freddie agreed. He was sitting on his rolled-up clothing, trousers on the outside of the roll, but the country road still jounced him pretty solidly against the hard floor of the van. And AstroTurf, as any professional ballplayer can tell you, is no fun to bounce on.

"Well, at least," Peg said, slowing but not stopping for a stop sign, then making the right onto another small twisty bumpy county road, "now we know for sure there isn't any paper out on you."

"I told you Barney was working off the books," Freddie said. "So now we're safe and clear. All we have to do is stay away from Dudley."

"There's not much there," Peg said. "We can do our shopping in the other direction."

"Fi-*hine!*" Freddie said as they went over one particularly brutal bump. "How much longer till we get home, Peg?"

"Ten minutes, maybe less."

"Good."

"And then we can relax."

"I keep thinking," Freddie said, bracing himself with both hands on the AstroTurf, "about that chief back there, and how he damn near got me."

"Well, he didn't get you," Peg said, braking not very much at a yield sign. "So don't worry, Freddie, you'll never see that guy again." She laughed. "And Lord knows, he won't see you."

31

Monday afternoon, three-thirty. Mordon Leethe watched Jack Fullerton the Fourth set flame to a cigarette from a Greek Revival lighter the size of a football. There was then a delay in the conversation for the ritual coughing, hacking, wheezing, gasping, spitting, eyeball-rolling, weeping, snorting, snot-spraying, drooling, and braying, Jack the Fourth being held and succored and rubbed down and wiped off all through it by his two silent dark-suited assistants. Then, once the storm had subsided and Jack was again capable of speech, the cigarette smoldering like some outlying district of hell in that huge ashtray on his desk, the oxygen tube once again in position beneath his nostrils, he turned his wet pale red-rimmed eyes on Mordon and said, "Where is he? I want to see this fellow."

"Well, that's the thing," Mordon ventured, fingers pointing toward various nonexistent fireflies, "you *can't* see this fellow. No one can. That's what makes him so hard to find."

"And so useful, dammit." Jack the Fourth thumped a meaty fist against his clean desktop, making the ashtray and Mordon jump, but not the stoic assistants. "I want that fellow *now*! I need him! So why don't I have him?"

"Being a thief," Mordon hazarded, fingers searching for a lost contact lens in a shag rug, "makes him adept, I presume, at hiding out. But I'm sure we'll find him eventually."

"I don't have eventually. What I *have* is an idea."

Mordon's hands climbed the escape rope of his tie. "Yes?"

"These mad medicos," Jack the Fourth wheezed, "they know now, don't they, if they put their two potions together, they make an invisible man?"

Surprised, his hands turning like sunflowers, Mordon said, "Well, yes, I suppose they do."

"Then let them make *us* one," Jack the Fourth demanded. "Keep looking for the original, but make us a copy."

The sunflowers grew. "They could, couldn't they?" But then the sunflowers died, and Mordon said, "But *who*? Who would take such a risk, and wind up like, like *that*?"

"One thing I've learned about money," Jack the Fourth wheezed. "If you have enough of it, somebody's gonna volunteer. And I need an invisible man, dammit. I need him right away!"

"Congressional hearings?" Mordon suggested. "Competitors' pricing plans?"

"All that, too, of course," Jack the Fourth rumbled, with a massive shrug of shoulder. "But that isn't the most important. I need him for something else, closer to home."

Suspected infidelity? Jack the Fourth's fifth wife? Mordon looked alert. "Yes?"

"The doctors!" Jack the Fourth cried, with sudden passion. "The doctors are lying to me!"

"Which doctors?" Mordon asked.

"You're right," Jack the Fourth told him. "They're *all* witch doctors!"

"No, I meant, which doctors are lying to you?"

"*My* doctors! Who the hell other pill pusher do you think I'd talk to? Do you think I *like* to talk to doctors? Grubby little handwashers? Don't you know I quit *two* different country clubs in my life because they let the pill pushers in? Measly little body mechanics, they get two dimes to rub together, they think they're *class!* Effrontery!"

"Uh, Jack," Mordon said. "What have your doctors been lying to you about?"

"*Me,* of course! What the hell do I care what their opinions are on anything else? They're lying to me about *me,* and I damn well know it. You think I look any better today than the last time you saw me?"

If it were possible for Jack the Fourth to look worse, he would look worse. Since it was not, he looked the same. "Uh—" Mordon said.

"Neither do I!" yelled Jack the Fourth, and paused to cough a lot of red foam into a handkerchief held by one of the assistants. When that attack was over, he resumed, telling Mordon, "They tell me I'm improving, if you can believe it. Oh, they admit I'll never play tennis again, they don't go so far as to promise a *cure,* the rotten sycophants, but they claim I'm *holding my own,* that's how they phrase it, as though I could even *find* my own anymore. I need this goddam spook of yours, or one we make ourselves, to sneak in there and listen when I'm not around. I *know* they're lying, I *know* it!"

"Then why do you need the invisible man's confirmation?" Mordon asked, blessing the multitudes.

Jack the Fourth turned his melting iceberg eyes on Mordon. "I want to know," he rasped, "if they're laughing."

32

Sometimes it seemed to Peg she'd been born in the wrong century. Sometimes it seemed to her she should have been born back in the Middle Ages, when people liked their white women white, when *alabaster* was a word that showed up in the poetry a lot, referring to women, not mausoleums, and was considered a compliment. Sometimes she thought it had been a mistake on her part to be born at a time when white women were supposed to color themselves like french toast.

Even when she was a little kid, she felt the same way. The other little kids were at Coney Island or Jones Beach, spread-eagled on the sand like victims of a hostile tribe, and where was Peg? Under the beach umbrella; wrapped inside the beach towel; in the shade of the hot dog stand; home, reading a book. "It's such a beautiful day out, whyn't you go out and catch the sun?" well-meaning but mortally mistaken grown-ups would say, and five minutes later Peg would be sneaking in the back door.

Now, of course, with ozone, everybody knows that tinting yourself the shade of a tennis racket handle is a dangerous affectation at best. Now, with the sunblocks steadily thickening toward three figures, Peg no longer had to justify herself to the rest of the world. "I'm keeping out of the sun," she'd say, and people would nod and say, "Ozone," and Peg would smile and let it go at that, but it wasn't ozone. It was her skin. She liked it the color she was born with.

So she hadn't expected to be spending much time at, in, or near the swimming pool that had come as part of the rental house, though she knew Freddie liked to swim and would probably drift up there by himself without a bathing suit from time to time. But then she discovered how much fun it was to watch Freddie swim, and that changed everything.

Yes, watch. In the pool, he was still of course invisible, but nevertheless he was a palpable substance, a mass, and he did displace the water he moved through. The clear water could be seen to bunch and roil and stream all around him, reflecting the light in another way, making forms and shapes of its own as Freddie passed by. When he swam the length of the pool underwater, a thing he liked to do, it was eerie, almost frightening, to see that thick rippling disturbance move ghostly and fishlike down there, occasionally emitting streams of bubbles from . . . from nowhere. And when he burst through the surface, leaping up, blowing water like a whale, it was just astonishing: water exploding, all by itself.

The pool was behind the house, and up a slight slope, and off-center from the house just a bit to the right. An enclosing fence framed the pool and its stone-and-wood surround; it was made of vertical wood slats four feet high, with a two-foot latticework above that, to catch the breeze and permit the people inside to look out while retaining their own privacy. At the right end of the pool, where a round Lucite table and four white plastic chairs stood under a large blue-and-white-striped umbrella that stuck up like a Martian plant from the middle of the table, you could look through the lattice and down past the side of the house to the driveway in front, to see people arrive without their seeing you.

Here they were spending most of their time, when not in Dudley. The sun was warm, the air not too hot, the pool heated. Freddie frolicked like a walrus, a dolphin, but one you couldn't see, while Peg sat under the umbrella, wore a straw hat with a big brim, and white slacks and sleeveless blouses (she wasn't a maniac on the subject), and read *Bleak House*. (Having been a dental technician had led Peg to the Good Books; she liked to give book reports aloud while working on her patients. They couldn't say anything anyway, their mouths being full of slender chrome instruments, so if Peg was going to be reduced to monologues, they might as well be on something worthwhile).

The morning after their encounter with the police chief in Dudley they spent up by the pool. Freddie swam sometimes, and other times lay out on a beach towel spread in the sun on the duckboard surround; he said he wasn't worried about getting a burn. Peg alternatively hung out with the lawyers in *Bleak House* or, whenever Freddie enthusiastically and invisibly cannonballed back into the pool, she watched that spectral surge as it lashed and plunged through the heaving water.

The sun was high, and she was just beginning to think about lunch, when she heard a car door slam. The chief! At once, she slapped down the book onto the table and jumped to her feet. The chief! He found us!

Of course, there was no way. Even if the chief knew their license number, which was unlikely, all it would lead him to was the address in Bay Ridge. Still, it was the chief she fully expected to face when she hurried to the fence and stared through the lattice, and so it was with great relief that she saw, moving away from his red car in the driveway toward the front of the house, the real estate agent, Call Me Tom. "Up here!" she cried, and waved her hand above the fence.

He looked back and up. "Oh, hi." Waving, he reversed his route.

Peg turned back to the pool, hissing, "Freddie! Freddie!"

He was already coming out of the pool, which she could

tell by the splashing, and then the wet footprints, and all those water drops suspended in the air, vaguely in the shape of a man.

"No, no!" She hurried toward him, with frantic shooing gestures. "Back in the pool!"

He went, dropping backwards, making a great splash, the idiot. Peg, shaking her head, ran over to open the wood-and-lattice door, just as Call Me Tom got there, smiling. He wore a short-sleeved white shirt with a pale green necktie, but he must have left his briefcase or sample book in the car. "Hi, Peg," he said. He was all the salesmen in the history of the world rolled into one and placed in bright sunlight, to see what would happen.

"Hi, Tom. Come on in."

"Thanks. Just checking, see how you're coming along," he said, as he entered the pool area.

"Fine, thanks."

He stopped and looked around. "Where's your friend?"

The footprints on the duckboards were fading fast in the dry sunny air. "He's in New York," Peg said. "He still has to work, poor guy."

"Oh. I thought . . ." Call Me Tom looked at the still-wet duckboards, the empty pool, the book on the table under the umbrella, and decided to give it up. "Catching up on your reading, eh?"

"Sure, why not? Good weather, nothing to do, no interruptions—"

"Except me," he said, and stopped smiling long enough to look sheepish.

"No, no, I didn't mean that," she assured him, though she had meant that, and they both knew it.

"Well, I won't take you away from your—oh, *Bleak House!* God, I read that years ago."

"First time for me."

"Jarndyce and Jarndyce," Call Me Tom said, and chuckled, and shook his head. "I could tell you some lawsuit stories," he threatened. "Real estate, it honestly brings out the worst in people, I believe that's true."

Beyond him, in Peg's line of sight, a wet forearm print appeared on the duckboard beside the pool. "You may be right," she said. "But not here, we're really happy with the place."

"I'm glad to hear it." Call Me Tom cast a look around, to be sure they were alone, and failed to notice the knee print that now appeared next to the forearm print. Nonetheless, he lowered his voice as he said, "You told me about the legal troubles your friend is having. The divorce and all."

It was hard for Peg to concentrate on what Call Me Tom was saying, when over his right shoulder she could see those wet footprints appearing one after the other along the duckboards on the other side of the pool. "The reason we're paying in cash and all that, you mean," she said.

"Exactly." Call Me Tom moved closer, being more confidential, as behind him a beach towel picked itself off a chair and whipped around madly and soundlessly in the air. Peg knew Freddie was doing this only because he was sore at the interruption, but it was so *dangerous*. "I just thought you ought to know," Call Me Tom murmured, managing to remain ebullient while expressing sympathy and concern and solidarity, "that I got a phone call this morning, first thing, some finance outfit in Syracuse, looking for *you*."

This made no sense. "Syracuse?" Peg repeated, astonished. "For *me?* I've never been in Syracuse in my life." Meantime, that damn towel was still doing its dance, as though Call Me Tom might not turn around at any second.

And yet he didn't. Maintaining eye contact with Peg, "My hunch is," he said, "it has something to do with your friend's divorce. *I* think they know the two of you rented a place somewhere around here, and they're calling all the brokers, trying to track you down."

The towel opened itself, sailed briefly, then made a magic-carpet landing on the duckboards. At the same time, Peg suddenly realized what that phone call must mean. "Oh, my God," she said. If she'd permitted her face to pick up any color before this, it would have drained away now.

"*You're* my client," Call Me Tom assured her. Parts of the beach towel flattened more than other parts. "I have no complaint with you, and I trust you have no complaint with me."

"Complaint? What complaint?" I must not get hysterical, Peg thought hysterically, and used up some of the tension by waving her arms around as she said, "Look at this great place you found us!"

"Well, thanks. It is nice, isn't it?" Call Me Tom said, and now he did turn in a half-circle, taking it all in: the day, the pool, the beach towel. Smiling at Peg some more, he said, "Mention me to your friends."

"I will."

"I got"—he took several folded pieces of paper from his pants pocket, went through them, selected one, put the rest away, and handed that one to Peg—"the fellow's name and phone number, in case you want to call him and tell him to leave you out of it all. Sometimes that works, when they're bothering somebody other than the person involved in the case."

"Good idea," Peg agreed, taking the piece of paper but not yet looking at it. She couldn't help herself; even with this bad news, her concentration was still broken by that goddam towel, lying there so innocently. I'm going to hit him with a stick, she promised herself, as she said, "I really appreciate this, Tom. Thanks a lot."

"Anytime. Well, I'll let you get back to your book."

They walked together over to the door in the pool-area

wall, Call Me Tom smiling at the scene, then frowning slightly. Had some corner of his brain noticed that there hadn't been a beach towel lying there in that position the last time he'd looked?

"I'll call Freddie tonight," Peg said, talking fast to distract him. "Tell him about this. He'll know what to do."

"Or his lawyer. Well, enjoy your summer," Call Me Tom said, and waved, and went away.

Peg stood inside the wall, door closed, and watched through the lattice as Call Me Tom returned to his car and backed it down the driveway. When, in the middle of that, a wet hand touched her arm, she didn't look around—what was the point in looking around?—but merely said, "I'm not speaking to you."

"He wasn't going to look away from those big eyes of yours, Peg. I get cold in the water after a while."

"It's a heated pool."

"Still. I seem colder, now I'm invisible. Anyway, it turned out our friend Barney set some skip-trace outfit loose on us, huh?"

Peg looked at the folded piece of paper in her hand, opened it, and read the names aloud: " 'Stephen Garmainster, Equity Research and Retrieval Corporation.' We aren't going to phone this guy."

"Barney's got some money behind him, to do this," Freddie said.

Call Me Tom was gone; pocketing the piece of paper, Peg walked back over to her chair and her table and her book. Freddie, from the sound of his voice, followed, saying, "This checking-account business you're gonna do. Better use the apartment in the city for the address."

"I'm glad Call Me Tom told us about it, anyway," Peg said, settling into her chair, resting a hand on her book, wishing she were back in nineteenth-century London.

"Yeah, well." The chair across the way recoiled from the table, then sagged.

Peg gave it a jaundiced look. "What do you think, he's after my body, that's the only reason he told me?"

"That's one possibility," Freddie agreed, from somewhere in the air. This was exactly the sort of thing Peg hated, she reminded herself, as he went on, "Another possibility is, he had a guilty conscience."

She frowned. "What kind of guilty conscience?"

"What if he *did* tell the guy something? Then afterward he thought it over, he thought, maybe you should at least get a warning."

"Oh, gee, Freddie, do you think so? Is that what it was all about?"

"I don't know. He's tough to read."

"*You're* one to talk."

"Yeah, but Call Me Tom's such a friendly guy, you can see him and you still can't see him."

"I don't think he'd lie about it," Peg said.

"I hope not." Freddie's voice floated in the air. "But, maybe, just to be on the safe side," he said, "we ought to each pack one little bag, leave it in the van. Just in case."

Peg sat there, alone but not alone. There were no more words from Freddie. Her hand rested on the book, but she didn't pick it up. The sun didn't seem as bright anymore.

33

"Not possible," Peter said, and David said, "What do you think we are?"

"Scientists," the lawyer Leethe said, which of course couldn't properly be refuted.

Still. "You come here unannounced," Peter began.

"Of course," Leethe said, shrugging his shoulders, playing the piano. "Had I called, you would have refused to see me."

"Absolutely," said David.

"Or insisted on your friend Cummingford being present."

"Our *attorney* Cummingford," Peter said.

They were standing together, all three, in the front hall, under the amused gaze of Shanana. When she'd buzzed up to them in the lab to say that Mordon Leethe had made an unexpected entry—rather like bubonic plague making an unexpected entry, that—they'd decided at once to come down here, meet the man as close to the front door as possible, and repel this invader before the pestilence could spread.

And now, when he'd told them the reason for his presence! He and his masters wanted Peter and David to make them another invisible man! Out of the question!

Peter said, "Don't you think enough trouble has been—"

"Excuse me," Leethe interrupted, stopping traffic with one raised palm. "I don't believe you're thinking this through as clearly as you might. We are talking here about volunteers, about the very experiment you were already undertaking, about—" He broke off and looked around. Almost plaintively, he said, "Couldn't we sit comfortably somewhere? In that nice lounge room upstairs?"

"We don't want you here at all," David said, but Peter had been listening more closely to Leethe's words, and so he asked, "What do you mean, volunteers?"

"I mean," Leethe said, "you needn't hold anyone at gunpoint."

Oh, dear, Shanana hadn't known about that. Her eyes were widening, weren't they? Yes, and her ears, too, no doubt. Peter said, "We can spare you five minutes. Come to the conference room."

"Oh, well," Leethe said, looking sad. "Mayn't I be permitted to sit in the nice lounge? Mr. Cummingford isn't present."

They both blinked at him. Peter said, "Did you say 'mayn't I'?"

Apparently surprised, touching his chin with a fingertip as though to identify himself for the onlookers, Leethe said, "So I did. Doesn't that mean I *deserve* the nice lounge?"

"Oh, very well," Peter said, rolling his eyes in David's direction. "Come along."

They went upstairs, and sat on the sofas the same way they had two weeks ago when Leethe had shown them Freddie Noon's police pictures. This time, no one offered the man refreshments; instead, Peter said, "Maybe you'd better explain this proposal."

"Certainly. You have two experimental medicines—"

"Formulae," Peter interrupted. "Not medicines, because untried."

"Very well, formulae. You had hoped that one or the other would help in the struggle against melanoma, but now you *know* that the two in combination create invisibility. You have in your possession an invisibility formula."

David said, "Peter, that's right! I never even thought about that." His mind had been too full of the other ramifications of the problem.

Peter was less thrilled. He said, "Go on, Mr. Leethe."

"NAABOR, for its own purposes, would like to employ the services of an invisible person," Leethe went on. "You, for your purposes, would like volunteers upon which to test your med—formulae. NAABOR is prepared to present you with two volunteers at this time, to be made invisible. As an inducement, NAABOR will undertake, in the near future, to provide you as many volunteers as you require for more normal study."

David, all agog, said, "Peter, do you think—?" But Peter was saying to Leethe, "What's the catch?"

"Catch?" Leethe smacked his right fist into a catcher's mitt, then tossed the ball into the dugout. "What catch can there possibly be? NAABOR will supply the volunteers, both now and for later, with all releases signed. You can observe your new guinea pigs, if you can be said to *observe* an invisible—"

"For how long?" Peter asked.

Leethe showed how long the fish was he'd almost caught. "How long do you want?"

"A week."

"Oh, come," Leethe said, reducing the fish to a minnow. "You were only hoping for twenty-four hours with the first one."

"The circumstances were different."

"We have a time consideration, on our side," Leethe admitted. "We could agree to forty-eight hours."

Peter considered that, then nodded. "Acceptable," he said,

then added, "We'll want a contract," and David looked stern and said, "That's right!"

"Of course," Leethe said.

"Prepared by Bradley Cummingford."

"Less work for me," Leethe said. "Why not phone him right now? The sooner we get the paperwork out of the way, the sooner we can get started, and the sooner we'll see some results." He smiled at himself. "Or not," he appended. "As the case may be."

34

It was Tuesday morning when Mordon Leethe put in his request for more invisibles; the rest of Tuesday, how those phones and faxes flew. Documents were drawn up, sent, revised, sent, argued over, sent, signed, and sent. Meanwhile, the vast machinery of NAABOR was grinding through who knew what contortions to select, approve, and induce the two volunteers. At last, at ten minutes past six that evening, in the lab, long after Shanana had left for the day and Bradley's last contractual nit had been picked, David put down a retort and answered the telephone himself, to hear someone say, "This is Ms. Clarkson from Personnel, wishing to speak to either—"

"I beg your pardon?"

"—Dr. Loo—I say, this is Ms. Clarkson from Personnel, and I wish to speak—"

"What personnel? I don't know what you mean."

"Is this the Loomis—"

"Heimhocker, yes."

"I'd like to speak to—"

"This is Dr. Loomis."

"—either Doctor Loo—oh. *You're* Dr. Loomis."

"I know who I am," David said. "Who are *you?*"

"Ms. Clarkson of Personnel, as I *believe* I said before."

From across the lab, Peter said, "Who is it, David?"

"I'm trying to find out," David told him, and into the phone he said, "I'm sorry, I have no idea what you're talking about. What is personnel?"

"The department I'm in!"

"Department? Macy's?" Away from the phone: "Peter? Did we order anything from Macy's?"

"The department of *NAABOR*!" screamed the woman.

"I don't think so," Peter said.

"Oh, for heaven's sake," David told the phone. "Why didn't you say so?"

"I thought I had." The woman seemed to be panting now.

"Well, you didn't," David said.

There was a little silence down the phone line then, which David didn't intrude on, having nothing to say—*she* was the one who'd made the call, after all—and then, in a much more controlled manner, she said, "May I speak to Dr. Heimhocker, please."

"Of course," David said, and held the phone out toward Peter, saying, "It's for you."

Peter approached, hand out. "Who is it?"

"Somebody from NAABOR. It's you she wants to talk to."

"Huh." Peter took the phone, spoke briefly into it, wrote a couple of things on the pad near the phone, then said, "Fine. Thank you very much. Good-bye," and hung up.

David said, "What *was* that all about?"

"Our volunteers. They'll be here at nine tomorrow morning."

"Oh, the volunteers!" David clapped his hands. "Peter, it's actually going to happen!"

"It would seem so."

David gave him a look. "Peter," he said, "I know we're both being calm and collected about all this, but in fact, it is *very* exciting."

"I suppose it is," Peter said. "And especially for"—he

added, looking at the names he'd written on the pad—
"Michael Prendergast and George Clapp."

George Clapp was black, but that wasn't the surprise. The surprise was that Michael Prendergast was a woman. And a beautiful woman at that, astonishingly beautiful in her flowered
summer dress, a tanned and healthy blonde of about twenty-
five, the Playmate of the decade, with bright blue eyes and delicious cheekbones and a body as strokable as a kitten's.

George Clapp on the other hand was probably forty years
of age and barely five feet tall. A skinny gnarly sort of guy, he
wore a shiny black suit, thin black tie, white shirt, and big
black river-barge shoes. His skin was a dull brown. Two thick
ropes of old scar tissue angled across his face, from just under
his right eye down his right cheek, across his chin and on
down to the side of his neck under his left ear.

Beforehand, Peter and David had decided to speed the
process by each doing the preliminary interview with one
subject. Peter had drawn Michael, so he took her up to the sitting room that Mordon Leethe craved so much. As they sat
facing one another on the sofas there, Peter took her through
her medical history, and he simply couldn't find anything
wrong. Not a junkie, no history of mental problems, no serious or chronic illnesses. Married twice, divorced twice, never
pregnant. Healthy siblings, healthy parents, healthy grandparents. Finishing, Peter said, "This is not a question on the form,
but I feel I have to ask it, anyway."

"Why, you mean," she said.

"Yes. You do understand what the idea is here, don't you?"

"Perfectly," she said. "I am a willing volunteer in a medical
experiment, at the end of which I either will or will not be invisible." She smiled briefly, a dazzling sight. "My guess is
that I will not be," she said, "but I don't want to spoil anybody's fun."

"Thank you."

"The corporation I work for is paying me a great deal of money over my remaining lifetime, no matter what happens with the experiment. If it turns out I *am* invisible, they'll have other well-paying uses for me."

"So you're doing it for money," Peter said. He felt vaguely disappointed.

"Not entirely," she said. "Dr. Heimhocker, would you say I'm attractive?"

"Anybody would say you're attractive," Peter told her. "You're probably the most beautiful woman I've ever been in the same room with. You understand you aren't my type—"

She smiled, and nodded.

"—but I certainly recognize beauty when I see it. Which is really why I'm asking the question. Why risk what—why risk anything?"

"Doctor," she said, "I am a nuclear physicist and a theoretical mathematician. I was third in my class at MIT, but when I left school I simply could not find a job to match my capabilities. My record was enough to get me many interviews, but that was always the end of it. Women hate me. Men find it impossible to think when I'm around. Today I am a drudge in the statistical section of the American Tobacco Research Institute, bending the cancer numbers. It's the equivalent of you being a janitor in a hospital."

"Surely," Peter said, "it can't be—"

"As bad as that? Which of us is living my life, Doctor?"

"You are," Peter said.

"Nobody has ever *seen* me," she said. "Seen *me*. Neither of my husbands ever saw me; they both felt cheated whenever that trophy on the shelf acted as though it were an actual living creature. The last time my looks gave me pleasure I was probably nine years old. I can't scar myself deliberately, that would be stupid. But this? Why not? No one can see me anyway, so why not be invisible? Make the rest of my life a phone-in? With pleasure." That dazzling smile had something too shiny in it. "Let's hope your invention is a success, Dr. Heimhocker," she said.

Meantime, in the conference room downstairs, David was having a very different conversation with George Clapp, who didn't so much have a medical history as a medical anthology. He had been shot, he had been stabbed, many of his bones had been broken in accidents and fights. He had been an alcoholic and drug addict, but had been clean—he swore—for six years. "After thirty-five, man," he said, "either it's killed you, or you get tired of it. I got tired of it."

"Any diseases?" David asked.

"Name it," George said.

David did, and George had at one time or another suffered from just about every nonfatal disease known to man, but was now passably healthy. He was a chauffeur with NAABOR, had been for the last four years, and when David asked him what had decided him to volunteer for this experiment George said, "This just between us?"

"Oh, of course," David said, and put down his pen.

"Couple states, they still got paper out on me," George explained. "Texas and Florida, you know, they're these death-penalty places, they like to kill people. Now, I'm not saying I *done* what they say, but the way I look at it, we leave them there sleeping dogs lie, we ain't gonna get bit. You see what I mean?"

"I think so," David said.

"All the time, these days," George said, "I'm kinda scared. I figure, some cop gonna pull me over, when I'm chauffeurin, you know, they run the computer on me, bang, my ass is in the southland. This way, if what you're gonna do works out, I'm home and dry. They can't fry what they can't see, am I right?"

"Oh, I'm sure you are," David said.

"And if it don't work, what you're doin here," George said, and spread his hands, his big smile making that awful scar writhe like a brown snake across his face, "they *still* gonna pay me so much money I don't ever hafta work again unless I don't want to. A cop that can't see me can't compute me, don't that make sense?"

David worked his way through the negatives, and finally nodded. "I believe it does," he said.

35

"Forty-eight hours exactly," Mordon said on Friday morning, when the doctors emerged from their elevator and came forward to meet him once again in their front hall. "I'm here to see your results. Or should I say, not see them?"

"No, you'll see them, all right," Heimhocker said.

Now Mordon looked more closely at the doctors, and realized they were not at all cheerful. They did not look like men who'd just had a triumph. They looked, in fact, quite glum. Shaking his head, thinking already how unpleasant it would be to bring bad news to Jack the Fourth, Mordon said, "You failed?"

"They aren't invisible," Heimhocker said, and Loomis, extremely defensive, said, "Which doesn't mean we *failed*. The experiment had too many variables."

"Exactly," Heimhocker said. "Without Freddie Noon, without knowing exactly when he took the second formula, what else he ate or drank that night, what he *did* the rest of the night, there's no possible way to duplicate the experiment, and therefore no possible way to duplicate the results."

"If that's the case," Mordon said, opening a combination lock, "why didn't you mention it before?"

"We didn't know it before, obviously," Loomis said, and Heimhocker said, "It was worth the effort, we've certainly learned from the experience. We now know, for instance, that we do not have a guaranteed invisibility formula."

"This is very bad news," Mordon said, wringing a washcloth. "Where are the volunteers?"

"In the conference room," Heimhocker said, and Loomis said, "Did you want to see them?"

Mordon had met the two volunteers briefly Tuesday afternoon, while the details were being worked out. Did he want to see them again? He wasn't sure. His hands fluttered by a buddleia bush, looking for pollen, and he said, "What do they look like now? Did it do nothing at all? Or do they look like the cats?"

"Not a bit like the cats," Loomis said, and Heimhocker said, "Nor like one another. Until we can study Freddie Noon, the only thing we can say is that the combination of formulae is both volatile and unpredictable."

"That doesn't sound good," Mordon said. "Are they likely to sue?"

"I doubt it," Heimhocker said, and Loomis said, "Come see for yourself."

"Perhaps I'd better."

Mordon followed the two doctors back to the conference room, that unlovely fluorescent-lit space, where a tan man in a blue bathrobe sat playing solitaire. He looked up when they entered, smiled at the doctors, then looked at Mordon and said, "You're one of the lawyers. I remember you."

Mordon approached him. "Well, I don't remember *you*," he said. This was hardly the George Clapp he'd met three days ago in NAABOR's corporate offices in the World Trade Center. This fellow was several shades lighter and several years younger. And—good God. Mordon said, "Where's the scar?"

"Gone," George Clapp said, and grinned. "All my scars went away, all over my body. Aches and pains gone. I feel like I'm nineteen years old."

Mordon turned wide-eyed to the doctors, and Loomis said, "It ate the scar tissue everywhere on his body."

Heimhocker said, "Fasting will do this, too, over a long term. When the body has nothing else to eat, it will eat its own dead tissue. But I've never heard of it happening this fast."

Clapp put down the deck of cards, lifted his hands palm out, grinned all over his face, and said, "Tell him about my prints."

"Yes, his fingerprints," Heimhocker said, and Loomis said, "We put their fingerprints on their medical sheets," and Heimhocker said, "George's have changed," and Loomis said, "They're much simpler and fainter than they were. Not at all the same."

"*Run* that computer on me," Clapp said, and laughed.

Mordon said, "And the woman? Miss Prendergast? Did it do the same to her?"

"Not exactly," Heimhocker said, and Loomis said to Clapp, "Where is she, anyway?"

"Went to the ladies'. She'll be back."

Heimhocker said to Mordon, "Her fingerprints didn't change. As I say, this formula is so unknown, we're not sure *what* it will do."

"Not without Freddie Noon," Mordon said. "I take the point."

"Precisely," Heimhocker said, and movement behind Mordon made him turn around.

Michael Prendergast had come in. Mordon stared at her. "Oh, my God," he breathed. His hands didn't move.

She was no longer the lushly healthy California-style beauty Mordon had met on Tuesday. Her skin was pale and pink now, almost translucent. A kind of ethereal glow surrounded her, as though she were an angel, or one of the lost maidens mourned by Poe. She looked fragile, unworldly, uncarnal, and absolutely stunning. She was ten times the beauty she had been before.

"Ms. Prendergast," Mordon stammered, poleaxed. "You are the most beautiful thing I have ever seen in my life!"

She burst into tears.

36

"Hold still," Peg said.

"I am holding still," Freddie said, though of course he wasn't.

Peg knew he was twitching because the brush tickled him, particularly under the nose, but there was no help for that. He just had to stand it for a minute, the baby. "I don't want to stick this brush in your nose," she pointed out.

"That makes two of us," he said.

The problem was cabin fever. It does exist, and not just in snowbound log huts in the frozen north. You can have cabin fever in a nice house in upstate New York in the summer, too, even with a swimming pool and a VCR and all the rest of it, if you can't *go* anywhere.

They both felt the same way about this. That is, Peg felt this way, and Freddie assured her he did, too.

So it was time to do something about it. And the something was a meal in a restaurant, a nice candlelit dinner that did not come out of their own kitchen. A restaurant meal was all either of them asked for. That was all, in fact, that either of them talked about or thought about these days. They had all this money, they had all this leisure, they were living in the middle of a resort and vacation area speckled with charming restaurants, and all they did was eat at home, and not even together. In separate rooms, gloomily, not even shouting stuff to one another anymore.

How to do it. How to have a nice dinner out. They could always go for drives, with Freddie inside one of his heads, but he couldn't very well eat a meal with a latex head on, and if he took it off in the restaurant there'd *really* be hell to pay.

He even volunteered at one point to just come along and escort her and sit there and watch her eat, only pretending to join in the meal himself, but she wouldn't let him do it. It would drive them both crazy, and she knew it.

So here was the idea. It had come to her this morning when she woke up, three days after Call Me Tom had come by with his warning that the forces of evil were still out and about. "Hmmmmm," she said, sitting up.

"Nothing's happened yet," the voice of Freddie said, from over by the dresser. "So maybe Call Me Tom did keep his mouth shut."

"Of course he did," Peg said, looking at a different corner of the room. "I told you he would. And I got an idea."

"What kind of an idea?"

"A way, maybe, maybe a way we can go out and have dinner somewhere."

"Peg?" Hope and skepticism battled in his voice. "Are you serious?"

"I think we could try it."

"Try what, Peg?"

"Makeup," she said.

"What?" Now disappointment and scorn battled there in that voice. "Come on, Peg."

This time she looked directly toward where she thought he probably stood. "Women wear makeup all the time," she explained.

"Not all over their face," Freddie objected.

"That's what you know. There are women you see on the

street, in stores, you aren't seeing one speck of their actual facial skin, not their real face, not even a teeny little bit. Maybe some of the forehead, but that's it."

"Are you putting me on, Peg?"

"We are talking about women," Peg went on, "who wake up in the morning all wrinkled, and when they leave the house there's no wrinkles on their faces at all. *That's* the kind of makeup I mean."

"And you could do my whole face?"

"Sure. And your neck, and your ears. That's not normally done, but I don't see why not. And we'll buy you a wig."

"What about my hands? Can I eat with makeup all over my hands?"

"Oh," Peg said, and suddenly crashed. "No, you can't." She hadn't thought about his goddam hands. A great weight that had just begun to lift from her shoulders now dropped down on her again, heavier than ever. "Forget it," she said. Slumped in seated position on the bed, she sighed and said, "Nobody's gonna think those Playtex gloves are real hands, not up close in a restaurant."

There was a little silence, in which she gazed at nothing at all, and then he said, "Burns."

She frowned in his general direction. "What?"

"What I'll do," he said, "I'll explain to the waiter, whoever, when I go in. I got burned, I got scalded or something, I got ointment on, I gotta wear these gloves."

The smile that spread across Peg's features was like daybreak. "Could you do that, Freddie? Say that?"

"Why not? Could you do the thing with the makeup?"

"Why not?" she said, and bounded out of bed with fresh enthusiasm and hope.

Makeup was easy. In a drugstore—not in Dudley—while Freddie waited in the van, Peg went through the displays of

Cover Girl and Max Factor. Freddie would have to wear sunglasses in the restaurant, of course—another result of that horrible accident that so messed up his hands—but the eyebrows would show (or not show), so she bought black and brown eyebrow pencils, on the assumption that if she painted his invisible eyebrows, the color would show on top of the invisible hairs, and look realistic enough for a dim-lit restaurant after dark.

Let's see, what else? Skin-tone lipstick. Blush. But not too much stuff; she wasn't up for a night on the town with Bozo the Clown. So she paid for her purchases—they were paying for everything these days, they were gonna need some more cash soon—and went back out to the van. It was parked under a tree down the block, windows open, Freddie invisible in back. "Now the wig," she said, sliding behind the wheel, as though that would be just as easy.

No. Men's wigs were not easy. They were expensive, and there weren't very many places that sold them, and they had to be fitted. That last was the killer.

They were driving around, Freddie consulting various telephone Yellow Pages in the back of the van, and it wasn't looking good. "There *are* places," he said, "they say here for chemotherapy patients and like that, but they all say 'fitting.'"

"Women's wigs are easier, I guess," Peg said, driving aimlessly around Columbia County, "because they've got more hair and they can do different styles and things."

"I dunno, Peg," Freddie said. He was sounding gloomy again. "I don't think I can go as Kojak," he said, "with makeup all over my whole head."

"I don't think so, either," she agreed, and thought a while as she drove, and then she said, "I think I got an idea. Another idea. Can you find a shopping mall in those Yellow Pages?"

"What's the idea?"

"I'll tell you later," she said, because she was afraid he'd say no if he knew what it was.

He said, "You're afraid I'll say no."

"No, come on, Freddie, it's just to be a surprise, that's all. Find me a mall."

From where they were at that moment, the nearest mall was over in Massachusetts, in the Berkshires, miles and miles away. They went there, and of course there were no trees or shade of any kind in the parking lot, baking in the July sun, so Peg said, "I'll be as quick as I can," and left both windows open, so he wouldn't roast in there.

She was as quick as she could be, and came back with a purchase in a plain brown paper bag. When she got into the van Freddie said, "Some guy tried to steal the radio."

"Freddie! He did?" The radio, she saw, was still there. "What'd you do?"

"I guess he figured," Freddie said, "the windows being open, might as well. So he got in, and he lay down on the seat there, facedown, so he could reach under the dash."

She had the windows rolled up now, and the engines and air-conditioning on, but she didn't drive yet. "Yeah?"

"So first I picked his pocket," Freddie said, "and then I pulled his hair."

She giggled. "You did? What'd he do?"

"He jumped, and hit his head on the steering wheel, and sat up, and looked all around, and then he decided it wasn't anything and he was gonna go back to the radio again, so I tapped him on the shoulder and when he looked back I poked him in the eye."

"Ooh," she said. "That wasn't nice."

"He's boosting our radio, Peg."

"Well, then what?"

"He *still* didn't get out of the van," Freddie said. "He had one hand up over his eye, like he's reading the eye-chart, and he's lookin around and lookin around with the other eye, and I figured, time to make this guy get out of here, so I slapped him on both ears at the same time. The palms, you know, *whack* against both ears. You know what that's like?"

"I'm not sure I want to know."

"It's like a firecracker went off in the middle of your head," Freddie told her. He didn't sound at all penitent. "So *then* he got out of the van."

"I bet he did."

"And took off running. I bet he's halfway to New Jersey by now. What's in the bag, Peg?"

"I'll show you when we get home," she said, and shifted into "drive," and steered out of the parking lot.

"Pretty crummy wallet that guy had," Freddie commented from the back, once they were on the road. There came the sound of money rustling, and then, his voice disgusted, Freddie said, "Twenty-seven dollars."

"I was just thinking," Peg said, as she watched the road, "we'll need more money soon."

"Off of radio-stealing guys at the mall is not where we'll get it," Freddie commented. "We'll make another trip to the city. Open your window a little, will you?"

She opened her window a little, and a pretty crummy wallet sailed past her ear and out onto the roadway. She shut the window, and they drove on.

He did *not* want to wear the wig, just as she'd expected. "It looks like a horse's tail," he said. "And the horse's tail goes on top of the horse's ass, and that ain't me."

"It isn't that bad, Freddie," she insisted, even though his description was more or less accurate.

The thing is, for women, but not for men, there are inexpensive wigs for sale in low-cost department stores, many of them with a famous person's name attached, like Zsa Zsa Gabor. Most of these wigs are short and curly, like the Zsa Zsa Gabor, but a few are long and straight, like the Cher. The one Peg had chosen was long and straight, shoe-polish black, thick coarse fake hair coming down from a narrow almost invisible part in the middle. If you were to cut it a little shorter, and wear it with armor, you could look like a roadshow Prince Valiant.

"I am *not*," Freddie announced, "gonna wear that thing. I'd rather make believe I was scalped by the Indians."

"They don't do that anymore, Freddie," Peg said. "In fact, I think it hurts their feelings if you remind them."

"I am not gonna wear that thing."

"Listen to my idea, will you?"

"I'll listen," Freddie agreed, "and then I still won't wear it. But I'll listen."

"Thanks, Freddie," she said, once again wasting sarcasm on an invisible man. "What we'll do," she told him, "we'll make up your face first, and then we'll fit the wig to see how it works, with these Velcro things on the inside here to get the size right, see them?"

"Oh, God, Peg."

"*Then*," she insisted, "I'll cut some of the hair off, to shape it a little, and we'll put it in a ponytail, with a rubber band. There's a lot of guys going around with ponytails."

"Wimps. Nerds. Guys with peace signs on their four-by-fours."

"Not all of them. Now, come on, Freddie, cooperate with me on this. It's worth a try, isn't it?"

"If I'm gonna look like an idiot," he warned her, "I won't do it."

"Freddie," she said, "if you look like anything at *all*, it'll be a step forward. Now sit down, and let me start." She waited, hands on hips. "Go on, don't argue anymore, just sit down."

"I am sitting down," he said.

Slowly, stroke by stroke, the face began to appear. It was like magic, or like a special effect in the movies. Cheeks, nose, jaws, all emerging out of the air, the slightly woodsy tan color of Max Factor pancake makeup. Freddie complicated matters by flinching away from the brush a lot, and even sneezing twice, but nevertheless, slowly and steadily, they progressed.

Partway along, with just the major areas roughed in, the forehead and on down, Peg reared back to study him, and said, "I don't remember you like that."

"Like what?"

"That that's the way you look. Freddie? I think I'm beginning to forget what you look like."

The parts of the face that now existed contrived to express surprise. "You know what?" he said. "Me, too. I was just thinking this morning, when I was shaving. I'm not sure *I* really remember what I look like, either. If I saw me on the street, I don't know that I'd recognize me."

"This is really strange, Freddie."

"It is. You don't have any pictures of me, do you, Peg?"

She shook her head. "Of course not. You never wanted any pictures, remember? You said they didn't go with your lifestyle."

"Well, I guess that's true, they didn't."

"Maybe what we'll do," she suggested, "when we get you all set here, I'll take a Polaroid."

The partial face now conveyed extreme skepticism. "It's gonna come out that good, huh?"

"Let's wait and see," she said, and went back to work with the brush.

"It doesn't look half bad," she said.

Then I must be looking at the other half," he told her.

They were standing together in the bedroom, in front of the floor-length mirror on the closet door, Peg and the Creature from the Fifties Horror Movie. With that sandalwood skin color, and sort of pinkish-gray lips, and bristly dark eyebrows (the paint had stiffened the eyebrow hairs), and the black fake hair swagged around his ears—the ears were a bitch to make up, with all those curls and convolutions—and the dark *dark* sunglasses, he didn't actually appear to be a human being at all. The way drag queens manage to stop looking like men without ever really looking like women, Freddie now looked as though he might be some sort of extraterrestrial in human drag. Or as though the Disney people had decided, next to their moving lifesize Abraham Lincoln doll at Disneyland, to put a Bobby Darin doll.

Peg was determined to put the best possible face on things, even if the best possible face was this store-window Freddie. "We're talking about after dark," she pointed out, "in a restaurant. Freddie, we've got to at least give it a try."

"Well, I'm all dressed up," he acknowledged, the pancake furrowing on his brow. "Might as well go for it."

"Thank you, Freddie."

"But, Peg."

"Yeah?"

"We can skip the Polaroid," Freddie said.

Peg called five different restaurants before she found one that sounded like it would work out okay. Yes, they prided themselves on their dim candlelit romantic atmosphere. Yes, they had high-backed booths, if that was what madam would prefer. Yes, they understood that madam's husband had been in an industrial explosion recently and was self-conscious about his appearance these days, and this would be his first time out in public since he came home from the hospital, and they would bend every effort to make his dining at the Auberge a pleasant and relaxing experience. And would that be smoking or nonsmoking? "Are you kidding?" Peg asked. "After my husband's explosion?"

"Nonsmoking, then. See you at nine, madam."

There are three kinds of restaurants in the country. There are the joints that are really just bars with kitchens, and that's where the local citizenry goes. There are places that try to be trendy by doing what the city restaurants were doing ten years ago, and that's where the weekenders and the summer people go. And there are very pretentious places with dim echoes of Maxim's, with tassels on the huge menus and too much flour in the sauces and too much sugar in the salads, and that's where everybody takes Mother on her birthday.

It wasn't Freddie's birthday, but here they were. It was true the maître d' was in a tux, and true the busboy sported a bow tie, and true the waitress was dressed like Marie Antoinette in her milkmaid phase, but these were people who were used to making mothers feel at home away from home on that special day, so they were very good with an explosion victim, hardly looking at Freddie's gloved hands at all, not acknowledging by word or glance that there might be anything odd about his face, and not even acting surprised when he moved and talked like a normal human being.

They were shown to a dim booth in a corner, high-backed purple plush seating, dark paisley tablecloth, and a low candle inside a gnarly glass chimney of such thickness and such dark amberness that the light it produced looked mostly like the last sputtering effort of energy from a galaxy that had died long long ago, on the other side of the universe.

"We can be happy here," Peg decided.

"I can't see my menu," Freddie complained.

"Good. That means your menu can't see you, either."

"Aw, Peg, is it that bad?"

"No, Freddie," she lied, reaching out to take his Playtex and give it a squeeze. "I was just doing a gag."

Through experimentation, they learned that if they held their menus just so, there was almost enough illumination from the indirect lighting in troughs up near the ceiling so they could make out a lot of the words flowingly scripted there. But then it turned out, when Marie Antoinette came back, that they hardly needed to think about the menus anyway, since she had forty-two specials to describe.

Slowly, Peg relaxed, grew easier in her mind. Slowly, she got back into the swing of things, the idea of being out at a restaurant for a nice dinner with your guy, and candlelight, and even pretty good music piped in, ballet stuff, Delibes, and like that. They ordered drinks, and they ordered wine, and they ordered special appetizers and special main courses, and they began to talk together like any normal couple out on a date, discussing the house they were living in, and how the summer was shaping up, and what they might do the next time they dropped in to the city to develop some fresh cash, and the whole evening was just being very nice.

Their drinks came. An extraspecial little treat from the chef came, being a kind of pâté on toast points that wasn't half bad. Their wine came, and Freddie forgot to be self-conscious while he went through the tasting-and-approving ritual. They toasted one another, and Freddie said, "I'm glad you talked me into this, Peg."

"Me, too," Peg said. "I love to be with you, Freddie, but not in the same place all the time."

"To getting out and about," he said, gripping his wineglass with some little difficulty. They clinked glasses, and drank.

Their appetizers came. They ate; they had a little more wine; they made funny remarks and laughed at them. The busboy in the bow tie cleared, and here came the main courses. Everything was just great.

Peg looked up, at the wrong moment. Halfway through the meal, eating and drinking had by now removed almost all of Freddie's lipstick, plus some of the makeup around his mouth. When Peg looked up, therefore, at precisely the wrong moment, with Freddie's mouth open and a forkful of food on its way, what she saw was a guy with a hole in the middle of his face, and in the hole she could just make out, way back there, the inside of the wig.

Peg closed her eyes. For good measure, she put one hand over her eyes. I'll forget that sight, she promised herself. Sooner or later, I'll forget what that looked like.

In the meantime, there were other considerations to consider. "Freddie," Peg said quietly, "when the waitress is around, keep your head down."

Instead of which, startled, he lifted his head. Amber candle-glow glanced dully off those dark sunglasses. Peg refused to look lower than the sunglasses, as Freddie said, "Peg? A problem?"

"A little. We'll take care of it. You go ahead and eat."

"What is it, Peg?"

"You're losing a little makeup, not bad. No point fixing it now, we'll do it when we're done eating."

"Now I'm nervous," Freddie said.

"We're both nervous, Freddie."

"No no," he said, "that's not what I mean. I'm not used anymore to people seeing me, Peg, you know? I'm like a teenager again, self-conscious, afraid people are staring at me."

"Nobody's staring at you," Peg promised him. "Believe me, if anybody was staring at you, we'd know."

"I don't want to know what you mean by that."

"Just eat," she advised.

Neither of them had much to say after that, though they both tried to recapture the spirit. But awkwardness had taken a seat at table with them, and wouldn't get up.

Peg did the talking with the waitress after that, saying the meal had been delicious, thank you, politely refusing dessert and coffee, asking for the check. All while Freddie posed like *The Thinker* with his gloved fist against his jaw on the waitress's side.

After Marie Antoinette went away to get the check, Peg slipped Freddie the little zipper bag containing his lipstick and makeup, and he went off to the gents' to reconstruct himself. That's what the girl does, Peg thought, not the guy, and decided not to pursue that thought, and then Marie brought the check.

Peg was counting out cash into the little tray when Freddie returned. Standing beside the table, he said, "Okay now?"

She considered him, squinting a bit. "It'll do to get to the car," she decided.

Freddie gave her back the makeup bag. "A guy in there saw me putting on the lipstick," he said.

"Did he make a remark?"

"I think he was going to, so I smiled at him, and he went away."

"I bet he did."

Freddie sighed. "Peg," he said. "I'm turning into something you scare little kids with."

Not just little kids, Peg thought, but she wasn't mean enough to say that out loud. "So we'll keep you away from playgrounds," she said instead. Getting to her feet, the bill paid, she said, "Lighten up, Freddie. Didn't we have fun tonight?"

"Yes," he said, without enthusiasm.

She took his long-sleeved arm, twined hers around it. At least he still *felt* like Freddie. "Pretty soon," she murmured, as they headed toward the exit, "we'll be back in our own bed, in the dark, without a care in the world."

"*That* sounds good."

The maître d' wished to bid them farewell, and wanted to know how they'd enjoyed the experience. "Let me do the talking," Peg muttered out of the side of her mouth, and then she praised the maître d' and the ambiance and the food and the service and the thoughtfulness of everybody concerned, until the maître d' squirmed all over with pleasure, like a heat shimmer. Then they left the place and crunched across the gravel parking lot in the dark, and at last got into the van.

"Oh, boy," Freddie said, sighing, sagging back against the passenger seat.

"It was worth the try," Peg said.

"I guess it was. Yeah, you're right, it was."

"Needs fine-tuning," she suggested.

"Back to the drawing board," he agreed.

"But we proved it's possible."

He thought about that. "Okay," he decided at last. "Not probable yet, but possible. But I tell you, Peg," and before she could react he'd reached up and whipped the wig right off his head and into his lap, "this wig here is *hot*."

There wasn't much light in the Auberge's parking lot, but there didn't have to be. Peg looked at him, at the makeup and the lipstick and the eyebrow pencil and the sunglasses, and then above that at nothing, and all at once, astonishing herself, she started to laugh. Then she couldn't stop laughing.

Freddie looked at her. "Yeah?" he asked. "What?"

"Oh, Freddie!" she cried, through her laughter. "I do love you, Freddie, I do love to be with you, but oh, my God, Freddie, right now, you look like a Toby jug!"

37

The funeral was on Sunday. Wouldn't you know it? Spoiled the entire Fourth of July weekend, putting the funeral on Sunday the second. Can't do anything before it, can't do anything after it, have to *stay in town*. You might as well be poor, or something.

It was three-thirty on Friday afternoon when Shanana buzzed upstairs, to where Peter and David were just beginning to pack. Mordon Leethe had at last departed, taking the volunteers with him, George Clapp practically singing "Happy Days Are Here Again" and Michael Prendergast weeping bitter buckets, and now Peter and David could prepare to leave, having been invited to Robert and Martin's place way up in the Hudson Valley for the holiday weekend. Then the distinctive buzz of the in-house phone line sounded, and they both looked over at it, and for some reason, some inexplicable reason, something told David to say, "Don't answer it."

Peter gave him a scoffing look. "Don't answer it? Why not?"

"I don't know, something just told me to say that. A premonition or something."

Peter shook his head. "And you call yourself a scientist," he said, and picked up the phone, and said, "Yes, Shanana, what is it? Put him on." Cupping the mouthpiece, he told David, "Amory," then said into the phone, "Archer, how are you?"

David moved closer to Peter and the phone, forgetting his premonition. Dr. Archer Amory, head of NAABOR's research and development program, was their only real link to the tobacco industry that funded them, if you didn't count the attorney, Mordon Leethe, and David certainly did *not* count that fellow. This was the first they'd heard from Dr. Amory since they'd turned to him with their invisible man problem a month ago and he'd passed them on to Mordon Leethe, who had told them, in an unnecessarily harsh manner, that NAABOR (and Dr. Amory, by implication) had "cut them loose."

And now here was Archer Amory on the phone, and Peter was listening, looking somber, saying, "Oh, too bad," saying, "Let me write that down." He jotted something on the pad beside the phone, said, "Thank you, Archer," said, "Yes, we'll see you there," and hung up. Then he just stood there and brooded for a while.

"Peter? Peter, may one know?"

Peter started, as though from a trance. "Oh," he said. "Sorry. Jack Fullerton is dead."

"Who?"

"The Fourth."

"*Who?*"

"The head of NAABOR, the man who ran it."

"Oh." David shrugged. "So what?"

"The funeral is Sunday."

"Yes?"

"We're expected to go."

David stared. "Sunday? *This* Sunday? The day after tomorrow?"

"Yes, of course. He died this morning. On the toilet, apparently."

"Peter, we can't go to a funeral on Sunday, we're spending the weekend with Robert and Martin!"

"Amory said the new head man specifically asked that we be there," Peter said, and the in-house line buzzed again. Peter raised an eyebrow at David. "Any more premonitions?"

"That last one was right, wasn't it? Go ahead and answer, apparently the weekend's ruined anyway."

"Apparently. Yes, Shanana? Yes, put him on." Cupping the mouthpiece, "Bradley," he told David, meaning of course their own wonderful attorney, Bradley Cummingford, and then into the phone Peter said, "Hello, Bradley. Yes, we just heard. Yes, Archer Amory said so. No, I have no idea. Yes, I suppose we must. Will you be—? No, I see, of course not. Well, say hello to Robert and Martin for us. And the whole gang. Yes, do that. We'll think of you, too, dear." Hanging up, Peter said to David, "Bradley says we should go to the funeral."

"We never even *knew* the man."

"Nevertheless."

David stamped his foot, a thing he did rarely. "I will *not* wear black," he said.

They were both in light gray, like the sky. Hazy, hot, and humid had been the forecast, and for once the Weather Service had gotten it right. The whole funeral party looked dead.

The initial proceedings took place in a Park Avenue church of so high and refined a tone their fax number was unlisted. Though of course Gentile, it was too genteel to admit to a specific denomination, and would certainly not have permitted itself to be named after any grubby sheet-wearing saint: The Church of Lenox Hill was good enough, thank you. A brownstone pile taking up half a really good Park Avenue block, surmounted by a few spires, it steered a delicate course between Roman Catholic–cathedral ostentation and Methodist-chapel humility, managing to make itself and everyone connected with it seem utterly insincere from any angle.

The sidewalk out front, when David and Peter emerged from their taxi, was dense with smokers, all puffing away in the heat-haze, a miasma rising from them into the dank air like the fog over a city dump, their low conversations polka-dotted with coughs. Hoping the interior of the church would be cooler, knowing its air would at least be cleaner, David and Peter made their way through the undulous crowd and up the steps to the main arched entrance, where a burly tough-looking man with a clipboard asked their names, checked them off on his list, and said, "You'll be in car three."

"Oh, we're not going to the cemetery," David said.

The man with the clipboard gave him an unadorned look. "Yes, you are."

"But—" David said, and felt Peter's hand squeeze his arm. He permitted Peter, by that hand, to steer him past the tough fellow with the clipboard, and heard Peter, behind his back, say to the man, "Car three. Got it."

On into the church, high-ceilinged, dim, and relatively cool. Peter released David's arm, and David hissed, "What was *that* all about?"

"Something's going on," Peter told him, quietly. "They insisted we come here, and now they're putting us in car three. They don't count those cars from the *back*, David, think about it. We're being treated like VIPs."

"I don't want to be a VIP. I want to be in North Dudley with Robert and Martin."

"Some other time. For now, let's keep our eyes open and our mouths shut."

And here came a slender young blond woman in a snug black above-the-knee dress. She too carried a clipboard and wanted to know their names, and when Peter responded, she led them to a pew very near the front on the right side. There was no one else yet in that pew—all out front, no doubt—so David and Peter sat down and looked around and watched the church gradually fill.

When Harry Cohn, the tyrannical well-loathed head of Columbia Pictures in the thirties and forties, finally passed away, there was a huge turnout at his funeral, which led Red Skelton to comment, "It just goes to prove the old saying. Give the people what they want, they'll come out for it." On that basis, the demise of Jack Fullerton the Fourth had to be considered a resounding success. Slowly the church filled, with more and more coughers, but fill it did, with men and women and even children in expensive dark garb, all maintaining a low decorous hum in deference to the surroundings, and not a wet eye in the house.

Peter and David's pew gradually filled, with complete strangers. Not to one another, judging by the low-pitched chatter all about, but certainly to Peter and David, who had deferentially slid over to the farthest end of the pew, where the low oak partition separated it from the servants' pews fed by the side aisle. Then, at the very end, a truly familiar face took up the aisle position: Mordon Leethe himself, his expression finally finding its appropriate venue. Peter and David raised their eyebrows at one another, but kept their opinions to themselves.

The service could not have been more nondenominational if Carly Simon had got up and sung; she did not, but a chorus group from *Nana: The Musical,* the current Cameron Mackintosh Broadway smash, did, and sang "Smoke Dreams," the thing that passed for a love ballad in that show.

Then the minister, or pastor, or parson, or deacon, or whatever he called himself, stood up and delivered the eulogy. Peter and David didn't listen to the sense of it, because they were trying to figure out the accent. Where *was* the man from? Nowhere in America, certainly. Nowhere in Great

Britain they'd ever heard of, though sometimes there was a trace of something very BBC audible down in there. Not Australian, not South African, obviously not Canadian.

But still it wasn't a foreign accent, either. It was as though, through all his formative years, this person in this cassock had never had the opportunity actually to listen to any human beings in conversation, but had merely watched an indiscriminate mélange of movies from all over the English-speaking world, so that he emerged from the experience at the end with a pudding of accents, in which every word was recognizably from the mouth of a native English-language speaker, but no string of words had any geographic coherence.

It was a pity, though, that the delivery system so distracted David and Peter, because the eulogy was in fact well worth listening to:

"You all know Jack Fullerton. You all, that is to say, knew Jack Fullerton, one way and another, most of you, I suppose, which is why you're all here today. To remember, to recall, Jack Fullerton, the man. Whom, in our own fashion, we all knew. Some in business, some . . . not in business.

"Jack was a family man. That needs to be said, one thinks, particularly in this day and age, particularly at a time when the family, the concept of the family, perhaps the family itself, is not what it was, once upon a time. But that was not true of Jack, no, never true of Jack. Jack Fullerton was a family man. He himself came from a family, and he went on and produced a family of his own, a proud and full family of his own, of which he was proud, mightily proud. Often expressed, proud.

"If Jack could be here today, as of course he cannot, but if he were somehow here as well as not being here, he would, I think, still be proud, yes, proud of that family I see, here and there among you, proud of his friends, his associates, his position in the world that he has now left, and we the poorer for it.

"Jack was a philanthropist. Ah, yes, that large word which merely means good. Good-hearted, good-intentioned, good in one's dealings with one's world. Jack's contributions are many and legion and many. Perhaps more than many of you are aware, because Jack was also a modest man, in his way, his own idiosyncratic very personal way of being a modest man, as many of you are aware. His support, for instance, for example, his support of the television episodes of great moments in the histories of the southern American states on public television is perhaps not as well known as it should be, and I would correct that if I could, and possibly do, here.

"Speaking personally, and with great and undimmed gratitude, I well remember the generosity with which Jack responded to our own fund drive, here at the kirk, when we had all that trouble with the roof, which some of you may remember. The more communicants among you. Those days with buckets in the pews, all that, well behind us now, gone and forgotten, and we have Jack Fullerton as much as anyone, except of course DeMartino Roofing, who did the actual work, to thank and thank we will. Did at the time. Do now. Remember Jack in our, er, thoughts.

"Jack Fullerton was a man of vision, who came to us from a family rich in men of vision, and who leaves in his wake, in his path, in his, behind him, more of the same. The Fullerton vision. Wealth carefully husbanded, largesse generously distributed, honor maintained, the law obeyed, and the family upheld.

"And so we say, from the deepest bottom part of ourselves, good-bye, Jack. We are all better men—and of course better women, and better children, too—for having known you. You enriched our lives, in so many ways: Jack. Farewell. Please bow your heads."

The sidewalk was covered by a lumpy layer of cigarette butts. The mourners, if that's the word, crunched over all those filters on their way to the cars, many of them lighting up the instant they emerged from the sanctuary within.

Car number three was a stretch limo, gleaming black, with darkened side windows. The blue-suited, uniform-capped chauffeur stood beside the closed rear passenger door, hands crossed at his crotch, face unreadable behind sunglasses. "Peter," David muttered as they crossed the sea of cigarette butts, "there must be some mistake."

"We'll find out," Peter said, and strode forward, David in his wake. When they reached car number three, Peter said, as though to the manner born, "Drs. Loomis and Heimhocker."

The chauffeur glanced down at the three-by-five cardboard card held discreetly in his left palm. "Yes, sir," he said, and stooped to open the door.

Well, well; not bad. Peter climbed in first, and then David, and in the low dim interior they found a lot of black leather upholstery on a bench-type seat across the rear, and facing that seat, more black leather on two separate seats just behind the driver's-area partition, flanking a console veneered to look almost exactly like wood.

Peter went for the broad bench seat at the rear, but David, as the chauffeur clicked shut the door behind him, slid into one of the rear-facing separate seats, the one nearest the sidewalk. Settled there, he said, "I wouldn't sit back there, Peter. Someone more important than us is going to get into this car."

Peter looked mulish for just a second, but then shrugged and said, "You're probably right," and shifted his long skinny body around to the other single seat, across the console from David.

The limo's engine softly purred, and its air-conditioning was switched on to a very comfortable level: decent temperature, low humidity. Outside the gray-tinted windows they could see the humidity-laden people move heavily through the real world, and they couldn't help but grin. Whatever chance it was that had led them into this vehicle, they were happy for it.

"Not bad," Peter said.

David turned and winked. "Stick with me, baby," he said.

Peter looked past David at the sidewalk outside the window, and his expression changed, became more sour. "If this is the garden of Eden," he said, "here comes the serpent."

David looked, and saw that it was true. Crossing directly toward their limo was the dark cloud of Mordon Leethe; was he going to be in their lives constantly from now on? They watched him speak to the chauffeur, who consulted his cue-card, and then opened the door. In came an ugly puff of hot wet city air and its moral equivalent, Mordon Leethe, who nodded at them, slid over to the far corner of the rear seat, and the chauffeur shut the door.

What was there to say? They'd finished with Leethe on Friday. Still, David could not help but be polite. Therefore, "Hello," he said.

"Hello," Leethe said.

Duty done, David looked out the window again. Who else were they waiting for? If someone more important than themselves, certainly someone more important than Mordon Leethe. Who probably knew, come to think of it, but David wouldn't dream of asking.

"Did you enjoy the service?" Leethe asked.

David turned his head, startled, but apparently Leethe had directed that question at Peter, who answered, "Enjoy? Do we enjoy funerals?"

"Frequently," Leethe said, and the limo door opened once more.

David had been distracted by Leethe, and had not seen these people arrive, so they burst onto his awareness all of a heap. First, the woman: thirty-something, blond, expensive dark clothing, expensive tanned face, expensive expression and manner—all in all, a property with a high fence around it and a sentry at the gate.

Entering, sleek knees together, this woman slid over next to Leethe without glancing at him or anyone else. She was then followed by the man: forty, at most. Trim, muscular, thick-necked but narrow-jawed, as though a greyhound had coupled with a malamute. Light brown hair in a furry low cap beyond a very high forehead. Ears tight to the skull, almost inset. Full mouth, slender nose, ice-cube eyes, eyebrows so pale as to be almost nonexistent. An aura of control, command, importance, that David found discomfiting in the extreme, a reaction that embarrassed him. Aren't we all equal, dammit? Oh, if only they could be upstate right now, with Robert and Martin, where nobody ever frightened anybody.

This time, once the chauffeur had shut the door, he went around to get in behind the wheel. Apparently the cortege was gearing up, almost ready to roll.

Leethe said, "Merrill, may I introduce—"

But the new man said, "No, Mordon, wait till we're on the road." To the woman, he said, "Wake me when we get to the Hutch."

She nodded, not looking at him. She had a black shoulder bag, now in her lap. While the man—Merrill, apparently—stretched out his legs so that David had to move his own out of the way, settled himself comfortably, and closed his eyes, seeming to go at once to sleep, the woman rooted around in the bag, came out with a slender appointment book and a tiny pen, and proceeded to read the entries, occasionally adding something or drawing a line through something.

David and Peter looked at one another. David looked at Leethe, who was gazing out his window at the mess of Park Avenue traffic.

Smoothly, the limo moved forward.

At the legal speed limit, once they reached the FDR Drive, the mortal remains of Jack Fullerton the Fourth and its train of twenty-seven cars sped northward up the eastern hem of Manhattan, across the Triborough Bridge without paying the toll—it looked as though they had motorcycle policemen with them—up the Bruckner Expressway and over to the Hutchinson River Parkway, the truck-free conduit to New England. Still technically in the Bronx, but with every outward indication of having left the city behind, the Hutch is the psychological watershed; beyond this point be suburbanites.

"Merrill," said calmly and quietly by the woman in a low but pleasing voice, was the first word spoken in car number three since it had pulled away from The Church of Lenox Hill. Instantly the man's ice eyes opened, he sat up, retracted his legs from David's space, stretched a series of muscle groupings without shifting very much in his place, and then pointed at the console while saying to David, "Get me a Perrier, would you?"

"What?" David leaned forward to look at the front of the console, and it contained a door, which he opened, feeling suddenly and foolishly like Alice in Wonderland. And there, inside the console, was a small refrigerator, full of not only little green bottles of Perrier but also beer, soft drinks, and splits of champagne.

"Of course," David said, and took out a Perrier, and handed it to the man, who had opened another secret compartment, this one in the door, containing short thick glasses.

"Take something for yourself," the man said, in lieu of thanks.

"Thank you," David said, because he would. He turned his head. "Peter?"

They both chose Perrier as well, and took glasses from the man's cache. David said, "Mr. Leethe?"

"Perrier."

David looked at the woman: "Anything for you?"

She very nearly looked directly at him as she replied with the most minimal of headshakes.

The four men sat with Perrier water fizzing and sputtering in glasses in their hands. Leethe said, "Merrill, may I now present—"

"Delighted."

"May I present Dr. Peter Heimhocker and Dr. David Loomis of the American Tobacco Research Institute. Doctors, may I present Merrill Fullerton, nephew of the late lamented Jack, and heir apparent to the chairmanship."

"Well, not quite apparent," Merrill Fullerton said, with a faint smile. "Not quite yet, though soon, we hope." He turned his smile and his ice eyes on David and Peter. "With the doctors' help, in fact. Or their friend's help."

David said, "Our friend?"

"The invisible man," Merrill said.

Peter said, "We won't discuss that except in the presence of our attorney."

Merrill Fullerton gazed almost fondly at Peter. "The reason we are having this conversation in this setting," he said, "far from your little attorney, and far from my feverish family, and far from the spies and wiretaps and bugs of our friends and enemies, is so that I can make it plain to you just what the situation is now that Uncle Jack has gone to the great ashtray in the sky. You needn't discuss anything for a while. I'll do the talking for all of us."

David and Peter watched Merrill Fullerton like birds watching a cat. Mordon Leethe watched the traffic out on the Hutch. The woman read a paperback novel by Danielle Steel.

Merrill Fullerton said, "Uncle Jack was all right in his way, in his day, but he had slowed down, you know, he wasn't the man he used to be, he was letting things slide, and one of the things he was letting slide was your invisible man."

"We haven't been able to find him," David said. "That's—"

The ice eyes looked at David. "I believe I said it was my turn to talk."

"Sorry."

"I understand from Mordon," Merrill said, "that the invisible man is not at this point replicable. So I want the original. I want him now, I want him doing our bidding, and I want him under *your* control."

"So do we," said Peter.

Ignoring that, Merrill said, "I want him, of course, for all the same reasons Uncle Jack wanted him, but Uncle Jack's vision, I must say, though not wishing to speak ill of the dead, his vision was rather limited. I will need the invisible man initially to consolidate my position as the new head of NAABOR, which shouldn't take long, once I have my own absolutely indetectable spy in the very bosom of the councils of my family, but after that, gentlemen, after that I have much bigger plans for both your invisible man and your own good selves."

"What," David said.

"In the first place," Merrill told him, "this melanoma nonsense is finished. Forget all that, throw out your research, no one now or tomorrow or ever in the history of the world will give a good goddam."

Stiffly, Peter said, "I can't believe that—"

"Believe what you want to believe," Merrill interrupted. "I'm telling you that your research, as you very well know, was never anything more than a public relations dodge, and I no longer need it or want it or will fund it or have anything to do with it."

David's mouth and throat were terribly dry. He drank Perrier, aware of Peter drinking Perrier over there to his right, but it didn't help. Liquid didn't help. He was just terribly dry.

"What you are going to do instead," Merrill told them, "with my financial backing, extremely generous financial backing, and with the assistance of your invisible man, is nothing more or less than save the entire cigarette industry from annihilation and collapse."

David blinked. He couldn't help it, he had to ask. "How?"

Merrill, a born orator, raised one finger. "Let me," he said, "give you just a bit of the background. It was more than forty years ago that the industry first had to confront the fact that the only product it had to sell was, in fact, a deadly poison."

Peter abruptly said, "Do you smoke?"

Merrill gave him a look of astonished contempt. "Of course not! Do you take me for an idiot?"

"The rest of your family smokes."

"Yes, and look at them."

"You're going to go on selling cigarettes."

Merrill smiled. "That's all I have to sell, isn't it? In fact, that's been the quandary ever since nineteen fifty-two, when Dr. Doll, in England—charming name—first laid out the evidence linking benzoapyrene to lung cancer. Since then, bad news has followed bad news, and by now the scientific world knows—we in the industry don't know, of course, but everyone else does—the existence of forty-three separate carcinogens in cigarette smoke. Quite an army in that field, don't you think?"

Faintly, David said, "I hadn't known it was that many."

"Could be more before they're done rooting around," Merrill said, and shrugged. "Dead is dead, as Uncle Jack could tell you, so it hardly matters if you're killed once or forty-three times. The point is, the industry has known about the problem for forty years or more, and has struggled with it, and has failed to solve it, and the situation has got blacker and blacker and blacker. As black as a smoker's lung, you might say. In the sixties and seventies, the industry tried everything it could think of to make its product less lethal; face it, no businessman in his right mind wants to kill off his customers. But nothing worked. All kinds of filters were tried, and failed. Different tobaccos, different additives, even substitutes for tobacco. If they were at all safe, smokers wouldn't go near them. Finally, within the last ten to fifteen years, when it became clear that there was *no* solution, there was *no* way to make cigarette smoking anything other than suicidal, the industry fell back on its last weapon: denial. That's where we are now, but the denials are getting weaker and weaker, the evidence is getting harder and harder to refute, and the lawsuits are getting more and more dangerous, and unless something is done, I stand to inherit a mighty ship just as it sinks to the bottom of the sea. Doctors, I don't intend to be the first president of NAABOR to lose a war."

"I'd heard," Peter said delicately, "the industry might shift over to marijuana. Might encourage legalization and—"

"For several reasons, no," Merrill said. "The zeitgeist is against that, to begin with. In the years since nineteen thirty-six, when marijuana was first made illegal in the United States, to give employment to those government enforcement officials put out of work by the repeal of Prohibition, marijuana has unfortunately become wedded in the popular mind with actual narcotic drugs, like heroin and cocaine. Also, marijuana contains even more tar than tobacco and may have just as many, though different, negative implications for the human respiratory system. There's nothing to be gained by switching from a legal health hazard to an illegal health hazard."

David said, "You still want to sell tobacco."

"It's what I have in the shop."

"And the invisible man comes into this? How?"

Merrill seemed to consider that question, as though for the first time. Then he answered it with a question of his own: "What do you know of the Human Genome Project?"

"Nothing," David said promptly.

"It sounds," Peter said, "as though it's outside our area of expertise."

"So far," Merrill agreed. "But it is about to *become* your area of expertise. Every cell of your body contains a complete strand of your DNA, the chain of information—the instruction manual, if you will—that went into constructing you in the first place. Genetic scientists—which is what you two are about to become—have begun to pick apart that chain of information, the human genome, and have learned how to isolate sections of it for study. The Human Genome Project is financed by the United States government, through the National Institutes of Health. They tried to patent a few genes a couple of years ago, but the patent office turned them down, on the basis that they couldn't describe what the things they'd discovered were good for. Read Cook-Deegan on the subject. So far, they've—"

He broke off, and frowned at them. "Shouldn't one of you," he asked, "be taking notes?"

Instantly, David and Peter both lunged into their inner jacket pockets, but then Peter said, "David, I'll do it," and David subsided, smoothing his jacket again, watching Merrill Fullerton, wondering where the man was headed, convinced that somehow or other, wherever this would lead, he and Peter would hate it. And what then?

"The genetic scientists," Merrill was saying, "can study *your* genes and tell you the percentage of likelihood that a child of yours will get Huntington's disease. Or one form of Alzheimer's. Or cystic fibrosis. They're working to identify the piece of chain that indicates breast cancer. Or homosexuality. Or alcoholism. Eventually, if it all turns out the way they expect, the Genome Project will be able to describe the probable health history and time and cause of death for every human being in the world, in embryo, in the womb. In the first trimester. If Junior is going to be the runt of the litter, you'll know in plenty of time to off him." Merrill Fullerton's smile was as thin as his eyes were cold. "What a healthy race we're going to be," he said. "The Aryan dream come true at last."

"It sounds horrible," David said.

"And marvelous," Merrill told him. "Horrible and marvelous. Knowledge. How much we want it, and how we're afraid of it. You, for instance, might want to know all about *my* future health history, and I might want to know all about yours, particularly if I were thinking of hiring you or marrying you or going into business with you, but neither of us would be comfortable seeing our *own* genetic report card."

Peter said, "Is this science, or science fiction?"

"Fact," Merrill answered. "You'll read the literature, of which there isn't as yet much. And you'll see that, like your friend here, the scientific part of the project is already well hemmed in by emotional and moral and ethical doubts. Will the project break the DNA code entirely, and then will the government do its best to keep us from that knowledge, for our own good? In a survey not long ago, eleven percent of the respondents said they would abort a fetus if they learned the child carried the gene for obesity. You can see that this is not going to be a simple ride."

"Not at all," Peter said. He was on, David noticed, the second page of his notebook.

"Whatever the government may do," Merrill told them, "to hem in this new knowledge, to confine it the way they confined the information about the atom bomb for so long, *I want it*. Already they're shrouding the project in secrecy, and I need to penetrate that shroud. I want the information, and I want to be able to lead the research, or at the very least influence the research into areas of interest to *me*."

"I'm sorry," Peter said, tapping his pen against the notebook. "I don't see what all this has to do with you at all."

"You don't?" Merrill smiled. "I want you both to prepare yourselves on this subject," he said. "I want you to know as much about it as the scientists in the project themselves. I want your invisible man in their laboratories, in their discussions, in their diaries and workbooks, bringing back to you every bit of information they have. I want to guide their research away from breast cancer and chronic liver disease, matters that I don't give one shit about."

It was astonishing, David thought, how through this whole tirade the woman just sat there, beside Merrill Fullerton, and read her book.

Merrill leaned forward, his eyes now hot ice. This was the gist, at last. "I want the code for lung cancer," he told them. "I want the code for emphysema. I want the code for congestive heart failure. I want the codes that tobacco taps into. And then I want a reeducation program, aimed directly at our consumers, not just here, but around the world. *Abort* the lung cancer cases! *Abort* the emphysema cases! Never let the little bastards see the light of day!"

David and Peter both blinked. Merrill sat back, as though after an orgasm, and smiled. "We've spent the last forty years," he said, "trying to make cigarettes safe for the human race, and we failed. We can spend the next forty years making the human race safe for cigarettes!"

A flunky informed them, midway through the interminable mumbling graveside ceremony on its breezy knoll with its one old oak tree and its green views of Connecticut and the purple haze over New York far away, that they would not be traveling back to the city with Merrill Fullerton and the woman of mystery, but in a different car. "Why am I not surprised?" Peter said, sounding peevish.

The flunky shrugged—what did he care?—and said, "You'll be in car nineteen," and went away.

David felt relieved, and said so. "Peter, you don't want to travel with that man again. God *knows* what he'll say next."

"He's already said too much," Peter agreed. But then he looked past David and murmured in his ear, "People are leaving."

What? David looked toward the grave, and the mound of earth next to it covered by that horrible Easter-basket-green tinsel fake grass they always use, a sort of Hawaiian welcome mat to the next world, and the minister was still mumbling over there, people were still standing around in attitudes of grief or boredom or paralysis, the service was certainly still going *on*.

But then he turned his head the other way, down the slope behind them, and he saw a car discreetly purr away along the gravel road toward the exit, leaving the line of waiting limos and cars, in which there were several gaps, suggesting that other cars had already departed. Between here and there, two women and a man, all in black, picked their way quietly down over the grass toward the cars. An exodus had begun.

"We've done our part," Peter murmured in David's ear, like Satan suggesting a new and interesting sin. "This Fullerton doesn't want to talk to us anymore, and we never even *knew* the other one."

"You're right," David whispered, and at once they faded back from the oval of mourners, turned in their pale gray suits, and headed for the cars.

They never did find car nineteen, because standing next to car eleven was George Clapp, who grinned when he saw them and said, "My doctors. Best doctors in the world. You wanna go back to town?"

David said, "We're supposed to be in car nineteen."

"Oh, don't worry bout that," George told them. "These systems always break down, people work it out. Climb aboard here, I'm ready to call it a day myself."

Car eleven was not a limo, but was what was known as a town car, being an ordinary sedan, but with black leather seats. David and Peter slid into the back, George shut the door behind them, and as they grinned at one another and looked up the hill at the people still standing there, outlined beside the oak tree against the sky as though the passing of Jack Fullerton the Fourth were meaningful in some way, George trotted around to get behind the wheel and drive them out of there.

As they headed southwest, a few minutes later, on the Connecticut Turnpike, Peter said, "George, I'm surprised. I thought they were paying you enough so you didn't have to work anymore."

"Oh, they weaseled out of that," George said, with no apparent ill feeling, "once it turned out we wasn't gonna be invisible after all. I figured they would, you know. That lawyer—"

"Mordon Leethe," they both said.

"That's the one." George laughed and said, "He's the one let us know, yesterday morning in his office, in there on a Saturday to tell us they ain't gonna pay anybody for being useless, and except for driving vehicles I'm useless, so that's that. Am I gonna take them to court? What are they called, The Five Hundred Fortune companies? They got five hundred fortunes and I got no fortune. Am I gonna *sue* them?"

"That's terrible," David said.

"Aw, it ain't so bad," George said. "If I'd *got* all that money, all that time on my hands, I'd justa got myself in trouble anyway. Fact is, I like driving, like talking to the passengers." He waved a hand in the air, grinning in the rearview mirror. "Now I got these new fingerips, this new face, nothing scares me, man, I can go on driving the rest of my life."

"So long as you're happy," Peter told him.

"Count on it," George said.

David said, "But what about Michael? Michael Prendergast. Did they cheat her, too?"

"Oh, sure, man," George said. "They're an equal opportunity fucker. They done her like they done me."

David said, "What is she going to do about it, do you know?"

"Oh, yeah, she told me," George said, "when we left the lawyer's office yesterday. There's this country, Iran, Iraq, one of those, been after her to head up their nuclear power program. She wouldn't do it before, on account it's against our law, her being there to do that, but now she says she's had enough. She's taking the job, probably already gone in the plane now."

Peter said, "To Iran?"

"Or Iraq, or one of those others over there. She says, the great thing is, she gets to wear that black thing the women wear, covers them all up . . ."

"The chador," David suggested.

"That's it. She gets to wear the chador, so that's good. And the other thing, running that program for them," George explained, "she says she should be just about ready to blow up the whole world in about eight years. I think she'll probably do it, too."

David and Peter stared at George's merry eyes in the rearview mirror. Neither could think of a thing to say. George winked at them. "What I figure," he said, "we might as well enjoy life while we got it."

38

Wednesday, July 5, the day after the long hot exhausting holiday weekend, was a quiet one at the Big S Superstore on U.S. Route 9, the main commercial roadway on the east side of the Hudson River. A few retirees with nothing else to do wandered the cavernous interior of this warehouse-type store, the no-frills successor to the department store, where mountains of items were piled directly on the concrete floor or stuffed to overflowing on unpainted rough wooden shelves. Once you became a "member" of their "club" (not a hard thing to do), you could buy everything in here from a television set (and the unpainted piece of furniture to hide it in) to a goldfish bowl (and the goldfish) to put on top of the set for those times when there's absolutely nothing to watch on TV. You could buy canned and frozen food, truck tires, toys, books, washing machines, flowers, tents (in case your house fills up), small tractors, bicycles, benches, lumber to make your own benches, double-hung windows, storm windows, snow tires, dresses with flowers on them, blue jeans, and baseball caps honoring the team of your choice.

Here in the Big S ("the Big Store for Big Savings!"), in other words, you could get everything you used to be able to get in the Sears Roebuck catalog, except now you have to go to the warehouse and pick it up instead of phoning in and having them send it to you. People enjoy a new wrinkle, and the warehouse you go to instead of phoning it is a very successful new wrinkle indeed. Even the day after the big Fourth of July weekend, there were people in the place; not many of them, but some. And in among the retirees with nothing better to do was an attractive young woman talking to herself.

This is what she was saying: "Freddie, be careful. That old lady just looked around at us."

"What did she see?" apparently asked the mountain of toasters the young woman was just then walking past.

"You know what I mean," she hissed.

This young woman, whom we already know as Peg, was pushing a shopping cart here and there around the warehouse, but she wasn't putting anything into it, because she wasn't in truth a member of the club. She and her invisible partner, whom we already know as Freddie, were merely casing the joint. Just looking it over.

An army of Barbies watched goggle-eyed as Peg pushed the shopping cart by, and then they all said, in Freddie's voice, "My feet are cold."

"It's hot outside," she reminded him.

"That's there, this is here. Concrete, inside, is cold. Hard, too, but Peg, you'd be surprised how cold it is. I wish I could put on a pair of those slippers there."

"Who knows how many heart attacks you could give people."

"I won't do it, I'm just saying."

"Well, do you want to get out of here, have you seen enough?"

"No, I gotta look at the rest of it, the offices and all. Tell you what, give me an hour here, okay?"

"Sure. I can go to the supermarket, do my shopping."

"Good idea."

"Should I come back in?"

"No, I'll find you in the parking lot."

"Okay. So you're going now, right? Right? And I might as well leave the store. Cause I'm alone here now, right?"

She listened, but answer came there none. At some point, he'd gone away, right? He wasn't here now, was he? Watching her, just goofing around. He wouldn't do that, would he? He'd say something if he was here, wouldn't he?

"Oh, I give up," Peg said, this time really and truly talking to herself, and left the shopping cart in the middle of that aisle, and left the store.

Freddie padded along the concrete floor, pausing at the intersections of aisles to look this way and that, wondering where the offices were, where the loading docks were, where there was a nice floor around here with a soft warm carpet on it. And also wondering, Is there a caper in here? Is there something for me in this place?

It was true that this was the most merchandise Freddie had ever in his life seen all together in one place, and that a truckload of almost anything out of here would make Jersey Josh Kuskiosko as happy as it was possible for Jersey Josh Kuskiosko to be, but the question was, how to make the transfer. An invisible man can't be seen, that's true. An invisible man carrying a television set still can't be seen, but the television set can, and any customer or clerk or guard seeing a television set float down a Big S aisle would be bound to have questions, and would be very likely to investigate the matter.

Then there was another consideration. Freddie Noon hadn't gotten into this line of work in order to engage in heavy lifting. To shlep several tons of merchandise out of this building all by himself was not an idea with strong appeal. Was there some other way?

"Hello, sonny."

Freddie looked around, startled out of his contemplations,

and over there was an old man, sharing this particular inter-section of aisles with him. A grizzled old guy leaning on a walker, he was smiling, and he was looking straight at Fred-die.

Whoops, was he visible all of a sudden? Was he standing naked and visible in the middle of the Big S? Freddie looked down at himself and, reassuringly, he was not there.

"Cat got your tongue?"

Freddie looked up, and the old man was definitely talking to *him*. Looking at him, and talking to him. There was nobody else nearby. What kind of magic old guy was this?

"You don't say hello to a person?"

There was no way out; the old guy was sooner or later going to draw the wrong kind of attention. "Hello," Freddie said.

The old guy's smile widened. "There you go," he said. "That wasn't so hard, was it?"

"I was distracted," Freddie said. "I was thinking about what I'm supposed to buy here today."

"Gotta check that shopping list, huh?"

"Yeah, that's right," Freddie said, and suddenly understood: the old guy was blind! Must have been blind for a long time, years and years. His other senses were sharper, to help com-pensate. Everybody else in the store, since they couldn't see Freddie, would assume he wasn't there, but this old guy could-n't see anybody anyway, and had to dope out presence or ab-sence by some other method—smell, heat, air currents, the tiny noises of human movement—and had not only known there was another person sharing this intersection with him, but had figured it out that the person was male and probably young. And naturally had to show off what a whiz-bang he was. *Hello, sonny.*

Freddie said, "I guess you don't have a shopping list, huh?"

"My daughter's got it." The old guy cocked his head, listening. "I think this is her coming now."

Freddie looked, and down the aisle from the right marched a thickset woman in her fifties, sour-faced, pushing a really full shopping cart. "Yeah, here she comes," Freddie said.

The old guy said, "Probably too old for you, but you want me to do the introduction?"

"No, that's okay," Freddie said, "I gotta get going. Nice talking to you." And he veered away to the left.

"So long, sonny," the old guy called after him, and Freddie then heard the woman say, "Pop, who you talking to?"

"That young fella over there," the old guy told her. "In a hurry, like everybody."

Freddie turned a corner and heard no more. He slowed down, then, and thought about the old guy, and realized it had been nice, that, to have a normal conversation with another person. He wasn't getting much of that these days. Maybe he should hang out with blind people a lot, go to their conventions and all.

Musing like this, Freddie found himself at the end of an aisle, and there was the front of the store, with a broad line of cash-register pods, like the world's longest highway tollbooth plaza, or like the Maginot Line that was once upon a time supposed to keep Germany out of France. Beyond the cash registers, most of them closed today, the main exit from the building was off to the right. The rest of the space at the front was occupied by a building within the building, a two-story vinyl-sided structure that didn't quite reach the ceiling of the warehouse and had some sort of flat roof of its own. In this building's ground floor were a restaurant, a video store, a foreign exchange window, and a drugstore, while upstairs were what looked to be offices, behind plate-glass windows covered by venetian blinds.

There had to be a way to get up there. Freddie went over

and sat on the counter of an unoccupied register—the metal was also cold, against his rump, thank you very much, but at least it got his feet off that cold floor—and waited, and watched, and observed, and pretty soon he saw the way it went.

There was no cash moving through these cash registers. People were buying in bulk, and they were paying by check—no credit cards. From time to time, an employee would come down the line and take all the checks and put them into a black cloth bag with a zipper, then carry the bag over to a door at the far left corner of the building-within-a-building, just beyond the drugstore. The person would press a button there, and a few seconds later would push the door open and go in, the door remaining open just long enough for Freddie to see the flight of stairs leading up, before it closed itself.

That was where Freddie wanted to go. The question was, How? The stunt with the doors that he'd pulled at the diamond-exchange place wouldn't work here, not with one person and a spring-closing door. There didn't seem to be any other way upstairs, like an emergency fire exit, which was a pity, because an exterior fire escape, for instance, would be just perfect access for an invisible man. But no.

The person who collected the checks from the registers was not the only one who went through that door and up and down those stairs. There were other people as well, all in the blue-and-white caps and smocks and ID buttons of employees—HI! MY NAME IS LANA HOW CAN I BE OF SERVICE TODAY?—who went in and out of there, mostly carrying sheafs of papers, invoices, order forms, various kinds of documents. The letters of transit. Those people were more interesting to Freddie than the check-carriers; he wanted to know exactly what they did and how they did it.

Well, maybe the thing to do was track them in the other direction first. Freddie waited until he saw a gruff-looking older guy—HI! MY NAME IS GUS HOW CAN I BE OF SERVICE TODAY?—go up to the office and then come out again, carrying a different sheaf of papers when he came out. Freddie then jumped off his register counter and followed Gus on a straight line all the way back to the very rear of the store.

Interesting. Since the whole setup was a warehouse, they didn't actually have a back room for stock. What they had instead was a series of tall garage doors across the back of the building, some open and some shut. Back up against the open doors were the trailers from tractor-trailer rigs, and they were being used as stockrooms, with goods on pallets and guys using forklift trucks to bring mounds of goods out of the trailers and across the floor to where they'd be put on display.

But it was more complicated than that. Inventory control must be a real bitch with an operation like this, so sometimes they just shifted pallets of stuff from one trailer to another—particularly if the garage door was going to be lowered so an emptied trailer could presumably be taken away—and he even saw a couple of instances of pallets of stuff coming *back* from the display area, most likely either to make room for sale items or because they were unsold sale items themselves, after the sale was over.

Gus had brought with him orders that moved some pallets out and some pallets over, and he spent a lot of time now yelling at his crew of forklift operators and waving the hand holding the sheaf of invoices. Watching him, Freddie saw that Gus kept doing something weird with his mouth, something ripply and faintly disgusting, and at last he realized what it was. Gus, a true Gus in a world that has lost much of its Gusness, was chewing an invisible cigar.

Freddie grinned, feeling a sense of camaraderie. There the cigar was invisible, here the whole man was invisible; it was a link. (Freddie, in his increasing isolation from humankind, would take his links where he found them.)

Having learned much from Gus, Freddie made his way back to the front of the store:

"Hi, Pop."

"Hello, sonny."

"Who *are* you talking to?"

This time, he decided to heck with it, just do it. So he went past the registers, over to the door beyond the drugstore, found the button, and pushed it, and a few seconds later was rewarded by a buzzing sound. He leaned the door open just barely wide enough to slide quickly through, then let it shut behind him, and waited, looking up.

There was no one visible at the head of the stairs, just a glimpse of ceiling up there, with an egg carton–style fluorescent light fixture. A hum of voices, a chitter of office machinery. The person up there who operated the buzzer was undoubtedly, like most such people, on automatic pilot; they hear the call, they respond.

Up the stairs Freddie went, very well pleased, because these stairs were carpeted. Scratchy industrial carpeting, but nevertheless carpet, and warm.

At the top, he found the second floor was mostly one large room, with a vaguely underwater feel. The industrial carpet was light green, the walls and ceiling cream, the fluorescent lighting vaguely greenish, the office furniture gray. They could be on the *Nautilus,* and out beyond those venetian blinds could be the deep ocean itself, with giant octopi swimming through the submarine's powerful searchlights.

Instead of which, of course, this was the command center of the Big S, a long low-ceilinged air-conditioned humming space full of clerks, mostly women, with an enclosed office at the far end for the manager. Freddie looked around and saw, positioned atop the desk nearest the stairs, a small TV monitor showing the space in front of the door below. The woman seated at that desk was entering an endless series of numbers into her computer terminal, reading from a two-inch-thick stack of pink vouchers. While Freddie watched, an employee appeared in the monitor and pushed the button; a buzzer sounded here, just like the one downstairs; the woman at the desk never looked away from the vouchers but just reached out, pressed a button in front of the monitor, and went on with her typing.

Routine is the death of security.

Freddie now spent a lot of time wandering around this office, watching over people's shoulders as they worked, reading the forms, studying the charts on the walls, getting to know a lot about the operation of this place. He learned that on weekdays the store closed at eight, but that clerks remained in the office until ten, and the cleaning crew came in at eleven, and there were four guards on duty all night, but no dogs, which had been a worry. (Invisibility wouldn't faze dogs; they trust their noses more than their eyes anyway.)

He also learned that the clerks arrived up here at eight in the morning, so there were two overlapping shifts of clerks, so nobody could ever be absolutely certain that such-and-such a decision had not been made by the other clerk on this desk. He learned that the store opened for business each morning at ten. And he learned a lot about the flow of goods in and through and out of the store. He saw what he could maybe do, and it looked nice.

And then he saw the clock on the wall, and he'd been up here an hour and a half! And who knew how long downstairs before that. He'd told Peg he'd see her in one hour. It had to be at least two hours by now, maybe more.

No no no; things were tough enough for Peg these days as it was, having to live with somebody she couldn't see. There was no point making her also sit forever in the hot sun in an exposed parking lot. Time to get out of here.

Freddie was in such a hurry to get going that he started

down the stairs without looking, and then he looked, and here came Gus, tromping upward. Frowning at the invoices in his fist, chewing his invisible cigar, boot-shod feet clomping one step after another upward toward the second floor.

Too late to go back. To late to do anything but make a run for it.

Holding his breath, grimacing in terror, Freddie scraped past, downward, between Gus and the wall.

"Sorry," muttered Gus, not looking up.

"Sorry," Freddie told him.

Both kept going.

The reason Peg didn't notice the time going by was because she was making plans. She had come to a decision, and now she had to make her plans, work out her timing, figure out exactly what to do and what to say and when to do and say it.

She did love Freddie, dammit, and she did like being with him, but only when she was with *him*. Being with his voice and some clothing and latex masks and Playtex gloves wasn't the same. Knowing you did not *dare* turn on any lamps once you were in bed at night took some of the fun out of having fun. Being tense all the time was bad for a girl's complexion, digestion, and posture.

The disastrous experience last week, that doomed effort just to go out and have a normal date and eat dinner at a restaurant, was the last straw, really. That had been last Friday, the restaurant fiasco, the beginning of the July Fourth weekend, and she'd spent the whole time since brooding about what to do, sitting up by the pool, under the umbrella, with *Silas Marner*, while that invisible whale surged back and forth in the pool.

Of course she already knew what to do, she'd known for some time what the only possible option was, but she stalled, she held off, and she was still stalling. And she knew all this was bad for their relationship, if you can call hanging out with the little man who wasn't there a *relationship*.

It wasn't Freddie's fault he had this condition, and she knew it, and yet she found herself blaming him, feeling as though he *could* be visible if he just wanted to, that he was being invisible just to be a smart-ass. In some ways, of course, Freddie *was* a smart-ass, which gave the accusation a little credibility; more credibility than Freddie himself had, these days.

I'll stick through this caper, Peg told herself. I won't distract him by talking about it now, but once this caper is done and he's got a bunch of money and he's set up here for a while, I'll explain it to him. "Freddie," I'll say, "this isn't working out. It's straining my love for you, Freddie, being stuck here in the backwoods with you when I'm not even *with* you. What we have to have, and I'm sorry about this, Freddie, but what we have to have is a trial separation. I'll go back to Bay Ridge, and you stay here, and we'll talk on the phone, and maybe from time to time I'll come up and visit, and if you ever get your visibility back I'll be here for you, you know that. But this way, honey, it's just too much of a strain. I'm sorry, but."

Peg sighed. She was sorry. But.

The passenger door opened. Indentations appeared in the passenger seat and backrest. The passenger door slammed. A passing mother on her way to the Big S didn't even look around, but her three tiny dirty-faced children all stared and stared, hanging back until their mama whacked all three of them on the top of the head. Then the entire group progressed on to the store, yelling and wailing.

Freddie's voice, out of breath, said, "Gee, I'm sorry, Peg, I lost all sense of time in there."

She smiled at where she figured his head would be. She might as well treat him nice, until she pulled the ripcord. Give him nice memories. After all, she really did love him, or what was left of him. "That's okay, honey," she said. "I was just sitting here thinking, that's all."

"I didn't mean to be away so long."

"Don't worry about it. Is it gonna be okay?"

"It's gonna be wonderful!" The enthusiasm in his voice gave her yet one more reason to be sorry she couldn't see his face. "All I gotta do," he told her, "is spend one night in there, and in the morning I walk off with half the store."

"That's terrific, Freddie."

"What we'll do, when we get home, I'll call Jersey Josh, ask him what he would most like a truck of—and the truck, too, he might as well take that along with—and then we do it."

"That's great."

"And then we can come back here," he said, bubbling over, "and take it easy for the summer. We got it made, Peg."

Something touched her right leg. She knew it was Freddie's hand, and didn't even flinch. "That's wonderful, honey," she said. "Why don't you go in the back and get dressed now?"

"Let me kiss you first."

She closed her eyes.

39

On the Wednesday after the July Fourth weekend, while Freddie Noon was casing the Big S upstate, Mordon Leethe was continuing, in New York City, to concern himself with Freddie's affairs. It began first thing in the morning, right after Mordon had parked his car in the untaxed parking space in the basement of his office building. Hearing another nearby car door slam, he knew even before he turned around that he was about to have another encounter with Barney Beuler.

Yes. Here he came, the hard fat man, making his way between the cars toward Mordon, smiling his hard smile, saying, "Morning, Counselor. Have a nice weekend?"

What a question. Ignoring it, Mordon said, "Barney, please tell me you've located Freddie Noon."

"Well, I could tell you that," Barney said, "but I'd be lying. Come on into my office, let's hit our heads together."

Mordon, heavy-footed but fatalistic, followed Barney to today's car, a burgundy Daimler. As Barney opened its rear door, Mordon said, "Do you intend to test-sit every car in this garage?"

"Call me Goldilocks," Barney said, unfazed. "Could be I'm in the market for new wheels. Get in, Counselor."

There was, surprisingly, a bit less space inside the Daimler than in the other cars Barney had chosen. Mordon found himself uncomfortably close to the other man, who slammed the door, heaved around to grin at him, and said, "I hear you've had a death in the family."

At a loss, Mordon said, "Me?"

"The Fullerton family."

"Oh, yes, of course."

"So my first question is," Barney said, "is the guy that's taking over, is he just as hot for Freddie Noon as the old guy was?"

"Even more so, Barney," Mordon assured him. "Even more so."

"Good. That's a weight off my mind. Now, here's something I been thinking about."

"Yes?"

"I put myself in this Freddie Noon's place, you see?" Barney nodded as he spoke, looking past the front seat and out the windshield, as though it were Fredric Urban Noon he could see out there, and not the rump of a parked purple Lexus across the way. "At first, this guy," Barney said, "he had to worry, maybe he was gonna die, maybe he was gonna stop being invisible, maybe something was gonna happen. But nothing did. We know that, because we know he pulled two quick heists here in the city within a week of getting invisible. And we know he was *still* a no-see-um, the son of a bitch, a week after that, when he waltzed out of his Bay Ridge place right under our nose and then knee-capped me upstate."

"He would appear," Mordon said, "to be in a stable condition, so far as being invisible is concerned."

"That's right," Barney said. "So now he's not so worried anymore that somethin bad is gonna happen. Now what he is, he's startin to get worried that *nothin* is gonna happen."

"I don't follow you," Mordon admitted.

"Face it," Barney said, "is this guy gonna wanna stay invisible the rest of his life? Would you? Would I? No."

"It's useful to him, though," Mordon suggested, "in his line of work."

"Sure. That's why he's hittin big and hard and often. Two major heists in a week. He's probably done more by now, but if he's working outside the city it's gonna be harder for me to keep track. If I was him—and this is the only way you can be a cop, you know, a detective, which in fact is what I am, and fuck the shooflys—if I was him, and I'm looking through his eyes, and I'm thinking with his head, what I'm thinking is, pull a lot of jobs quick, stockpile a whole lotta cash, then get visible again and retire."

"How? Get visible again how?"

Barney waggled a finger unpleasantly near Mordon's nose. "This brings me to my subject," he said, "the reason I'm here today. The doctors."

"The doctors."

"The doctors. Sooner or later, our friend Freddie is gonna make contact with the doctors."

Mordon hadn't thought about that, but now he did and slowly he nodded. "I see what you mean. Make a deal with them, finish the experiment for them if they promise to put him back the way he was. The status quo ante."

"You said it. He is gonna call the doctors." Barney nodded, satisfied with his own deductions. "Or," he said, "maybe he already did. You think about that at all?"

"You mean if he contacted them, they might not tell me about it?"

"Not without being asked."

Again Mordon thought it over, and again he had to concede that Barney was right. "The relationship between the doctors and myself," he allowed, "in fact, between the doctors and NAABOR generally, is not perhaps as good as it might be."

"I bet it isn't."

"Well," Mordon said, "as a matter of fact, I'd meant to call the doctors today anyway, make an appointment with them, to discuss some proposals that were made over the weekend. I can include this as a second topic."

"Yes, you can," Barney agreed. "And you can include me as a second participant."

"You want to come along?" Mordon asked, surprised. "Meet the doctors? Have them meet you?"

"Right."

"Why?"

"Well, first," Barney said, "you'll discuss the situation with the doctors, and why they should cooperate, and the legalities and their responsibilities and all that. And then I'll come on," Barney finished, and smiled, "and scare them."

The black receptionist, Shanana, recognized Mordon this time, seeing him through the oriel beside her desk, and started to smile, but then she saw Barney. Her expression clouded, and she looked at Mordon with fresh doubt; still, she released the door lock and let them in.

"An equal opportunity employer," Barney commented, as the buzzer sounded.

"I wouldn't underestimate that girl," Mordon told him, pushing the door open, holding it for Barney.

Shanana had come to her office door. "Good morning, Mr. Leethe," she said. Mordon saw that she was prepared to pretend that Barney didn't exist, as though he were an embarrassment she wanted to spare Mordon having to acknowledge.

More than willing to go along with that concept, Mordon smiled his nearest-to-human smile and said, "Good morning, Shanana. The doctors are expecting me."

"Yes, I know. I'll tell them you're here." She gestured with a slender graceful dark hand. "You remember where the conference room is?"

Mordon looked mournful. "Not the pleasant room upstairs, eh?"

She was amused, sympathetic. "Afraid not," she said, and retired into her office.

Mordon led the way toward the conference room, and Barney followed, saying, "You get along pretty good with that one."

"I get along with everyone, Barney," Mordon said.

Barney stared at him. "Do you really believe that?"

Mordon didn't bother answering. They entered the fluorescent-flooded conference room, and Barney looked around and said, "Okay, I confess. Where do I sign?"

"It does lack an amenity or two," Mordon agreed.

Barney spread his hands. "Here we are in the Asteroid Belt," he said, and the doctors entered.

Barney and the doctors were meeting for the first time, of course, and it was interesting to Mordon to see how immediate and instinctive the loathing was on both sides. The body language alone was enough to set off seismographs in the neighborhood, if there were any. Mordon was watching two herbivores meet a carnivore on the herbivores' own ground, and the rolling of eyes and curling of lips and stamping of hooves was thunderous.

Mordon, as though nothing at all were wrong, made the introductions. "Dr. Peter Heimhocker, Dr. David Loomis, I'd like you to meet Detective Barney Beuler of the New York City Police."

"Harya," Barney snarled.

Loomis remained wide-eyed and mute, but Heimhocker looked Barney up and down, raised an eyebrow at Mordon, and said, in a you-rogue-you manner, "Oh, really."

"Barney," Mordon explained, "has been helping us in the search for Fredric Noon. We thought it would be a good idea if we all got together."

"Did you," Heimhocker said.

Mordon gestured at the bare conference table. "Shall we sit down?"

"Yes, of course," Heimhocker said, remembering his manners.

Loomis, also remembering his manners, said, "Did Shanana offer you soft drinks? Coffee? Anything?"

"Not necessary," Mordon assured him. "Thank you just the same."

They sat at the long table like labor-management negotiators, two on each side, facing one another, hands clasped, elbows on the table, mistrustful eyes shaded from the fluorescents by furrowed brows. Breaking a little silence, then, Loomis said to Mordon, "To be honest, when you called this morning, we thought it was about Merrill Fullerton and *his* ideas."

"I do want to get into that," Mordon agreed. "Perhaps we should cover it first." Glancing at Barney's unpleasant profile, he said, "Barney, if you wouldn't mind?"

"Be my guest."

Mordon turned back to the doctors. "About his project, whatever it was called."

"The Human Genome Project," Loomis said, and Heimhocker said, "It does exist." He didn't sound as though he entirely approved.

"And it's what Merrill said it was?"

"In a way," Heimhocker said, and Loomis said, "That man is crazy, you know. Talk about megalomania."

" 'Think big,' I think, is the business phrase," Mordon said. "You've looked into this Jerome project?"

"Genome," Heimhocker said. "From the word *gene*. The Human Genome Project is the most expensive United States government scientific enterprise since the Manhattan Project."

"Is it really."

"I'm amazed," Loomis said, "at how little it's known."

"Well, of course," Mordon pointed out, "the Manhattan Project, inventing the atomic bomb, wasn't very well known while it was going on, either."

"True," Heimhocker said, and Loomis said, "But that was wartime," and Heimhocker said, "It may merely be too hard a story for the press to explain to the great unwashed," and Loomis said, "True."

"But the project does actually exist," Mordon said, "and it is doing something with DNA chains—"

"Mapping," Heimhocker said. "As your friend Merrill said. And it is finding disease tendencies. But this is a *government* project, you know, it's not something you can sneak around inside, or influence, or co-opt."

"But now, already this morning," Loomis said, with a hint of a wail in his voice, "we received a hand-delivered letter from this Merrill Fullerton, with a covering letter from Dr. Archer Amory, informing us our melanoma researches are finished! Just like that!"

"Unfortunate," Mordon murmured.

"And we were so close!" Loomis cried.

Heimhocker said, more calmly, "Whether we were close or not, we were always, in the company's eyes obviously, no more than window dressing. They have no more use for that false face, so they're throwing it away."

"We feel so *used*!" Loomis cried.

"And we also feel," Heimhocker said, "frustrated. We're told in the letter that our research facility will be permitted to continue on as before, but only with a *restructuring of goals*, and that our goals are now in the area of *genetic enhancement of tobacco safety.*"

"How do you like *that* for a euphemism?" Loomis demanded.

"I think it's rather wonderful," Mordon admitted.

"But," Heimhocker said, "how are we going to do this? Even if we find the invisible man—"

"We will," Barney said.

"Yes, no doubt." Heimhocker sneered at him, and spoke to Mordon again, saying, "But even if we find him, and even if we convince him to work with us, and even if he manages to pussyfoot around government laboratories without getting caught, or implicating us—"

"I've never wanted to commit a federal crime," Loomis confessed.

"Exactly," Heimhocker said. "So, Mr. Leethe, I realize you represent the other side in this matter, but it seemed to me you were as appalled as we were in that limo, listening to that man—"

"Not really," Mordon said. "I've listened to businessmen dream before. But what you want to know is, how are you going to continue to live off NAABOR if NAABOR insists on you doing something illegal."

"*Impossible* is the word I had in mind," Heimhocker said, and Loomis said, "Impossible *and* illegal, and unethical, and immoral."

Mordon nodded. "Everything but fattening. Gentlemen, I want you to understand this suggestion is not coming from me, but don't you think you could work on this new project for some time to come without having any actual finalized data to report? I mean, how often do you report progress on your melanoma research?"

"Never, in fact," Heimhocker admitted, but Loomis said, "That isn't precisely true, Peter. We do prepare an annual report for the stockholders' brochure, restating our goals and so on, indicating areas we've concentrated on during the previous fiscal year."

"Other than that," Mordon said.

"Other than that, nothing," Heimhocker said, and Loomis

said, "But we were just about to, we were on the verge of a breakthrough, we're convinced of that, that's why we were so eager to test one of the formulae on that burglar."

"Speaking of whom," Barney said, "do you mind if we do?"

"Please," Heimhocker said, patting the air to calm Barney down (which, of course, would do just the reverse), "let me just finish this other matter first." To Mordon, he said, "What you're suggesting, without the suggestion coming from you, we understand that, is that we simply go along with Merrill Fullerton's ideas, as best we can, without getting ourselves into trouble with the law. Not protest, not argue."

"If you protest or argue," Mordon told him, "you'll be replaced. There are a lot of researchers out there who'd like a lab of their very own. If you make waves right now, you'll lose your funding. You'll probably lose this building."

Loomis said, "But what about our melanoma research?"

Mordon shrugged. "Continue it. Call it something else in your financial statements. The accountants who pay your expenses have no idea what you're doing anyway."

Heimhocker and Loomis looked at one another. At last, Heimhocker said, "We could probably give him little bits of information from time to time."

"Not enough," Loomis said, "for him to do any real damage."

"Of course," Mordon said.

Heimhocker gave Mordon a hunted look. "It's a frightening way to live, though," he said.

"All ways to live are frightening," Mordon consoled him. "Imagine living like Barney here, for instance, who has been very patient, and who wants to talk about Fredric Noon now. Go ahead, Barney."

Barney frowned at Mordon's profile. "What's wrong with the way I live?"

"Nothing. You seem very content in it. Talk to the doctors about Noon."

Barney thought it over, and decided to move forward. Turning to the doctors, he said, "Has Noon been in touch with you two yet?"

"No," Heimhocker said, and Loomis said, "We wish he would!"

Barney beetled brows at them. "You sure about that? Not even one little phone call?"

"Of course not," Heimhocker said, looking insulted, while Loomis looked astonished, crying, "Every time the phone *rings*, we hope it's him! For heaven's sake!"

"Because he will," Barney said, and glanced at Mordon. "Right, Counselor?"

"His invisibility doesn't seem to be ending," Mordon told the doctors. "So far as we can tell, he's still absolutely unseeable."

"Well, of course," Loomis said, and Heimhocker said, "That's what we expected."

Mordon raised an eyebrow. "You expected it? That he'd still be invisible? Unharmed by your potion, but invisible?"

"Absolutely," Heimhocker said, and Loomis said, "There isn't the shadow of a doubt. Or a shadow of Noon, come to think of it."

Barney said, "And that's why he's gonna call you. One of these days, one of these nights, he's gonna have piled up all the cash he wants, he's gonna want to get visible again so he can live like a normal guy, and he's gonna call you two and try and make a deal."

"That," Loomis said, "is what we've been praying for."

"When it happens," Barney said, "we want to know. Mr. Leethe here, and me, we both want to know, right away."

"That depends," said Heimhocker.

"The hell it does," said Barney, and Mordon held Barney's

arm a moment, saying, "Easy, Barney, let me explain it to them." Back to the doctors. "Here's the situation. At this moment, you're worried about your funding, you're worried about the future of your legitimate and no doubt very useful research here in this facility. You know you can't go forward without NAABOR. I am in a position to make life easier for you at NAABOR, or to make life impossible for you there. You have my assurance that no one, none of us, not Barney, not me, not even Merrill Fullerton, has any intention of harming Fredric Noon. We all want to make use of him, true, but so do you. You will be given every opportunity to continue your experiments on him—"

"Observations," corrected Heimhocker.

"Observations. There is no reason for you not to work with us, and therefore I have no reason to make trouble for you at NAABOR. Do we understand one another?"

"I'm afraid we do," Heimhocker said.

"So when Mr. Noon calls," Mordon said, "you'll make arrangements with him—"

"You won't lose him," Barney said.

"Exactly," Mordon agreed. "You'll keep your contact with him, and you'll inform us at once. Yes?"

Both doctors sighed. Both nodded. Heimhocker said, "Yes."

Barney said, "And you don't make him visible again without clearing with us. The both of us."

The doctors looked at him in surprise. Loomis said, "Make him visible? Not possible."

Barney said, "What?"

Mordon said, "You can't undo it?"

"Absolutely not," Loomis said, and Heimhocker said, "The computer models were very clear on that."

Mordon said, "You're positive."

"It's a one-way street," Loomis said, and Heimhocker said, "Freddie Noon's invisibility is irreversible."

"Irreversible."

"Think of albinos," Loomis said, and Heimhocker said, "That's a loss of pigmentation in a different way," and Loomis said, "Not as thorough, not as severe," and Heimhocker said, "But just as irreparable," and Loomis said, "You can't *paint* an albino and expect it to stick," and Heimhocker said, "And the same is true, forever, of Freddie Noon."

"In the movies," Barney said, "once the guy is dead, you can see him again."

Heimhocker curled a lip. "I have no idea what the scientific basis for *that* would be," he said.

"Invisible forever," Mordon said. He was still getting used to the idea.

"I'm afraid so, yes."

Barney cleared his throat. "I tell you what," he said. "When Freddie Noon calls you guys, you don't mention that part, you see what I mean?"

"You can call me a worrywart if you want," Barney said.

They were on the sidewalk in front of the Loomis-Heimhocker Research Facility. Mordon said, "Why would I do that, Barney?"

Barney jabbed a thumb at the pretty little townhouse they'd just left, where Shanana continued to observe them from within her oriel. "I'm gonna tap their phones," he said.

"Do," said Mordon.

40

Freddie waltzed into the Big S at five minutes to eight on Thursday evening, two days since he'd first cased the joint and five minutes before it would close for the night. Since being here last, he'd called Jersey Josh for his order—Josh had grumbled about the truck, but finally admitted he could resell it and would therefore buy it—and he'd made his plans, and now Peg had let him off at the front door and he was ready to go.

The first place he went was the rear of the store, where all the garage doors were, some of them shut and some of them open to reveal the insides of big trailers being used as storage. Skipping around workmen on and off forklift trucks, Freddie studied the contents of the various trailers and finally decided that the sixth one from the right would be the most useful. At the moment, it was less than a quarter full, with Japanese VCRs on pallets, stacked to the ceiling at the far end of the trailer.

Outside each trailer, taped to the wall beside the garage-door opening, was a yellow trip sheet that gave that trailer's identification number and a lot of other news. Freddie memorized the number of the sixth trailer from the right—21409—and then went on to make the rest of his selections. Since he couldn't carry stuff around with him, not even a pencil and a piece of paper, he had to memorize everything he needed to know, but that was okay. He had a good memory, and nothing to distract him.

He was maybe half an hour at the rear of the building, and then he legged it to the front, headed for the office, and it just seemed as though everything was going to be with him tonight. For instance, he didn't even have to press the button to be let into the stairwell. There was a guy just coming out, papers in hand, a younger and less cigarlike Gus, and Freddie managed to reach behind the guy and stop the door just before it snicked shut. The guy walked on, frowning at his new orders, and Freddie slid inside and upstairs, where clerical crew number two was finishing up the last two hours of the workday, mostly with gossip, and most of the gossip about people on soap operas instead of people they actually knew.

It was easy for Freddie to make his own order, adding a line to a work sheet here, a work sheet there, tapping them out on the computer terminals, whenever the clerks were distracted, which they usually were. By ten past nine, according to the big clock on the wall, his paperwork was finished, and down the stairs he went, and along the row of shops to the restaurant, closed for the night, with a lock on the door that Freddie merely had to caress to get in.

This restaurant was just a sandwich-and-coffee place, which was fine by Freddie. He made himself a nice big sandwich, had a glass of milk, had a piece of pecan pie and another glass of milk, and sat at a booth near the back, where the moving fork and glass couldn't be seen, but he could watch the clerks leave. He did not look down at his stomach.

Ten o'clock. Here they came, in little clusters, moving by the plate-glass windows of the restaurant on their way to the main exit, still talking soap. Then the last of them were gone, and the illumination out there on the selling floor changed as most lights were switched off, to leave just enough for the guards to see what they were doing as they moved around.

On a little two-man electric cart. That was cute; Freddie was sitting there, twiddling his thumbs, waiting for dinner to finish its disappearing act, when *whirrr,* that little golf-cart sort of thing went by, with two rent-a-cops on it, talking sports to each other. Their uniforms were navy blue, almost black, imitation police in style. They carried walkie-talkies in holsters where police carry guns, and they wore their police-type hats farther back on their foreheads than regular cops do. They didn't look as though they expected trouble.

Well, so far as Freddie Noon was concerned, they weren't about to have any trouble, at least not from him. Checking to make sure he was invisible again, leaving his dirty dishes behind to cause an argument among staff tomorrow morning, he let himself out of the restaurant and paused to check things out before heading back to look-see truck 21409.

He could hear the electric cart whirring around here and there, the buzz of it bouncing back at him from the metal rafters up by the roof. Apparently, there was only one cart in operation, with two of the four nighttime guards on it. Moving forward from the restaurant, looking back and up, he saw lights on in the upstairs offices, and one venetian blind raised, and a guard seated at the window there, looking out, which made a lot of sense—good place to station a sentry. The fourth guy he didn't see yet.

No problem. Freddie loped away to the rear of the store, avoiding the electric cart, and truck 21409 was *full.* Yes, sir. Giving it as much of the double-o as he could from outside, it seemed to Freddie that his orders had been carried out to the letter. The heavy lifting in this caper had been done by others, which was only proper, and now, in addition to the Japanese

VCRs that had been in this truck in the first place, there was everything else Jersey Josh had requested: personal-computer terminals, boom boxes, and, God knows why, washing machines. (Jersey Josh could not possibly have wanted those last for himself.)

But here Freddie found guard number four, which created a bit of a snag. The guy was seated in a chair leaning against the rear wall of the building, between two of the open garage doors, and he was doing the puzzles in a crossword-puzzle magazine.

The problem was, Freddie had wanted to pull down and close both the door of truck 21409 and the garage door fronting it, neither of which he could do with that guard sitting there. The truck, maybe, almost, since all he'd have to do was reach up to the dangling leather strap and tug on it, and it might not make too much noise as it rolled down, if he did it slowly and carefully. But the garage door was electric, and clanked; he'd heard these doors clank open and shut his last time here.

Well, so he'd adjust. Leaving those doors open and the guard at his puzzle, continuing to avoid the electric go-cart as it whirred around and around in random patterns, Freddie made his way back to the middle of the store, where he'd noticed a ten-foot-high display of pillows, all in a big wire basket, its sides open enough so the customers could reach in and pull out the pillows they wanted. Freddie now climbed up this basket—the wire was sharp and painful against his bare feet—and when he got to the top he flopped onto the pillows and wallowed around until he was really nestled in, and then he lay there gazing up at the ceiling as he waited for the cleaning crew to arrive. He was as comfortable as he had ever been in his life, but he was pretty sure he wouldn't fall asleeeeeeeeee—

Eleven o'clock. The cleaning crew was here. Freddie

knew it was eleven o'clock, and he knew the cleaning crew was here, because the sudden racket they made was so loud and so god-awful that he jumped out of sleep like a deer into your headlights, kicking and flailing in such a panic that he was well and deeply buried in the basket of pillows by the time he got his wits about him. Then he struggled back to the surface and lay there gasping a while, listening to all that noise.

No, it wasn't that the building had fallen down. It was just the cleaning crew, that was all, with their vacuumers and compactors, advancing through the aisles like an invading army in tanks.

Freddie lifted his head, cautious, trying to orient himself, and far away, above the aisles, beyond the phalanxes of weed-whackers and battalions of work boots and soft explosions of furry pink slippers, there remained the lit window of the second-floor office, at the same level as himself atop his pillows, and the impassive guard was still seated in there, looking out, directly at Freddie, and not batting an eye.

Right. Time to go to work.

Climbing back down the basket to the concrete floor, the din of the cleaning crew in his ears, Freddie realized he was going to have to make one extra stop along the way, but when he found the men's room it was full of cleaning crew. He could have startled those people if he'd wanted to, but he used the ladies' room instead, then forgot and flushed and that did startle them. He was just barely out of the ladies' when they all piled in, staring, awed.

The puzzle-working guard had abandoned not only his post but his puzzles; the magazine and pencil sat on the chair instead of him. Maybe he'd gone off to have a word—a shouted word—with the cleaning crew.

Eventually that guard would return, if only to get his magazine. Zipping over to truck 21409, Freddie pulled down its

door, and if it made any noise even he didn't hear it. Then he
pushed the button for the garage door, and down it came, no
doubt clanking and squealing, but who cared?

The next job was to get out of here. Freddie made his way
to the front, and there was guard number four, now in a chair
near the main entrance. So this must be his routine; because
the cleaning crew had to go in and out several times in the
course of their work, this guard moved from his regular position to cover the unlocked doors while they were here, both to
keep unauthorized persons from coming in and to keep members of the cleaning crew from cleaning the place out a little
too enthusiastically.

Easy as pie. Freddie walked by the guard, waited till a
cleaning-crew guy in his green coverall went out to get something from his truck, and eased through the doors just behind
him.

It was July, but it still got cool at night. Feeling a little
chilled, Freddie jogged around to the back of the building,
which took a long time, because it was a very big building.
He and Peg had driven back here last time, which hadn't
taken any time at all, and had seen the arrangement, and it
was still the same now. Snuggled up against the rear of the
building were the trailers, and in the spaces where there was
no trailer there was a closed garage door instead. A pair of
large floodlights, one at the top of each rear corner of the
building, created a flat landscape in sharp white and deep
black, with conflicting shadows. The blacktop parking area
back here was smaller and scruffier than the one in front,
fading off into weedy plane trees and shrubbery at the back,
where half a dozen big blunt cabs for those trailers were
parked.

Freddie had been involved in hijackings before (though
never completely on his own) so he knew how to do the
next part, which was to jump the wires on one of the cabs,

back it up to trailer number 21409, and switch off the engine. Then, after double-checking that this actually was trailer number 21409, as a pink trip sheet taped to its side confirmed—he wouldn't want to remove the wrong trailer, from an open garage door, which might cause comment—he attached the electrical and hydraulic hoses from the cab to the trailer, restarted the engine, drove very slowly forward a few feet just to be absolutely certain that was a closed garage door he would see back there in his outside mirror—it was—and then he checked the lights and brakes, and everything seemed fine.

It was unlikely the people inside would be able to hear this truck engine anyway, but they certainly weren't going to hear it while the cleaning crew was at work. Freddie slipped into low, did some massive turning of the big wheel, and eased that heavy trailer on out.

He did not go past the front of the building, but turned the other way, diagonally across the empty parking lot and out an exit to a side road, then from there to the main intersection, where the light was red. No traffic went by. No traffic went by. No traffic went by. The light turned green. Freddie made the turn, and drove away from there.

The agreement was, they would meet at the burned-out diner at one o'clock, but Peg was too keyed up to stay at home, not after the eleven o'clock news, when there were no more distractions. She wanted to know how things had worked out for Freddie, and she also had this momentous announcement to make to him once the night's work was done.

If there were no problems, that is. If there was a problem, she certainly couldn't compound it for the poor guy by giving him bad news. So she certainly hoped there weren't going to be any problems, and for that reason and all the other reasons she just couldn't hang around the house waiting, so finally she piled out the front door and into the van, and as a result she reached the burned-out diner forty-five minutes early, and of course he wasn't there.

She parked around behind the diner, lights off, as they'd agreed, and sat in the dark, practicing how she would tell him, her exact words and his exact words, and twenty minutes later headlights appeared over there on the road side of the diner. So he was twenty-five minutes early, if it was him. And if it wasn't him, she hoped at least it wasn't state cops, either here to coop or to check on this van parked in the darkness back here.

But it was Freddie. That is, when the passenger door of the van opened there wasn't anybody there, so that meant it was Freddie. Hardly even noticing that kind of thing anymore, Peg said, "How'd it go?"

"Great," his floating voice told her, as the van dipped and swayed because Freddie was getting in and climbing over the seat and going to the back where his clothes were. "No problems at all. I even got to sleep for a while."

"Terrific," she said, listening to the slide and slither of him getting dressed back there, and then Dick Tracy joined her, wearing pink Playtex gloves and a long-sleeved buttoned shirt and khaki slacks and pale socks and loafers. "Hi, Freddie," she said.

"What a snap, Peg," he said, the Dick Tracy face puffing and collapsing as he spoke. "I think I could hit a different one of those stores every week, up and down the Eastern Seaboard."

"Let's just do this one," she suggested.

"Right. One thing at a time."

"That's right."

"Follow me," he said, and got out of the van.

Peg started her engine, switched on her lights, and drove around to the front, and what a *big* trailer that was out there!

For Pete's sake. "Wow," she whispered, peering up at how tall it was, how way up off the ground were those yellow lights along its top edge. And how long it was. And it had more yellow lights on the sides, and red lights at the back, and red and yellow lights on the cab, and great big head-lights out front. It was more like a steamship than a truck, like a great big cargo ship on its way around the world.

She beeped to let him know she was ready, and the big rig slowly started forward, grinding upward through the gears, moving out onto this empty country road in the darkness, Peg in her van easing along in its wake.

They had to cross the Hudson River, which they did on the Rip Van Winkle Bridge, which was all right, because twenty years did *not* go by before they got to the other side. They kept driving west until they got to the New York State Thruway, where the Dick Tracy mask and Playtex gloves would get their first of several tests tonight. This was the first time they were going anywhere that Peg couldn't do Freddie's driving, which made for a great unknown. So, just to be on the safe side, while waiting behind the truck for Freddie to take his toll ticket from the guy in the booth, Peg opened an extra button on her blouse, and when she drove forward to get her own ticket she was kind of leaning forward a little, smiling.

And the guy in the booth had the *weirdest* expression on his face, as though asking himself, What the hell *was* that? But then he saw Peg, and he saw the shadows within her open blouse, and he forgot all about the previous driver. "Hi, there," he said, handing Peg her ticket.

"Hi." She smiled some more.

"Nice night," he suggested.

"Sultry," she said, rolling the *l* around in her mouth like a strawberry, and took off after Freddie.

They were over a hundred miles from New York. Freddie

tucked the big rig into the right lane and kept it at the speed limit, fifty-five miles an hour, not wanting to attract any official attention. Peg tucked in behind him, turned on the radio and settled down to the long and boring drive.

All the way down the Thruway, with traffic very light the whole way (mostly trucks). Then, when they were near New York, they switched over to the New Jersey Turnpike, which meant two more toll-people Freddie left stunned and Peg left happy. Down the turnpike through New Jersey to the spur over to the Lincoln Tunnel, and two more toll-people, one of whom (at the tunnel) was a woman, so Peg's wiles wouldn't do any good. On the other hand, this woman was a toll-taker at the New Jersey side of the Lincoln Tunnel, so she hadn't seen anything odd at all about the guy driving that big tractor-trailer; in fact, if you asked her, he looked more normal than most.

Freddie had told Jersey Josh he'd probably phone between three and four in the morning, and it was in fact about a quarter past three when, reaching Ninth Avenue in Manhattan, Freddie pulled the big rig to a stop at the curb in a no-parking zone, and Peg pulled in behind him. Getting out of the van, stretching, stiff and sore, she walked forward to the cab, looked up, sighed, and said, "Freddie, put your head on."

"Oh. Sorry. I remembered for the tollbooths."

She watched Dick Tracy reappear. "You mean, you drove all the way down with your head off?"

"It gets hot, Peg."

"I'm surprised we didn't leave a hundred accidents in our wake."

"You can't see up in here at night," Dick told her. "It worked out, didn't it?"

"Sure. I'll call Josh now, right?"

"Yeah." The Playtex glove pointed. "I parked where there's a phone booth. If it works."

It wasn't a booth, it was just a phone on a stick, but it did work. Peg dialed the number, and after about fifteen rings it was finally answered. "S?"

"Hi, Josh," Peg said, with absolutely false friendliness. "It's Peg, calling for Freddie."

"O." He didn't sound happy.

"We're here with the stuff. We'll meet where you said, right?"

"Meet Freddie."

"The both of us, Josh."

"S," he said, sounding bitter, and hung up.

A long long time ago there was an actual slaughterhouse in Manhattan, way down below Greenwich Village, near the Hudson River. In the nineteenth century, they had cattle drives down Fifth Avenue, bringing the cows to the slaughterhouse, but then they built a railroad line that was partly in a cut between Tenth and Eleventh Avenues, which is still used by trains from the north coming down to Penn Station, in the West Thirties. Going down from there, the old train line was elevated, at second-floor level, and ran all the way downtown, the trains that carried the doomed cows trundling south and south, as buildings were constructed all around the track, and neighborhoods grew up, until here and there the elevated train line was actually inside buildings along its route.

Then it all came to an end. The slaughterhouse shut down and there was less and less manufacturing of other kinds in lower Manhattan, and fewer and fewer cargo ships from Europe that unloaded there, so there was no longer a need for a railroad line down through Manhattan south of Penn Station. But that old elevated line had been constructed of iron, and built strong enough to carry many tons of train and beef, and it was not an easy thing to tear that big old monster down, so for the most part it was left standing. Here and there, when new construction was under way, it made sense to remove a part of the old line, but most of it is still there. It's there today, just above your head, black old thick iron crossing the street, out of that old building and into that old building, an artifact from an earlier and more powerful time.

Down in the West Village, a block-square brick factory building had long ago risen around the railroad line, incorporating the track inside the building. After World War II, when that factory was converted to apartments, the old loading docks and other access to the tracks were all sealed up with concrete block and finished on the converted side with Sheetrock walls. The unlit unfinished ground-floor area beneath the track was used as parking space by a few neighborhood businesses, a plumber and a locksmith and one or two others, but over the years that cubbyhole down there became a hangout for the kind of people who have only good things to say about anonymous sex. There were some robberies down in there, and some assaults, and then two fatal stabbings within a month, at which point the city sued the corporation that owned the building, which was the first time the corporation had had to confront the fact that the filthy grungy hellhole beneath the old railroad track was actually a part of the structure they owned. So they concrete-blocked one end of it, and put a high chain-link gate at the other end, with razor wire on top, and only the supers had the key to the gate, which meant that, within six months, half a dozen of the worst felons in the neighborhood had keys to the gate.

One of these was an associate of Jersey Josh Kuskiosko. He

it was to whom Jersey Josh would deliver the truck and its goods, for a nice profit on the evening's work, it having been agreed that Freddie Noon would be paid forty thousand dollars if the truck and goods were as advertised, whereas Jersey Josh's associate would then pay Jersey Josh one hundred thousand. That is, once the truck, and its contents, were safely locked away inside that gate, inside that apartment building, under those old railroad tracks.

Freddie had not had that much experience maneuvering a monster this large around streets as small and narrow and bumpy as those in the West Village. Every time he made a turn, at least one tire climbed the curb. That he didn't hit any parked cars was a miracle. Peg, trailing along behind him, had to keep closing her eyes and waiting for the crash that never came.

But then Freddie saw it, out ahead; the old railroad line, the black iron terrace of the Nibelungs, a black bridge spanning the street from one nineteenth-century brick factory to another, with the murky expanse of New York Bay in the background, beneath a clouded sky.

That creature hulking in the deeper darkness under the span was more than likely Jersey Josh; the truck's headlights somehow seemed to avoid shining directly on him. The two guys with him maybe actually were Nibelungs: brutish, nasty, and short.

Freddie wasn't used to thinking in terms of the height of the vehicle he was driving, so it wasn't until later, after he was out of the truck, that he realized that, when he'd driven under the railroad bridge, he'd had less than three inches' clearance. Which, of course, was as good as a mile.

In any event, Freddie drove the truck under the bridge and beyond, stopping with just the very rear of the trailer still underneath. Then, as he climbed down from the cab, feeling very stiff and sore after all that time in the same unnatural position, Peg drove the van into the narrow lane left between the truck and the line of parked cars at the curb, and stopped next to Jersey Josh, who was standing between cars, frowning at the big trailer as though he'd expected something smaller, maybe pocket-size.

"Hi, Josh," Peg said.

Josh looked at her and said nothing. The two henchmen—born henchmen, those two—stood back on the sidewalk, near the chain-link gate, and said nothing. Freddie approached, in his Dick Tracy head and Playtex gloves.

Perky as she could be, Peg said, "You got the money, Josh?"

"Check," Josh said.

Peg shook her head. "We don't take checks, Josh," she said.

He pointed a blunt and filthy finger at the trailer. "Check *truck.*"

Freddie had reached them by now. "Josh," he said, "you know it's all there. Everything you asked for. In fact, even two extra washing machines. I'm throwing them in for free."

Josh turned his head to look toward Freddie's voice, and then recoiled at what he saw, bouncing his butt off the hood of the car behind him. "What U?" he cried.

Freddie waved a Playtexed hand at the henchmen. "You trust these guys because they're your pals," he said, which was patent nonsense. "But do I know them? No. So I don't want those guys to know who I am."

"I know who you are," one of the henchmen said. "You're Dick Tracy."

The other henchman said, "How come a cop?"

"If a real cop stops me," Freddie explained, "he'll think I'm on his side."

"Gloves," Josh pointed out, pointing at them.

"Fingerprints."

Josh shook his head, bewildered as usual by the antics of the human race.

"Money," Peg said, extending a graceful arm out of the van.

Josh ignored her. Pointing his right hand at the truck and his left hand at Freddie, he said, "Back in." Then pointed both hands at the chain-link fence, which one of the henchmen was now unlocking.

The other henchman stepped forward and said, "We'll move these cars, they're ours," meaning the ones blocking entrance to the dungeon.

But Freddie said, "Not me, Josh. You got guys know how to baby these babies. I couldn't back one of these monsters anywhere if I had to."

"Deal," Josh said.

"No, Josh. The deal is I bring it here. You want me to back that up? I'll knock the whole building down, the first thing you know you'll have cops here, wanting to know what's going on."

It's the little things that change history. Josh had been prepared to honor his side of the bargain, but on the other hand, Freddie and Peg had bested him in a couple of encounters recently, leaving a bad taste in his mouth in addition to the bad taste that was always there. Also, one was always up for betrayal, if the situation looked promising. And now Freddie wouldn't back up the truck.

"No deal," Josh said.

"You mean, you want me to take the truck away?"

"It stay."

"We keep the truck," said one of the henchmen, catching on fast.

"*You* go away," said the other henchman, also a quick study.

Peg said, "Without our money?"

Josh gave her a nasty smile. "Revenge," he said.

Both henchmen drew pistols from under their Hawaiian shirts. "Maybe," one of them said, "we keep the broad."

Freddie said, "Josh, you got three seconds to get smart."

Josh looked at him in gloomy satisfaction. "U could die," he said.

"Peg," Freddie said, "go around the block," and he was already ripping off the head and gloves when he dove down and went rolling under the trailer.

The henchmen shouted, as Peg accelerated, and Josh missed her wrist by a millimeter. The van went tearing away down the block. The henchmen ran around both ends of the truck. Josh bent to peer under the trailer, seeing nothing, hauling out his own very old and well-used pistol, just in case Freddie decided to come rolling back.

The henchmen met at the far side, and stood over a pile of clothing on the sidewalk there. "He's naked," one of them said.

"Duhhh," the other one said, and fell down.

The first henchman stared. It was a brick, is what it was, a big dirty brick, waving around in the air all on its own, and now it was coming after *him*. He backed away, stumbling over Freddie's clothes, dropping to one knee in his panic, and took a shot up at the damn brick, and the bullet zipped away up into the understructure of the railroad, binging and caroming off the metal up there for quite a while.

With a moan, the henchman dropped his pistol, swung about, and tried to escape on all fours, which meant he didn't have far to drop, when he dropped.

Josh remained crouched on the other side of the trailer. He could hear activity over there, but didn't know what it meant. Then there was a shot, which he didn't like; if there were seven or eight more like that, somebody might call the cops. But then there was silence, which was better, but not informative. Josh waited, and waited, and then something cold and hard touched his right cheek, and when he rolled his eyes down and to the right, it was a gun barrel. He froze.

"Josh, I'm beginning to lose patience with you."

Freddie, behind him somehow. Where were the henchmen? Josh remained frozen.

"Straighten up, Josh."

Josh did so.

"Do you even *have* the money, you jerk?"

"In car," Josh said, moving nothing but his arm as he pointed away to his right and behind him, at one of the cars blocking access to the gate.

"Is it locked?"

"Dough no. Not mine."

The van returned then, having circled the block, and stopped next to Josh. Peg said, "Freddie, is that you?"

"Yeah. My clothes are the other side of the trailer, would you get them?"

"Sure."

While Peg got out of the van and trotted away, Josh stared and blinked at the side of the trailer, stared and blinked, afraid to turn around. Freddie was naked? Why?

Peg came back with the pile of rumpled laundry and latex and tossed it into the van, then said, "Now what?"

"He says the money's in the car there. Is it locked?"

Peg went over and tested. "No."

"Trusting."

"There's three big manila envelopes on the backseat."

"F!" cried Josh. "F! F!"

Peg said, "One of the envelopes has an *F* on it."

"Freddie!" cried Josh.

"Is there money in it?"

"There's money in all three."

"Take them all."

DONALD E. WESTLAKE

"Just F!" Because the other two envelopes contained the extra sixty thousand earmarked—or dogeared—for Josh.

"Shut up, Josh."

Josh, tried beyond endurance, spun around to remonstrate, to argue, to put his case, and found himself staring at the brick wall beyond the sidewalk. He goggled. "What? What?" Then he saw the pistol, hanging in the air, pointed at his face. Automatically, he thrust out a hand, and it hit something where there wasn't anything: flesh, a chest. "Aaaa!"

Low and dangerous, Freddie's voice sounded from the air directly in front of the trembling Josh: he could feel the warm breath on his face. "Now you know a secret that nobody knows, and lives."

At that point, Josh fainted. And then Freddie had to drag the big flea-covered hulk closer to the curb, so the van could get by.

"A hundred thousand dollars," Freddie said, in satisfaction, and dropped the last of the three envelopes onto the floor behind the passenger seat. He was in his messy clothing and the latex again, beside Peg as she drove.

"That's great, Freddie. That'll set you up for a good long time."

"Set *us* up."

"Freddie, uh, there's something I want to—"

"Peg." They were driving north on Tenth Avenue, and Freddie said, "Peg, I don't think we should try to drive all the way back upstate tonight."

"You don't?"

"No. It's almost four in the morning, we been at it all night, we're both whipped. Let's go home to the apartment, get a good night's sleep, go back up there tomorrow."

"You may be right," she decided.

"I know I am."

"Okay." She turned right on Forty-second Street.

He said, "There was something you wanted to tell me?"

"It'll keep," she said.

41

Due to various matters that were proceeding along in several cloudy corners of his life, Barney Beuler was at the moment operating seven different wiretaps within the five boroughs of the City of New York, every one of them illegal. Which meant he didn't have the advantages of unlimited manpower he'd enjoy if these wiretaps had been ordered by a competent authority and blessed by a judge.

Still, Barney had friends on the force who were experts in this sort of thing, who for a fee would provide him with the off-the-record man-hours and the borrowed official equipment and the expertise to set it all up, and then, with the wonders of modern technology, he didn't even have to go personally to the bugging locations to retrieve whatever phone conversations the tapes might have picked up. It was as easy as collecting your answering machine's messages when you're away from home.

The trickiest part, in fact, was finding a safe phone. Once he had one—a pay phone in an unexpected neighborhood, the home phone of an unsuspecting citizen away at work—he would attach to it his small portable digital recorder, then call his well-hidden little bugaroos in their locations all over town, and the voice-activated little darlings would give him, with no dead air, everything that had been said on that line by everybody using it since his last call, erasing themselves as they went. If there'd been no activity since his last harvest, the bugaroo would say so with a double beep and hang up.

All in all, the seven bugaroos were a grand toy, and frequently of great use, and Barney's only regret at the moment was that they were not yet eight. He'd spoken to his friends about adding Drs. Loomis and Heimhocker to his radio theater, and it would happen eventually, but these things always took time. He'd put in his request on Wednesday, after leaving Mordon Leethe and the doctors over at their research facility, and his contacts now told him the bugs would probably go in sometime over the weekend—weekends are the easiest times to fool with telephone equipment—and be operational no later than Monday morning. So all he could do was hope the doctors didn't say anything really interesting this week, and meanwhile continue on with the seven bugs he did have in place.

Two of the seven were, and had been for some time, inactive, or damn near to it, and one of those two was the bug on the phone of Peg Briscoe, in Bay Ridge. Would she ever come back? She still had the lease on the apartment, she still had the phone and the electric in her name, but did that mean anything? Maybe not, but if she did one day return, Barney wanted to be the first to know. So, three times a week, whenever he made the rounds among his bugaroos, he always included Peg Briscoe, listened to the double beep, and moved on.

But not today. Today, Friday, July 7, at eleven in the morning, Barney worked his way through his taps, recording everything (he culled it all down to the most useful stuff later, at his leisure), and when he reached the Peg Briscoe number he got: "Dr. Lopakne's office."

Barney sat up straight at the desk. He had settled today into the office of an insurance salesman in Woodside, Queens, a man who had announced on his street-facing office door that he would be away for these two weeks on vacation. Barney, his elbows splayed over the insurance man's application forms, listened avidly for the next voice, and bingo:

"This is Peg Briscoe. Is the doctor there?"

"He *is* with a patient right now."

"I used to be his dental technician, and—"

"Yes, I know. This is Hilda."

"Oh, Hilda, hi! I didn't recognize your voice."

"I recognized yours."

"Well, I told you my name. Anyway, what I was calling about, do you think the doctor might need me again?"

"We've got a part-timer that's not so—"

"Part-time would be fine."

"Starting when?"

"Next week, whenever."

"Can the doctor get back to you?"

"No, I'll be in and out. I tell you what, I'll call back Monday morning. Is that good?"

"Fine. Be nice to have you back with us, Peg."

"Thanks, Hilda, be nice to *be* back."

Then the robot voice, male, vaguely southwestern: "Friday, July seven, nine-oh-four A.M."

beep beep

Two hours ago.

"May I ask who's calling, please?"

"Barney."

"Mr. Barney, may I ask what your call is in reference to?"

"No, you may not. You may just tell Mr. Leethe that Mr. Barney is on the line. He'll want to know."

A long silence, dreadfully long, three minutes, four minutes on hold. Rotten bitch. Barney's fingernails tap-tap-

tapped on the insurance man's forms, leaving little scimitar-shaped indentations.

"Barney?"

"*There* you are!"

"What on earth did you say to my girl?"

"I told her I'd sew shut every opening in her body if she didn't put you on the phone."

"I almost believe you."

"Write down this number. Seven one eight, seven nine seven, seven, nine, three, three. Go to a pay phone. Call me. *Fast.*"

Barney hung up. He stood and paced the floor between the filing cabinets and the blinds over the windows concealing the view of—and from—Roosevelt Boulevard.

The phone rang. Barney leaped to catch it on the first ring, before the insurance man's answering machine could come into play. "Yes!"

"Barney, I hope this is worth the—"

"Briscoe's back."

Satisfying silence from the pay phone.

Barney smiled. "I thought that would get your attention. She made a phone call from the Bay Ridge apartment two hours ago, trying to get her old job back. Do you tobacco people have goons?"

"I beg your pardon?"

"Tough guys. Muscle. What do you college-educated boys call such people?"

"All right, all right, I understand."

"We don't want him slipping by us. We gotta go in and cover everything, fast and hard. You come along, and two, three, four—"

"Me? Barney, I'm not—"

"You're not clean, Leethe, don't hold your skirts up. You be there with as many soldiers as the tobacco company can give you. It's—shit, it's twenty after eleven. Can you be there at one? At the corner where the bodega is."

"We'll be there," Leethe promised.

Muscle in suits; will wonders never cease. Lightweight summer suits, and light summer ties, and short-sleeved white shirts. Barney looked at the three guys Leethe had brought along, and all of them had, when you looked past the Little Lord Fauntleroy uniforms, necks wider than their ears, foreheads with shelves, and hands and arms that looked like fence posts. Barney laughed. "I like your style, guys," he said, and turned to Leethe. "Do they know the story?"

"I'm not sure *I* know the story."

"Do they know he's *invisible*?" Barney demanded, getting impatient.

One of the tough guys said, "Yes. We don't believe it, but we know it."

"Believe it," Barney told him. "What we're going to do, we're going to bust straight in. It's the third-floor rear, with an air shaft that doesn't help anybody, but windows at the back. We go in, we quick shut the door behind us, Leethe, you sit on the floor with your back against the door, you holler if anything happens."

"I'm sure I will."

"The rest of us, we secure the windows. We make sure nobody leaves when we come in, not out through anything you can use for an exit. Once we've got the place secure, we will find Mr. Invisible Man."

"Sounds good," said the skeptic.

"No time like the present," Barney said, and led the charge.

Barney had long since acquired keys that would fit the Briscoe building's front door and the Briscoe apartment. If you could ease in quietly, surround your subject before your subject knew what's what, why not? Why go crash-bang, if you didn't have to? Why not leave that stuff to the feds?

Of course, these thugs in suits weren't exactly quiet, not even just walking up the stairs. They did sound as though demolition was going on somewhere in the neighborhood. Barney, leading the way, had the two keys in his hand, and had both locks of the apartment door unlocked when the thugs arrived, so they didn't even have to break stride.

Barney pushed open the door and moved fast, looking neither left nor right, running like the fat man he was straight into the bedroom and across to stand with his back pressed against one of the two closed windows there. One of the thugs took the other window. Leethe had presumably obeyed orders and was now seated on the floor in the living room, his back against the closed front door. The windows in the living room looked out on the useless air shaft—no way up, no exit below—and the other two goons would be at the other two windows, one each in the kitchen and bathroom.

And Briscoe wasn't here. Barney hadn't concerned himself at first with anything but securing the apartment, but now, having accomplished that part, he could consider the fact he hadn't seen Briscoe on the way in, and didn't hear her yelling in either the kitchen or bathroom. So she wasn't here.

Gone to lunch? Both these windows, in the July heat, were closed, though the room wasn't very stuffy. *Been* here, recently, like the phone tap said. Gone again? Freddie Noon still here?

Moving away from his window, Barney told the thug at the other one, "Go get that chair. If either of these windows starts to open, swing the chair at the space in front of it, and give me a holler."

"Right."

Barney left the bedroom, stuck his head in the bathroom, and saw the goon there standing in the tub, which was the way to cover that window, which was also closed. "Good," he said to the goon, who looked faintly embarrassed, like an elephant with its foot stuck in a bucket.

Barney went on to the kitchen. Window closed. Refrigerator turned on, but nothing in it. Ice-cube trays in the freezer, slushy water, not ice yet. He picked up a wrinkled dish towel with deep long vertical pleats in it from the counter beside the refrigerator, and knew what that meant. They'd turned the refrigerator off, expecting to be gone a long time. They'd propped the door open, then kept the freezer open by tying the handles of both refrigerator and freezer doors together with this towel. Then, this morning, Peg Briscoe filled the ice-cube trays, switched on the refrigerator, and tossed the towel on the counter.

Barney tossed the towel on the counter. She had been here. She was gone now. She would come back.

The kitchen goon leaned his back against the kitchen window, folded his arms, and watched Barney at work. This was the skeptic, and nothing so far had dimmed his skepticism. Which Barney couldn't care less about. "Okay," Barney told him, "let's us go outa here arm in arm."

The goon obediently linked his arm with Barney's, and they moved to the kitchen door, both with their other hands out to the side walls. "He isn't here," Barney decided, and shut the kitchen door.

"I guess not," said the skeptic.

Barney grunted. "Wait in the bedroom."

The skeptic raised an eyebrow, but went away to the bedroom while Barney collected the elephant from the bathtub, the two of them exiting the bathroom in such a way that nobody invisible could slide past them.

Once outside, Barney shut that door as well, then he and the elephant went into the bedroom, where first Barney searched the nearly empty closet while one of the goons made sure by swinging a broom handle that there wasn't anybody under the bed, and then the four of them scanned the room and came back out to the living room, where Leethe sat slumped on the floor like an earthquake victim trying to decide who to sue.

"One room to go," Barney said, shutting the bedroom door behind himself.

From where he sat, Leethe would be able to see all the closed doors, while Barney and the three goons did a modified version through the living room of the World Famous Radio City Music Hall Rockettes, at the end of which they were all gathered around the crumpled Leethe as though they were the cowboys and he the fire.

Leethe looked up, his expression as skeptical as that of the skeptical goon. "Having fun, Barney?"

"She was here this morning," Barney said.

"She isn't here now."

"Neither's the guy," said the skeptic.

Barney said, "She told the place where she wants her job back, she'll call Monday morning. She just started up the refrigerator here, she'd had it off for a while. She's coming back. Where's she going to make that call from, Monday morning? Here. Where are *we* gonna be, Monday morning, Mr. Leethe? Three guesses."

42

Two cars drove north out of New York City, even as Barney and his friends prepared to toss the Peg Briscoe apartment. One of them was Peg's van, driven by Peg, with Freddie beside her, completely dressed. He'd decided to be the Ayatollah Khomeini today, God knew why. Or maybe Allah knew. The other car was a Hertz rental, obtained at the deep discount offered executives of NAABOR, and driven by Dr. Peter Heimhocker, with Dr. David Loomis in the passenger seat beside him.

Living in New York, Peter and David had no need of an automobile of their own. In the normal course of events, an automobile would merely be a constant hassle and expense, with garaging and insurance and repairs and all the rest of it. On those rare occasions, mostly in the summer, when they had need of a car, they simply ordered up a shiny clean air-conditioned sedan from Hertz, using the deep discount arranged for them by Dr. Archer Amory. (So *much* would be lost if they severed their relationship with NAABOR; it didn't bear enumeration.)

Peg and Freddie and the van left Bay Ridge not long after ten on Friday morning, maneuvering through city streets over to the Brooklyn–Queens Expressway, then taking that road all the way up through Brooklyn and Queens to the Triborough

Bridge, avoiding Manhattan entirely. Just as their van was crossing from Brooklyn to Queens, David received a phone call from Martin, of Robert and Martin, saying, since they hadn't been able to come up last weekend because of that ridiculous funeral, about which Martin wished to hear *everything,* why not come up this weekend instead, to which David said yes, without even consulting Peter, and then called Hertz. *Then* he told Peter, who was delighted as he was, and they both passed the good news on to Shanana, giving her the phone number where they'd be over the weekend, and telling her she could shut up shop and send home the two lab assistants—borrowed from NYU Medical Center, after a generous contribution to that worthy health-care institution from NAABOR—at the same time. Then they phoned their cat-sitter person, packed their ditty bags, and cabbed up to their nearest East Side office of Hertz, where today's magic carpet was a bright red Ford Taurus, with a sunroof, which turned out later to be a mistake, since the opaque sliding panel to shield them from the sun was broken; fortunately, they'd both brought caps. In any event, by eleven they were in their shiny newish car, and they were headed north on the FDR Drive up the eastern shore of Manhattan Island when Peg was paying the toll on the Triborough Bridge to a toll-keeper who kept trying to look past her at the Ayatollah Khomeini.

Shortly afterward, Peter and David passed the exit for the Triborough Bridge, but they weren't going that way, and continued on up the Harlem River Drive, did a jog east on the Cross Bronx Expressway, then headed north again on the New York State Thruway. Peg and Freddie, somewhat farther north and a bit to the east, had taken the Bruckner Expressway to the Bronx River Parkway, and left the actual City of New York, crossing the invisible line from the Bronx into the city of Yonkers, about fifteen minutes before Peter and David had a similar experience on the Thruway, just a bit to the west.

With Yonkers to the left of them and Mount Vernon to the right of them, Peg and Freddie drove north, and the Bronx River Parkway became the Sprain Brook Parkway with no discernible change in the road at all. The Sprain, however, at first angled northwest, and soon tangentially touched the Thruway, before curving northward again. Ten minutes later—Peter and the Ford traveled slightly more rapidly than Peg and the van—Peter and David reached the same tangent, where they switched from the Thruway, which would soon cross the Hudson River and be of no further use to them, to the Sprain Brook, and now both cars were on the same road, heading in the same direction.

Peg waited until they were on the Sprain, where the traffic was lighter, now that they were well beyond the city, to start the dread conversation. "Freddie," she said, "we have to talk."

"Sure," he said. The Ayatollah face gave nothing away.

"You know I love you, Freddie."

"Uh-oh," he said.

There went the first half hour of her planned speech. Flipping ahead a lot of pages in her mind, feeling miserable now that she'd started, she said, "I just can't go on this way. You know that yourself, Freddie."

The Ayatollah's cheeks filled with air, as Freddie sighed. He looked as though he might either start praying or declare a holy war, hard to tell. "I know it's been hard on you, Peg," his voice said, slightly muffled as usual by the mask. "I've done my best to make it as easy as I could."

"I know you have, Freddie, that's the only thing that's kept me going *this* long. But the strain of it, you know? I mean, you know, you're not really *there*, Freddie. I mean, you are, and you aren't."

"Dinner at that restaurant," he said.

"That's one thing," she agreed.

He sighed again, giving the Ayatollah mumps, then curing them. "Let me think about this," he said.

"I already did think about it, Freddie."

"Well, let *me* think about it a minute, okay?"

"Okay. Sure." And she concentrated on her driving.

In the red Ford Taurus, David was saying, "A part of me, Peter, you know, a part of me doesn't want to go back at all."

"I know," Peter said.

"Just keep going, not even stop at Robert and Martin's, just drive right on up into Canada and just . . . *go*."

Peter smiled, ironically. "Into the north woods?" He sang, "I'm a lumberjack, and I'm okay."

"Oh, you know what I *mean*."

"Yes, of course I do."

"Before this," David explained, even though Peter did know what he meant, "we didn't have to think about tobacco at all, did we?"

"Charles Lamb wrote," Peter quoted, " 'For thy sake, tobacco, I/Would do anything but die.' "

"Well, so would we, apparently," David said bitterly. "Do anything."

"But smoke the stuff."

"We're *living* on the stuff, Peter. We never had to think about that before, but we have to think about it now. The American Tobacco Research Institute is nothing more nor less than a public relations piece of puffery for NAABOR. Before this, I never even *thought* about NAABOR, never thought we had anything to *do* with NAABOR, not really."

"I know," Peter said.

"But now, this new fellow, Merrill Undertaker, or whatever his name is."

"Fullerton, as you well know."

"He'll always be Merrill Undertaker to me. Peter, even if we never give him what he wants, we've agreed to do his bidding, We're *selling out* to him."

"I'm afraid, David, we sold out long ago, if truth be told."

"But we never had to *notice* before!"

"David," Peter said, becoming just the slightest bit irritated, "what do you want to do? Do you want to pay full price for this rental?"

"No, of course not. Isn't there anywhere *else* we can go, anyone else we could work for?"

"Maybe the government," Peter suggested, "falsifying evidence of cancers downwind from nuclear test sites. Or the insulation industry, struggling to unprove the effects of asbestos. Or a chemical compa—"

"Stop!" David shrieked, clapping his hands to his ears. "Isn't there anybody *good* in this world?"

"You," Peter told him, "and me. And possibly Robert and Martin, I'm not sure."

David stared out the windshield, trying not to think, and thought.

Eight miles ahead, Freddie broke a long silence in the van. "You want to leave me, don't you, Peg?"

"In a way," Peg admitted. "Kinda."

"I saw you start up the refrigerator, in the apartment."

"You did?" Exasperated and embarrassed all at once, she cried, "Do you *see*? Do you see, Freddie? How can I live like that? I never know where you are, and when I *do* know where you are, it's because you look like something in a horror movie."

"Aw, it isn't that bad, is it?"

"Sometimes. I've gotta admit it, Freddie, sometimes it's very very hard to open my eyes in the morning."

"Ah, hell, I suppose it is," Freddie said. "Jeez, Peg, I do wish sometimes this thing, this, whatever it is, invisibility—"

"The disappearing act," she suggested.

"Up in smoke," he agreed. "I wish it was over."

"Boy, so do I, Freddie."

"I mean," Freddie said, "it was just that one shot they gave me, and the antidote that wasn't worth a good goddam, but how long before it wears off? With the hundred grand from Jersey Josh, and the stuff from before, we're set now for a good long time, we could take life easy, travel, go out together, have some fun."

"Not with you like this, Freddie. Believe me."

"I know. I know." The Ayatollah brooded out the windshield, as the straight highway beneath their wheels changed its name again, this time to the Taconic Parkway.

Peg drove, the speed slackening a bit because she was trying to think. "We can talk on the phone a lot," she said. "And I can come up and see you sometimes. Watch you swim. Stay over, go home in the morning."

"Go home where?" Freddie asked. "Back to the apartment?"

"Sure," Peg said. "Why not?"

"Because that cop is still looking for me. And the lawyer. And they know about the apartment."

"They also know we're not there," Peg objected. "They know we came upstate."

"If I was that cop," Freddie said, "I'd keep an eye on the apartment sometimes, just in case one of us came back for a clean shirt. He's got to know you're still paying the rent on it."

Peg hadn't considered that possibility, but now she did, and she didn't like it. Not have her apartment back? Get chased around by those bad people? She said, "They can't watch an empty apartment every second, Freddie. I already fixed it so I'll go back to work for Dr. Lopakne—"

"You did, huh?"

"I'm surprised you didn't listen to the call." But then she realized they were both getting irritable, which they shouldn't do, and she said, "It's just part time, just for a while, till I figure out what I'm doing."

"Sure," he said, also making the effort to be reasonable. "Makes sense."

"So I'll stay over tomorrow night, I can take that much of a risk, and go in to Dr. Lopakne Monday, and then find a new place after that. I mean, I got nowhere else to spend tomorrow night."

"Well, you do, if you think about it."

"Come on, Freddie," she said. "I *have* to make this change, I just do. And I have to be in the city tomorrow night so I can go over to Dr. Lopakne Monday morning, I already promised I'd be there."

"Uh-huh."

"Listen," Peg said, "it won't be as bad as you think, it really won't. It'll work out, you'll see."

"With me up here, and you down there."

"Mostly. It'll make life a lot easier, Freddie, it really will. For you, too. If you want to walk around in just shorts and sneakers, there wouldn't be anybody there to scream when you walked into the room. You could relax."

Freddie seemed to think about that for a few minutes, and then he said, "At least you don't want to call it off completely."

"Oh, *no*, Freddie, absolutely not. We're still together, only just not so *much* anymore."

"I know you tried, Peg," Freddie said. "I know you did your best."

"Thank you, Freddie. We need gas."

"Take the exit at Route Fifty-five, there's that good gas station there."

Seven miles south, Peter and David were traveling now in their caps, having learned what a mistake they'd made in accepting the sunroof. David said, "Peter, I could not be more thirsty. I feel like we're in one of those Foreign Legion films."

"There's that convenience store and gas station at the exit by Fifty-five," Peter said. "I'll pull off there."

"You don't need gas?"

"No, Hertz fills it right up."

Peg and Freddie didn't discuss their situation any more before they reached the Route 55 exit, where she swung off the Taconic and across the state road to the large gas station. "Sit back, kind of," she advised Freddie, and got out of the van to pump gas.

Freddie, sitting back, reflected on the complexities of life. The same thing that's a boon and a benefit is also a bane and a complete drag. "If I had it to do over," he muttered inside the Khomeini head. But what was the point? He didn't have it to do over.

The van took eighteen gallons of gasoline. Peg waited while a red Ford Taurus crossed her path, then walked over and into the convenience store to pay, where she had to wait behind two other customers.

David and Peter got out of the Ford, stretching and bending. David glanced at the old man slumped in the passenger seat of the van over by the pumps, but hardly registered him at all. They went into the convenience store and Peter got a Diet Pepsi while David chose a lemon-lime seltzer. They stood on line behind a young woman paying for gasoline, then paid for their drinks.

Peg went back out to the van, got in, and started the engine. "It'll be okay, Peg," Freddie told her. "Don't worry."

She smiled at that frowning madman mask. "Thank you, Freddie," she said, touched, and put the van in gear.

Peter and David came out of the convenience store, backed the Ford out of its parking place, then had to wait while the van with the old man in it went by in front of them, the young woman at the wheel. They followed the van out of the station, to the right, under the Taconic, and then right again. Peter, impatient, wished the van would move a little faster. The two vehicles came up the curving ramp, back toward the Taconic northbound, and at the merge the van put on its left blinker and slowed to a crawl, while the young woman checked for oncoming traffic.

"Get *on* with it," Peter muttered.

First the van, then the Ford, rejoined the light traffic flowing northward. For a couple of miles, the Ford stayed behind the van, but then Peter pulled out and passed it, just at a moment when Peg had slowed again, because she was saying, "Freddie, can I tell you what I think we ought to do?"

"Sure. Go ahead."

Peg watched the red Ford pull back into the right lane. He didn't really want to go that much faster than her, she could tell. She said, "When we get to the house, I think we should collect some cash and then go to a used-car lot, and buy you a car. Maybe one with the smoky side windows."

"Because you want the van?"

"Because people know about the van," Peg said. "The cop that followed me up here to the railroad station, and the police chief in Dudley. I think you're better off, driving around in the country, if you're not in the van."

"You may be right about that," Freddie admitted.

"I think we should do it this afternoon," Peg went on. "Soon as we get there, so they can do the paperwork and the insurance and the license plate and all that."

"Why? Peg? When do you want to leave?"

"To . . ." She'd been going to say *tonight*, but at the last second she found herself stumbling, and saying instead, "Tomorrow."

Another sigh from Freddie. "I'm really gonna miss you, Peg."

"I'm gonna miss you, Freddie," Peg said. "But, truth be told, I've already been missing you for quite a while now."

Up ahead, David said to Peter, "Peter, what if they find the invisible man?"

"Our Freddie? What if?"

"They want us to enslave him, don't they? Into their own nefarious designs."

"Well," Peter pointed out, "he's fairly nefarious to begin with."

"Not *their* way. Not *our* way, Peter."

Peter gave him a long hard look, before once again checking the road out front. (The van remained well back in the rearview mirror.) "David," he said, very cold, "do you intend to be a sodden sack of guilt the entire weekend?"

"No. I intend to forget my troubles the instant we get there."

"With drink?"

"I'm not going to be sodden, Peter, all right?"

"Thank you," Peter said.

They drove for a minute or two in silence, and then David said, "*And* they want us to lie to him."

"Well, David," Peter said, "I must admit I'm not looking forward that much to telling him the truth."

In the van, Freddie said, "What if I call the doctors?"

"What?"

"When we get there. You go off to a used-car lot, you don't need me along anyway, you'll be more comfortable if I'm not there—"

"Are you sure? You don't want to pick out what you're gonna drive?"

"You know my taste, Peg. Smoky glass, that's nice, but maybe not too flashy after that. Not something the cops automatically look at. I trust you to pick the right thing, we know each other *that* good."

Peg thought it over. "Okay," she said. "Then we can go back to the place together in the van, later today or tomorrow, whenever they got it ready, I'll get out of the van a block or two away, go pick it up, drive it back to the house."

"Perfect," Freddie said. "And today, when we get there, while you're off to get the car, I'll call the doctors."

"You won't tell them where you are, will you?"

"Of course not. I'll just say I'm ready to discuss a deal, and do they by any chance know when this thing is gonna wear off. And then play it by ear."

"Anytime you need me, Freddie, any help, drive you places, pick things up, whatever . . ."

"I know that, Peg. I appreciate it."

Four miles ahead, David broke a long silence in the Ford by saying, "A great weight has been lifted from me."

Peter glanced at him. "Good."

"You don't have to worry, Peter, I will not be a wet blanket all weekend. Or any of the weekend."

"Very good."

"I just had to say it, that's all, get it off my chest. And now it's gone. Look how beautiful it is up here."

Peter looked. Green trees, blue sky, gray road. It was beautiful. "Yes, it is," Peter said.

"I've left the cares of the city behind me," David said, as they drove on by Freddie and Peg's exit, their own exit to North Dudley being some miles farther north.

Five minutes later, Peg slowed again to take that exit from the Taconic onto the county road. Following its twists and hills, she at last, eight minutes later, turned in at their own little hideaway. They got out of the van and went into the house, which for both of them was already becoming home, familiar and comforting.

While Peg looked in local phone books for used-car dealers, Freddie called information for the number of the Loomis-Heimhocker Research Facility, then called that number, and a young woman answered, saying, "Loomis-Heimhocker Research Facility," so that part was okay.

He said, "I'd like to talk to either one of the doctors." Across the room, Peg, two local phone books under one arm, waved as she left, and Freddie waved back.

"I'm sorry, the doctors have gone away for the weekend."

Trust doctors to take off early on a Friday. Yanking the hot Khomeini mask up off his head, Freddie said, "This is kind of an emergency."

"An emergency?" She sounded doubtful. "The doctors here are not in regular practice."

"No, no, I know that. You see, they gave me one of their experimental formulas, about a month ago—"

"They *did*?" Absolute astonishment.

"You didn't know about that?"

"As a matter of fact, I've—there've been certain things that—" With sudden suspicion, she said, "Did you have anything to do with our burglary?"

"Uhh . . ." It was so unexpected an accusation he didn't have a real answer at first, but then he said, "That's part of what I've got to talk to the doctors about. Do you have someplace where I can get in touch with them?"

"Give me your phone number, I'll have them get in touch with you."

"Miss," Freddie said, "I'm not gonna give you my phone number. But I promise you, if you give me a number where *I* can reach *them,* they'll thank you. Honest to God."

There was a long pause, while the young woman thought that over, and then she said, "All right, I'll take the chance." And she gave him a number that started with the area code 518, which was the exact same area code as where he was calling from!

It's an omen, he thought, finally a good omen. "Thanks a lot," he said. "I really appreciate this, and so will the doctors."

"Mm-hm," she said.

Freddie hung up, and called that number, and a man answered, saying, "Skeat residence."

"I'm looking," Freddie said, "for Dr. Loomis or Dr. Heimhocker, either one. Makes no difference."

"Oh, they're not here yet," Skeat said, if that was his name. There were party sounds in the background. "They're expected soon."

"Okay," Freddie said. "I'll call back."

"Why not give me your number, and they can call you when they get here?"

"No, that's okay, I'll be kinda in and out. I'll call back in, what? An hour?"

"Oh, less, I should think. Half an hour."

"That's what I'll do then," Freddie said.

"Who shall I tell them called?"

"Tell them—tell them Freddie, from last month."

"Freddie, from last month," Robert repeated, intrigued. "I'll tell them," he said, and hung up, and went back to the rowdies in the front room.

This group now were the stay-overs, the weekend guests. The actual *party* would begin at around five, when the first of the other guests would arrive, a mixed bag of straight and gay, New Yorkers mostly, though some West Coast film people as well, all with country places within an hour's drive of here.

Much frolicking would take place in the pool, and frivolity here and there, and drinking generally. Dinner would be served, buffet-style, at eight, cleared at ten, and the staff gone away to their own country homes—mostly mobile—by eleven. A few of these stay-overs, to judge by the way they were knocking it back now, would be unconscious long before dinner, and a few of the party guests would find friends, or at the very least soft places to lie down, and would still be here in the morning. The summertime Friday parties at Robert and Martin's tended not to be over, not to be really *over,* until around seven Sunday evening, though Sunday afternoons did sometimes have about them something of the air of the roving bands of penitents in Europe during the plague, self-flagellating and doomed.

Twenty minutes later, interrupting a general conversation about global warming—the consensus appeared to be guarded approval—Martin looked past Robert's left ear toward the front windows and said, "This must be Peter and David now, at last."

Robert turned to look, out the window and past the four cars already here, and saw the red Ford Taurus inching in to join the herd. And yes, here came Peter and David out of the car, wearing their cute yachting caps and carrying their bags as they moved toward the house.

Robert met them at the door. Cheeks were kissed, and then Robert said, "You just missed your friend, on the phone, but not to worry."

"Friend?" Peter said, and David said, "Who?"

"He says he's Freddie, from last month. He does sound like fun," Robert said, and then stopped, astonished, as Peter went off into gales of hysterical laughter and David burst into tears.

43

Robert was Robert Skeat and Martin was Martin Snell, and they were something very important on Wall Street that involved them having a fax machine in their Land-Rover and a pied-à-terre in Paris and a private airstrip out beyond the barns on which small planes and sometimes helicopters landed, merely to bring Robert and Martin things they were to sign.

Robert and Martin had been together forever, which was why they had the logo of entwined *S*'s on the archway over the drive leading to their house. It was a family joke that Robert always answered the phone, "Skeat residence," while Martin always answered, "Snell residence," and it was also true that they had never declared themselves openly on the Street. There were certainly rumors about them in their place of employment, had been for years, but, "Don't ask, don't tell" had been their byword since ages before those nervous Nellies in the Pentagon had stopped playing with their G.I. Joe dolls. And so long as they were so good at doing whatever it was they did, no one in their firm had the slightest desire to make trouble for Robert and Martin.

Weekends, particularly in the summer, Robert and Martin let it all hang out up at S&S in North Dudley, twenty-eight acres of rolling wooded countryside up a blacktop private drive from a dirt county road off a two-lane blacktop county road just a snap of the fingers from the Taconic Parkway. The house was large and sprawling, with seven bedrooms, plus a three-bedroom apartment in one of the barns. The pool was large and heated. The tennis court was clay, and magnificently maintained, as was the wine cellar. Robert and Martin had many friends, from a variety of worlds, including a number of straight worlds, and their country weekend parties were, in a word, notorious.

So that's Robert and Martin; usually, as you might suppose, the center of all eyes. But not today, not just this minute. Just this minute Robert and Martin and the nine other people here in the big front room of the main house were all staring hungrily, avidly, at Peter and David, waiting for them to get themselves under control, so they could *tell all.*

Both had been borne, had been half-carried, to this long sofa facing the fireplace with the brilliant flower arrangement in it, and both had been plied with drink, someone remembering that Peter liked vodka and grapefruit juice, and someone else remembering that David liked Campari and soda with a slice of lemon, and now everyone waited to find out *what* was going *on.*

Peter recovered first, and in fact had settled down to gasps and hiccups even before his vodka arrived, but then everybody had to wait while Peter did a miserable job of helping David recover, snapping at him with such useful lines as, "Pull yourself together," and, "Stop it, David, for God's sake," while David just kept on keening and sobbing in the most heartbroken manner you could imagine.

"Oh, do shut up, Peter," Martin finally said, and hunkered down beside the distraught David, holding up the cheery glass of red liquid and clear ice cubes and bright yellow lemon slice for David to see, saying, "David, come along, try to drink some of this, you'll feel much better, I promise, listen to Nurse Martin, now."

That did make David laugh, or at least giggle or snicker or something, through his tears, but the tears kept flowing, and David remained far too unstrung to hold a full glass of anything in those trembling hands.

Martin said, "David, we have the most wonderful new snorkel gear for the pool, it's phosphorescent, you *glow* in the *dark*, it's the most fantastic thing, you'll have to see it for yourself and advise us on it, it's probably madly carcinogenic, what do you think?"

David looked at Martin. His eyes were welling with tears, but they were grateful, too, and even amused. He gasped a bit, struggling to catch his breath. "Don't," he managed.

"Yes?"

"Don't . . ."

"Yes? Yes?"

"Smoke underwater!" David blurted out, and smiled through his tears, and looked up with comforted pleasure at his friends when they laughed, and the phone rang.

Utter silence. All eyes turned to Robert, as he crossed toward the phone. "If this is Susan," Robert said dangerously, "asking if she can bring dessert . . ." and left the threat unfinished, as he picked up the phone and said, in an amazingly normal tone of voice, "Skeat residence."

Pregnant pause.

"Yes, he is. Hold on." Robert turned and extended the phone toward Peter, at this point the more able-bodied of the two. "It's Freddie."

Peter knocked back half his vodka and grapefruit juice at a swig, put the glass on the floor, got to his feet, and strode over to Robert. David took the Campari and soda from Martin and drank it *all* down, his eyes never leaving Peter, who took the phone, cleared his throat, and said, "Dr. Peter Heimhocker here."

Everybody waited. Peter pointedly turned his back on the

room, as though he would be permitted privacy at this moment in the exercise. "Yes, I recognize your voice." Accusingly, he added, "You took our things."

"Peter!" David hissed. "That hardly matters now!"

Gesturing violently at David to shut up, Peter said, "So would we, of course. Naturally." Then he seemed troubled, and said, "Well, that would be hard to say, we'd really have to examine you before we could do that sort of prognosis . . ."

"Oh, God," David said, brokenly, and handed his empty glass to Martin, who handed it to the canapé waiter, who knew what to do with it and went away and did.

Peter was saying, "We'll be back in the city Monday, we could— Well, if you don't trust us, I don't—oh, come now, *you're* the untrustworthy one, aren't you? I mean—" He took a deep calming breath, listening, and then apparently answered a question. "We're upstate. North of the city. A hundred miles north." Deeply troubled, Peter put a palm over the mouthpiece and turned to Robert. "He wants to know can he come up?"

"Yes!" said everybody in the room, all at once, except David, who cried, "God, no!" but was ignored.

Into the phone, Peter said, "If you really want to—all right, fine. Where are you now? I *know* you're in New York City, I mean *where* in New York City? Freddie, I just want to know where I'm giving you directions *from*, all right? I swear to God, you're the most paranoid heterosexual I ever met in my life."

"Pity," Robert said.

"All right, fine," Peter said, making no effort to hide his exasperation. "Do you know where the Taconic Parkway is, north of the city?" To the others, he said, "He says he'll find it." Into the phone, he said, "Do not cross the Hudson River. Stay to the east, as though you were going to New England. Come up the Taconic to the North Dudley exit, then drive east toward North Dudley, oh, about half a mile. Then turn left on County Route Fourteen, take that to Quarantine Road, take a—*I* don't know why it's called Quarantine Road, they named it two hundred years ago, it's perfectly safe. Freddie, the condition *you're* in, I don't think you need to worry about anybody else."

That made the other people in the room raise their eyebrows at one another. In the little silence, the canapé waiter gave David his new Campari and soda, and David wept quietly into it.

"All right, you take a right on Quarantine Road, it's a dirt road, and about three miles along on your left you'll see a very tasteful wrought-iron archway with entwined *S*'s over a blacktop drive going—entwined *S*'s." Peter exhaled, not calmly. "An *S,* Freddie, the letter *S,* and another letter *S* facing the other way, and they twine together, like vines. Freddie, it's the *only* archway on Quarantine Road. You come in there, about a mile—"

"Seven-tenths of a mile," said Robert.

"Seven-tenths of a mile," Peter said, through gritted teeth, and showed his tension even more by adding, waspishly, "If you were to go a full mile, of course, you'd drive right through the house without noticing. What? Nothing, I'm just—" Peter closed his eyes, swayed slightly, clutched the phone, opened his eyes. "I apologize to everyone," he said, into the phone and into the room. "I've merely been under something of a strain lately."

"Oh, God," David moaned, in agreement, and slurped Campari.

"It will take you—" Peter said, and broke off, and said, "Well, I don't know where you are, do I? It will take you two to three hours to get here, depending where you're coming *from.* Are you going to leave now?" Peter looked at his watch. "It's twelve-thirty-five."

"I'm forgetting lunch," Martin murmured, and beckoned again to the canapé waiter.

"Let's say," Peter said, "you should get here sometime around three. All right? What are you driving? A van. I don't suppose our lab equipment is still in it."

"Peter!" David hissed. "Don't antagonize him!"

"Yes, that's what I thought," Peter dryly told the phone. "You wouldn't, would you, like to give me a number I could call, in case you don't show up? No, I didn't think so."

Peter hung up, and gazed sardonically across the room at David. "Don't antagonize *him*?"

"The time has come, boys and girls," Robert said, "for class to hear today's story."

Peter came back over to stand beside David, but didn't take his seat on the sofa. David didn't stand, but he did look up, and say, in a half-whisper, as though he thought he couldn't be heard by everybody standing around, "What do we do?"

"What timing," Peter said.

"*Pee*-ter!" David cried, and waved his nondrink hand around to indicate the entire bright-eyed crowd. "We can't swear eleven people to secrecy!"

Martin, kindly Martin, kindly as ever, said, "David, you can, when you think of the alternative."

David blinked at him. "Alternative? What alternative?"

"There is none," Martin said, and smiled in sympathy.

44

Of all times for Peg to be away with the van, unreachable, and who knew when she'd be back. Maps spread on the dining table, Freddie's invisible finger moved along the colored road lines, but he couldn't keep track of anything that way, so he got a spoon from the kitchen, and used the end of the spoon handle to follow the road lines.

County Route 14, right up there, not far at all. Quarantine Road; gotcha, little black windy line goes over that way. Fifteen minutes from here, no more, north and a little east.

Fifteen minutes in the van.

What a pain. He could be there before one o'clock, could be there two hours before they expected him, could hang around, listen, watch, see what they were up to, if they were calling the cops, get the lay of the land. But, no.

Freddie went to the kitchen and put on the Playtex gloves so he could make himself a quick sandwich. He'd found it was easier, working around the kitchen, if he could see his hands. Putting the sandwich together, pouring a glass of tomato juice, Freddie tried to think of what to do. Then he removed the gloves and, carrying his sandwich, went out to the two-car garage that had come with the house, and there, as he remembered it, was the 1979 white Cadillac convertible, and it was still up on blocks. A *car*, and no damn use at all.

What? What? What?

The sandwich appeared to float in the open garage doorway, slowly converting itself into sludge as it oozed two feet lower. At last the transition from sandwich to sludge was completed, and Freddie started to turn away, to shut the garage door and go back to the house, and then he saw the bicycle.

Peter, being the calmer of the two, was elected to tell the story. "You all know," he began, "about Buffy and Muffy."

But then it turned out that, no, they did not all know about Buffy and Muffy. Seven of the eleven people in the room, including Robert and Martin, did know about the translucent cats and had seen them trotting around Peter and David's private quarters on the top floor of the research facility, but the other four had not, and so Peter had to start from the very beginning, and explain what melanoma was, and what science was, and what research was, and even what tobacco public relations was, all before finally getting to Buffy and Muffy, which didn't even begin to get them to Freddie.

It is very tricky for a naked man to ride a bicycle.

"He was a burglar," Peter said; they'd gotten that far at last. "He seemed like the answer to our prayers."

"If only we'd known," David said.

"Yes, but we didn't. And he did agree, we did have an agreement with the fellow."

"A crook," Robert said.

"Point taken," Peter admitted. Much of the tension had left him, now that he was getting it all off his chest. "Now," he said, "I'm afraid comes the difficult part, where I must say I do feel to some extent responsible. We both do. We share the blame."

"Thank you, Peter," David whispered.

Peter was again on the sofa, perched forward on the very edge of it, while David slumped back beside him. Peter took David's hand and squeezed it, and then said to the group, "We had these two formulae."

It was a thirty-gear bike, a virtual thesaurus entry of power and speed, adaptable to any terrain known to man; there was probably a gear for going across ceilings. Once Freddie'd figured out how to sit on the thing without pain or damage, it fairly flew along the verge.

These were country roads, and not heavily trafficked, but *some* vehicles used them. On an average of once every two minutes or so, a car, or more often a pickup truck, would come along, in one direction or the other, and the first few times Freddie tensed up a lot, waiting for who knew what to happen. After all, the people in those vehicles would be seeing a bicycle travel along beside the road all by itself, at a pretty good clip. The bicycle was on the right side, to go with the flow of traffic, but that was all that was even remotely right about it. (The sandwich sludge, growing fainter, was a minor element in the scene.)

So he'd expected cars to slam to a stop. He'd expected part of this exercise would be him from time to time racing away into the woods, or into the forehead-high cornfields, or otherwise eluding pursuers, before being allowed to proceed peacefully on his way. But in the first ten minutes of his journey half a dozen cars and trucks went on by, north- or southbound, and nobody at all stopped, though he did see some surprised faces in passenger windows, and a couple of times he saw brake lights briefly flick on. But then every car or pickup continued on its way, some even faster than before.

Maybe country people, Freddie thought, are calmer than city people. Maybe they take odd things in stride, since living in the country is already such an odd thing to do. Maybe they figured it was a remote-control robot bicycle, like the remote-control robot airplanes that go sputter-sputter-sputter over every park in America in the summer, when you're trying to relax, or like those remote-control robot automobiles people give their kids at Christmas and the first thing the kid does is drive it into the tree and knock the tree over. Or maybe they were just people who mind their own business.

Well, no. Up ahead, the road dipped down, and then dipped up again, and then way up there it went around a curve. And that was where, headed this way, the police car appeared, coming around that curve, some kind of dark-colored state police car. No siren or lights or anything, but moving fast.

Somebody'd made a phone call.

To Freddie's right was a cornfield, the corn about five feet tall. The state-police car disappeared into the dip. Freddie turned right, and pedaled into the cornfield, as the state-police car reappeared, much closer.

They'd seen him, dammit; he heard them squeal to a stop. Sounds of car doors opening and closing. They couldn't see the bicycle, because it was shorter than the corn. And they couldn't see Freddie because they couldn't see Freddie. But Freddie could see them, two state troopers in uniforms and Smokey the Bear hats, conferring briefly beside their car.

Freddie, having driven fifteen or twenty feet into the cornfield, had turned left, and was now going between the rows, parallel to the road. There was almost room enough between the lines of corn plants for the bicycle, particularly if he held on to the handlebar in from the outer edge grips. The ground in here was hard as a rock, pretty smooth, and weedless; these are not organic farmers, you know.

Freddie worked his way through the gears until he found the one for cornfields, and then legged it, occasionally looking back toward the cops. They had apparently spotted his wheel tracks where he'd crossed the scrubland into the field, but once inside he'd left very little spoor on this hard dry soil; certainly not enough for anybody to track him. They were now moving around aimlessly back there, looking down.

What would the cops do next? They must have received more than one report about a bicycle traveling all on its own, because one report they would have figured was a nut. These two officers had been sent out to check into it. They'd seen the bicycle, or they'd seen something, far away and indistinct, and they'd seen it go into the cornfield. Now they'd look around in here for a while, and then they'd radio in that they thought they'd seen it but had lost it, and they'd be told there's no point hanging around, let's see if there's any more reports, and in any case a bicycle riding by itself doesn't actually break any man-made laws, only natural ones. So they'd go away.

That was Freddie's theory, anyway, and he liked it. What he didn't like was that, as he moved into the dip in the land, he saw that just ahead the cornfield gave way to pasture with cows in it, surrounded by barbed-wire fence.

There was nothing for it but to turn left and go back out to County Route 14. He was in the dip now, and the state-police car was out of sight. May it stay out of sight. Freddie coasted to the bottom of the dip, switched to the climbing-out-of-a-dip gear, and sped on.

There was no rearview mirror on this thing, unfortunately. Freddie had to keep looking back over his shoulder. Up to the top of the dip, and he saw way behind himself to the police car still stopped beside the cornfield. Around the curve he went, shifted into the good-level-road gear, and hit forty-five without working up a sweat.

Robert said, "Peter, if I didn't know you have no sense of humor—"

"Well, thank you very much."

"You're welcome. *And* if I hadn't seen those two ghostly cats of yours with my very own eyes, I would think, when you tell me an invisible man is on his way here to this house from the city, that you were pulling my leg."

David said, "Robert, I would *give* my leg for this not to be true."

One of the four who had just heard the whole story for the first time, a talent agent named Gerald, said, "Peter, what I still don't understand is, if you never considered using these potions togeth—"

"Formulae."

Gerald smirked a bit, but nodded. "Whatever you say, dear. If you never put these things together on purpose, in your lab, how can you be so sure what their combined effect might be?"

"Computer models," David answered.

"Also, I'm afraid, empirically," Peter said, and looked mournful. "On the phone just now, Freddie asked me when the invisibility would fade off and he'd get to be visible again."

David made a low moaning sound. "Lunch," said the canapé waiter.

Martin got to his feet. "We have an hour and a half, at the very least, before this fellow gets here. We'll have our lunch, and then we'll decide what to do."

"I *know* what to do," Peter said, also standing. "Once we've got our hands on Freddie, I want to *keep* him. Not lose him stupidly, the way we did last time."

"And not," David added, "turn him over to those awful to-bacco people."

"Nor," Peter said, "that even worse policeman."

"Oh!" David cried, at the very memory of Barney Beuler. "Certainly not!"

"We'll capture him," Robert decided. "Thirteen of us, one

of him. I don't care how invisible he is, or how clever, we can surround him and capture him and tie him to a piece of furniture if we have to."

"A large piece of furniture," Peter advised.

"First," Martin said, "lunch."

The car that squealed to a stop in the middle of the road was full of drunken teenage boys. It came down Route 14 from the north, weaving back and forth in the road ahead of Freddie, polluting the air with terrible rap noises, and then it stopped so suddenly its front bumper kissed the blacktop, and five teenagers piled out of it, leaving the doors open and the rap snarling as they ran with drunken intensity straight at Freddie. That is, at the bicycle rolling along all by itself at the edge of the road.

Damn, damn, double damn. By Freddie's calculations, Quarantine Road would be just a little beyond that next curve up there; he was almost to it. But these drunken clowns were too close and coming too fast for Freddie to take any evasive action, even if he'd had a friendly cornfield beside him instead of these hilly, rocky, underbrush-clogged woods. No time to swing around and head the other way, and no profit in it, either, since they could always catch up with him in their car, and probably run him down with it, too.

Freddie jumped off the bike and gave it a shove toward the woods. It was still rolling, though with a distinct wobble, when the first of the drunken louts reached it, and launched himself through the air and tackled it, which must have hurt.

Freddie was already through them, running toward their car, the blacktop hot beneath his bare feet. The car was an old Ford LTD that had apparently been used as a stable for several years. The driver had not only left the rap crap blasting and the key in its ignition, he'd left the engine running as well, merely shifting into "park" before he'd leaped out in pursuit of the bike. Sliding behind the fuzzy-cloth-covered wheel with its eight-ball speed-turner mounted on it, feeling his body immediately stick to the vinyl fake-zebra seat cover, Freddie grabbed the eight-ball-topped gearshift with one hand while slamming the driver's door with the other, shifted into "drive," and *drove*.

The assembled meatheads looked up from dismembering the bicycle to see their former chariot execute a fast hard K-turn, its other doors slamming as the LTD shot forward, its wheels smoking as it reversed, and the whole car bouncing like something in a demolition derby when it slashed away, northbound.

How they yowled! Like hyenas disturbed over carrion. Freddie couldn't hear them, because he was leaving so fast and also because he couldn't figure out at first how to stop that strident yawp out of the LTD's oversize speakers. Then he was around the far curve, the throwbacks were out of sight, and he slowed down long enough to discover the racket didn't come from a radio station but a tape. He ejected the tape from the player, and then from the car.

Quarantine Road. Freddie made the turn, and on this narrow dirt road there was no other traffic at all. If he'd only made it this far on the bike, he'd have been absolutely safe.

On the other hand, this LTD was faster, if grubbier. Freddie drove along, and in no time at all he passed the archway with the double *S*'s. A blacktop road went in under it, but no structures could be seen from here in those woods.

Freddie kept going, and a quarter mile later he found a weedy dirt track that wandered away to the right. He drove in there, went far enough to be invisible from Quarantine Road, turned off into the scrubby woods, and kept going until the bottom was torn out by a rock. That seemed far enough.

Most people wanted to talk about the invisible man during lunch, but Martin would have none of it. "Our digestions come first," he said. "We can wait, and take our time, and have a nice lunch, and then, over coffee afterward, we can discuss exactly what to do about Peter and David's invisible man."

Of course Nurse Martin was, as usual, right. So everybody *thought* about the invisible man, but spoke, if they spoke at all, disjointedly about other things that didn't matter a bit.

At last lunch was finished, coffee was served, and the plates and staff were removed to the kitchen. Robert said, "Now, does anyone have anything they've been dying to say?"

A clamor of voices arose, but through them drove the Kissingeresque basso of Edmond, a corporate attorney in his other life, who said, "I would like to say a word about kidnapping."

That shut everybody up. They all stared at Edmond, a bearlike man famous in his group for having more hair on his shoulders than on his head. At last, William, an antiques dealer, said, "Edmond, this isn't kidnapping. This is an invisible man!"

Edmond spread his meaty hands. "Hath an invisible man no rights? Hath he not hands, organs, dimensions, senses, affections, passions, even if you can't see them? If you prick him, doth he not bleed?"

"Not so's you'd notice," said Peter.

Edmond said, "I just think you should consider the ramifications, from a legal point of view, before you proceed."

"Fine," David said. "*Then* we'll proceed."

"And it isn't kidnapping," Peter insisted. "We had an agreement with the man."

"Which he abrogated," Edmond said, "when he left your house."

"And which he reinstated," Peter said, "when he phoned me. *He* phoned *me*, Edmond, not—"

"Us," said David.

"Exactly," Peter said. "He phoned *us*, he asked for either of *us,* so he was returning to the original agreement, and in fact he said so on the phone, offered to go on with the observation pattern we'd agreed to in the first place."

"An interesting question," Edmond said. "Unlikely, I suppose, to go to court."

"Freddie is very likely to wind up in court," Peter said, "but hardly as the plaintiff."

Robert said, "I know we have an hour, or more than an hour, but let's figure out now what we're going to do when he gets here."

"How will we *know* when he's here?" asked Curtis, a set designer. "I mean, if we can't see him."

David said, "I suppose he must have some sort of car, to come all the way up from the city."

"*That* should be something to see," Daniel, an architect, said. "An empty car, speeding along the highway."

David said, "Maybe he has a friend who can drive him," and Peter said, "Or possibly he wraps his head in bandages like Claude Rains in that movie."

"That *would* be spooky," Curtis said.

Robert said, "All right, he gets here, we see his car or he rings the bell or whatever. Peter and David, you two discuss the situation with him, see if you can persuade him to cooperate, but if it becomes clear he isn't *going* to cooperate, we ought to have a plan."

Martin said, "Here's what we'll do. Peter, if you decide he's planning to give you the slip again, say, 'Harvey,' as though that were somebody's name here—"

Peter said, "Why Harvey?"

"Because that was the six-foot invisible rabbit in the play of the same name," Martin said. "Don't worry about it, Peter, just say 'Harvey' if you think we have to hold the fellow here against his will. Then we'll all jump up and block the exits, and imprison him in this room."

"I'm not very happy about that idea," Edmond said.

"But you'll go along with it," Robert told him.

Edmond shrugged those hairy shoulders. "If I must. But, Peter, if you can get his willing agreement to stay, that would be so much better than using restraint."

"We had his agreement last time," Peter pointed out, "and we saw what it was worth."

"Besides," David said, "when he finds out, you know, he's going to be mad at us."

"I'm afraid he is," Peter agreed.

"He's likely to go away," David said, "just out of spite, and then that awful policeman will get him."

"Or the tobacco-company people," Peter said.

"When he finds out what?"

"That it's permanent, of course," Peter said, then looked up and frowned at everybody, to see them all frowning at him. "Who said that?" he asked.

They all went on looking at him.

"It's *permanent*?"

"Oh, my God," David whispered. "He's here."

"Impossible!" Peter cried.

"Peter," David whispered. "Can he *fly*?"

"I'm *never* gonna get myself back?"

All the faces in the room were now ashen. Hair stood up on the backs of necks, throats grew dry, eyes grew wide. Everybody stared all around, even though everybody knew there would be nothing to see.

Martin leaned toward Peter. "Speak to him," he whispered.

Those first two shouts had seemed to come from over by the fireplace, but the next one sounded from the vicinity of the hall doorway: "You dirty bastards! You can't bring me *back*!"

Everyone was afraid to move. With nothing else to gape at, they gaped at Peter and David. Turning to gape toward the doorway, Peter said, "You shouldn't have taken the other formula, Freddie. You should have been honest with us, and none of—"

"*What* other formula?" The loud angry voice came now from near the front windows. "I didn't take any formula! All I took was that goddam useless antidote!"

"There *is* no antidote!"

"*Now* you tell me? You *said* it was the antidote!"

"I'm sorry, Freddie," David said, and Peter said, "We did lie to you, we're both sorry, but we had no idea you'd be in a position to take that other formula."

"You *said* it was the antidote."

"To calm you down," David said, and Peter said, "You said it first, remember? It was your idea. 'Oh, yeah, the formula's the shot and the antidote's the thing you swallow.' Remember?"

"You lied to me."

"We were wrong to do that, Freddie," Peter agreed, "but *you* were wrong, too. You promised you'd stay, and you *didn't* stay."

"So what *was* that other thing, if it wasn't the antidote?"

"We had two formulae," Peter said, and David said, "You took them both," and Peter said, "If you'd just taken the one, none of this would have happened," and David said, "You'd be your old self now."

"I can't believe it," the bodiless voice said. It seemed to be moving steadily around the room, like a lion in a cage. "My girlfriend's leaving me because it's driving her nuts I'm like this, and now I have to tell her I'm *always* gonna be like this?"

"I imagine," said the other William, the screenwriter, "sex is rather odd, the way you are now." He managed to sound at the same time both sympathetic and prurient.

"We keep the lights out."

"Oral, in particular," the other William mused.

Peter said, "Freddie, if you'll come back to the lab with us, we'll work on it, I swear we'll work on it day and night. We'll devote our entire lab time to *finding* an antidote. I'm sure, if you'll just give us some time—"

Edmond said, "I could draw up a preliminary agreement for you all right now. There'd be profit in it, too, of course, for all of you. Film and television rights, a sort of super magic act onstage—"

"You're gonna make a *freak show* outta me?"

"Oh, hardly anything that tasteless," Edmond assured him.

"The rose room was nice, wasn't it?" David asked. "You wouldn't mind staying there again, would you?"

"You could put the door back on," Peter said.

"Your girlfriend could come visit you all you wanted," David said.

"We'll study you," Peter said, "we'll show you to the scientific community and we'll *all* study you, we'll study the effects, and I'm *sure* we'll find the antidote in no time."

"That's right," David said, blinking, looking hangdog.

"You're lying, aren't you?"

"Freddie, what else are you going to do?" Peter demanded.

"Stay the way I am." The bravado obvious in that voice, he went on, "I'm doing okay, don't worry about me."

David said, "The policeman will get you, the really nasty one," and Peter said, "They know about the robberies you did."

"What robberies?"

"The fur place, and the diamond place. You can't wear gloves, Freddie, you leave fingerprints wherever you go."

"What?" The discorporate voice sounded more exasperated than ever. "Invisible hands leave *prints*?"

"I'm afraid so, yes," Peter said.

"God*dam* it!"

A champagne bottle lifted itself out of its icer, rose into the air, and tilted itself upside down. They all heard the glug-glug-glug, and they all watched in astonishment as the amber fluid flowed down a twisty curvy route through the air and made a bowl of itself three feet from the ground.

The bottle lowered, and waved around. The swallowed champagne moved tidally, like the sea. "Son of a bitch!" Freddie cried, and the bottle leaped *crash* back into the water and ice, without breaking. "You are some goddam guys," Freddie snarled.

Peter said, "Freddie, for your own good, please don't leave," and David said, "We're on your side, honest we are."

Everybody watched the bowl of champagne.

"With friends like you . . ." said the bitter voice. The bowl moved toward the door. "Good-bye."

"Wait!" cried David, and Peter cried, "Stop him!"

"Harvey!" shouted Martin. "Har—*wait*! That's very very valuable!"

A Ming vase had just jumped up from its stand and hung in midair over by the door. The visible people in the room were all frozen in odd postures, half-seated and half-standing. Martin's hand was out imploringly toward the vase.

This tableau lasted one second, two seconds, and then the voice cried, "You'll want to catch it, then!" and the vase went arching up into the air in the middle of the room.

Everybody ran for it, arms outstretched. Everybody crashed into everybody else, and the vase crashed into the floor. Everybody stared at four hundred thousand dollars in tiny pieces, and the front door slammed.

45

Roving the outside of the house, while the thirteen pursuers went haring off in all directions—or, hounding off in all directions, since they kept baying at one another—Freddie felt a deep and total bitterness, very unlike his normally sunny personality. He had to keep reminding himself that violence wasn't part of his MO. Right now, he wanted to bust up a lot more than some stupid vase that wasn't good for anything but to throw your old pennies in.

He couldn't leave here, not yet; he was stuck in this place for a while. They were all running around, hither and yon, beating the bushes with brooms and cue sticks, looking for that telltale bowl of champagne, and every once in a while finding it: "There he is! There he is!" And off he would bound once more.

He shouldn't have drunk the champagne. The news had just been so sudden and so bad, that was all. The realization of what had been done to him, and why.

In the first place, and he couldn't really articulate this very well, but he instinctively understood it, in the first place, this was a matter of *class*. Not sexual orientation, that wasn't the issue here. What they'd done to Freddie, those two doctors, they would not have done to anybody they considered their equal, and it wouldn't matter if the guy swung this way or that way or both ways or no way at all. They had looked upon Freddie as being underclass or lower class or working class or however they might choose to phrase it, and therefore they could treat him any damn way they wanted because the civilized rules didn't apply.

That's right. The civilized rules only applied to people who talked like them, had their kind of education, read the same newspapers and magazines, had the same *attitudes* toward things, including the attitudes toward people like Freddie. To know that you've been fucked over not because science needed it, or nobody else was available, or it was the luck of the draw, but only because you're scum, can take some getting used to, and can move a nonviolent guy very near to the edge of the envelope of his MO.

In the second place, Peg. Already, he and she were about to begin a trial separation just because of the way he already was, and figuring this problem had to be temporary and sooner or later he'd be getting back his regular self again. And now what? How could he tell Peg he didn't *have* a regular self anymore? She'd have to write him off, wouldn't she? Give up on him entirely, find some other guy she could look at over a candlelit table. Leave him completely alone.

He wasn't exactly in a state to meet girls, was he?

Over there by the house, they were coming to the conclusion that he'd gotten away. He couldn't leave the property yet, though, and in any case he was in no hurry to go away from here, to go anywhere, to do anything; not with what he knew now.

He kept roaming, wishing the champagne would hurry up and finish digesting—it hadn't improved his mood, *and* it kept putting those guys on his trail—and then he came across the swimming pool, out behind the house. He and the champagne could both hide in there, couldn't they, while he waited? They could. Freddie eased himself down into the pool, and morosely began to do laps.

It was Curtis the set designer who saw it. They'd all come back inside, barricaded themselves in here to some degree, and were gathered around the living room trying to decide what to do next.

Was the invisible man still somewhere on the property? If so, did he plan some sort of awful vengeance for what Peter and David had done to him? And if he did have such plans, would he be willing to restrict his vengeance to Peter and David, who after all did deserve the fellow's wrath—"Thank you I *don't* think"—or would he make the Draconian decision that the friend of his enemy is also his enemy, and thus wreak his awful vengeance indiscriminately on the whole crowd?

"And with thirty-four people more invited for this evening," Robert said. "This is some little contretemps you two brought us, I must say."

"You *wanted* him to come here," Peter said, and David said, "You all just thought it was going to be *fun*."

Curtis didn't like squabbling; he got enough of that in the theater. So he roved the living room while the others bickered, and after a while he picked up the bird-watching binoculars and casually looked through them, adjusting the focus, wondering what sort of bird one might watch in this neighborhood, and all at once he stiffened. "Robert," he said, half-afraid to breathe. "Robert, there's something . . . in the pool."

Freddie loved to swim. His body moved through the buoyant water, resisting him and helping him at the same time, urging him along. Below the surface, he swept along, pushing through the clear slightly warmed water, surfacing only when he needed to breathe, then rolling like a dolphin down again beneath the air.

Time disappeared. The hot thoughts in his brain cooled. He knew he was an adaptable sort of guy, inventive, basically positive. He was giving those qualities their most severe test at the moment, and he was pleased to see his better side coming through. If this is who he had to be from now on, he realized, somehow he'd figure out a way to handle it. The only real insoluble problem he could see was Peg.

What did please him, in this whole mess, was that he hadn't the slightest urge to go back to dope. Not that finding a vein would be at all easy, even if he wanted to; though on the other hand he wouldn't have that much trouble finding his nose. But he didn't want to, not even in this extreme situation, and he was glad to see that in himself. I may be disappearing, he thought to himself, but at least I seem to have grown up.

Out of air. He rolled to the surface, took in a lungful of air, heard the motor sound, and had already slip-slid back down into the moving water when the echo of what he'd just seen and heard came back to him.

The thirteen guys. They were all around the pool, looking at him. And some kind of motor was running.

Staying underwater, Freddie fishtailed on, remembering what Peg had said about being able to see him, or at least find him, in the pool. Time to get out of here. Then, as he thought that, the world around him darkened; not black, but suddenly much dimmer than before. He rolled over onto his back, and couldn't for a second figure out that darkness up there, spreading inexorably from one end of the pool to the other. And then he understood.

The pool cover! The bastards were closing their electrically run pool cover over him!

He swam ahead of the advancing darkness to the far end of the pool, but the second his wet hand touched the top of the coping around the pool's edge half a dozen of the bastards yelled, "There he is! There he is!" And came running, to surround that wet handprint.

Can't get out, not here. Freddie pushed away from the edge as people risked falling in fully dressed to reach for him. He flowed away, faceup, kicking, and here came the pool cover, right over him.

Hell! Hell and blast and damn son of a *bitch*!

Narrr, said the pool-cover motor, as Freddie quartered beneath it like a goldfish in a too-small aquarium. Click, said the pool-cover motor, and Freddie was completely roofed in, floating in a big room of water with no exits.

"Turn off the heater!" one of the bastards yelled.

Oh, you bastard, Freddie thought, I'll get you for this, I'll get you all for this. The rage that had consumed him, back in the house, when he'd first learned the truth, came back into him now in full force, as though it had never gone away. Go ahead and turn off the heater, he thought, my *brain* could heat this pool.

"Freddie? Freddie!"

It was one of the doctors, he recognized the voice, the blond baby-fat one, Dr. David Loomis. Freddie was damned if he'd talk to the bastard. To conserve his strength, he moved down to the shallow end of the pool, sat there on the lowest step, his head just below the thick tarp of the cover, and considered his situation.

Not so good. The cover was loose down both long sides of the pool, only fastened tight across the ends, but the bastards were watching the sides, they'd see the cover lump up if he tried to get out, and they'd see his wet prints on the pool surround.

Trapped. And, face it, his brain would not heat the pool. With the cover on, the sun's warmth no longer reached the water. There was no place under here that he could go without being in water. After a while, this was not going to be a pleasant place.

Crap. Freddie rested a wet elbow on a wet knee, cupped a wet chin in his wet palm, and waited.

Martin knelt beside the pool, holding up the edge of the cover so he could look in at the shadowed grotto within. It had been nearly two hours now, and the invisible man had so far refused absolutely to respond. He won't speak, he won't move, he won't do a thing. He just sits there, on the steps at the shallow end.

Martin called, "Freddie? Wouldn't you like to come out now? Isn't it getting a little cold in there? We could give you towels, a robe, we have lovely terry-cloth robes, one size fits all. No? Would you like a cup of coffee? Tea? A drink? We have a nice Spanish red that might warm you if you're feeling a bit chilly. Freddie? Forgive my informality, but I don't know your last name. You're going to make yourself sick if you stay in there much longer, you really are. Trust Nurse Martin, please do. Freddie? Darn it, you know, I can *see* you there, the parts of you that are under water, I can see you sitting there on that step, the least you could do, I mean, it *is* our pool, the least you could do is give us the courtesy of an answer. Freddie? No? Oh, Freddie, this isn't going to get you anywhere but a good case of the flu."

Reluctant, saddened, Martin dropped the pool-cover edge and got to his feet. He shook his head at Peter, nearby. "He's just stubborn, Peter, he's just very very stubborn."

Peter had decided to be coldhearted; it was the only way to handle the situation that he could see. He said, "Let him stay in there as long as he wants. Let him get really exhausted down in there, and when he finally does come out he'll be that much easier to deal with."

"I suppose so," Martin said, sorry to treat a fellow human

being in such a way, and a gray van came tearing around the end of the house, over the lawn, through the hedges, with a sudden blaring squawk and ruckus of horn.

"Good God!" Martin cried. "What now?"

The van drove straight for the pool, horn screaming, regardless of whatever else was in the way. "My delphiniums!" screamed Robert.

People ran toward the van, but then they turned and ran away from it, because it was *not* veering out of the way. And the horn of the thing just kept blaring and blaring and blaring.

"There he is!" screamed Peter, pointing at the sudden bulge that had risen up at the side of the pool cover, and then the spray of moving water drops in the air, the sudden wet footprints on the deck.

"Stop him!" a lot of people cried, and a few tried. Gerald the talent agent happened to be nearest the expanding line of wet footprints; he ran over there, arms widespread to capture the invisible man, and suddenly he went, "Whooofff!" and doubled up, clutching his midsection.

William the screenwriter stuck out a foot in front of the advancing prints, to trip the fellow, instead of which his ankle was grabbed by a hard hand, his leg was yanked up over his head, and he was dumped ass-over-teakettle over a folding chaise longue that then folded around him like a Venus flytrap.

Peter came running at an angle to intercept the footprints, yelling, "Freddie, listen! Freddie, listen!" until he abruptly flipped over and fell on his back. When he sat up, his nose was bleeding. "He *hit* me," Peter said, in utter astonishment.

Meanwhile, the van was circling around and around, as near the pool as it could get, running roughshod over all sorts of plantings, while the grim-faced young woman at the wheel kept everybody from getting too close. Then all at once she braked to a stop, which did the lawn no good, and the passenger door snapped open and shut, and the van shot away, which did the lawn even less good.

It was gone. The van was gone. Without question, the invisible man was gone. The pool was covered, the lawn and the gardens were a wreck, the guests were staggering around in filthy disarray, the hosts were furious, nobody remembered the van's license number, and Peter's nose was bleeding.

And the weekend had just begun.

46

"How are you?"

Peg waited to ask that question until after they'd bounced over a lot of shrubbery and plantings and railroad ties and pebbly Japanese gardens and a lot of other stuff all the way around to the front of the house, and then out the weaving blacktop driveway, and then the sharp squealing rattly right turn onto the dirt of Quarantine Road, with all this time Freddie somewhere in the vehicle, no telling where, probably just holding on for dear life. "How are you?" she asked, as they settled down to the more or less straight and more or less even dirt surface of Quarantine Road.

"Iiiiii'mm *freezing!*"

"Oh, you poor baby!"

The voice had come from the passenger seat, and sounded much frailer and weaker than Freddie's normal voice. She reached out and touched a leg, and that was cold flesh she was feeling there. Cold and clammy. "What did they *do* to you?"

"In the pool," he said. "Forever, Peg."

"I saw them there," she told him. Here was the end of Quarantine Road; she made the left onto County Route 14. "I got back to the house," she said, "and saw your note, and the little map you drew up, and I came up here as quick as I could."

"Th-th-thank you."

"There were all those cars parked there, and I went first to the front door, but then I saw everybody was around back, so I snuck over and saw them around the pool, and listened, and finally figured it out they had you trapped in there."

"Boy, did they."

"When we get home, you'll take a nice hot tub, and I'll grill hamburgers, how does that sound?"

"Better than anything else I heard today."

Peg drove another half mile or so before *that* penny dropped. When it did, she said, "Oh? You got to talk to the doctors?"

"I got to listen to them. They didn't know I was there."

"And what did they say?"

"Well, the first thing I learned," he said, and she didn't have to see a face or body language or anything like that to know he was stalling, so that bad news must be on the way here, sooner or later, "the first thing I learned, if they *do* talk to me, they're gonna lie to me. They said they were, they told those other guys that."

"Who *were* all those people?"

"I dunno, some kind of house party. I got the feeling it was like Dracula's house, you wouldn't want to go there after dark."

"*You* don't want to go there in the daytime. What was the other thing you learned, Freddie?"

Long silence. Very long silence. How bad could this bad news be? And then at last he said it: "Well, Peg, what they told those other guys, this situation is permanent."

She stared at the road, appalled. Out there, five drunken teenage boys, flopping around beside the road, made some hopeless attempt at hitchhiking; she didn't give them a second's thought. "Permanent?"

"What they say now," came his deeply gloomy voice, "was

that the thing they told me was an antidote *wasn't* an antidote, so they lied to me from the very beginning, it was their other experiment, and they never figured to put those two experiments together, so they're trying to put it around it's *my* fault."

"*Your* fault! Doctors!" Peg cried, curling her upper lip, a thing she rarely did because it didn't look good on her. "Blame the patient!"

"That's it. They lied to me before about it being the antidote, and they told their pals they were gonna lie to me about it being permanent. So the only way I can trust those guys is when they don't know I'm around."

"That's probably true of all doctors," Peg said. "But what about it, Freddie? Why not get a second opinion?"

"I wouldn't trust *anything* they said to me."

"From a different doctor, Freddie. Have a different doctor examine you, as best he can."

"Peg, those are the guys *made up* those experiments, they're gonna know better than anybody else what's what with them."

Peg scrinched up her face, as though at a bad taste. "So you really think they're right, huh?"

"Well, Peg, I've had this thing a month now, with no booster shots or nothing like that. If it was gonna wear off, wouldn't it start by now?"

"I guess. Probably."

Another silence, each of them alone with troubled thoughts, and then Freddie said, "I know what you got to do, Peg, and I don't blame you. I'd do the same. I mean, with men, a woman's looks are more important than a man's looks to a woman. Imagine if I couldn't see that nice face anymore." Then, perhaps realizing the other implication of what he'd said, he added, "I mean, if you were invisible."

"I know, Freddie."

"Here, but I couldn't see you."

"I *know*, Freddie."

Something touched her right forearm; she couldn't help it, she flinched, but then immediately pretended she hadn't. Freddie said, "This doesn't change anything, Peg, not between you and me. You still got to go away, see how you feel, get away from this situation for a while."

She sighed, long and sincere. "Yeah, I do, I really do."

"We can still talk on the phone, you can still come up and see me—Jeez, Peg, the language is full of land mines—you can come up and visit me when you want, we won't have to worry about what happens long-term, just take it one day at a time."

"Okay, Freddie," she said, grateful to him and loving him and sorry for him and absolutely unable to go on living with him—not right this minute, anyway.

Some of their silences together were comfortable, but not this one. It was with a real grinding of gears being shifted that Freddie suddenly said, in a bright new artificial voice, "Well, anyway, did you get me a car?"

"I got you wheels," she said.

"What do you mean? It isn't a car?"

"No no no, it's a car."

"It's not a truck, or a hearse, or a school bus."

"Come on, Freddie, I'm not going to get you anything stupid. It's a car, okay?"

Did you ever have that feeling, even though you can't see anybody, you know eyes are watching you?

"What is it?"

"It's called a Hornet. An American Motors Hornet. It's eighteen years old, and in perfect mechanical condition, except the right window doesn't roll down."

"It's *green,* Peg."

"So?"

"The green Hornet, Peg?"

"You worry too much, Freddie," she told him.

This was Saturday morning, around eleven o'clock. Yesterday, when they'd gotten home, Freddie had taken a long hot tub, he'd had two big cheeseburgers and two ears of corn on the cob and two bottles of beer from Pennsylvania, and then he had slept until eight that evening, and woke up just in time to eat his way through a complete dinner, after which he'd announced he was beginning to feel a little better.

This morning, Peg had called the dealer over in Putkin to be sure the car was ready, which it was. Freddie, in Dick Tracy mode, then rode in the van with Peg to Putkin, left her there outside the used-car lot, and drove on back to the house. Half an hour later—even when the dealer says it's ready, it isn't ready—Peg showed up in this thing.

The green Hornet was very low, about elbow height, and small, with two doors and a backseat just big enough for two bags of groceries and one—not two—six-pack. The front and rear windows were both so steeply slanted they almost looked straight up. The rear and side windows were covered with smoky film, and even the windshield had a faint coppery gray tinge to it. The interior was very hard to see. Freddie said, "What's with the windshield?"

"It's bulletproof. All the windows are."

"Who owned this thing? Al Capone?"

"It's not *that* old, Freddie. I've got the car's whole history, and it only ever had one owner, and she was a little old lady—"

"Who only drove the car once a week."

"Well, yes," Peg agreed.

"To go to church on Sunday."

"Well, no," Peg said. "Actually, to go visit her son the ax murderer in the state penitentiary."

"That's what the dealer told you."

"He showed me the newspaper clippings," Peg said. "There's a law, there's a lemon law, if a car has anything unusual in its history that you oughta know about, like a bad accident or a dead body stuffed in the trunk for a couple months, anything like that, the dealer has to tell you."

"I've heard of a lot of laws," Freddie said, "and none of them have ever made a hell of a lot of sense, if you want my personal opinion, but that one there is just about the dumbest yet. You're makin a law that mice can fly."

"Nevertheless," Peg said, "he had to tell me the history, and that's why the car was so cheap. Three hundred bucks. With a one-year guarantee on everything except tires."

"Peg," Freddie said, "there's bumps all over this car, dents and bumps."

"Well, according to the news clippings," Peg said, "the ones the dealer showed me, the people in the neighborhood hated the family, especially because the mother always kept saying her son was a good boy—"

"They always do."

"So people would throw rocks at the car every time she went by. That's why the bulletproof glass, too. And that isn't the original paint."

"No, I could see that," Freddie said. "You don't usually get brush marks on a factory job. Peg, when I drive this thing around, people are gonna throw *rocks* at me?"

"No, no, this all happened in Maryland. They had to move the car far away to a different state so they could sell it at all. When they auctioned it."

"Who auctioned it?"

"It was a consignment from the state of Maryland. Apparently, this dealer in Putkin is the only one even put in a bid."

"How come it was up for auction? What happened?"

"Well, the son's prison time was up, so they let him go."

"Yeah? And?"

"And he went home."

"And?"

Peg shrugged, looked away, looked back. "And," she said, "he took the ax to his mother, so now he's back inside forever, no parole, and the car came on the market."

"The car came on the market," Freddie echoed, looking at the lumpy green Hornet.

"It's a very hard sell, all in all," Peg said. "But I figured, a guy like you, a story like that wouldn't bother you."

"Oh," Freddie said. "Right. Not a bit."

Peg smiled fondly on the little green monster. "And if you don't think about its history," she said, "it's perfect, right?"

"Right," Freddie said. The Dick Tracy head nodded and nodded. "Perfect," he said.

47

The worst thing was knowing they'd never be invited back.

Well, *was* that the worst thing? Wasn't the worst thing losing Freddie, the invisible man, *twice*? This time, no doubt, for good? Wasn't that the worst thing? And if not that, then wasn't the worst thing losing their funding for their melanoma research and having to do the bidding of a monomaniac out of James Bond, who wanted to genetically alter the human race so he could sell *cigarettes*? Wouldn't that be the worst thing on a whole lot of lists?

Well, yes, of course. And both of those are extremely bad and terrible and horrendous and unfortunate. But nevertheless, when you come right on down to the nitty-gritty, the worst thing was knowing they'd never be invited back.

Not that Robert and Martin displayed by the merest iota of a scintilla that anything was even the teeniest weeniest bit wrong. They were as polite and civilized as ever, or almost; the destruction of their landscape had necessarily dimmed their sparkle somewhat.

And there had been an extra moment of trouble, unfortunately, when Peter—and then David, just a few seconds later—had tried to limit the damage by insisting that none of the thirty-four guests soon to arrive for the dinner party should be told about the invisible man. "And just *what*," demanded Robert, waving a hand that quivered over the moon-scape of his former lawns, "am I supposed to say happened here? A remake of *All Quiet on the Western Front*?"

"You can say," Peter suggested, "you're redoing the exterior."

"And *that* wouldn't be a lie."

But there was no hope for it. Even if the physical evidence hadn't been so extreme, there was the fact that the eleven people already present were absolutely bursting with the story, bubbling over with it, half-wanting to end the weekend *now* so they could go away and regale someone who hadn't been here. If gossip is the fuel of social interchange, this was rocket fuel, and no power on earth would keep it from going off.

"All I ask, then," Peter said, when everything else he'd asked for had been refused, "is to make the announcement. At dinner, let *me* tell the story."

"When at dinner?" Robert asked, suspicious. "Over coffee? Believe me, everybody will *know* by then."

"No no no, before dinner is served."

Dinner would be buffet-style, and announced, so people could get on line. Peter said, "They'll be waiting for you to announce dinner, so announce me instead, and I'll tell them what happened, and then we'll have dinner, and that will be that."

"Please, Robert," David said. "Our future hangs on this. Robert, Martin, you've always been dear friends, you know how *horribly* we feel about what happened here, please let Peter tell everybody in his own fashion."

"Put his spin on it," Robert suggested.

"If you like," Peter said, who would have agreed with anybody about anything at that point.

Well. It was easy to refuse Peter, no problem, but everybody had always found it hard to refuse David, so it was finally agreed, with great reluctance, that no one would tell the new arrivals anything about the invisible man before Peter stood up and made his general announcement.

And that, a few hours later, was what he did: "Thank you, Robert, thank you, Martin. Thank you for a lovely weekend, as usual, for charming and exciting guests, for a dinner that we already know is going to be superb. And thank you both for being so understanding and sympathetic and forgiving about an experiment that went so very very wrong."

Peter sipped his vodka. There was so little grapefruit juice in it by now it looked pretty much like the invisible man himself. Peter went on: "You all saw that horrible destruction outside, when you came in."

They had. The murmuring the last half hour had been about nothing else, with those privy to the story merely giggling or sighing or shaking their heads, saying only, "We promised to let Peter tell."

So here it came: "As most of you know, David and I are scientific researchers, and skin cancer, melanoma, is the area of our research. An experiment on a willing—and I must emphasize *willing*—volunteer subject went terribly awry. It affected his body in the way, well, somewhat in the fashion we'd expected and hoped, but it seems to have, well, affected his mind as well, making him angry and mistrustful, and possibly even violent. I'm sorry, I don't mean to tell you a wolf-man story here, but the fact is this fellow, who happens to be a convicted felon, by the way, and his name is Freddie, is, well, he's, you can't see him."

Everybody looked around. Can't see whom? So what?

Robert called out, "Say the word, Peter, say the goddam word!"

"Oh, all right!" Peter cried, and finished his vodka, and announced, "He's invisible! All right? He came here because he knew *we* were here, and he wanted us to help him *stop* being invisible, and we can't! And he's, he's extremely angry! And he had a, he had a cohort here—"

"Peter," David interrupted, "I don't think one person can be a cohort."

"I don't care!"

The newcomers were wide-eyed, disbelieving, asking quick whispered questions, getting quick whispered answers, yes, yes, it's true, it's all true, an invisible man, in *this* very room!

Peter drank from his empty vodka glass, rolled his eyes, took a deep breath, and said, "This man, this Freddie, is invisible. Yes, he is. He was here, and now he's gone away, we don't know where, we *wish* we could help him—"

"Oh, yes, we do!" David cried.

"—but we can't, and he's probably gone for good, and we're just so sorry that Robert and Martin's beautiful house and beautiful grounds were just so *wantonly,* wantonly, that everything here was so, so, so . . ."

Peter was floundering by now, which Martin saw and understood, so he got to his feet and stood in front of Peter, faced the openmouthed guests, and said, "Peter and David asked if they could invite this person here, this man who'd been a volunteer in their experiment and was turned invisible, and we said yes, of course, because *nobody* realized, and certainly not Peter and David, just how much trouble this individual would be once he understood that the effects of the experiment were irreversible. It did upset him terribly, and I'm sure we can all sympathize with what he must have been going through, even while we do regret the certain amount of damage that resulted. And now that's the whole story, and I believe dinner is served, and now we can forget all this and go on and discuss other things."

Not one word was said, on any other topic, the entire weekend.

"A fantastic weekend," David said, on Sunday afternoon, as he shook Robert's hand and then Martin's, out by the cars in the sunshine. "You rose to the emergency *so* well."

"And so did you, David," Martin assured him. "And Peter, too."

Robert, with a gruff and hearty false laugh, said, "The landscaping was due for a makeover anyway. You get tired of the same old fountains."

Peter said, "We still feel terrible about the whole thing. You two have always been such dear friends, I'd hate to think of something like this coming between us."

Martin, with his sweetest smile, said, "Peter, please, don't think another thing about it."

Smiles; air-kisses; waving farewells. Peter and David climbed into the red Ford Taurus, which seemed smaller and nastier than on Friday, in a more garish and plebeian red. In silent misery, they put on their yachting caps.

David was driving, for the return to the city. He steered out to Quarantine Road, made the turn, and Peter said, "That Martin. What a slimy creep he is. Nurse Martin indeed. Did you hear him? At least Robert comes out and tells you what he thinks."

"No, he doesn't," David said.

"You know what I mean. 'Don't think another thing about it,' " he simpered, mimicking Martin. "You know what *that's* all about. Don't think you're ever coming *back* here."

David sighed, but saw no point in discussing their ouster from Eden any further. They were on County Route 14 now, and he looked at the remains of a bicycle by the side of the road; it must have been in a truly ghastly accident. I'd hate to have been riding *that* bike, David thought, trying to find somebody in the world worse off than himself.

"And now the story's out," Peter complained.

"Oh, not really," David said. "That part doesn't worry me. Already it's just an anecdote. People who weren't there won't really believe it, they'll think it's just another of those urban legend things."

Peter brooded. "I'd like to see that Freddie now," he growled.

David sighed. "Well, that's the problem in a nutshell, isn't it?" he asked.

48

Sunday afternoon. No more stalling. It was time to leave. "Freddie," Peg said, looking mournfully at Frankenstein's monster, "I wish you'd chosen another head."

"This didn't seem like anybody else's moment, Peg."

She should have left here yesterday, after she'd done the test spin with Freddie in the green Hornet and he'd pronounced himself pleasantly surprised with its comfort and handling. But somehow neither of them could permit it to end there, just like that. They stood on the driveway blacktop beside the new car, Freddie at that time, yesterday, still in his Dick Tracy mode, and they hemmed and hawed together for a while, and at last Freddie said, "I have a little idea, Peg. Come on to the pool."

"What for? I've *seen* you swim, it's the only time I *can* see you, or something like you."

"Just come along, okay?"

His Playtex hand took her hand, and she allowed him to lead her around the house and up the slope to the pool, where he carefully closed the door in the fence and said, "Come on *in* the pool, Peg."

"*In?*" That would truly be exposing herself to sunlight, with no protection at all. Water was no protection. "I didn't bring my suit," she said.

He laughed, as he peeled off his own clothing. "You don't need a *suit*," he told her.

That was so strange, to watch him disappear like that, to watch a complete human being turn into nothing more than a pile of clothing on the deck. Then there was a giant splash as he cannonballed into the water, and there it was, the ghost dolphin again, coursing through the pool.

"Come on in, Peg!"

It was along the lines of a last request, after all, she told herself, so she decided to go along with it, stepping out of her clothing, leaving it all more neatly on a chair than he had on the deck, and then stepping gingerly into the pool to find it not cold at all, the water first warmed by the pool heater and then by the sun. She descended into the sparkling water, and the giant dolphin swept toward her through the pool, and put his warm wet arms around her, and kissed her on the mouth.

"Mmmmm," she said.

"It's nice, isn't it?"

"Mmmmm," she said.

Sex in the swimming pool, in the buoyant warm water, languorous and slow. This was the first time since Freddie's transformation they'd been together like this when it wasn't pitch black, and it was kind of terrific. Very sexy, very loving that was, to be turned and stroked by a giant ghost dolphin in the water, someone you couldn't really see, but almost, and finally, when all was said and done, it didn't matter. Peg and Freddie and the warm moving water flowed together into one being, loving and content.

Well, after that she couldn't just put her clothes on and go home. They spent the afternoon together, for a while with Freddie in a terry-cloth robe—one size fits all, as Martin had pointed out—and espadrilles, with a white towel tossed over his head. That wasn't so bad, seeing the spaces where there ought to be a person. Maybe, if she had small doses of it like this, particularly with pleasant interludes like the one in the swimming pool as part of the arrangement, maybe eventually she could begin to get used to this new Freddie. In small doses.

It was Peg's idea they try a candlelight dinner at home, with only two candles. That made it a bit hard to find the food, but Freddie was now in a short-sleeved polo shirt and slacks, no gloves or head, and in the dimness she hardly minded the fork as it moved in and out of the candle glow, or the lack of anything at all above the shirt's soft collar. They had wine with dinner, and it was impossible for Peg to leave after that, and in any case the pool experience and the romantic dinner, and the protected solitude of their hideaway house here in the country, suggested a different ending for the evening, so that was what they did.

But now it was Sunday afternoon, and they could stall no longer. Peg could not bring herself to kiss Frankenstein's monster's cheek, but she patted the cheek, and that was no good either: cold, and not at all lifelike. "Freddie," she said. "I'm going to close my eyes now, and I want you to kiss me good-bye."

"Hell and damn," he said, but she closed her eyes, and she heard the rustle of latex, and then he kissed her for a long time. Then she opened her eyes, and the morose monster was back. "I'll call you tonight," she told it, and got into the van quickly, before she would start to cry in front of him.

Which was another advantage he had, she told herself, as she tried to be hard and cold. If *he* cried, who would know?

The monster stayed in her rearview mirror, waving its Playtex hand. She honked as she went around the curve that put him out of sight.

Driving south, she thought furiously but profitlessly about herself and Freddie and their problems and their options, and nothing seemed to make sense, nothing at all. She drove much faster than usual, because she was upset, and it was lucky she didn't get a ticket. At one point, on the southern part of the Taconic, she zipped past a red Ford Taurus poking along moodily in the right lane, with two long-faced guys in white yachting caps inside it, illuminated like a stage set because of their sunroof, but she didn't even give them a glance. She had troubles of her own.

The apartment was hot and stuffy and dusty and empty. There was a window air conditioner in the bedroom closet, which she lugged out and installed in a bedroom window, sweating gallons along the way. After she showered, the bedroom was a little cooler, but the rest of the apartment was still hot.

She called Freddie from the bedroom phone, but it turned out they had very little to say to one another. Both felt extremely awkward, and both were happy to end the call, with, "Talk to you tomorrow." Then Peg went out to a deli to get some necessities, went home, called a Chinese take-out place, carried the TV set into the cool bedroom, and spent the evening eating anonymous foods in front of anonymous reruns.

She went to bed early, but it was very hard to get to sleep. On the other hand, she had no trouble at all waking up when Barney Beuler kicked the leg of the bed and snarled, "Rise and shine, Sleeping Fucking Beauty."

49

Like the valet in *Sullivan's Travels*, Mordon Leethe viewed the entire proceedings with a sense of gloomy foreboding. It was not his desire to be here, aiding and abetting the commission of any number of felonies not normally associated with the partners of corporate law firms, but on balance his situation was so impossible in every direction that it was probably best, all in all, that he be here, present and culpable in these acts of breaking and entering, kidnapping, coercion, and possibly even battery upon persons, because if he weren't physically in this place he'd still be a coconspirator, still just as guilty in the eyes of the law—and in his own eyes as well—and without even the hope that he might somehow influence events, blunt the worst excesses of Barney Beuler, this associate in crime to whom he found himself so inextricably lashed, or that he might help steer the fragile ship of his own good name through these felonious reefs toward the barely visible shore of early retirement, a beaching that was coming to seem more and more advisable with every passing moment. Or, as Henry James might have put it, he was in it now, up to his neck.

At six on Monday morning, they had let themselves into Peg Briscoe's apartment, Mordon and Barney and the three cigarette-company thugs. Creeping, silent, they had observed the woman asleep in her air-conditioned bedroom, with no second body shape mounded beside her and with no male clothing to be seen anywhere. Nevertheless, reclosing her bedroom door, they had swept the apartment just as they'd done last time, to be absolutely sure the invisible man was not here. Only then did all five invade the bedroom once more and Barney wake the Briscoe woman with his patented charm.

Her eyes popped open. She sat bolt upright, staring at the five men in her room. Under a sheet, she seemed to be wearing some sort of long T-shirt. Instead of aroused, Mordon felt embarrassed. Before Barney could do or say anything else crude, he stepped forward, saying, "Miss Briscoe, it's Freddie we want."

"Oh, *Christ!*" she cried, in apparently genuine exasperation. "It's *you* guys again. For a second there, you had me terrified. Hold on while I use the bathroom," she said, sliding out of bed. Yes, a long white T-shirt, not quite opaque enough. "Make some coffee, will you?" she said, and sloped out of the bedroom and into the bathroom, slamming the door behind her.

Now it was Barney who looked embarrassed. His fearsome authority had just been deflected as though it didn't exist. "Well, whaddaya thinka that?" he said.

"I think she's right," Mordon said, and told one of the thugs, "Why don't you make us all some coffee? You remember where the kitchen is, don't you?"

"Sure." The thug looked around. "Everybody want?"

Everybody wanted. He went away, and the toilet flushed. Then the shower ran.

Barney and Mordon and the other two thugs wandered out to the living room, which was hotter and stuffier than the bedroom. They left the bedroom door open. "This is ridiculous," Barney said. "What we gotta do is *lean* on this bitch, not make her coffee."

"Freddie Noon isn't here," Mordon pointed out. "Peg Briscoe will know where he is."

"Damn right she will."

"We want her cooperation," Mordon reminded him. "It seems to me we should at least begin on a calm and civilized plane."

"That's fine," Barney agreed. "You be Good Cop. I'll jump in a little later."

It was after seven before they were all gathered in the living room, with toast and coffee. The only air conditioner was in the bedroom, but with it turned on full and the door open, it did help in the living room a bit. It seemed to Mordon that the fruits of Freddie Noon's crimes should have been juicier than this, but Mordon wasn't here—none of them were here—to enquire into the economics of burglary. They were here to find the burglar.

Mordon said, "Miss Briscoe, where is he?"

"No idea," she said. She was dressed now in jeans and a polo shirt and tennis shoes, and didn't look intimidated at all by this hostile mob in her house.

Mordon said, "Miss Briscoe, would you look at Barney here?"

Obediently, she looked at Barney, though clearly she didn't want to. Barney looked back at her, and smiled. Her confidence could be seen to slip a little, like a hat on a drunken song-and-dance man. Turning away from Barney's smile, she busied herself with her coffee cup, which had been empty for a while.

Mordon said, "I received permission from Barney, Miss Briscoe, to ask you these questions first."

"Uh-huh," she said. She was studying the empty interior of her cup, as though looking for tea leaves to read.

"If you don't answer *me*," Mordon said, "Barney will ask

you the questions himself, and you won't say to *him,* 'No idea.' I'm doing my best to make it easier for you here."

"That's nice," she said. She put the cup down and crossed her legs and clasped her hands around the upper knee and looked at Mordon. He could see her willing her face to be blank.

He shook his head. "I'll ask you once more," he said, "and please consider your answer very caref—"

"No idea."

"Oh, Miss Briscoe, if you would only—"

"My turn," Barney said, getting to his feet. "You guys hold her," he said to the thugs, and took a black handle out of his pocket. He did something, and a long knife blade popped out of the handle.

The thugs stood, alert, but didn't immediately approach Peg Briscoe, who sat up straight, staring at the knife. Barney turned the knife this way and that in his hands, admiring it, and then he said, "All I need from you is a mailing address, that's all. A box number, whatever it could be. Just someplace I can send the finger."

Her eyes widened. "I don't know where he is."

"What a waste that's gonna be, then," Barney told her. "See, what's gonna happen is, every day I'm gonna cut off one of your fingers and mail it to our friend Freddie, with a note with a phone number where he could call me if he felt like it. Now, if I don't have an address to send the finger it's a real shame and a waste, cause you're still gonna lose the finger. Hold her steady, guys. Better put a hand over her mouth."

"I don't know where he is!"

As the thugs closed on Briscoe, Mordon also got to his feet, saying, "Barney, we don't have to—"

"Sit down, Counselor," Barney said, and looked at Mordon, and the look all by itself knocked Mordon back into his chair. "Hold her, now," Barney said, turning again toward Briscoe.

"Waitwaitwaitwaitwaitmmmpmmmpmmmpmmmp—"

"Oh, all right," Barney said, weary, the knife poised over her left hand. "Let go her mouth, let's see what she's trying to say."

"I know where he is!"

"Well, yeah, sure you do, *I* know that. Hold steady, now."

"I'll tell you where he is!"

"Where I send the finger, that's right. Otherwise, it's a shame, right?"

"No no no, I'll tell you where he is right now, you don't have to mail him any—"

"Peg, Peg, Peg," Barney said, "I don't want to make you betray your best friend, you know what I mean? Let *him* come to *me,* of his own free will, after he gets a couple fingers in the mail. Hold steady now, I don't wanna take more than one."

"You don't *have* to!"

Barney paused. He seemed genuinely perplexed. He said, "What do you mean, I don't *have* to?"

"I can tell you exactly where he is, exactly how to find him!"

Barney chuckled. "And we leave here and we go to this location, and he isn't there. And then we come back here and guess what? You didn't wait for us. Hold the hand steady, guys."

"I'll take you there!"

Again Barney paused. He thought that one over. "I dunno," he said. "You probably had plans for today, this'd use up hours and hours of your time—"

"It's all right! It's a free day, I got a free day!"

Barney shook his head. "The finger in the mail, you know," he said, "it's a pretty surefire system."

"I'll take you there," she promised. "I'll take you right to him."

Barney sighed. He looked at the knife as though at an old

friend, then turned to look at Mordon. "I don't know, Counselor," he said. "Traveling with her for hours, and then maybe she's planning something—"

"I'm not! I'm not!"

"—and then we still got *her* on our hands at the end of the day." Barney shook his head, troubled by the complications. "What's your opinion, Counselor?"

There was no way to tell to what extent Barney Beuler was bluffing, or to what extent Barney Beuler was insane. Mordon judged it safest to go along with the insane part of Barney, so he said, in his most sober legal-counselor manner, "There might be some advantage to it, Barney, to have her with us. If we use her van, with all the rest of us in the back . . ."

"Hmmm," Barney said. "Trojan horse, like."

"Exactly. Then we let her talk to him, let him see we have her under our control."

"If we *have* her under our control." Barney turned back to the girl, who was following the conversation very intently. "Do we have you under our control?"

"Yes! Yes!"

Mordon licked dry lips. He said, "If things don't work out, Barney, we can always fall back on the finger option later."

"That's true." Deciding, Barney smiled and pressed the knife between his hands, and the blade disappeared back into the handle. Pocketing the handle, he shook his head and said, "You're makin a softie outta me, Counselor."

50

When Geoff Wheedabyx saw the van, he was on his way home from this morning's emergency, a barn that had caught fire out on Swope Road. His was one of four fire companies that had responded and, as usual, all they'd managed to save was the foundation. You get one of these old barns, that old dry wood with all its nooks and crannies packed full of dry old straw and sawdust and crap—literally crap; the stuff they use for fuel in the Middle East—and when the fire starts, there's really nothing to do but break out the marshmallows. Well, and make sure the fire doesn't spread to the house or the fields or anything else. But once a flame takes hold in a barn, you can be sure that barn is *gone*.

The reason for this fire, as for most of the outside-of-town fires Geoff and his people responded to, could be summed up in one word that has yet to appear under "Cause" on any insurance report form: *Farmer*.

The problem is, your farmer will never call a mechanic, no matter what the job. Your farmer is his own carpenter, and he isn't a good carpenter. He's his own plumber, electrician, mason, roofer, auto mechanic, and midwife, and he's pretty bad at all of them. Geoff had seen wiring in some of these old farmhouses and barns that would give you nightmares; in the one that burned down this morning, for instance. If you ever see anything that's built to Code, you know a farmer didn't build it.

The farmers will tell you the reason they do everything themselves, instead of calling in somebody who knows what the hell he's doing, is because they're poor, which isn't exactly true. Oh, they're poor, all right, but that isn't the reason they do everything themselves. The reason is, they're proud; and we know what pride goeth before, don't we?

Geoff, in his ruminations, was just at the point of brooding on pride and its aftermath when he saw the van, definitely that selfsame gray van, owned by one Margaret Briscoe of Bay Ridge, Brooklyn, New York, and last seen zipping away down Market Street out of town with Margaret Briscoe at the wheel and an invisible man named Freddie as the passenger.

And now the van was parked in front of Geoff's house. Geoff, in his pickup and still wearing his smoke-permeated firefighting gear, drove on by his house and reached first for his police radio, switching it over to the frequency it shared with Cliff's Service & Auto Repair out on County 14, Cliff being one of his two part-time deputies. "Cliff," he said into the mike. "Tell me you're there."

Geoff drove to the end of Dudley, made a U-turn, and parked behind his police cruiser. "Come on, Cliff," he said into the mike. "*Be* there."

"I was under a car, dammit. What's up?"

"Cliff, get your badge and your gun and go on down to my house. Out front, you'll see a van, gray. Do not let *anybody* into that van."

"Do I use lethal force?"

Clearly, Cliff had been watching too many action movies on his VCR. "Only if you absolutely have to," Geoff said.

"Roger."

Geoff switched off the police radio before he could hear Cliff say *over and out,* and picked up his walkie-talkie. "Hi, guys," he said into it. "Somebody turn off the damn radio and pick up."

The walkie-talkie connected him with his construction crew. Having finished the porch conversion here in town, they were at work now installing two rest rooms out at the Roeliff Summer Theater. The summer-theater operators having been given an anonymous grant for this purpose, their patrons would no longer have to use the Portosans out in the parking lot; at least not once Geoff and his guys got finished installing the wheelchair- and handicapped-access, water-saving, energy-conserving, unisex, washable-wall interior rest rooms.

"Is that you, Smokey?"

"If this is a dumb joke," Geoff said, "this must be Steve. Yeah, Steve, it's me. I want you guys to down tools—"

"Missy's gonna be mad."

"That's Missy's problem. I want you to down tools and come over to my house. All of you. There's somebody in there, I'm not sure who, not sure how many. Bring your walkie-talkie, and stay just down the block. Park in front of Whalens'. Don't come in or show yourselves unless I call you."

Steve, his joking ways forgotten, said, "Geoff? You got a real problem there?"

"Don't know yet. Goin in to find out."

"We'll be around."

"Cliff's watching a van out front. Don't let him shoot you."

"He might shoot *at* me."

Geoff got out of the pickup. He was in his tall firefighting boots, and black water-repellent coat, and now he put back on his fire-chief helmet, pocketed the walkie-talkie, and crossed Market Street to come at his house from the rear, as he'd done the last time he'd encountered Freddie and Peg.

Letting himself quietly into the house through the back door, he paused to remove his firefighting boots, but kept his helmet on, and eased forward slowly through the house. Not a sound. Nothing visible out of place.

His office door was closed and, when very quietly and cautiously he tested it: locked. He palmed his key, eased it into the keyhole, slowly turned it, and eased open the door.

Nothing. Office empty. Office chair not tilted back, so the invisible Freddie was not in it.

So what was going on? Where were they? Turning away from his now-open office doorway, standing in the middle of his front hall in his tube socks and firefighting gear, arms akimbo, Geoff looked this way and that and up the stairs, and nothing was to be seen, nothing was to be heard. "Peg?" he called. "Freddie?"

A smiling fat man with a pistol in his hand came out of the parlor. The pistol was pointed at Geoff's chest. The smiling fat man said, "You lookin for Freddie, too? What a coincidence, so are we. Let's look together."

51

This was not what Peg had had in mind, not at all.

When she had realized, back home in the apartment in Bay Ridge, that this guy Barney was either too mean or too crazy to stand up to, that he *would* do terrible things to find out what he wanted to know, that in fact he might even be serious about cutting off her finger and sending it to Freddie, she had done her best to think fast. Not easy, under the circumstances.

She would have to give these people *something*. Not Freddie, but something. A place to go, and they would certainly bring her along. She absolutely would not turn poor Freddie over to the tender mercies of Barney and his friends, but if she took them somewhere and Freddie wasn't there, then what? Wouldn't they get mad? Wouldn't this guy Barney be both meaner *and* crazier? If she wouldn't be able to stand up to him when he was calm—and she knew she wouldn't—how could she possibly stand up to him when he was upset?

That was when she'd thought of the little town of Dudley, and its he-man police chief. *There* was a hero for you. He already knew about Freddie, so no long explanations would be needed, and in fact, they'd already explained to him that Freddie was some kind of scientist, she could no longer remember exactly what kind, and that bad guys were chasing him, so *here* would be the bad guys.

That's the way she'd seen it in her mind's eye, their arrival on the front porch of that big old house on the main street of Dudley, knocking on the door, and Chief Whatsisname answering, and her popping him a wink as she'd say, "These fellas are here looking for Freddie." And let him take over.

Instead of which, the bad guys captured the hero in the first second of play, just like that.

So now, with the bad guys seated around this old-fashioned parlor, and the he-man that failed standing in the middle of the room with Peg beside him, Barney questioned him, and Peg listened to the answers.

His name was Geoff Wheedabyx. He was police chief, and also fire chief and a lot of other stuff in this town, maybe even Indian chief as well. And he said he didn't know where Freddie Noon was. "This is the first I'm hearing his last name," he said. "Thank you for that."

"You know him, though," Barney said. "You know Freddie."

"I've seen him," Geoff Wheedabyx acknowledged, then chuckled sheepishly and said, "I've met him, I mean."

Mordon Leethe, the awful attorney, said, "He knows Freddie, all right."

"So why doesn't he know where he is?" Through his maddening perpetual smile, Barney was beginning to exhibit dangerous signs of frustration.

Leethe said, "Barney, there's another question that comes first."

Barney showed by a raised eyebrow that he didn't think that was possible. "Yeah?"

"This is the fire chief, is that correct?"

"That's what his costume says."

"But he's also the police chief, Barney. Is he armed?"

"No," Geoff Wheedabyx said.

Barney grinned. "You don't mind," he said, "we don't take

your word on that. Search him," he told one of the thugs, who rose obediently to his feet.

Spreading his arms, Wheedabyx calmly said, "I don't lie."

The thug patted him down, and said, "No gun, but here's a walkie-talkie."

"No kidding," Barney said. "I wonder who's at the other end of it, do you think. Freddie? Give it to the chief." To Wheedabyx he said, "Say hello into it."

"I'm not in touch with Freddie Noon."

"Say hello into it, Chief."

"I don't see what you hope to—"

"Say hello!"

Obviously reluctant, Wheedabyx lifted the walkie-talkie to his lips. "Hello."

Immediately the room was filled with the staticky broadcast voice saying, "Geoff, everything okay in there? We're out here, man, we're ready. Everything okay?"

"Everything's okay," Barney prompted.

"Everything's okay."

"Come on in, all of you," Barney suggested.

Wheedabyx made a sour mouth, but repeated the words.

"Fine," Barney said. "Take the walkie-talkie away from him. Greet our guests when they come in, and lock them in the basement."

Two thugs left the room, drawing guns from inside their suitcoats. Wheedabyx called after them, "They aren't armed, they're my construction crew."

"No construction today, Chief," Barney said. "Where's Freddie?"

"I don't know."

"And you don't lie," Barney said.

Some noise in the hall; not much, and not for long.

Barney nodded. "I'm beginning to believe you, Chief. The last guy Freddie Noon is gonna hang out with is a straight-arrow police chief from some hick town. He probably dodged you one time, that's how you know about him. Right?"

"Yes," Wheedabyx said.

"There, you see?" Barney said, as pleased as if he'd invented Wheedabyx himself. "The man doesn't lie. But Peg might," he said, and leered at her. "Is that right, Peg? Like you didn't happen to mention this house belongs to the chief of police in this burg. You led us to this place because you figured Captain America here'd come to the rescue, is that it?"

Peg didn't answer, but she felt her face grow red. And when she glanced sidelong at Wheedabyx, his face was red, too. And he wasn't looking at her.

Barney gave an exaggerated shake of the head and said to Wheedabyx, "Sorry to involve you in this, pal. Is there a post office in this town?"

"Other end of Market Street. Why?"

"I got a little package to mail." Heaving himself to his feet, Barney said to Peg, "Let's take care a this in the kitchen, not get stains all over these nice antiques here."

Wheedabyx said, "What's that?" He was looking very alert, and as though he was thinking of doing something stupid and heroic after all.

So Peg gave up. "Okay," she said. "You win."

"Come on, Peg. Kitchen," Barney said.

"Fuck you, Barney," Peg said. "I told you I give up. I'll give you Freddie, dammit to hell, but I won't play your stupid fucking games anymore."

Barney beamed at her. "Peg," he said, "I admire you. You fought the good fight. And as long as you do what I want, you can use every curse word in the book. Is Freddie around here?"

"About ten miles away."

"What town?"

"Not a town, a house in the country."

"What I always dreamed of," Barney said. "We'll take the van, to keep him calm."

"Er," said Wheedabyx.

"No," said Peg.

"Hold it," Barney said to Peg, and to Wheedabyx he said, "Whadaya mean, *er*?"

Wheedabyx seemed very tired of this whole situation. "I have a man outside," he said, "keeping an eye on the van."

"Well, aren't you full of surprises," Barney said. "A fireman?"

"No."

"Is he armed?"

"He's just a part-time deputy, he's got a gas station out on—"

"So he's armed."

Sounding frightened for his deputy, Wheedabyx said, "Except in the qualifying sessions, he's never fired his weapon."

"Well, he won't start today," Barney promised. "Does he have a radio out there?"

"No."

"How do you get in touch with him, if you want him?"

"I go out on the porch and say, 'Hey, Cliff.'"

"Ha ha," said Barney, without mirth. "You stand in the doorway, with these two friends of mine just out of sight, and you say, 'Hey, Cliff, come in here a minute.' And if it turns out his name isn't Cliff, and he heads in some other direction, Mr. Wheedabyx, he will *never* get to fire that weapon of his, we will disqualify him completely."

"His name is Cliff."

"Good." To the thugs, Barney said, "Disarm Cliff, and put him with the construction crew."

Wheedabyx and the two thugs left the room, and Barney turned back to Peg. "You're making a lot of trouble for a lot of people today, Peg," he said, "and I don't know how big the basement is in this house, and it seems to me the last word I heard you say was *no*. Now, why's that, Peg?"

"We can't go there," Peg said. "Freddie knows you guys are after him. He knows you even had skip-tracers looking for *me*. So we've got a signal, if I show up in the van, just show up, he'll disappear, he'll know it's not my idea I'm there. I mean, he won't let you find him or talk to him, he won't let *me* find him. If Freddie decides to disappear, you know, he can really do it."

"So we'll take some other car," Barney said. "The chief'll loan us something."

"A strange car pulling in? He'll be off like a shot."

Mordon Leethe broke a long and troubled silence, saying, "You said you'd give him to us, Miss Briscoe."

"I'll phone him," Peg said. "I'll tell him you guys have me, I'm your prisoner, and it's gonna get tough for me if he doesn't come here and talk it over."

Barney said, "And you think he'll show up, on your account?"

"If I'm wrong," she said, "I'm in deep trouble."

"You certainly are."

Wheedabyx came back in, then, looking disgusted, trailed by the thugs. Everybody ignored him. Leethe said, "Barney, I think it's worth the try. If Peg Briscoe is the hook that'll hold Freddie Noon to us, let's use it. If she isn't, let's find out now and go kidnap his mother next."

With a surprised laugh, Barney said, "Counselor, I'm beginning to rub off on you!"

"In for a penny," Leethe said. "Once she brought us to this police chief. . . . What happens when we leave here, Barney, and all these people start identifying us?"

"First they have to find us," Barney said. "Peg's the only one who knows who we are, and she isn't gonna tell, are you, Peg?"

"Not unless I can get away from you," Peg said, seeing nothing to be gained by trying to soft-soap these people. What she was up to would work, or it wouldn't work, that was all.

And Barney loved her answer. Laughing, he said, "That's right, Peg, not unless you get away from us, and that ain't about to happen." To Leethe he said, "Anyway, Counselor, I got *my* alibi all firmed up. Don't you have yours?"

"Not yet," Leethe said. He didn't look either happy or well.

"You'll be all right," Barney assured him, and turned back to Peg. "What's Freddie driving these days?"

"An orange Subaru station wagon. I bought it for him used."

Barney turned to Wheedabyx. "Chief, I need a phone for the lady, and an extension for me." He grinned at Peg. "Not that I don't trust you," he said.

52

Freddie was moping around the house, was what he was doing. He didn't feel like swimming in the pool, he didn't feel like watching a movie on the VCR, he didn't feel like sitting in the sun or in the shade or indoors or outdoors. He didn't feel like much of anything.

He had got dressed this morning, putting on summer shorts and a T-shirt and espadrilles, because we do spend most of our lives in clothing, so he just felt more comfortable that way. But no long sleeves, and no gloves, and no latex head, because who for? Not for himself. In those rare instances when he caught his own reflection, that passing image of the self-animated pale blue T-shirt and maroon shorts, in a mirror or a window or the face of the microwave, it just amused him. He kind of liked the look of himself in clothes; he thought it suggested something interestingly quirky about his personality.

When the phone rang, he was just about to put his gloves on, however reluctantly, so he could make a lonely sandwich just to keep his strength up. Then the phone rang, and he decided it was probably a wrong number or somebody trying to sell him something, so why answer. Peg wouldn't call in the middle of the day, she'd wait till this evening. In fact, as he remembered it, she planned to spend today probably getting her old job back, so she could look again into the mouths of people who had mouths you could look into.

(I hope I never have to have dentistry, he told himself, while the phone rang. Or surgery, come to think of it. Important life-threatening surgery. "Nurse, we must remove this spleen at once!" "What spleen is that, doctor?")

Four rings, and the answering machine kicked in, Peg's voice saying we're out, leave a message, see what good it does you; no, not the last part, that was implicit. Freddie took cold cuts and mayo and mustard from the refrigerator, noticing again how rapidly his hands got hot in these gloves, even when he was reaching into the refrigerator, and Peg's voice stopped on the answering machine, and then Peg's voice started again, saying, "Freddie, aren't you there? Oh, hell, if he's up at the pool, I don't know what to do. Jesus. Can I leave this number, he could call back?"

By that time, Freddie had the refrigerator door closed, the gloves off, and the phone in his hand, floating in space. "Peg?"

"I mean, he doesn't know *where* the number is, if I tell him this number."

"Peg?"

"What? Freddie, is that you? Are you there?"

"Hi, Peg," he said, smiling, happy to hear her voice, only faintly snagged by the realization she'd been talking to somebody else for a few seconds there. "I didn't think you'd call so early," he explained, "so I wasn't gonna answer."

"Well, this isn't a regular call," Peg said.

Then he heard the strain in her voice, and paid more attention to that memory of her speaking to somebody else wherever she was—not home, that was for sure—and he let the silence go by for a few seconds, during which time he heard breathing on the line that wasn't Peg—heavier, raspier.

"Freddie? Are you there?"

"Oh, I'm here, Peg. Where are you?"

"I'm at the chief's house."

Chief? What chief? Freddie's invisible brow furrowed; he could feel it. He said, neutrally, "Oh, yeah?"

"You remember. The guy with all the hats."

Then he did; the police chief, in Dudley, the guy they were going to keep clear of from now on. Feeling sudden concern for her, "Peg!" he said. "Did he nab you?"

"No, not him. In fact, he's nabbed, too. Remember that cop, moonlighting, followed me north that time?"

Oh, Freddie thought, so that's it. He said, "Is that him, listening on the line?"

"Yeah." Then, away from the phone, she said, "Why not? Am I supposed to pretend we're all stupid?" Back to Freddie, she said, fatalistically, "Yeah, it's him again."

"He gotcha at the apartment, right?"

"Right."

"Said lead me to Freddie, you led him to the chief instead, right?"

"Yeah, Freddie, right."

"That's pretty funny," Freddie said, grinning.

"Nobody here sees the humor, Freddie," she said.

"Ahhhh, yeah. I guess not."

"What this Barney wanted to do, Freddie, that's his name, he wanted to cut my finger off and mail it to you, with a phone number where you could call him and talk it over."

Barney is listening, Freddie reminded himself. Handle this situation. "Pretty drastic, Peg," he said, wondering was this Barney bluffing or was this Barney a maniac.

"There's other guys with—" Off, she shouted, "I'm telling him the situation, isn't that what you want?"

Freddie said, "Peg? Peg, never mind him, cut to the car crash."

"This *is* the car crash, Freddie."

"Okay. What do they want?"

"They want to talk to you."

"Then how come *you're* talking to me?"

A heavy male voice—this must be the maniac moonlighting cop, Barney—said, "We want you to understand, Freddie, what's goin on here."

"You're threatening a woman with a knife," Freddie said. "I think I got it."

"No no no, Freddie," said Barney's croaky wisenheimer voice, "that isn't the topic. *You're* the topic."

"Uh-huh."

"You're a valuable guy, Freddie, to whoever's got a handle on you. And what we think we got here, with Peg, we think we got the handle."

"They want you to get in the Subaru," Peg said, "and drive over—"

"I'll do the talking now, Peg," Barney said. "Hang up."

Click. Subaru: double-click.

Freddie said, "What do you want, Barney?"

"You, Freddie, workin for me and workin for some friends of mine. Light work, very easy, a little excitement every now and then. Good pay."

"I don't like to be an employee, that's always been a problem I had."

"That's too bad, Freddie, time you got over it. We got the idea you place a certain value on Peg here, and we got Peg, and we're gonna keep Peg, so that makes you an employee. So you'll get used to it."

"And what if I just say the hell with everything, and go someplace else? California, maybe."

"Gimme an address, to send the fingers."

"You can always shove them up your ass."

"Don't be silly, Freddie," Barney said, almost fondly. "You don't talk tough to *me*. And you don't leave Peg on her own, either, that's one of the nicest qualities about you." Off, he said, "Isn't it, Peg?" Back, he said, "She agrees with me. She's kinda counting on you, Freddie. So you come *here,* you come *now,* and you wear something so we can see you, and we give you the details of the situation."

Hogtie me, you mean. Other guys there, Peg said so, Barney didn't like her telling me that. Lean on me because they'll want me to do stuff I really and truly won't want to do. Peg's the hostage, and I'm the patsy, world without end. Don't even get to be visible again someday, so I could retire.

Well, screw that.

Aloud, Freddie said, "I want Peg sitting on the front porch, so I can see she's okay. All by herself."

"You know what'll happen, she decides to run."

"Yeah, we all know. If she's there, and she's okay, I'll come in."

"She'll come in with you."

"Okay, fine. After I see she's okay. I'll be there in twenty minutes."

"Peg tells me you're ten minutes away."

Oh, hell, Peg, what'd you say that for? Freddie said, "Did you ever know a woman with any sense of time?" Forgive me, Peg. "I'll be there in twenty minutes."

"Fifteen. If you aren't here, she loses a finger."

"Then make it the pinky on her left hand, she never uses that. I'll be there in twenty minutes," Freddie said. "And the first thing I'll do when I get there is count Peg's fingers."

And he hung up and ran.

53

Peg and Barney and one of the thugs had been in the chief's office for the phone call, there being two phones on the same line in that room, one of them cordless. Barney, using that one, had paced back and forth like a fat Napoleon all through the conversation, and when it ended he thumbed the phone off, slapped it onto the desk, and said to Peg, "Up."

She'd been seated at the desk, talking on the other phone there, and now she obediently got to her feet. She'd done what she could to help Freddie, so now it was up to him. If only Barney were less mean, less quick, and less maniacal. But he wasn't, so there you are.

Barney called, "Bring in the chief," and then started opening cabinets and closets, making small sounds in his throat that would have been humming if they weren't all on the same note. By the time Chief Wheedabyx came in, with a second thug, Barney had found a whole cache of handcuffs. They clacked like castanets as he motioned with them at the desk chair, saying, "Take a load off, Chief. Things are gonna slow down and get peaceful now."

The chief said, "This is going to end badly for you, you know."

"No, I don't know, Chief," Barney said. "But if you don't put the ass in the chair right now—"

"Language," the chief said, and sat in the desk chair.

Barney stared at him. "*Lan*guage? Chief, I hope you never meet up with any bad guys." Picking out two sets of cuffs, handing them to the thug who'd been appointed the chief's monitor, he said, "One wrist to each chair arm. If he gets a call, you hold the phone up to his head for him. If he says anything you don't like, hang up and shoot him in the head. Then come tell me about it."

"Got it."

Turning to the first thug, who'd been with them during the phone call, Barney said, "Grab down those rolls of twine from the closet there, bring 'em along."

"Uh-huh."

"Come on, Peg."

She followed Barney out of the office, the thug with an armload of rolls of twine following her, as the chief was cuffed to his own office chair. He looked grim and heroic still, like Mount Rushmore.

In the hall, they met the third thug and the attorney, Leethe. Barney said, "We're moving."

Leethe said, "What's happening?"

"He's on his way. Look in the tall cabinet in there, second shelf, you'll see boxes and boxes of thumbtacks and pushpins. I want 'em on the ground all around the property, and in the doorways, and on the windowsills. You and Bosco do that." Meaning the third thug.

Leethe looked surprised and displeased. "Barney," he said, "do you think I'm one of your henchmen?"

"No, I think you're one of NAABOR's henchmen, same as ever. We got no time to stroke egos, Counselor. Freddie's on his way."

Leethe made a bad mouth, but he went away to do Barney's bidding, followed by the thug now christened Bosco, while Barney led Peg and the remaining thug out to the porch, where they found the usual country assortment of wood and wicker furniture. The sturdiest of these was a straight-backed wooden armchair, long ago painted dark green, which Barney now dragged across the gray-painted porch floor closer to the door. "Park it," he told Peg, and as she sat he turned to the thug with the armload of twine. "Give me one roll," he said, taking it, "and go out there and string me trip wires all around the property, tree to tree."

"Right."

The thug left the porch and crossed the lawn over to a big maple, where he went to work. Barney opened the roll of twine, knelt beside Peg, and tied her right ankle to one chair leg and her left ankle to the other. "Slip knots," he told her, using the porch rail to help lever his bulk back up onto his feet. "If you bend down to touch the cord, I'll give you a warning shot in the shoulder. When Freddie gets here, ask him to untie you."

Leethe and Bosco came out, hands and pockets full of little boxes of thumbtacks and pushpins. They walked around like Johnny Appleseed, sprinkling shiny sharp things on path and lawn, so that when Freddie got here he'd have to move very slowly, clearing all the tacks and pins out of the way of his bare feet, if he was barefoot, or have to wear shoes. In either case, Barney and the others would see him coming.

Barney went back into the house. Peg sat in the chair and watched the preparations continue, Leethe moving around the house to the left, Bosco and the trip-wiring thug to the right. From time to time, a car or pickup truck went by on Market Street, and there were some curious stares, but not many. There was always some sort of construction work going on in town.

Bart Simpson drove by, in a green Hornet.

Barney had his crew add coffee cups and silverware and other noisemaking things to his trip wires, and make sure every door and window except the wide-open front entrance was locked and blocked and defended by thumbtacks. Then they stripped blankets and bedspreads from the beds upstairs and waited just inside the open front doorway. The idea was, when Freddie stooped or knelt to untie the twine around Peg's ankles, they'd leap out and wrap him in bedding and tie him up and *then* talk to him.

Maybe it won't be so bad, Peg thought, Freddie working for Barney and the lawyer. Steady employment, low risk. Probably no health benefits, though.

It's hard to look on the sunny side when you're in a shit-storm.

54

Freddie walked back to the house. He'd seen the preparations as he'd driven by, and now he took a closer look. Trip wires to make jangly noises. Sharp things on the ground for his bare feet. No windows open, on this nice sunny day, so probably everything locked up except that invitingly open doorway beside Peg, sitting there on the front porch. Was that some kind of cord or twine around her ankles? Very nice.

Freddie made a complete circuit of the house. It wasn't completely surrounded by trees, but there were enough large old maples spaced here and there to give comfortable summer shade. Also, at the moment, they made handy posts for the trip wires.

A big maple on the right side had branches going right up above the roof. Its lowest thick branch was a little more than seven feet from the ground, extending outward away from the house and trip wire. On his second jump, Freddie grabbed that branch and managed to pull himself aboard.

For a naked man, shimmying up a tree is even trickier than riding a bicycle.

Freddie didn't know it, of course, but the route he was taking now had been Geoff Wheedabyx's favorite path in and out of his house when he was between the ages of ten and twelve, sometimes traveling that way because his parents didn't want

him out so late at night, sometimes going by tree merely because it was fun.

The thick branch Freddie inched out on, when he had as-
cended high enough, bowed and swayed with his weight; fortunately, nobody was looking up. It led him to the porch roof,
which his bare feet touched so gently that even Peg didn't
hear it down below, but kept on looking out at the street, wondering when something would happen.

The upstairs windows were open (good) but screened (bad).
Freddie hadn't brought any tools with him. The screens were
the old-fashioned wooden-frame sort, with small slitted metal
bars at the top corners. These hung on metal tongues attached
to the window frame. In the winter, no doubt, the chief came up
here and took down these screens to put up old-fashioned storm
windows on the same hardware.

First unhooking the screens, of course. Yes, each screen
was hooked closed on the inside. The wooden screen frame
was flush with the wooden window frame: nothing to get a
grip on. And bare hands do not punch through well-made
screens like this, not without harming the hands and alerting
the already alert people just below.

This is very irritating, Freddie thought. Through one of the
open windows, he could hear Barney and the others talking
together downstairs. So near, and yet so far.

He walked over to the right corner of the porch roof, and
from there, on tiptoe, he could just see the steep slope of the
main roof. No trapdoor on this side; no, and there wouldn't be
one on the other side, either, *or* it would be locked. There was
a chimney over there, which he would not crawl down.

In trying to see the roof, he'd held on to the drainpipe that
went down this corner of the house. Now he considered the
drainpipe, shook it experimentally, and it was quite solid.
New, or not very old. The chief was also a construction guy,

so maybe he put his crew to work on his own house sometimes, when business got slow.

Freddie looked over the edge. The porch railing looked *very* far away, straight down. If he fell, of course, he'd just land on grass down there—no thumbtacks; they were all farther out—but he wouldn't land quietly, and then they'd know he was here.

Still, what choice did he have? He was *on* the house, and he had to get *in* the house. There was no silent way to get through those screens. There was no point going back down the tree. Time to do a little more Tom Sawyer.

Which meant, first, extending his right foot down so he could press his toes against the metal collar that held the drainpipe just below the porch ceiling. That metal collar was unexpectedly sharp and painful to his flesh, but there still wasn't any choice, so he gripped the drainpipe, shifted his weight to his extremely pained toes, lowered his right hand to a new grip, bent the right knee, pawed with his dangling left foot for the porch rail, lowered his left hand to a new grip, bent the knee a lot more, pawed a lot more, stubbed his toe on the rail, touched his toe to the rail, bent the knee more than he thought he could, shifted his weight to his left foot, pushed away from the drainpipe while still holding on to it, removed his extremely pained right foot from the sharp metal collar, went on holding to the drainpipe, turned on the railing, and saw Peg in profile, seated in that chair, arms on the chair arms, legs tied to the chair legs.

Freddie climbed down to the porch floor, braced himself against the wall of the house, and felt the bottom of the toes on his right foot. He was amazed to find that he wasn't cut or bleeding. He massaged the toes until they felt a little better, and then he moved.

He was sorry he couldn't whisper a word of encouragement to Peg on the way by, but he didn't want to risk her giving some sort of startled response that would alert the guys inside.

So he just eased on by behind her, then went through the open doorway, and here was the cop, hunkered over next to the wall, gripping a blanket in both hands like the child-eating ogre in a fairy tale.

With the cop was the guy who had been with him that day in Bay Ridge, the guy Peg later had told him was a lawyer, though he didn't look or act much like a lawyer at the moment. He had a nice old antique quilt bunched in his fists and hanging down his front, and he looked like the evil brother in a fourth-rate touring company of *Arsenic and Old Lace.* And also present, also holding blankets at the ready, either to douse a fire or capture an invisible man, were two plug-uglies in suits and white shirts and neckties. They looked like pit bulls that had been made to wear fancy collars.

As Freddie walked in to study this diorama, the lawyer said, "How long?"

The cop looked at his wrist. "Fifteen minutes. We'll give him the twenty he asked for."

Thanks, Freddie thought.

The lawyer said, "What if he doesn't show?"

"Then it's Plan B."

"Barney, I don't—"

Sounding almost sorry about it, but not *really* sorry, the cop said, "Mr. Leethe, we got no choice. If we say we're gonna take her finger, and then we *don't* take the finger, we lose all credibility. Freddie wouldn't have any reason ever to believe us again. And I want Freddie to believe, to really know and believe, that when I tell him something is going to happen, that's what's gonna happen."

Uh-huh. Freddie left them to their plans and stratagems, and went exploring, and the first thing he found was the chief, handcuffed to his own chair in his own office, with a third plug-ugly in suit and tie in another chair nearby, watching over him. The chief looked bitter, and the plug-ugly looked bored.

Freddie explored on. He found nobody else on the ground floor, and didn't expect there'd be anybody upstairs, so didn't look. He was going through the kitchen when he heard voices, arguing together, and in a minute realized there were some people in the basement and the basement door was locked.

Okay. Those are good guys, apparently, the chief's friends. For the moment, we'll leave them out of play.

Freddie went back to the chief's office, and nothing had happened, nobody had moved. He went over to the wall behind the plug-ugly, where all the hats were hung, and under the hats he found a lot of the chief's equipment. There was a very nice fire ax, but that seemed extreme. Oh, here was a nightstick.

Freddie picked up the nightstick, and the chief jumped a mile. Or he would have jumped a mile, if it hadn't been for the cuffs holding him to the chair.

The plug-ugly frowned at him. "What's with you?"

"Mosquito," the chief said. "Could you wave a magazine around my head or something?"

"Don't worry," the plug-ugly said. "You won't itch for long. Just sit there and—"

The chief winced.

Freddie held the plug-ugly so he wouldn't crash to the floor, adjusted him in the chair, then went over behind the desk and whispered in the chief's ear, "Key. Whisper."

The chief was quite wide-eyed. "Hook," he whispered, and pointed with his nose and chin at a small board of hooks, most containing keys, on the opposite wall.

Freddie crossed the room, and the keys all had neatly lettered little cardboard tags attached to them with white string. He started to read the tags.

"He says the time is—hey!"

Freddie spun around, to see another of the plug-uglies in the doorway, staring at his unconscious friend. Hell and damn.

The guy turned and left the doorway at the run, yelling, "He's here! He's here!"

"Later," Freddie told the chief. Dropping the nightstick, he ran from the office before he could be trapped inside it, and got out just as the doorway filled with the whole crowd of them.

The cop was a fast thinker. "Bosco!" he cried at one of the plug-uglies. "Keep an eye on the broad! The rest of us, let's see if he's still in here. Freddie?"

They moved forward into the room, the three men, spreading out, holding hands. "You here, Freddie?"

Freddie was not there. Freddie was approaching the guy who'd been left to watch the broad.

In the old days, when people knew what they were doing, plug-uglies did not wear neckties. Plug-uglies wore turtleneck sweaters, as you can see from looking at all the old photographs, and plug-uglies knew *why* they wore turtleneck sweaters. It was because turtleneck sweaters have nothing on them an enemy can hold on to.

A necktie is a *handle*. Freddie grabbed this clown by the handle, ran him full speed across the front hall, and drove his forehead into the stairway newel post with such force the wood cracked.

The clown kissed the carpet.

Immediately the cop was in the office doorway, looking up from the guy on the floor, glaring around the hall, saying, "Freddie, Freddie, why be so unfriendly? Do you want the *law* to get you? Would you rather explain your life of crime to the chief in there?"

Too late, Freddie realized the cop wasn't just talking, he was also moving; suddenly he made a dash for the front door, Freddie scampering after him.

Too late. When Freddie got to the porch, the cop was crouched over Peg, and a long knife was pressed to Peg's throat, and Peg was looking very worried. "Listen to me, Freddie," the cop said, staring at the doorway. "If I feel one thing, one *touch*, she's dead."

"Then so are you," Freddie said.

The cop swung his eyes to where Freddie had just left. "Maybe," he said. "Second. But she goes first. Are you ready to talk?"

Why wouldn't somebody passing by see a man on a porch holding a knife to a woman's throat? Why weren't people more *observant*?

The cop was saying, "Peg, untie those knots now, they're real easy, just pull the loops. Move slow, Peg, then we're all going back inside."

Freddie was already back inside, where the lawyer and the last plug-ugly were standing around in the hall, blinking a lot. Freddie went around them and back into the office, and this time he found the right damn key and used it to undo the chief's right cuff. Pressing the key into the chief's hand, he whispered, "Do something, okay?"

The chief nodded, and Freddie turned, and the lawyer was in the doorway. "He's in the office, Barney!"

"That's it," Freddie said, crossing the room toward the row of hats. "I've had enough of you, pal." He picked up the fire ax and headed for the lawyer.

Who screamed, and flung his hands in the air, and ran from the room. Freddie followed, the fire ax out in front of him, and in the front hall were the cop and Peg, he behind her, one arm round her waist, the other hand still holding the knife to her throat as he backed them both into the parlor.

"Leethe!" the cop yelled, forgetting to say "mister," as the lawyer ran right by him and out the front door and off the porch and down the walk and away, his shoes apparently having thick enough soles so the thumbtacks and pushpins didn't bother him. Or maybe they bothered him but he was too busy running away to be bothered by something bothering him—that was also possible.

"Leethe!" the cop yelled. "Come back!"

But Leethe was long gone, and Peg was staring in shock at the ax in midair, and then she shouted, "Freddie! Look out!"

A heavy weight tackled him from behind. The ax went flying, and Freddie was driven face first into the carpet, very near the unconscious plug-ugly.

He'd forgotten the third one, dammit, and the guy had snuck up behind him, guided by the ax. Of course, he couldn't see Freddie, but now he could sure feel him, and had him in a bearhug on the floor.

The cop was still backing away into the parlor with Peg, and he called, "Bring him in here! Hold on to him, and bring him in here! Alive!"

Freddie writhed and twisted, and got his left arm free, and swung it up and back, and his elbow connected with something or other. He did it again, and hit the same something, so he did it again. On the fourth whack, the weight above him shifted, and he managed to twist around, and now he was faceup, with this bulky monster straddling him, trying to hold on to him with both hands.

Freddie punched the guy in the face. The guy responded by taking a swing where Freddie's head should be, and getting it absolutely right. Freddie's head spun. He reached up, blindly, and his hand found the guy's necktie, and he grabbed it in his fist and turned his fist over, tucking the fist in under the guy's chin, then grabbing that fist with his other hand to make a bigger mass that he was pressing into the guy's Adam's apple while the necktie pinned him there, and now he was strangling the son of a bitch.

Who reached down, pawed his fingers over Freddie's face,

found his neck, and now the son of a bitch was strangling Freddie. Neither would let go, and Freddie had no confidence that he would win this contest, but then all at once the son of a bitch said, "Ah," and fell facedown on top of Freddie, and over his unconscious shoulder Freddie saw the chief, with the nightstick.

"Ah-hah," Freddie said. "You *are* good for something. Get this guy off me, will you?"

The chief pulled, and Freddie crawled out from under, and looked over toward the parlor, and in the doorway were the cop and Peg, same as ever.

"I'll call the state boys," the chief said, backing away toward his office.

"Wait!" Freddie said, staggering to his feet. "Not yet."

The cop gave a sour laugh. "You don't want *more* law, Freddie," he said, "any more than I do."

"Chief," Freddie said, "why don't you handcuff those guys, before they wake up. And the one in the office, too."

"Good idea."

Moving toward the cop and Peg, as the chief went into his office for handcuffs, Freddie said, low and fast, "You're screwed here, cop, it isn't working. Let Peg go and I'll get you out of here. Otherwise it's a standoff until the state cops come, and then what? We're *all* screwed. I don't want law all over me and you don't want law all over you."

The chief came back out to the hall and went to one knee, to handcuff the sleeping palookas. The cop stared at the chief while he tried to think out his alternatives, and of course, one of his alternatives was simply to use the knife on Peg, who'd caused all this trouble by bringing him here to the police chief; then maybe he could make a run for it in the confusion.

Freddie didn't want the cop to give serious consideration to that option, so he pressed a little, saying, "You don't have weeks to make up your mind here. You let Peg go, she goes out and starts the van, and then we follow."

The chief was done with the handcuffs. Getting to his feet, he said, "I'll let the fellas out of the basement, then call the state boys."

"Not yet, Chief, okay?"

The chief looked toward Freddie's voice, bewildered. "Why not?"

"I'll explain," Freddie promised. "Just go along with me for a minute, will you do that?" To the cop, he said, "I know you're just gonna keep after me, so when we get outta here we'll talk it over, we'll make a deal. Let her go, let's get out of this place."

The cop glared into the air. "I wish I could see your face," he said.

"So do I, pal."

The cop made his decision. Lowering the knife, stepping back one pace, he pushed Peg forward and said, "Go start the van."

"Put the knife away," Freddie said, as Peg ran out of the house. "You don't need it."

The chief said, "What's going on here?"

"In a minute, Chief," Freddie said, while the cop, still suspicious, closed up his knife and put it away. Freddie said to him, "You know I'm a thief, right?"

"It's what I like about you," the cop said. "So far, the only thing I do like about you."

"Well, there's another thing about me you oughta know," Freddie said.

"What's that?"

"I'm also a liar," Freddie said, and punched him in the face.

55

It was the damnedest thing Geoff Wheedabyx had ever seen. For about three minutes, the fat bad guy called Barney apparently beat himself severely with parts of Geoff's house, throwing himself on the floor, dragging himself backwards into the hall, flinging himself madly against the walls, knocking himself down repeatedly and repeatedly jerking himself back upright again, while making a lot of sounds like *oof!* and *uh!* and *aak!* Then, after having done a final tattoo of the back of his head against the office-door frame, Barney collapsed on the floor without a sound and stopped moving, a marionette when the show's over.

Geoff was still staring at this battered unconscious man when the voice of Freddie sounded over by the open front door, yelling, "Peg! Go home!" Then the door slammed itself.

As if that weren't enough, something grasped Geoff's elbow and propelled him back into his office, while Freddie's voice, now very close to him, said, "Chief, we gotta talk."

"What I've got to do," Geoff said, "is let my crew out of that basement, doggone it. They've got toilets to install."

"In a minute, Chief. Do you know what happened here today?"

"I'll be damned if I do," Geoff said. "But after a couple

weeks' intense interrogation, I believe I'll begin to get some idea of it."

"That bunch of guys came to this town to rob the bank."

Geoff wished he could give this fellow Freddie the look of scornful disbelief that remark deserved; it wasn't anywhere near as satisfactory to give the opposite wall a look of scornful disbelief. "They never did," he said.

"And there's no invisible man here," the invisible man said.

"I'm talking to myself, I guess." But Geoff was too straightforward a guy to make sarcasm really work.

"No, you're not talking at all, you're listening. And I'm telling you those guys came here to rob the bank, and they figured to neutralize the local law first, which is you, so they came over here and captured you and your construction crew—"

"And my deputy, he's down there, too."

"Your deputy, that's good. But then you turned the tables on them, all by yourself."

"I can't say a thing like that," Geoff said, "even if there was a reason for it, and what's the reason?"

"I probably saved your life, Chief, how's that for a start?"

"I was thinking about that," Geoff admitted, "while I was handcuffed to the chair there, and they sure didn't act like they planned on leaving any witnesses."

"I just found out I'm gonna be invisible the rest of my life," Freddie said. "Found out from the doctors who did it to me. So I could stick around here with you and tell the invisible man story and be a freak in a cage the rest of my life, doctors poking at me. Or I can take off and *really* disappear, you'll never hear from me again, and Peg and me'll have a quiet life somewhere."

"I sympathize with you," Geoff admitted, and added, "Freddie, I do. But I can't claim I beat up and knocked out and captured four tough guys all by myself."

Freddie, or the air around him, sighed. He said, "You don't lie, is that right?"

"That's right, that's the problem, I'm just no good at it."

"Chief, did you ever lie to your mom, when you were a kid?"

Geoff felt his face turning red. He stammered, "Well . . . I suppose . . . you know . . . kids . . ."

"With the construction company, ever lie to a customer?"

"Well, you know, there's things people don't entirely understand, in a business like, you got your scheduling and your parts delivery, and, uh . . ."

"Ever lie to a woman?"

Two days ago, most recently. Geoff shook his head. "You want me to lie," he said.

"You bet I do."

Geoff thought about it. "I just can't see it," he said, "that I can look one of the state boys in the eye and tell him I did all this by myself."

"Just keep telling the same story, you'll be all right."

"And what about the story *these* fellas tell?"

"You mean, how they came up here to kidnap an invisible man? You think they're gonna *say* that?"

"They gotta say something," Geoff pointed out.

"They'll claim misunderstanding, innocent victims, and they won't get away with it. Chief, I bet you not one of them says a word about any invisible man. And if they do, they'll be talking to nothing but psychiatrists the next twenty years."

"All right," Geoff said, having thought it over. "I tell you what maybe I could do. I'll explain things—I'll explain some of the things—to the fellas in the basement. And then I can say I managed to unlock the door and free them, and that's three, plus one, plus me, the five of us overpowered these fellas."

"Will they keep their mouths shut for you?"

"We pretty much take care of one another," Geoff said.

"Fine." The voice trailing away toward the door, Freddie said, "I'll get out of the way now."

Geoff went out to the hall, where the fat man was stirring, half sitting up. "Barney's coming around," he commented.

Whap! "No, he isn't. So long, Chief. And thanks."

The front door opened and closed. Geoff went back into his office to get handcuffs for Barney before talking to the guys in the basement, but then he heard a sudden shout from outside. So he went back to the hall, and the front door opened, and Freddie's pained voice said, "Could I borrow a broom, Chief? I forgot about those damn tacks."

"Better let me do the sweeping," Geoff said. "I wouldn't want the neighbors to think I'm doing *The Sorcerer's Apprentice* over here."

Geoff was just bringing the broom back into the house, where the tough guys were now conscious and rolling around on the floor, helpless because their hands were cuffed behind their backs, and here came Cliff and the construction crew, boiling in from the kitchen. "Where are they? Geoff, what's happening? What's the story here?"

Geoff said, "You got out! That's great!"

The crew looked a little sheepish. One of them said, "We kinda had to go through the wall beside the door. Kinda demolition, you know."

Another one said, "We did it as neat as we could."

The third one said, "We can patch it up, Geoff, no problem."

"Well," Geoff said, "this makes it a lot easier. Come on in the parlor and sit down, guys, let me tell you a little story before I call the state boys."

56

When Mordon awoke, he watched the oval spot of sunlight rise slowly to the teak cabin wall, then sink slowly to touch the mounds of his feet beneath the creamy blanket, then rise again; and so did Mordon, shaking, pale, staggering as he went into the bathroom.

It wasn't the gentle slow roll of the yacht that had so unmanned him, nor drink (though last night he had taken onboard much drink), but fear. His fear of the floating ax, when yesterday he had run pell-mell from Chief Wheedabyx's house and all the way out of the town of Dudley, had soon been replaced by the even stronger fears of exposure, ruin, and prison. His fears had been so powerful that his flight took place in a terrified daze, so that he barely remembered the pickup truck that had given him the lift, the diner in which he'd made the phone call to the car service in New York, the hours spent quivering over undrunk coffee in a rear booth of that diner, the hours spent quivering in the back of the town car that returned him to New York, the hours spent quivering in his office while he waited for Merrill Fullerton to respond to his call.

But then Merrill did, at last, and agreed that Mordon should come to see him, not in the NAABOR offices in the World Trade Center, since Merrill had not yet consolidated his power there, but in Merrill's apartment atop Trump Tower.

When Mordon, in abject despair, related the events of the day to Merrill, fully expecting to be thrown into the street, his heart to be eaten by dogs, Merrill had instead leaped magnificently to his defense, saying, "Beuler *will* betray you, we know that much. Leave it to me."

And an hour later Mordon and Merrill and a dozen other people were sailing past Miss Liberty, out of New York Harbor, into the choppy Atlantic on the good ship *Nicotiana,* where all aboard were prepared to swear they had been disporting themselves for the last twenty-four hours, with distinguished attorney Mordon Leethe prominent in their midst.

Would it work? Could it work? Could even Merrill Fullerton rescue Mordon from this far down in the deep pit of ignominy? His sleep last night had been tortured, and so were his bathroom experiences this morning.

When at last he staggered back out to the bright cabin, with its roving spotlight of sun, as though the gods of rectitude were looking for him to wreak their own vengeance, there was a discreet tapping to be heard from the cabin door. "Come in," he choked, but no one could have heard that croaking, so he went over to open the door and found standing there a white-suited member of the ship's crew, who actually touched a fingertip to a temple in what looked rather like a salute as he said, "Mr. Fullerton's compliments. He awaits you on the fantail, sir. Whenever you're ready."

"Fan—?"

"Aft, sir. Stern. Back of the ship. That way, and up." He pointed.

"Thank you."

Mordon would never truly be ready, not fully ready, but in ten minutes he was sufficiently together to go in search of the fantail and his benefactor, who stood beside a groaning board of breakfast, a huge buffet table. No one else was around.

"Good morning," Merrill said, and gestured at the many foods. "Breakfast?"

"Perhaps . . . later."

The fantail was outdoors, but shielded by a canvas roof, striped blue and white. The sea was huge, and everywhere, and nowhere flat. The day was sharply lit, with acute edges.

"Probably," Merrill said, with a smile, "you'd like to know what's going on ashore."

"Yes."

"Sit down, Mordon, sit down."

They sat near each other and the white rail, on large and comfortable leather and chrome chairs. Mordon didn't so much want to sleep as merely to lose consciousness, but he forced himself to remain alert, alert enough to listen.

Merrill said, "I've been on the phone to New York a lot this morning. You were right about Detective Beuler, he did implicate you, and me, and poor old Jack the Fourth, and the doctors, and everyone else he could think of. However, we were lucky enough to get our people to Beuler's home on Long Island before the police got there, and what a *lot* of evidence he'd built up against you, Mordon!" Merrill beamed at the thought of it.

"He needed," Mordon said, "to protect himself from everybody."

"The other way around, I should say," Merrill commented, and added, "But not to worry. All of those tapes, all of that evidence that, I must say, could have disbarred you and probably put you behind bars for the rest of your life, is in my hands now, so you have nothing to worry about."

"You'll destroy it all, won't you? Or give it to me, so I can."

"Oh, there's no need for that," Merrill said. "It's safe with me. And so are you, Mordon. The upstate activities of yesterday are being treated as a simple failed bank robbery, Beuler's smearing of so many of his betters is being quite properly ignored, and we are all of us home and dry. Now let us talk about the invisible man."

Mordon slightly lifted his head. "Did he get away again?"

"For good this time, I think." Merrill's smile seemed quite savage for a moment. "It seems, those two blithering-idiot researchers managed not only to find the fellow and chat with him but, before they lost him again, they let him know there's no hope of his ever returning to his former self. He has no more reason to contact them, nor can any of us contact him. So he's gone."

"Too bad," Mordon said.

"Agreed. Also, after that one experiment, it would seem we can't replace him, either."

"Apparently not."

"So we must lean on our doctors more firmly than I had at first intended, Mordon, you and I."

Mordon squinted at his benefactor in the harsh bright air. "Me?"

"Think of that as your assignment from now on, Mordon," Merrill said. "Project director, we'll call it. The Human Genome Project. *You* will see to it the doctors don't dawdle or stall or waste their time on that ridiculous research they were doing. *You* will see to it that they concentrate on the genome project, that they make it their business to meet and grow friendly with the researchers in the field, that they themselves become an official part of the project within, oh, I know we can't rush these things, say eighteen months."

"Eighteen months."

"Do you think I'm being too generous? Well, if they can do it more quickly, more power to them. And to you." Merrill's mad eyes glittered in all that light reflecting from the sea. "What a future we're going to have, Mordon, what a future you and I."

57

Elizabeth Louise Noon had lived in this little house in Ozone Park, under the flight path for the big jets coming in from Europe or heading out for anywhere, all of her married life. Long ago she'd stopped hearing the thunder of the jets as they slid down their invisible chute over her house toward JFK or climbed the invisible ramp from JFK to the world. Long ago she'd stopped noticing the dark shadows of the wide bodies cross her lawn and house and yard.

Betty she was called by most people, but Louise by her husband, Norm, who in the first flush of their romance had wanted a private name for her and couldn't think of anything else. In her own mind, unknown to anybody, she was always Elizabeth Louise. She and Norm, a sanitation worker with the City of New York, had raised nine kids in this little house, all of them grown now, all of them living elsewhere, but most of them would come back from time to time to shout their hellos under the passing jets.

When you've got nine kids, you're going to have variety. Elizabeth Louise didn't believe she had any *bad* kids, not mean or nasty, but she did admit to having a few scamps in the mix. She also had proper kids who'd grown up to be proper citizens, one nurse, one bus driver, one third-grade teacher, one Wal-Mart stock clerk.

She liked it when the kids came by, and she missed the ones who didn't, fretted over them in a small way, not making a big deal of it. Lately, the one she'd been fretting about most was Freddie, who was maybe the worst scamp in the bunch. He'd already been in jail, and she suspected he'd done drugs at one point in his life, and she was pretty sure he didn't have any regular job. Then, last month, that fake official letter had come, claiming the state of New York owed Freddie money for some cockamamie reason, and she could see that meant somebody was trying to find Freddie for no good reason—not good for Freddie, that is—so she lit a few candles for him, and hoped that if she ever did hear from him again, at least it wouldn't be bad news.

When the doorbell rang, Tuesday, the eleventh of July, around three in the afternoon, it wasn't Freddie who Elizabeth Louise was thinking about at all. She had a pregnant daughter-in-law, and that was who was on her mind as she walked through the house, unaware of the vibration as another big jet went over, and opened the front door.

A pretty girl was on the stoop. I hope she isn't a Jehovah's Witness, Elizabeth Louise thought, and said, "Yes?"

"Hi, Mrs. Noon," the girl said. "I'm Peg Briscoe. I've been living with your son Freddie for a while."

Elizabeth Louise had heard the name, from Freddie and from his brother Jimmy (another scamp), and Peg Briscoe seemed calm and cheerful here on the stoop, but nevertheless Elizabeth Louise's first thought was that Freddie was in trouble again. "What is it?" she said. "Does he need bail money?"

"No, no, nothing like that," the girl said, laughing. "Freddie's fine."

"That's a relief. Come in, come in."

So she came in, leaning against the open door for a second as though she'd lost her balance, but then righting herself and moving out of the way so Elizabeth Louise could shut the door.

"Iced tea?"

"That'd be nice," Peg Briscoe said, and uninvited she walked back to the kitchen with Elizabeth Louise, saying, "What a nice house. Freddie's told me about it."

"Has he?" Pouring iced tea for them both, she said, "Where is Freddie these days? Keeping himself out of trouble?"

Peg laughed again; she was clearly an easygoing girl, the right type for Freddie. "Keeping himself out of sight, anyway," she said.

"Probably the best we can hope for. Let's sit in the living room."

They sat in the living room, and sipped their iced tea, and the shadows went over the house, and Peg said, "Freddie wanted to come see you, but he's in a complicated situation now—"

"Trouble?"

"No, not at all. That's what he wanted me to come tell you. The situation he's in is really awfully difficult to explain."

"Is he sick?"

"No. He isn't sick, and he isn't in jail, and he isn't wanted for any crime, he's just in a . . . a complicated situation. So that he has to go away and he has to be kind of alone. Mostly alone."

"You mean, a quarantine?" Elizabeth Louise was getting scared.

"No, honest," the girl said. "He's not *sick*. It's kind of a problem, but it isn't terrible. It took me a while to adjust, but it's gonna be okay now. He came and helped me when I was in trouble, and he didn't have to, and I realize we need each other, we've got to be together. So I want you to know I'm gonna stick with him, he can count on me."

She'd said that with such assurance and sincerity that it was as though she were saying it to Freddie himself. Elizabeth Louise found herself feeling reassured, even though everything Peg Briscoe had said so far was so vague and incomprehensible that she shouldn't be feeling reassured at all. She said, "Where's Freddie now?"

"Waiting for me, not far from here." A jet went over, and when it was gone Peg gestured upward and said, "We're gonna take a plane. Haven't decided where yet."

"He's on the run?"

"*No*, Mrs. Noon," Peg said, and laughed at her. "You keep thinking Freddie's in trouble."

"He usually is."

"Not this time. Not ever again." Peg got to her feet. "I'd better go. He's waiting for me, he just wanted me to tell you not to worry, even though you won't be seeing him anymore. And please tell the same to his brothers and sisters, especially Jimmy."

Elizabeth Louise also rose. "Well, give him my love," she said. "And I hope things work out for him. And if he gets the chance, he should come say hello himself."

"When we get where we're going," Peg said, "I'll make him write you a letter. Or at least a postcard."

They walked back to the front door, and as Elizabeth Louise opened it she felt something, some movement of air, some aura, some weird experience that frightened her all over again, and she said to Peg Briscoe, in the open doorway, "He isn't dead, is he?"

"I'm alive, Ma."

Peg Briscoe smiled a slightly nervous smile, said, "He's fine. 'Bye," and pulled the door shut.

Did I hear that? What was it?

Elizabeth Louise opened the door and watched Peg Briscoe cross the sidewalk to a little old green car. As Peg opened the driver's door, the passenger door opened by itself. She got in

and shut the driver's door and the passenger door shut by itself. She waved and smiled, and drove away, and another
wide-body jet's shadow crossed over Elizabeth Louise and the
house.

This one she noticed. She looked up, as the shadow went
by. One of those would be Freddie, with his nice girlfriend.
From now on, it could be any one of them, going over. One of
those shadows is Freddie.